I0672110

"... this fusion of soft science fiction and romance is well written, briskly paced, and utterly readable. Where other science fiction romances get bogged down in intricate—and at times, unnecessary—backstory, author Sara L. Daigle brilliantly avoids this and immediately concentrates on the protagonist's development and storyline.

"Romantic science fiction has been slowly gaining popularity for years: This is a perfect example of a successful blending of those genre elements. Powered by an identifiable and endearing heroine, this novel is just the beginning of what could be a long and fascinating series."

- BlueInk Review

"This novel is the perfect combination of everything—romance, controversy, futuristic planetary relations, love, new 'beliefs' ... totally awesome!"

- Meghann Conter, Mistress of Marketing,
MeghannConter.com, Denver, CO

"The storyline in *Alawahea* took me on a journey far beyond what I could have imagined. After living in Colorado for forty-two years, it was especially enjoyable to read about Denver, a place near and dear to my heart."

- Lisa Ford, Author, *Finding Her Claire*

"I have so enjoyed this book! The writing and characters completely sucked me into the story. I can't wait to see what happens in the next book! Sara Daigle's writing is wonderful. Her descriptions are captivating and her characters well thought out."

- Kirsten Wolpert, Scottsdale, AZ

"I believe everything in the book as fact; I'm not even kidding you. I love it!"

-Joshua Johnson, Theta Healer, JoshuaTree ThetaHealing

"*Alawahea* immerses you in a world of possibility. Intriguing characters make Sara Daigle's universe come to life and leave you anxiously turning the page to find out what happens next!"

- Jarrod Musick, Destiny Capital, Denver, CO

"I am not a reader, but this book had me from the start. I could not put it down, and I was sad when I came to the end. Sara has a unique vision. I can't wait to read the next book."

- Lauren Shrensky,
Nutritious U Bravo Bars, Denver, CO

"I had a feeling when I found out it was over 400 pages that I would not be putting it down … and I was right! I finished it in two-and-half days! And as excited as I am for the rest of the series, I will definitely be reading *Alawahea* again!!"

- Wendy Groves, Pueblo, CO

"*Alawahea* brought a sense of imagination and creativity back into my life. I cannot wait for it to be continued."

- Marie Makinano, WIRE Properties, Denver, CO

Alawahea

Alawahea

The Azellian Affairs
Book One

Sara L. Daigle

MERRY DISSONANCE PRESS   CASTLE ROCK, COLORADO

Alawahea
The Azellian Affairs, Book One

Published by Merry Dissonance Press, LLC
Castle Rock, CO

FIRST EDITION 2015

Library of Congress Control Number: 2015903351

Daigle, Sara L., Author
Alawahea: The Azellian Affairs, Book One
Sara L. Daigle

ISBN 978-1-939919-13-7
1. Fiction
2. Visionary & Metaphysical
3. Romance/Fantasy

Book Design and Cover Design © 2015
Cover Design by Elena Karoumpali
Book Design by Andrea Costantine
Editing by Donna Mazzitelli

To David and my mother
You never got to see the finished product,
but here it is … at long last

Chapter One

DISASTER. IT PROMISED to be a total disaster. Or else the very best thing that had ever happened to the world. Ellen Pearson snorted, almost laughing as she stared down at the harbringer of change in front of her. Couched in legal terms that nevertheless did not camoflauge the revolutionary intent behind the request, the précis in front of her seemed completely innocuous, yet *so very* complex.

A presidential election year loomed like a threat on the horizon, and the President of the United States had decided he wanted to push everyone's patience and promote goodwill toward all in an effort to create a positive image—hopefully. A part of that involved inviting alien students to Earth to study. And people like her had to make it work—somehow. She sighed, tapping her fingers on the desk. Of the many ambassadors on Earth available to consult with about this matter, only one had shown any interest at all in the project—the Azellian ambassador. Ellen had met

Merran Corina only once; unfortunately, he had not impressed her. Oh, he was certainly young, handsome, charming, and very polite, but he also dominated many of the tabloids with tales of his prowess amongst human women. She'd seen an article just this morning linking him with some new starlet. How he managed to have time to actually work, she had no idea, but shortly after the president made his announcement, Mr. Corina had indeed put in a request to be part of the exchange program, refining and improving upon the president's original suggestion. She pulled up his email, clicking on the attachment.

Somewhat to her surprise, Merran's request was organized, well-planned, and very short. The idea was to allow students to exchange from Earth to Azelle and Azelle to Earth. There would be limited exposure at first, initially through the University of Denver. Located a couple of blocks from the embassy, it would provide the perfect place for Azellian students to get familiar with their human counterparts. The exchange would last for one year—a small group only, of maybe four to six Azellian students to start with, all conversant in Standard English, who would choose a courseload in accordance with university policy. Then, a select group of students from Earth would be allowed to exchange back to Azelle. Merran Corina would oversee the whole process closely, and, if successful, this exchange could be expanded to include universities in other cities on Earth and Azelle.

Ellen drummed her finger against her computer screen. She glanced down at her watch. Was it too late to call the ambassador? Probably, but if she called the embassy's number, she could leave a message and have him return it in the morning. She clicked on the video portion of her computer and tapped the embassy's number.

"Azellian Embassy. This is Saudrina Marynna. How may I help you?" The video had been picked up by an actual Azellian, amazingly enough in this era of computer-generated answering services and endless hold times as calls were routed to overseas locations. The screen showed a young woman, maybe in her twenties, with regular features—brown hair and ordinary brown eyes. She spoke English with a perfect accent. Except for her name, which wasn't a human surname, she could have been Ellen's own assistant.

"Good evening, Ms. Marynna. I would like to leave a message for Ambassador Corina. This is Ellen Pearson of the Earth Liaison Office."

"Just a moment, Ms. Pearson. Let me check to see if Ambassador Corina is available to speak with you now." The screen went dark as she put Ellen on hold. Ellen leaned back and waited, surprised that she might actually be able to speak to the ambassador at this late hour.

"Thank you for waiting, Ms. Pearson. I have the ambassador on the line for you." She clicked another button and Ellen was suddenly looking at Merran Corina himself. His hair was a bit tousled, and he looked like he was wearing little else but a dressing robe.

Ellen felt the blush crawl up her cheeks and bloom into ferocious heat. "I'm so sorry, Ambassador. I didn't realize you would be disturbed by my request."

The young ambassador grinned. "You didn't disturb me, Ms. Pearson." An odd time-lag to his voice and his musical accent necessitated Ellen's focused attention to understand his words. "I am working from home today," he added.

Ellen blinked. "Uh, aren't you here in Denver, Ambassador? It's nearly ten o'clock in the evening. I'd intended to leave you a message because of the lateness."

"No, I am currently on Azelle where it is mid-afternoon." His impish grin faded to a more formal, appropriate expression for an ambassador. "What can I help you with, Ms. Pearson? I would imagine it is quite important that you should need to contact me at ten o'clock in the evening."

With some difficulty, Ellen collected herself. "Oh, no, Ambassador. Not at all. I am simply going through your request to exchange students between here and Azelle and I have a few questions for you about the details."

He said nothing further about the lateness of the hour, settling back in his chair instead. "Certainly. What can I help you with?"

She fought to remember what she'd been meaning to ask, trying to bring her brain back online. She might have met him in the past, but she'd never had to deal with him directly before, and the sensation that his eyes went right through her, even through the somewhat jerky online connection, was unnerving in the extreme. "Our strongest concern is your involvement. How closely do you intend to oversee this process?"

"I see myself taking a very active role in the choice of students who will be allowed to exchange in both directions. I plan to host regular excursions and meetings at the embassy on Earth, offer adjustment services for the Azellians who will be traveling to Earth, and facilitate the same services for humans who come to Azelle. I will personally interview all candidates who go to Earth and return to Azelle. Students will be picked based on the ones most likely to make the best transition between the two cultures. The students in both directions are going to be ambassadors, and we plan on treating them as such." His answer was smooth and practiced, and Ellen had the sudden feeling he'd delivered it many times in the recent past.

12

"So you will be the one the Liaison Office contacts in the event of trouble?"

"Yes."

"Well, Ambassador, there is no reason to refuse your request … the university is quite thrilled to be the first exchange school with Azelle. The new school year begins in one month. Were you planning on enrolling your Azellian exchange students this semester?"

The ambassador's smile made her heart stumble. She ignored its effect, calling on thirty-five years of dealing with ambassadors—some young, some old, some strange, some fantastic—to keep her expression smooth.

"We would love to, Ms. Pearson."

"Will you be returning to Denver soon, Ambassador?" Only a tiny quiver in her voice betrayed her, but that wasn't audible to someone who didn't know her. At least she hoped not.

"In a few days, yes. I can have the bio stats on the Azellians who wish to attend the university ready when I arrive. Do you need me to supply the university or you with a copy?"

"Yes, send over two copies. I'll review them and submit them to the university administration. It won't be easy, but we will have your students enrolled within the month."

Again the blinding smile, but Ellen braced herself for it this time.

"Thank you, Ms. Pearson. Can I help you with anything further?"

"No, Ambassador, I think that is all I need for now."

"Well then, good evening Ms. Pearson. Or should I say goodnight?" The ambassador's smile took on the edge of a grin.

"Good evening, Ambassador." Ellen firmly pushed the end button. Were they all that young? Had she ever been? Ellen sighed as she turned off the computer. She hoped the president knew what he was doing with this open exchange thing, because if all Azellians were like the young ambassador, human relationships were in trouble. Shaking her head, she leaned over her desk, sliding the précis away from her, and then pushed her chair back. Getting to her feet, she turned away from the dark mountains and the lighted skyscrapers and walked out of the room, closing the door firmly behind her.

❋ ❋ ❋

Several days later, in one of Denver's northwestern suburbs, Tamara Carrington stared at the book she was trying, rather unsuccessfully, to read. The blare of the television coming from the family room downstairs distracted her as she sprawled across the thick, oversized armchair where she sat in the formal living room upstairs.

"And now, our human interest section," the newscaster droned in his smooth, neutral voice. "In accordance with President Labord's new era of open communication, the University of Denver has announced its plans to welcome four students from Azelle to their campus this semester. Ambassador Merran Corina, one of Azelle's youngest and most active ambassadors, is going to oversee the program and will help integrate the Azellian students for the nineteen months they will be attending school on Earth. Lucy Parvinter managed to catch up with Ambassador Corina earlier today and has the details for us."

Tamara threw her book aside, launched herself out of the armchair, and flew down the stairs, hanging on to the rail as she skipped over several steps on her way down. She rounded the corner of the basement, clinging to the edge of the wall to make it around, and stared at the plasma televison that dominated the room. Her father watched the screen, his expression impassive. Her mother, with her mouth open in a little "o" of surprise, cupped a mug of tea and watched the screen intently. Her grandmother focused entirely on the knitting in her hands, seemingly ignoring the television with a ferocity that was nearly palpable.

"Thank you, Jim. I am here at the Azellian Embassy." A woman's face, pretty in a generic, television sort of way, with dark hair cut short in clean lines that framed her round face, appeared on the screen. Behind her, tall ornate gates surrounded a beautiful white mansion lit up brilliantly in the night. Spotlights highlighted specific areas of the mansion, giving it a ghostly glow. Not knowing why, Tamara suppressed a shiver. "A short distance from the university campus, it provides the perfect spot from which to coordinate efforts to introduce Azellian students to Earth."

The shot on screen switched abruptly to a room inside the mansion, focusing on Lucy Parvinter's face. "Thank you for agreeing to meet with me, Ambassador." The camera swung away from the generically attractive reporter to focus on the ambassador who was seated behind a large oak desk.

Tamara's breath caught as the ambassador favored the reporter with a brilliant smile. High cheekbones, firm jaw, a slender blade of a nose, generous lips, and a perfectly proportioned mouth, his face should have graced the cover of a men's fashion magazine. Wavy dark hair fell around his broad shoulders, and the camera caught even darker brown eyes. In the bright lights of the camera equipment, his skin was an olive color, tanned to a glowing bronze. The ambassador lifted long fingers to brush a wave of hair off his forehead. He wore a light gray suit, setting off his dark looks perfectly. "You are welcome, Ms. Parvinter. It is an honor to be here." His voice was light and musical, the words flowing off his tongue almost as if they were being sung. Except for the accent, he spoke English flawlessly.

"Ambassador, tell us a little bit about the program. What do you hope to accomplish?"

"Our purpose is to build a stronger relationship between our worlds. We have reached a new era of exploration and study for all of us. As this era continues, we cannot continue to isolate ourselves. We want to learn from you and hope you will also learn from us in a free exchange of ideas, thoughts, and behaviors. I have spent eight years here in Denver, and I must tell you, it has been absolutely fascinating to me. I hope my fellow Azellians will agree." The ambassador favored the reporter with another blinding smile. Tamara held her breath. How was the woman keeping her thoughts straight?

However she was doing it, she managed. Her voice didn't even waver as she replied in smooth, polished tones, "We are certainly glad to have you here, Ambassador. We know very little about our Azellian cousins. It is wonderful to have the opportunity to learn more."

"We're better off knowing nothing about those demons," Tamara's grandmother muttered, twitching the length of blanket across her lap and pointing her knitting needles as if she were ready to leap through the screen and stab him.

"Isn't that your dorm, Tammy dear?" Jeanine, Tamara's mother, interjected quietly. Sadie Carrington fell silent—a sour expression remaining on her face as she violently wrenched her knitting. It was as if it represented the attractive ambassador, each movement of the yarn wrapping more tightly around his throat.

Tamara focused on the screen. The news report had switched to the university and was showing scenes of university life voiced over by the ambassador's musical lilt and the reporter's calm questions. "That *is* my dorm! Wait a minute! Are they housing the students there?"

Sadie cleared her throat loudly and snapped the blanket on her knees with even more force. "I would have her moved immediately, Jeanine. She will be corrupted by those filthy animals."

Tamara hastened to answer, although she knew it was probably hopeless. Her grandmother had always had something against Azellians. It was apparent that she had something against Tamara as well, which made the fact that the old woman was living with them temporarily very unpleasant. "I have no choice in where they put me, Grandma. I don't imagine I'll be living all that close to them. Look, they're focusing on another dorm."

"You have nothing to do with them, child. Do you hear me? In fact, I would suggest you move her to another school, Peter." She took her angry gaze off Tamara and turned to Tamara's father. "Immediately."

"It will be all right, Mother."

"It will not be all right, Peter James! Of all of us, you should know that best." Peter's mother stared at him with cold blue eyes.

"You are overreacting, Mother."

"Am I, considering the way you behaved when you were younger?" Sadie hissed between her teeth. "Tell me I am overreacting, after the way both you and your bastard of a father behaved back then." Tamara blinked. She knew something large existed between her father and his mother, something that had soured their relationship over the years, but they had never spoken about it openly. Whatever had happened in the past was an ongoing point of contention for her grandmother. She knew better than to ask.

Tamara's mother stood up, breaking through the tension. "That's enough, Sadie, Peter. Tammy is going back to the university in a couple of weeks and I'm sure she doesn't want you squabbling the entire time she's home."

Her father got to his feet. Her grandmother glared up at him. "Mark my words. Letting those filthy creatures into our institutions will pave the way for immorality and the destruction of everything we know."

Tamara sensed that her father's temper was about to ignite. She watched as he tensed his jaw. She could feel his emotion building as he clenched his hands—his muscles visibly quivering. Her mother laid a gentle hand on his shoulder, and he restrained himself with visible effort. He turned on his heel and strode out of the room, taking a large portion of the tension with him as Sadie pointedly ignored Tamara and Jeanine.

Tamara got up and followed her father. He sat with his elbows poised on the kitchen table, his face buried in his hands. "Are you all right, Dad?"

Peter Carrington dropped his hands and looked up at his daughter. He gave her a small smile. "I'm fine, Tammy."

Feeling awkward but wanting to do something to help her father, Tamara ventured, "Why is she so hateful?"

She watched as her father shrank in on himself. "She was hurt badly years ago and she's never gotten over it." He lowered his hands. "Don't worry, Tammy. She's not going to be staying with us all that long."

Not sure she understood the explanation, Tamara shook her head. "I don't understand why, but she's never liked me much, Dad ... any more than she seems to like you."

Peter's expression darkened. "She doesn't dislike us, sweetheart." He rubbed his hand against the back of his neck. He seemed to consider something before speaking and finally repeated, "She's just hurting."

Tamara closed her eyes. "For all these years?" She muttered the words under her breath, almost whispering them to herself. She opened her eyes and spoke more loudly, "I just want to help, Dad. I'm twenty years old. I think I can handle a few family skeletons."

Peter looked up at her. He was silent for a moment and then opened his mouth to speak. A shiver skittered up Tamara's back as she leaned forward. He seemed tired but almost eager at the same time. Tamara tensed. Was he finally going to tell her about the deep dark secret?

"What's happening? Dad, I heard shouting—" Tamara's younger sister Andreya skidded around the corner. She saw Tamara standing there and gave her a glare. Tamara ignored her younger sister as best she could but knew the opportunity had been lost. Peter seemed to harden, his shoulders going back and his head coming up. "What did Tammy do now?"

"Nothing. It's not important, Andreya. Go to your rooms, both of you. I'm going out for a walk." Peter stood up, shoving his chair back. Tamara wanted to strangle her sister. Every time she and her father almost seemed to connect, Andreya waltzed in and destroyed the fragile communion. She seemed to have a sixth sense about it, careening into the conversation every time Peter seemed ready to tell Tamara about the past. For some reason, he would clam up as soon as Andreya came in and then dismiss them both.

She glared back at her sister. "Way to go, Andreya. Just chase him out of the house."

"Did not. What happened?"

Tamara shrugged, suddenly irritated. "Ask Mom, nosy. I'm going to bed." She walked down the hallway to her room and firmly shut the door behind her.

That night, she dreamed. In the dream, she ran after her father. "Dad, why does Grandma hate us?"

"You and I are different, Tamara." Her father's voice had a lilting accent he didn't have in life, morphing into the ambassador's handsome features as he spoke. Behind the ambassador an empty plain stretched in all directions, swept only by winds and sand. "Come home." The wind howled in the distance—an eerie, ululating call that made her long to run through the fine sand as it oozed between her toes. Her whole being vibrated, feeling the lure of the song. She stepped toward the ambassador. He took her hands in his, his hands large and warm in her fingers. He pulled her close and bent his head to kiss her, his hands suddenly exploring her body. New feelings built, pushing away the longing, a different kind of aching beginning …

She woke abruptly, breathing hard. Struggling to get free of the tatters of the dream, she sat up. Her heart raced; her nightgown clung to her shoulders and back. Outside, the wind howled as a weather front moved in, rattling the windows. She listened to the wind for a moment, trying to hear that note, the note that had permeated her dream, that siren's call. What had it been—that wild song that hadn't been external at all? She lay back down on the bed and listened to the wind shake the windows, sleep banished by the dream and the formless longing that followed.

※ ※ ※

Several days later at the Azellian embassy, Merran Corina leaned back against his chair and stretched, looking out his window at the early morning vista. Skyscrapers loomed against the majesty of the Continental Divide. The blue sky met the dark silhouette of the mountains, throwing them into stark relief. He rubbed his eyes and reached out with his mind. *Janille?*

The door opened almost immediately. "Yes, Ambassador?" An older woman with graying hair stepped into the office. Always very proper, his assistant, Janille, maintained a strict distance between them. Although he had been a little uncomfortable with the formality at first, Merran had since gotten used to their working relationship. It gave him something of a relief to know that she would not pry into anything she had no business knowing. Considering that the human media left him very little in the way of privacy, Merran appreciated her discretion.

"What's on the docket for today?"

Janille placed an electronic pad on his desk. "The Council reports are ready for broadcast this evening when you have your regular contact with them. You have to pick up the Azellian students at noon at the spaceport and escort them to the campus to help them get settled in. Then you have a meeting with the Earth Liaison Office this afternoon. Following that, you have a welcome dinner planned for the students, assuming they have the energy after the flight and settling into their rooms."

Merran sighed. "It begins. Why did I agree to this anyway?" Janille allowed herself a small smile, but she said nothing. He continued, "Did you happen to catch the newscast last week?" He straightened in his chair and looked down at his desk. "The one where they interviewed me?"

"I did, sir."

"Any reaction?" Merran stretched his neck one way, then the other.

"I think it went well, but it's the humans that matter and it's hard to say what they think about it. The question she raised about our mental abilities ... you glossed over that one very smoothly, sir."

Merran grinned. "I tried. Distraction seemed to be safest, as most of the humans I meet are either extremely terrified or quite fascinated by the idea of my possible ... abilities ... that they are hardly able to function around me."

Janille's mouth twitched. "I can imagine what form of distraction you chose."

His grin widened. "Would I be so unscrupulous as to capitalize on my looks to distract a truth seeker?"

Janille's expression was eloquent. "I have only one question, sir. Do I need to send flowers?"

Merran laughed. "Hmm, good question. It might be useful to call on her again, eventually. She's ... ah ... quite an interesting woman."

Janille's eyebrow shot up. "Did you wish to arrange another encounter with her?"

Merran shook his head. "Not really. Just keep her in the possible contact group." He glanced up at the clock on the wall. "The *aarya* damn it! Is it already so late?"

Janille smiled and held out a tablet computer. "The car is waiting out front, Ambassador. Here are the necessary documents for your friends. The flight is right on time."

"Thank you, Janille." Merran jumped to his feet as the tablet, guided by his telekinetic abilities, flew from her hand into his. He tucked it into the inner pocket of his blazer and headed out the door, hoping he had time to make it to the spaceport before his fellow Azellians arrived.

❋ ❋ ❋

Completely unaware of Merran's wild dash across Denver, Tamara leaned against the kitchen wall, watching her mother as she finished washing the counters. "I—I don't understand, Mom."

Jeanine looked at Tamara over one shoulder, her expression carefully neutral. "I need to go in for tests, Tammy dear."

"For the pain in your chest? I thought the treatment was working."

"The pain really hasn't gone away, honey. Your father and I thought we should get it checked out formally, with a specialist." Jeanine's mouth curved in a slight smile. "It's probably nothing, but it's better to be safe than sorry."

Tamara made a face. "God, Mom, I hope so." She stepped forward to hug her mother. "I have to get to work, but I'll see you later tonight. Call me at work if you need to."

Jeanine returned Tamara's hug with a tight embrace of her own. Her mother didn't say anything, but her eyes were wet with sudden tears that Tamara noticed as she stepped away.

Tamara left the kitchen, trying to control her own desire to cry. What would she do if something happened to her mother? She took a deep breath and went to her room to grab her jacket.

Andreya stood by the door to her room, arms crossed under her breasts. "Going to work?"

Tamara spared her fifteen-year-old sister a glance. "Yes." She would have added a sarcastic rejoinder, but Andreya looked like she was spoiling for a fight and Tamara had no desire to spar with her at that moment.

"You think you're so superior, don't you?"

Tamara brushed by her sister and grabbed her jacket, closing the door firmly behind her. "I don't have time for this, Andreya."

Unsatisfied by Tamara's refusal to give her the fight she wanted, Andreya followed her back down the hallway. "You're not one of us, you know." Unlike blond Andreya, Peter, and Jeanine, Tamara had dark brown hair, which she kept clipped short for comfort and ease. Also, unlike the rest of their family, Tamara had grey-blue eyes. She looked something like her father, but absolutely nothing like Jeanine. The accusation that she didn't belong had been a favorite taunt of Andreya's since they were kids.

Tamara sighed. "I know you're jealous, Andreya, but you'll get your chance to go to college and get a job."

Andreya glared at her. "I am not jealous."

Tamara just shook her head and walked away. "I'm gonna be late if I don't get out of here." She could feel Andreya's angry stare on the back of her neck and tried to ignore it. It wasn't until she had driven her car halfway to the university that she felt in command enough to let the whole conversation go. Occasional glimpses of the mountains beyond the looming skyscrapers of the downtown area helped, although she didn't have time to do much more than glance. The rest of the tangled downtown traffic demanded all her attention.

With the heavy traffic, the drive to the university took longer than she'd expected, and she had to force herself to be patient. On campus, Tamara maneuvered the car into a parking space between two other vehicles and got out, locking the doors behind her.

Since classes had not yet started, the walk to work was relatively peaceful, with few groups wandering the sweeping campus area. The old Southern Colonial style columns of the Administration building loomed over her head as she walked up the wide cement steps and entered, taking the elevator just inside the door to the third floor. Encountering no one in the building—most of the students would not be arriving for a couple more weeks—Tamara crossed the study lounge to the Registrar's Office.

She entered the office and saw her boss sitting at one of the computer terminals. "Hello, Kim. Have we got lots of new student cards to enter?"

Kim smiled at her. "Well good afternoon to you, Tamara. We sure do. Here's the stack to start on." She pushed a tall, wobbly stack of old-fashioned paper cards at Tamara.

"Yikes." Tamara snagged the box as she made her way to the other computer. "Are they actually returning their cards on time?"

"Those are just the new students. We've got a huge class coming in this year."

"Any chance the school's going to upgrade the computer system to voice recognition software?" Tamara settled into the chair and pulled the box closer.

Kim snorted and chuckled. "Are you kidding me? Why would they when they can get along with these ancient things? They haven't even let us use electronic clipboards for the students to complete. Too expensive, they say. Much better to have them write down their information on paper and pay us to enter it. But then, we wouldn't have a job if they actually updated their computer system, so I'm not really complaining."

Neither was Tamara, but she did have to admit that entering student data cards wasn't normally the most interesting task in the world. She didn't make any further comment and focused instead on entering the stack of cards in front of her, using the antiquated keyboard system to enter each card into the Registrar Office's software.

After an hour or so, Kim pushed her chair back. "I'm going to get a cup of coffee downstairs, Tam. Can you hold down the fort?"

It took Tamara a moment to realize Kim was talking to her. "Oh, sure." She gave a distracted wave. Not five minutes later, the door opened again. Expecting Kim, Tamara didn't look up right away.

"Excuse me?" an accented male voice said, sounding oddly familiar.

Tamara jumped and looked up. Standing in front of her was the young man she had seen in the news report less than a week ago, his dark brown eyes regarding her intently. Wearing a suit very much like the one he had worn during the interview, he was even better looking in person. She flushed, feeling the heat crawl up her cheeks. "I'm sorry. I thought you were my coworker coming back. How can I help you?"

"I am Ambassador Merran Corina of the Azellian embassy," he said, his words flowing with exquisite enunciation. She had to force herself to concentrate on his words rather than his accent; otherwise, she might have gotten lost in his voice. "I need to register these four students so they can get settled in their rooms today, if you could help me."

Tamara collected her scattered thoughts, pulling herself together and belatedly noticing there were four young people with him. "Oh, you must be the exchange students." She gave them all a warm smile, handing them each two cards. "We need you to complete a card like this and one like this. I think you've been pre-approved for your classes, but you need to let us know what they are." She motioned to the table. "There are pencils over there. Please give me your cards when you're done."

As they turned to comply, the ambassador walking away with them, Tamara studied the newcomers surreptitiously. The three young men and one young woman all had an air of comfortable confidence quite at odds with their new status here. The young man closest to her was a redhead. His features, even in profile, were delicate and chiseled—his nose a fine, straight blade on his face as he leaned over the table in the far corner. He rested an olive-skinned, tanned arm on the table, the muscles in his forearm etched in sharp relief by the pressure he exerted on his arm. Generous lips pursed as he read the card in front of him. His broad shoulders and chest, well-defined under a white t-shirt with some type of writing on it that she could not see, tapered down to a narrow waist and slender legs encased in light blue jeans.

The second young man leaned over the table facing her. Sandy-blond hair fell over a high forehead into amber brown eyes as he read—a slight frown between them. His features were much heavier than his companion's, with a slightly too-long nose and a jaw that was almost too strong. A good four or five inches shorter than the redhead, his dark blue t-shirt stretched across a well-muscled chest that, despite being stocky, had no spare fat on it at all. As he wrote on the card with his left hand, she observed that he was less tanned than the redhead. He nevertheless bore the same basic olive complexion. The dark-haired young man next to him nudged him and said something she couldn't hear. The one who spoke suddenly grinned—his wide, generous mouth flashing straight white teeth. Black hair fell into his blue eyes, and he tossed his head, catching Tamara's expression as she looked at them. He winked and returned his attention to the table in front of him.

Not wanting to get caught staring, Tamara looked away. After a few minutes, she snuck another peek at him. His face reminded her of someone's, but she couldn't place where she'd seen those features before. Relatively small and straight, his nose had a slight flare to the nostril. His jaw was fairly prominent, making his face look long. The generous mouth softened the hard, masculine features of his face. He wore a vividly colored t-shirt tucked into a pair of long safari shorts. His thighs were quite heavy and muscular. His upper body was broad and unfinished looking, a little more muscular than the redhead but not as stocky as the blond. Her eyes traveled around the table to the young woman. The same height as the blond, she bent over the table with her back to Tamara. She had wavy brown hair that was cut in an attractive, shoulder-length bob and swept behind one delicate ear as she bent over the paper. Tamara couldn't see her features from that position, but her lithe, slender body looked athletic.

Tamara's cautious regard swept on to the final member of the group. Standing at the head of the table, the ambassador leaned forward to answer a question posed by the woman. His expression intent on what the young woman was saying, Tamara got the opportunity to study him more closely. Taller than the other young men, the ambassador in his suit revealed less of his body structure than their jeans, t-shirts, and shorts. She had a moment of disappointment. Then, as if he noticed her attention, the ambassador looked up, caught her looking at him, and dodged around the desk to come up to her. Hastily, Tamara dropped her eyes to her desk as he approached, feeling the furious blush crawl up her face.

"You are a student here?" he asked in that musical voice.

Tamara looked up, her cheeks burning. She had a hard time meeting his eyes but forced herself to do so anyway. "Yes. Uh, my name is Tamara Carrington."

The ambassador leaned against the desk. "Carrington? Would you be any relation to James Carrington?"

"He was, uh, my grandfather."

"Ah, this is wonderful! We in the diplomatic corps know Ambassador Carrington well." He paused, then continued, "Was? Is he not still alive?"

Tamara ducked her head. "He passed away a few years ago."

"I'm sorry to hear that." The ambassador straightened and bowed to her, placing his hand on his chest as he did so. "He was well respected on Azelle. We knew he had been ill, but we had no idea he had actually transitioned." He rested his hands on her desk. Leaning forward, those dark eyes appeared intent on her. He gave her a charming grin that might have even melted her grandmother's cold heart. "Well now. Do you mind if I ask what you are majoring in?" Usually feeling fairly secure in herself, she wondered why she was suddenly blushing.

Tamara swallowed hard as she tried to regain her composure—and her ability to speak. "I am, uh, in diplomatic studies. Or I will be when I declare my major this year."

His grin widened, and he looked at her from under thick lashes. "Any specific planet you might be interested in?"

Dizziness assailed her as she struggled to remain calm. An odd pressure built behind her eyes and she lifted her hand unconsciously to rub the bridge of her nose. "Azelle is, um, interesting. I know more about it than my teacher does sometimes, mainly because my grandfather used to share stories with me. All the other planets are really great, too. I really like learning about other places. I'm not positive I want to be a diplomat like he was, but I do want to learn about other cultures and planets, and diplo studies is the best place to do that."

The pressure vanished abruptly just as it edged into pain. "Would you be willing to come to the embassy for a welcome party for these students tonight? It would give you an opportunity to mingle with embassy members and get you prepared for a possible diplomatic career." One side of his mouth lifted higher than the other as his voice took on an almost wheedling tone. "I can also get you access to other diplomatic embassies. I have several contacts in both the Atheran and Dorbin embassies."

Tamara hesitated only briefly. "Sure, that would be great! I'll come to the party tonight."

He straightened. "Seven o'clock, in the main lobby. Bring any of your friends too who you think might be interested in diplomatic studies."

Tamara blinked. A slight headache throbbed between her eyes. She managed to ignore it as the young woman stepped up to the desk carrying the eight cards. She smiled at Tamara. "Thank you. Here are the cards you asked us to complete." The words flowed out of her mouth more heavily accented than the ambassador's, although with the same musical lilt.

Tamara smiled back and collected her thoughts. "Now you need to go to the Dean of Students' office and get your room assignments."

The five Azellians left and the room suddenly seemed empty, as if there had been a lot more than just their bodies in the room. Tamara shivered, her head pounding. She flipped through the cards, reading the personal information listed there as she tried to figure out which was which. The only one she successfully identified was the woman, Mellis, since she was obviously the only female in the group. If Tamara attended the welcome party that night, she was sure she'd be introduced to the others—Greg, Justern, and Alarin—and learn who was who. Pushing aside her curiosity, Tamara focused on entering the data into the computer and tried not to wonder more about them. She'd probably get the chance to find out more, if she actually took the ambassador up on his invitation.

As soon as the five of them walked out of the office, Merran reached out to Greg on his private level so he could converse with him telepathically without the others hearing. *Did you pick up that she sensed me?*

I caught that she was becoming rather uncomfortable. I think you were hurting her. As a Healer, with a highly specialized sensitivity to others' suffering, Greg often could tell things about people that everyone else missed. *Is that even possible? Do humans even have psi?*

Theoretically, yes, they do. We talked about it a little bit in my training. I'm surprised Healers don't talk about this in theirs.

Healers aren't exactly all that interested in humans ... as you know ... considering the challenges I faced getting permission to come here. Back to Tamara Carrington. What did you pick up?

She was open on the surface, but her deeper levels are heavily screened by a very thick shield. When I pressed on it, it resisted me with surprising force.

Is that normal?

I don't know. I haven't run into a human with psi before. Whether they normally have it or not, Tamara certainly has a shield, at least on the deeper levels.

Greg was silent for a moment. *Shielded, huh? So, you actually think she's psi?*

Sure, why not? I think she very well could be.

Hmm. Maybe I should keep an eye on her.

Merran glanced at him. *Is she giving off a Call?* He had been friends with Greg long enough to know the Healer responded to things that Merran himself couldn't sense, but that those sometimes odd decisions and directions were important.

Not really. I just have a gut feeling.

I'm not one to argue with a Healer's gut feelings. Go for it.

Heads up, humans headed this way, Alarin sent on the public level, bringing their attention back to the group. Three women walked past them, laughing and talking, casting an admiring glance at the group of Azellians.

All five Azellians heard the comment clearly, easily picking up the mental admiration. "My, my, the students are getting better looking every year, aren't they, Jan? Makes you almost wish you weren't an employee."

"Since when has that stopped anyone? You know Lisa from accounting? She's going out with a senior. And James from admissions married one of the students last year," one of them added as the women rapidly passed out of sight and hearing range.

Wow, are these humans going to be a rush! Justern drawled on the public level. *They are so open it's like swimming naked.* He rolled his eyes and shivered. *You could get off just listening to their thoughts.*

Can't you think with anything but your hormones, Justy? Mellis, the female of the group, nudged him teasingly.

Why would I want to? Justern shot back as they entered the dean's office. *Wouldn't you want to walk around in a constant state of orgasm?*

Merran sputtered and coughed as they entered the dean's office and a distinguished looking gentleman came forward. "Excuse me, sir." He collected himself and gripped the man's hand. "Something caught in my throat." He ignored his friends as Mellis and Justern suppressed laughter, then turned back to the dean. "I'm Ambassador Merran Corina, and I'm here with the four Azellian exchange students."

32

The dean smiled—his warmth genuine, even if a bit overdone. "Welcome! We hope you will be comfortable here. Please, don't hesitate to ask any one of us for help should you need it."

Greg bowed. "We are honored to be here, sir. I'm sure we are going to have wonderful experiences. Our goal is to learn."

"Then you came to the right place. Our goal is to teach." The dean turned to the student seated behind the desk. "Ken, can you get the keys for these young people?"

"Sure." The young man hopped up and grabbed four sets of keys. "We have you set up in two different areas. Nearby, but not on top of each other. We hope that it allows you to mingle better with the hum—uh, other students."

They exchanged glances and Merran could feel the apprehension in all four of them. He hastened to reassure them mentally. *It will be fine. I'm planning on having many get-togethers at the embassy and you are always welcome to come to the embassy even when I'm not there. Remember the overt reason we're here. To foster understanding, which means mingling, guys.*

"Thank you," Mellis offered, recovering first. "It will help us settle in better, I'm sure. Start us off right."

"We've had quite a bit of experience with exchange students," the dean continued pleasantly. "And we find they tend to stick with their own groups rather than stretch and learn about the new one. This practice of separating our exchange students helps with that. You at least get to know your neighbors." He looked at the four of them and his mind oozed parental concern and high ideals. "It is up to you, of course, but I certainly hope you will all mingle with your fellow students and foster a better understanding of each other."

The aarya *take him, I think I'm going to be sick!* Justern shared mentally. Rather predictably, he was the most reactive to the pseudo-parental vibes the older man emoted. *How much more patronizing can he get?*

Alarin responded before Greg or Merran could. *Enough Justern. We are here to learn and he is genuinely concerned. Just smile, nod, and say thank you.*

Justern glared but he obeyed—reluctanctly.

Merran was glad to usher the group out of that particular office. "I have to go. I have a meeting with the Earth Liaison Office. Go to your rooms and get settled. We'll have our get together tonight. Be there at seven o'clock." They scattered, the four students heading for their individual rooms.

As he walked, Alarin extended a careful probe to his friends. His fellow Azellians were lost in feelings of overwhelm, even Justern, who was desperately trying to sidetrack himself by thoughts of sex and sarcastic little subvocal mutterings as they walked across campus. No one said anything, not even when they each reached their different dorms. In front of the blank wooden door that was to represent his home for the next nineteen months, Alarin felt the enormity of what he had done by coming to Earth at Merran's request, against his parents' wishes, against his other friends' wishes, even against his own inclinations. So many ifs. If his father hadn't been Leader of Azelle. If his older sister hadn't been a Healer and therefore ineligible to take up the family mantle of leadership, focusing all the family attention on him. If he hadn't been told over and over that he had no choice but to develop and highlight his family's genetically enhanced charismatic and coercive psi talent rather than the chemical engineering he wanted to study. If his mother hadn't been so forceful about his having to marry a woman she picked for him. If he hadn't been a Raderth, one of the eight ruling families of Azelle and the family that considered itself first among the ruling families. The pressure had ultimately been the deciding factor. He just hoped he'd done the right thing by leaving.

After looking down at the key in his hand, he glanced around. When he saw that no one was nearby, Alarin extended his mind and, with his telekinetic ability, clicked the mechanism. As the lock gave a satisfying thump, he turned the knob and opened the door. His little rebellion had gone unnoticed, of course, but it made him feel more like himself in the middle of this alien environment, so very unlike the majestic stone caverns of his hometown.

Standing in the doorway, he surveyed what would be his domain for the next several months. A bed, a dresser, a closet. A wall made of peculiar fabric-type material. A dark-brown, plastic-and-rubber chair pushed up against a scratched-up desk. Dragging his luggage behind him, he walked into the room, closed the door behind him, and threw himself facedown on the bed. Thin bands of sunlight striped the bare mattress—a western exposure of the window promised a good view, if he could gather up the energy and desire to go to the window. With his head swimming, he rested his forehead on his arms, trying to process everything that had happened to him these past few days. Along with the people and responsibilities he left behind, he'd traded the hot desert wind and near-white sky of Azelle for Earth's much bluer, although not much cooler, atmosphere, as well as the strangeness of how Earth felt to his psi sensitivity.

Every living, breathing planet had its own unique voice in the psi dimension, and although he'd never been to another planet before, Alarin instinctively thinned his shields to listen to the noisy, boisterous psi signature that was Earth's voice as a way of introducing himself. The sharp contrast of Earth's cheerful chaos to Azelle's soothing, harmonious song was jarring enough to make him homesick. He thickened his shields so that he could barely hear anything at all, even though the extra shielding made the bed spin unpleasantly. The tight, choked feeling of being cut off from the planet beneath his feet was enough to force him to open up again. Relaxing his shields, he lay on the bed and focused on nothing more than re-grounding himself, breathing slowly and deeply to reach his awareness past the cacophony of the upper levels of Earth's psi voice, deep into the thrum of the planet's very vibration. As he focused on his breath and the strong pulse of the planet's heartbeat, his body slowly relaxed and he let his awareness descend into the ground to bring himself into sync with the planet. To his surprise, Earth welcomed him, and he let the rest of his tension slide away into the ecstasy of communion.

❋ ❋ ❋

In another part of Denver, Merran strode up to the imposing skyscraper that housed the Earth Liaison Office. Inside the cool air-conditioned interior, people hastened by, carrying briefcases and folders, minds occupied with various errands or meetings. Out of habit, Merran checked the directory and stood in front of the bank of elevators, his own briefcase held loosely in his right hand.

A young woman joined him at the elevators. Merran glanced over at her and smiled. She met his eyes boldly, something few humans did when they knew who he was. Her eyes dropped from his eyes, travelling down his tie and shirtfront to the briefcase held in his hand. Merran raised his eyebrows, his smile increasing on one side.

The elevator door swooshed open. Merran stood back and let her in first, following her onto the platform. Her eyes checked out his backside; he could clearly sense her disappointment that the blazer he wore prevented clear viewing. He waited until the doors slammed closed and the elevator jolted upward before he spoke. "And?"

The woman jumped, startled by the fact that he had spoken. "And what?"

"Do you approve of what you see?" Merran shifted so he could see her but not face her completely, giving her plenty of space if the clear message pouring from her actually was unintentional. After so many years on Earth, he'd learned to treat human sexual messages carefully.

She leaned against the back wall of the elevator. "I can't see all that much, so I'm not qualified to make that judgment. Unless you'd be willing to ..." she trailed off suggestively.

Merran lifted his shoulders in an expressive shrug. He grinned and glanced at the cameras on the ceiling of the elevator. "I don't think an elevator with three cameras is quite the place."

"Pity," she sighed. "It would be an impressive end to a long day, with a very hot stranger in an elevator. A story to tell the girls. You don't work in this building, do you? If you did, I'm sure I would have seen you before now."

Merran wondered what she would say if she knew who he was. "No. I'm on my way to a meeting."

"Oh? On which floor?" She straightened and dropped the flirting. At least the obvious flirting.

"Thirtieth." Merran shifted against his hip as the elevator slid upward.

"The thirtieth floor? I'm headed there, too." Her boldness was the most attractive quality about her. Merran noticed that she dressed tastefully but aggressively, in a short black skirt and black tights, a red silk blouse with a fluffy red ruffle down the front, and three-inch heels.

A slow smile touched his lips. "Oh? For what meeting?"

She tossed her dark hair over a shoulder, pulling her hand through it in a move calculated to draw attention to herself. Her face was plain, although highlighted tastefully with makeup. Merran somehow doubted she would ever lack for partners. "Some boring meeting with an old fogey from the Azellian embassy, I think. We're going to grille him on some program he's been trying to foist on us for years."

Merran suppressed the grin that threatened to break through his control. "And your role is?"

"I'm assistant to Ellen Pearson, the Assistant Director of the Earth Liaison Office. My name's Lori Taylor." She extended a hand.

Merran took the delicate fingers and brushed his lips across the backs of them as he bowed, maintaining eye contact as he did so. "It is a pleasure to meet you, Ms. Taylor."

Her eyebrows shot up under the fringe of bangs that curled across her forehead. "Pretty manners too. My, my. Maybe we can hook up after the meeting."

Merran's smile broke through as the elevator stopped and the doors opened. "I could be convinced." With a small bow, he let her out first, holding the door open.

"Wait, how will I find you?" Lori stopped and twisted around to look at him. "What meeting are you going to?"

"The same one you are."

"Really? Well, that's good. What's your name by the way?"

They walked past the big desk in the front toward a conference room.

"You can call me Merran." He opened the conference room doors and let her through.

"Merran. That's unusual. It goes with your accent. Where are you from?"

Ellen, looking very trim in her business suit, not a strand of gray hair out of place, walked up to them and extended a hand to him. "Ambassador Corina, how wonderful to see you! I trust you had no problem finding this room."

Lori Taylor looked like she had just been kicked in the stomach. From her mental reactions, she felt something like it too, as her mind raced over their recent interaction, looking for a hint of his reactions to it. Merran bowed but managed not to grin. "None at all, Ms. Pearson. Your assistant here provided a wonderful escort."

"I'm glad to hear that," Ellen Pearson replied as she eyed her assistant. "I do hope she didn't behave inappropriately in any way."

Lori flushed a deep red.

Merran bowed. "It was a very enjoyable elevator ride. No offense was offered or taken. I did learn quite a bit about certain old embassy members however."

Lori choked and coughed. "Excuse me," she said hastily. "Do you mind if I go to the ladies' room before we get started?"

Ellen waved a hand, a slight frown between her eyes. "Go. But I need you back here to get set up so make it snappy. Ambassador, if you would?"

Lifting his briefcase, Merran strode to the front of the room, scanning with his mind and psi abilities as he moved. Except for the flirtatious Lori, whom he suspected would not want to have anything to do with him after this, the others in the room were all older, conservatively dressed, and conservatively minded. He had a moment of déjà vu—he'd had a hard time convincing the Azellian Council to allow this exchange, and now he faced another council, another day of hard arguing, and another endless war as the new tried to express itself through the old. Although the humans were on board with the idea of an exchange, he had no illusions that it would be easy. He suppressed his sigh and put his briefcase on the table.

Chapter Two

IN THE REGISTRAR'S OFFICE on campus, Tamara got ready to call it a day. She put the box of entered cards on the shelf behind the desk and pushed her chair back.

"Ready to go?" Kim asked her as she stood up.

Tamara stretched and nodded. Kim smiled at her as Tamara slipped on her coat.

"See you tomorrow?" Tamara asked over her shoulder.

"Tomorrow." Kim turned back to her work as Tamara pushed open the door and walked into the study lounge.

She didn't even notice the person sitting on one of the lounge chairs until he got up.

"Hi, are you done with work?" It was the dark-haired young man. Those luminous grey-blue eyes met hers and again Tamara was struck by a resemblance to—someone. She immediately felt a pressure behind her eyes. "I'm Justern."

"Hi, Justern." Tamara collected her suddenly scattering thoughts with some effort. "Are you all settled in?"

He nodded. "Better anyway. I finished unpacking everything and found myself at loose ends. Do you know any place where I could get something to eat? The campus seems to be closed down." His accent was as heavy as Mellis's, but his deeper voice made it seem a little less musical. Or maybe he was just nervous.

"The cafeteria will be opening for dinner in about ..." she checked her watch, "... forty-five minutes or so." He didn't seem quite so arrogant as he had earlier; in fact, he seemed almost desperate. "Do you know where it is?"

He shook his head.

"I can show you, but then I have to get home." Although she was in no mood to babysit a new arrival, there was something vulnerable about him that made her unwilling to chase him away. She motioned for him to get up. "How are you liking Earth so far?"

"Overwhelming." He sounded lost. She suddenly wanted to reach out to touch him and tell him it was going to be all right, but she resisted the urge. "And empty," he complained. "When are the other students going to arrive on campus?" He walked beside her down the stairs.

"In two weeks. You'll learn to appreciate how calm and quiet it is here right now. It's chaos for the first few days after the rest of the students get back. The other first-year students are going to be arriving tomorrow."

She could feel him look at her. "Regular classes don't start for two weeks then?"

Despite his accent, his English was really very good. Plenty of idiom. "Yes, two weeks from now. I noticed that you are all taking English as a second language, but you seem to be pretty fluent already."

42

"It was required to come here. The administration assumed that because we aren't human, we don't speak English." Justern's comment was tinged with an odd sarcastic lilt, quite contrary to the vulnerable little boy image she'd gotten from him a moment ago.

Sudden questions flew across her mind, dashing off into a tangent of uncomfortable thoughts. *Just how human are these Azellians? They are supposed to be closely related to humans, despite all their differences. But ... how closely?* Her grandmother had always claimed that her grandfather was unfaithful with Azellian women. *What would an Azellian look like naked? Maybe that ambassador*—she clamped down on her thoughts and pushed them away.

Justern looked at her strangely, and horror blanketed her thoughts. *Can he read my mind?* Her grandfather had always believed they could. She concentrated fiercely on counting, keeping her mind blank. "Are you all right?" he asked, but she was not at all sure whether he could read her mind or was just asking because she had done something weird to make him wonder.

"I'm fine." *What had Grandpa said? Repetitive counting would prevent a mind reader from reading anything they shouldn't?* Before now, she had never believed it as more than a story, but it couldn't hurt. *One two three four five! One two three four five!* "The cafeteria is over there," Tamara told him, pointing to a large Greek-style revivalist building on the north end of campus. "It will be open in about half an hour. I have to get home. See you later tonight ... at the embassy." She added the last quickly, as an afterthought, so he wouldn't think she was running away, even if she was.

Justern frowned at her, his head tilted slightly. "Okay," he said slowly. "Are you sure you're all right?"

One two three four five! One two three four five! One two three four five! Oh God, please make sure he wasn't able to read my mind. Tamara nodded. "I'm fine. I'm just late. My mother had an appointment and I have to get home." Across campus, she could see three people walking toward them. The glint of late afternoon sunlight on red hair made her realize the other Azellians were approaching. Too distracted to think up anything else and desperate to get out of there before the Azellians arrived, Tamara fled.

Alarin, Mellis, and Greg came up to Justern. "Was that Tamara speeding out of here as if a pride of sandcats was on her tail?" Greg asked in Azellian as they joined Justern.

Justern shrugged, his confusion apparent. "She was showing me the cafeteria, then just ... bolted."

Mellis scowled at him. "Did you hit on her?"

Justern put his hands up. "No!"

"What triggered the reaction, then?" Alarin asked, frowning at Tamara's escape route.

"We were talking calmly about the beginning of classes and getting oriented when her shields flared so strongly I thought she'd teleported away. They were solid, like stone walls, and they covered everything. Even her surface thoughts. I couldn't tell her mental signature ... nothing. It was like she wasn't there at all!" Justern sounded rattled. "Except she didn't go anywhere. She started acting funny and told me she was late for something, then ran off."

Have you scared her off from coming tonight, Justy? Mellis shifted to mental speech, frowning after Tamara. *We could really use a human to show us the ropes. I'd like to get to know her better—*

"No, she said she was coming." Justern shifted back to verbal speech, veiling his thoughts again from his friends.

Is she psi? Alarin sent to Greg on his intimate level. *Is it possible in a human?*

Merran says human psi exists theoretically, although he's never seen it personally. Did you read Justy's memories? If her psi is anything like Azellian psi, she's got the potential to be very powerful. She was open, like she was when we saw her earlier today, then her shield flared into place. Did you see her aura as her shield slammed closed?

Yeah, I think you're right. Whatever her abilities might be, she's powerful all right. No matter that she's human. She really frightened Justern. Did you see his reaction?

Justy isn't exactly stable at the moment, Alari. None of us are. We're space lagged and exhausted. I wouldn't read too much into his reactions.

Well, fine, that's true enough. Could you tell anything about what talents she might possess?

No, the shield slammed shut too fast and Justern is not experienced enough to have picked up anything from her aura before the shield covered it.

She's not Awakened, if she is psi. That shield isn't consistent enough.

That's assuming humans react anything like an Azellian to psi. I hope she doesn't, though.

Why not?

If she Awakens as we do, she's quite far beyond the normal and optimal age range for it.

Most of us manage to Awaken quite normally on our own, you know. Without Healer help.

Greg shrugged. *The pathways are more fluid the younger we are, and the channeling tends to be easier. The older it happens, it's usually because there are emotional factors involved that can create trauma and block the pathways. The later it happens, the worse it typically is.*

Speak for yourself. My Awakening was quite volatile and I was well within the normal age range.

Greg grinned at him. *That's just because you're a stubborn Raderth.*

Alarin grinned back. His family's reputation for arrogance and stubbornness was quite fitting with their status as the leaders of Azelle, although he himself was usually more easygoing. *That's what Kyla said, too, when she was trying to tell me to relax into it.*

Well, maybe Tamara won't Awaken like an Azellian does.

But just in case she does react the way one of us would … He expanded his mental sending to include Justern and Mellis. *We might want to tread carefully around her. From our time with her this morning, we know she's attracted to us and we all know the connection between sexual energy and psi. At least for us Azellians, anyway.*

Justern shuddered and answered verbally. "You don't have to worry about me. I'm not getting anywhere near her or her energy field." The fear generated from his exposure to her aura still oozed through his mind. Greg soothed him with a light mental touch.

Alarin spoke out loud as well. "Let's go get something to eat. Then we'll take tonight one step at a time."

❊ ❊ ❊

Merran's first hint that anything extraordinary had happened occurred later that night. He arrived back at the embassy after a four-hour, particularly grueling session with the Earth Liaison Office—the meeting had not gone at all the way he expected. Conservative-minded they might be, but the conference room full of high-ranking officials had decided to be *very* interested in the fate of Azellian students on Earth, especially a certain elected official who had encouraged the exchange in the first place. Merran had been grilled by the President of the United States before and didn't particularly want a repeat of the experience. Although humans had no obvious mental abilities, the president was a forceful person with as much willpower as any of the more powerful Raderths he had ever met. The president also possessed a sharp, keen mind that attacked him about Azellian "abilities" incessantly. Merran brushed a hand through his hair as he sat in his chair, remembering with some chagrin his evasive answers. He had probably just created larger rumors rather than answer the ones that were already out there. He sighed and reached over his office desk to flip a switch, turning on the digital frame that masqueraded as a window. Instead of the mountain afternoon, a dramatic view of the Azellian desert lit up. Resting his head back against the chair, he wondered for the first time if his fighting so hard to get the exchange to happen had been worth it. He tried to find the inner peace and security that would return him to confidence as he let his thoughts drift into the desert scene in front of him.

Instead, he got a quiet knock on the door and Greg's mind at his shields.

"Come in," Merran called out, keeping his deep fatigue and discouragement screened.

Greg came in, followed closely by Alarin. He stopped when he saw Merran. "Are you all right?"

Merran lifted his head from the chair. "I'm fine. Why? Do I look sick?"

"No, you just look like a shuttle recently landed on your head," Alarin observed. "What happened at your Earth Liaison meeting?"

"Nothing much," Merran replied with an airy, self-deprecating gesture. "No shuttles, although I might have preferred that. No, I just got landed on by a bunch of humans seeking the answers to life, the planet, and the burning Azellian question."

"Which are?" Greg asked, coming forward to settle in a chair in front of Merran.

"Do we have fearsome mental abilities or not, and how can we be of use to Earth?" Merran heaved a heavy sigh. "As much as I should have been prepared for the questions, I wasn't. My answers didn't really satisfy them, so I was grilled for four hours about our reasons for being on Earth and our hopes for the future. By the president himself, no less. He might have been present only by conference call, but that was bad enough."

"Is there going to be trouble over the whole issue?" Alarin asked, alarm creeping into his tone.

Merran shook his head. "No, no, I was able to convince them that we are much less than we are. But it wasn't pleasant. I tell you that president seemed to smell when I was being evasive." He leaned his head back. "And I have a flaming headache."

Greg got up and came around the desk. "I can help you with that." He moved to stand behind Merran. Touching his temples, rubbing lightly in concentric circles, then back down Merran's neck, Greg lightly massaged the tense muscles in his neck and head. Merran leaned into the touch, feeling the warmth spread from Greg's fingers up his neck and down his spine. The tension drained slowly out of him and he relaxed.

"Thank you, Greg," he murmured, closing his eyes. Then he opened one eye and looked at Alarin. "So what did you two come here to tell me?"

Alarin and Greg exchanged glances over his head. *How many people can hear us in here?* The comment came through to Merran's intimate level.

Merran opened his other eye. "None. I have my offices well screened from anyone seeking to hear thoughts or voices."

Then read my memories. Greg's hands stopped moving, but he continued to touch Merran's neck lightly. Merran used the contact to forge a link with Greg and absorb the information.

A few moments passed as he studied Greg's memories. "That's...interesting."

"Did your probe of her when we first met her reveal any potentials like that?" Alarin asked, leaning against the desk.

"Not actively. She was too shielded on her deeper levels for me to read anything. She was open enough on the surface, though, like any other human. If it hadn't been for her shield, I wouldn't have thought anything of it."

"Is it possible she'll Awaken the way one of us would?" Alarin asked intently.

"If she's human, highly unlikely," Merran replied. "From what little I know about the theory of human psi, it doesn't function the way ours does at all."

Greg tensed, suddenly very alert. "Is there any chance she's not human? That she's got Azellian genetics from somewhere?"

Alarin cleared his throat. "Azellian genetics? Are we even fertile with humans?"

"Oh yes, quite," Merran said to Alarin. "I suppose I'd better warn Justy too, but if either of you has sex with a human woman while you're on Earth, make very sure you're taking care not to impregnate her. Humans are odd about us. They find us extremely attractive, but long-term relationships between psi and non-psi don't really work well, especially with us trying to stay low-profile with our abilities. That doesn't stop them from trying, though, and there are human women who will try to trap us into relationships through pregnancy." He shook his head. "As for the progeny resulting from those interactions, fortunately it doesn't happen very often, but it does occur once in a while. One of my jobs here is to monitor those people with Azellian genetics, to see if they or their descendents show any signs of psi."

Merran paused briefly before adding, "The Carringtons aren't on the list of those I've been assigned to watch. Would it matter whether she has human psi or Azellian psi?" Merran asked, frowning at Greg.

He waved a hand. "Maybe not. It's just that if she does Awaken the way we would, she's very old for it. Azellians who don't Awaken until they're in their twenties usually are blocked and the Awakening process can become … difficult."

Merran shook his head. "Let's not borrow trouble. Let's assume she's human. I'm curious to learn more about human psi anyway."

"So you're willing to help?"

"She's very likely psi of some type, so yes. If there's any chance she has Azellian genetics, then I have to." He sighed and massaged between his eyes. "Can you give me some basics on Awakening protocol and psi training? I'm thinking it might be helpful if I'm going to play a part. Just to cover all the bases, even if she's human. Human psi might not work the way ours does, but having a little bit of training is better than nothing."

"Certainly," Greg replied. "You want some background too, Alari?"

"I'd better. I might have a Healer sister who's shown me quite a bit, but it never hurts to get some training from another Healer, and I'm curious, too. I'd like to help."

Greg glanced at the clock on the wall. "Now?"

Merran nodded. "We might as well take the next hour before the party starts. Otherwise, I won't have any spare time until later next week."

"You've got it. Open your minds and let me guide you."

Both young men complied and their training began.

✳ ✳ ✳

Not far from the embassy, Tamara sat in her family's kitchen, wrapping her hands around an empty mug that had once contained tea. It had taken her almost an hour to calm herself down after that rather embarrassing experience with Justern, but now she was once again feeling relaxed. It helped to see her mother. "What did they say, Mom?"

Jeanine shrugged and sipped her tea, wincing as she did so. "We won't know anything for a week or so."

"Do you want me to stay home? There's a new student welcoming party tonight at … at school and I was invited. But I can stay home and help out instead."

Peter was standing behind his wife with his hands on the back of her chair. He shook his head. "No, go, Tammy. You don't need to stick around here. We'll be all right. You can't suspend your life, and we don't know anything yet."

Jeanine reached out and touched Tamara's hand as she stood to leave. "Tammy, please make me a promise."

"What Mom?"

"Promise me that no matter what happens to me, you will finish school and get a career. I don't care what you choose, but I don't want me to interfere with your plans for the future, whatever they might be." Jeanine looked like she was fighting to hold back tears.

Tamara swallowed around a suddenly thick throat. "Don't talk like that, Mom."

"Well, promise me, Tamara."

"I promise, Mom." Tamara said finally, as tears burned at the back of her throat and eyes. She wanted to say more but was afraid of breaking down, so she fled.

Fortunately, she did not run into Andreya on her way to her room. When she broke down, she was able to be alone.

Again, it took her a bit of time to get composed, but when she came out of her room her eyes were clear, all signs of her crying gone. She kissed her parents goodbye and told them not to wait up for her, as she might sleep on campus. Feeling more at ease, she then left the house.

The embassy was not far from her parents' home, but the streets did not directly get her there. By the time she pulled up to the ornate gates, she had managed to work herself into a case of nerves.

The gates opened as she pulled up and a man—very likely an Azellian, although he wasn't dressed any differently than any other Denverite—came up to the car. "May I help you?"

"I'm here for the welcome party," Tamara replied. "Where do I go?" She thought she heard a murmur, but the man's lips did not move as he watched the pad in front of him. "I'm sorry, what did you say?"

With one eyebrow raised, the man focused on Tamara. His dark brown eyes, which were almost black, matched his dark hair. Because of his olive complexion, he could have passed for Mediterranean. "You may go up to the main lobby, Ms. Carrington. They are expecting you."

Tamara caught a glimpse of the pad as she drove in. It was blank. How had he known who she was? And how had he known that she could enter? An uneasy feeling crawled down her spine, but she ignored it, pulling her car through the gates. They closed smoothly behind her. She parked the car along the side of the curved drive and got out, walking along the edge of the pavement.

Her nerves increased as she came to the front of the huge mansion that served as the embassy. Much to her surprise, no one accosted her or did anything overt regarding security. She would have expected at least a metal detector, but maybe they weren't worried about terrorism. She walked up to the front doors.

The massive doors opened smoothly at her approach. She couldn't suppress a shiver, wondering suddenly if they had used a sensor, then berated herself. *Of course there's a sensor. How else would the doors open?*

The noise level from the party stopped her at the door. People stood in clusters and thronged the lobby entrance of the embassy. She halted just inside the doorway, blinking in confusion. It certainly sounded like thousands of people had been invited. The low murmur of voices swelled around her, making her dizzy, overwhelmed, and a little sick.

"Ah, Tamara," a voice greeted her smoothly. "Welcome to our little gathering." It was the ambassador, his hair pulled back and tied loosely at his neck. The sense of a thousand voices retreated and Tamara was able to catch her breath. The ambassador bowed to her, smiling warmly. She returned the bow, using one that her grandfather had taught her.

The ambassador looked surprised, but his smile widened. "I'm impressed. That was just the right response."

"Grandpa taught me a few of the most common bows before he died. I don't understand nearly all the nuances, though," Tamara admitted somewhat shyly. "How many people are here? I didn't think there were this many students on campus yet."

"Oh, this is mostly embassy workers and a few diplomatic humans. Maybe a hundred people," the ambassador replied, standing aside to let her pass in front of him. His arm came up to guide her, but he did not touch her as she thought he might. "Come, let me introduce you to the Azellian students formally. I know you saw them earlier, but we didn't have time to properly introduce them." Tamara passed in front of him. She thought she felt his hand brush her side as she passed. Someone laughed loudly beside her, cutting through the oddly muted sounds around her, and she flinched.

Unbeknownst to Tamara, as Merran guided her through the throng of people, he carefully kept a shield around her and himself. *Greg!* He called the Healer through his intimate level, reasonably sure Tamara could not hear it.

Merran? Greg's response came within seconds.

Where in hell are you? Tamara's here and she's wide open. Projecting like a son of a bitch, too. Mostly terror.

I'm trying to get Justern calmed down. It seems he's having an attack of something. Nerves or what, I don't know. I'll be there in a few minutes. Then, after a moment had passed, *Are you shielding her?*

What do you think? Merran snapped. *I'm just letting her project at everyone here? Do you know how many telepaths are here today? Damn, she's strong.*

The ambassador seemed oddly quiet as they walked through the room. Tamara got the strong impression he was distracted by something, although she couldn't tell what. "Is everything all right?" she asked him.

"Everything's fine," the ambassador said with a somewhat strained smile. "I am a little surprised at the number of people who've shown up tonight. I need to be more of a host than I thought I'd have to be. But then," he smiled and it seemed normal, as normal as she had seen up until now anyway, "that's what I do. And what I get when almost everyone accepts your invitation." He shrugged gracefully. "Of course, I will definitely limit the invite list when I ask the human students here to get used to Azellians."

Tamara laughed as she tried to relax and control her fear. The laughter helped. The ambassador gave her a look, one she could not interpret. In a flash, she became aware of a slight musky, spicy scent. *A rather nice smell,* she thought, breathing it in. He was wearing a robe, a very unusual garment for Earth, but it looked quite comfortable and appropriate for him. The robe outlined his wide shoulders, tapering to his narrow waist, and was cinctured by a wide, ornate belt. His body shape was not so much different than the redhead's she'd seen earlier, although Merran wasn't as lean. She wondered suddenly if he was wearing anything under the robe.

Merran closed his eyes briefly as a new sensation spread over him. She was still wide open, although patchy shields had appeared. The question that flew across her mind was not simply there for him to read—it was projected at him, followed by a powerful wallop of good old desire. Although he already knew she found him attractive, his own response took him completely by surprise. His body resonated with the vibration of sexual interest, strong enough to send him into immediate overdrive. He was not going to be able to shield her and control his physical reaction at the same time. *Greg!* He let the panic in his mind tone show. *Get in here!*

The response was from Alarin. *Greg's on his way. I'm here, though. Do you want help?*

You can't help her, Merran flashed back. *Not while she's open like this. You'll end up in the same boat I am.*

Let the shield go. I've got it. Alarin told him, walking up to them. *She's just projecting at the moment. I don't think she's particularly sensitive right now.*

Damn, she's strong. Whatever the hell she is, she's got enough power behind her projection to be a Corina, Merran managed to say through his discomfort.

For a moment, Alarin was silent. He sought to reach that part of her mind accessible behind the patchy shielding. *She certainly could be a projecting empath like you, if she can project her emotions out strongly enough to knock you off balance. You can usually roll with emotions that come in, except when someone equally strong projects them at you. If she were Azellian, I'd say she is for sure, but as I didn't even know humans had psi until a few hours ago, it might very well be something else. I don't think your reaction was entirely due to her projection, though. Find her attractive, do you?*

Merran's response was a low mental growl. He concentrated on draining the blood that filled him by opening the capillaries. He projected at Alarin just a hint of the pain caused by the forced draining of his erection. Alarin winced and shut up.

When Merran could speak again, he turned to Tamara. "Alarin, I'd like you to meet Tamara Carrington. Tamara, this is Alarin Raderth." Tamara recognized Alarin as the redhead that had come into the office earlier that day. "Now, as I have other duties to attend to, I'm going to leave you with Alarin, Tamara." He bowed to her. "Please feel free to visit the embassy at any time. We will certainly be having more get togethers. I hope you will attend many more of them." He knew he was being abrupt, but his body was more off balance than he'd expected. It had been a long time since he'd dealt with another projecting empath and he needed a moment to re-center himself. Otherwise, he knew he'd find himself leaking to the rest of the room. The last thing he needed to do was project sexual frustration at a room full of telepaths.

He left, trying not to feel like he was fleeing. Still fighting his body for control, he ran into Greg on his way out.

"Damn," Greg said in response to Merran's state.

"Tell me about it," Merran replied. "Alarin says she's possibly a projecting empath."

Greg blinked at him. "Given your reactions, I'd say that's more than a possibility. Is she only projecting at the moment?"

"She was sensing pretty hard when she arrived and projecting too. I think she could hear some of the mental conversation and it scared her. She started projecting stark terror so loud I went over and shielded her. Then she started to relax and got attracted to me. That's what undid me. I couldn't shield her and myself at the same time," Merran explained. Greg touched him lightly, doing something to his limbic system, and his body began to settle down. "Alarin's out there shielding her right now. If she becomes attracted to him, she'll put him into my state in moments too."

"And she has no idea she can do this?" Greg studied him.

Merran shook his head. "Not that I could tell. Her projection of desire at me was innocent. I don't think she's done this much."

"That would make sense if she's never had sex. Among Azellians, the awakening of psi energies and sex usually go hand-in-hand." Greg shook his head. "This particular incident should almost be over. I'll start getting her used to the idea of psi immediately, just in case there's a link between human psi and sex too." He studied Merran clinically and grinned. "Considering you seem to find her quite attractive and we know how much you love human women."

Merran waved a hand, ignoring the comment. "You'd better get out there, then. Oh. How's Justy?"

"Better. I think he's just a little freaked out and not used to the sensation at all. And space lagged besides. He'll be fine as soon as he settles down."

Merran nodded. "Is my office empty? I need a few moments to collect myself."

Greg waved his hand. "Be my guest."

It was with a tremendous sense of relief that Merran escaped into the quiet of his office.

❋ ❋ ❋

Across the lobby, Alarin guided Tamara unobtrusively to the edges of the crowd. Tamara's patchy shields thickened, laying a soft veil across her thoughts that protected her mind from the chaos around her. As her shields thickened, Alarin gently withdrew his shield from around her.

Pain built behind her eyes, a steady throbbing pressure that spread to the back of her head and thumped heavily in time to her heartbeat. Tamara didn't quite know what was happening or why, but suddenly the light stabbed at her eyes, nausea burned at the back of her throat, and the sounds of the talking people made her ears hurt. Tears eked out the corners of her eyes as she looked up at Alarin, barely even aware of his presence. Flashing lights danced across her vision and she wobbled on her feet. Strong arms caught her, picked her up, and carried her away. Her head started to whirl faster and faster, and she slid slowly toward complete black.

When she awoke, she was in a dark room. Disoriented and confused, she moved, but pain exploded through her.

"Don't move," a very soft voice told her. "Stay calm."

"Wh—" Her voice failed, nothing but a croak came out. "Who are you?"

"I'm Greg Tenricth." The young man was barely visible in the dark room, but his voice came out of the shadows from somewhere to her right. As he approached, she recognized him as the stocky, sandy-haired young man from earlier. "I can help you with your headache, if you cooperate with me. Do you mind if I touch you?"

Tamara fought down a sudden wash of nausea. She nodded gingerly, not having the ability to say anything right then. Greg could either see in the dark or took her silence for assent, because a light touch on her forehead soothed away the pain. With it went the nausea, until Tamara felt human again. Greg moved his hands and a low light sprang up.

"Where am I?" she asked, still feeling the need to whisper.

"Merran's office. It's the most shielded place I could bring you." Greg said matter-of-factly, but she did not understand his explanation. "How's your head?"

"Fine. H—how did you know? I w—was talking to—" She frowned. Nothing was clear since her arrival at this party.

"You were talking to Alarin. When you developed a headache, he brought you here to recover and called me to help."

"Wh—what did you do?" Tamara looked at him, suddenly nervous. She just remembered him touching her forehead, followed by a tremendous feeling of warmth, then the blessed cessation of pain.

"I healed you." Squatting at her side, Greg sat back against his heels. "It's something some of us Azellians can do. Comes in useful at times."

"Healed?" Tamara asked, fascinated despite herself. "What do you mean? Like Jesus?"

Greg laughed. "Not nearly so mystical or religious as that. You had inflammations in the muscles of your neck and it cut off a few capillaries, causing a very common phenomenon known as a migraine. I believe that's what you call it in English. I simply drained the inflammation and freed the blood flow again."

Alarmed, Tamara sat up and stared at him. "I had what? Oh no!"

Greg touched her shoulder lightly and her alarm faded. "Nothing unusual, just a typical migraine. I healed it. It doesn't matter exactly how."

Tamara stared down at his hand. "You mean like that? You're doing something to me right now, aren't you?"

Greg smiled at her, removed his hand, and looked harmless. "I'm calming you down. Encouraging your body to produce calming hormones."

"Do all the others here have these abilities?" Tamara asked. Deep down inside something clicked. Unbidden, a memory welled up of her grandfather's gruff voice telling her about fantastic things he had witnessed by the Azellian Healers. She had always thought the stories were exaggerations, especially because that was what her grandmother always claimed.

"No, I'm the only one on Earth right now who can do this. It takes a certain combination and fine tuning to make a Healer, and it's not actually all that common." Again, the explanation didn't quite make complete sense to her.

"The others do have abilities, though, don't they?" Something tickled at the back of her brain again. More of Grandpa's stories.

Greg nodded. "Different ones, in varying degrees. There's nothing mystical about these abilities, Tamara. They simply are very natural results of using certain parts of the brain."

"ESP has never been proven."

Greg smiled. "Psi exists, Tamara. Probably among humans, too, even if you don't know about it yet. Azellians aren't that different from humans. Our talents might be stronger than human talents because of environmental and acceptance factors, but we are all the same. Would you like me to show you about it?"

Fascinated despite herself, Tamara nodded. "But why would you? I'm just a human."

"Let's just say it may come in useful. Especially if you ever decide to come to Azelle to visit. You wouldn't be frightened or overawed. We aren't gods just because we can do things with our minds that others can't, Tamara. We still have frailties and feelings, just like humans."

"All right. My grandpa used to say that knowledge is power. And the more knowledge we have ... it's the only way to understand what we fear, right?"

"It's one way." He stood up and looked at her critically. "Are you sleeping on campus?"

Tamara nodded. "I've been sleeping at home the past couple of nights, but all my stuff's moved into my room."

"Then let's get you to it. I don't think you've got much energy left tonight." Greg turned away. "Merran's got a car for the group of us to use to get back to campus. Did you want to join us?"

It sounded better than walking home, or driving back to her parents' house tonight. She found herself completely exhausted. "What about my car?"

"Merran can make arrangements to have it delivered back to campus if you leave the keys," Greg told her.

Deciding to trust them and nodding wearily, she let him help her up. She dug her car keys out of a pocket, pulled the car key off the key ring and handed it to Greg. He placed it on the desk. She didn't see him leave a note or anything, but she was tired enough to be fading in and out. *I might have missed it,* she thought, as he led her down a set of back stairs that completely avoided all the other people downstairs. He pushed open the door—she didn't look too hard at whether or not he actually touched the door before opening it—and guided her out toward a long limo that was waiting in a back parking lot. She'd never seen this side of the embassy before. Unlike the ornate front, it was somewhat disappointingly utilitarian, not unlike any warehouse or office in the downtown area. Greg guided her to the car door, pulling it open for her.

As she bent over to climb in, she was startled to notice the other students already in the car. Alarin and Justern sat on the bench seat across from her, Justern resting his head on the seat, his eyes closed. Alarin gave her a sleepy smile but didn't say anything. He moved his legs out of the way so she could climb in. Mellis was curled up on the far side of the bench seat, her head leaning against the window. Tamara climbed in and settled beside Mellis. Greg got in beside her.

"How long was I out?" she asked, glancing over at Greg.

"A little while, but not really that long. It's not all *that* late. We're just not used to this diurnal cycle yet and none of us have the stamina we typically would at home. Our bodies feel like it's the middle of the night."

"To say nothing of the fact we just landed on this planet this morning. It's been a very long day," Alarin added, lifting his head.

The limo pulled out of the parking lot slowly, turning into the narrow alleyway at the back of the building more smoothly than Tamara would have expected for a long vehicle like this. The car managed to navigate the back alley, although doing so was a little nervewracking to her. She tried to frame her thoughts to talk, but she couldn't seem to focus long enough to think about any questions, and it didn't seem all that important anyway. By the time she thought up something to say, the moment had passed, so she said nothing. The other people in the back of the car did not seem disposed to talk much either. Breathing through his mouth, Justern snored slightly, seemingly in a deep sleep. The atmosphere in the car seemed relaxed, so she finally just let herself relax and drift.

Not long after, the car pulled up to the back of Tamara's dorm. Mellis stirred, uncurling herself from the position at the window. Tamara frowned as she tried to remember her contact with these four people earlier today. Had she ever told them where her room was? She decided it didn't matter, since they obviously knew. Mellis leaned closer to her. "Do you need help getting to your room?"

Tamara concentrated intently to attempt to speak a simple sentence. "I'll be fine." The words came out clear enough, but she wasn't sure of her ability to navigate four floors, since the limo had pulled in on the basement level.

Greg leaned over. The whisper of clothing against the leather seats seemed exceptionally loud in the quiet interior of the limo. "I'd suggest taking Mellis up on her offer. You just had an intense experience. She can help you get upstairs."

"A migraine?" Tamara wasn't tracking very well, but she didn't think a migraine would have this kind of effect.

"Just go to bed, Tamara. You'll feel fine in the morning." Greg patted the cushioned seat beside her. "Mel, why don't you help her get to her room?"

Mellis nodded and leaned over to pop open the door. Tamara protested, even though she felt like she had just been run over by a truck. Twice. Maybe even by a train. "No, I'm fine. I don't want to be a pain—" She hadn't felt this bad since she accidently ended up with a hangover once in high school. She tried not to glance at Alarin or Justern, but neither of the young men seemed to be paying any attention to her at all. Both had their heads back against the headrest with their eyes closed.

Mellis touched her shoulder. "It's no trouble, Tamara. You can show me around campus tomorrow. Sound fair?"

Abruptly, Tamara capitulated. "All right. Thank you." She climbed out of the car, trying not to trip over Alarin's legs. He opened one eye, gave her a sleepy smile, and pulled his legs up as she braced herself against the edges of the door. Mellis met her at the door—*how had she gotten out so fast?*—and was ready to help her up to her room by the time Tamara had pried herself out of the car. The limo zipped away as soon as they were free. Tamara fumbled a bit with her key but managed to get it out and get the basement door to the dorm unlocked.

Mellis held the door as Tamara made her way inside. "I live on the third floor," she told Mellis. "Just the thought of it is giving me a headache."

Mellis smiled. "That's what I'm here for. Lead on when you're ready."

The trek up the four levels of staircases was agonizing. Tamara clung to the rail and with Mellis's help managed to get her feet to carry her upstairs. God was she tired!

They entered the little lounge area around which five rooms were clustered. Tamara went to the easternmost facing room and stuck her key into the lock. She was only vaguely aware of Mellis helping her into the room as her stamina started to fade. She fell into bed and was out in moments, not even bothering to undress.

Her sleep was not dreamless, though. The wind howled through her dreams again, a tantalizing siren call. Music wove under it, a formless melody shot through with a throbbing beat. She stood again at the edge of a windswept, sandy plain that stretched to eternity in front of her. "Where am I?" she shouted.

"Come. Come home." The words were whispered in her ear, a breath of wind under the wild scream, infinitely seductive and achingly beautiful. "Join us, Tamara."

"Who are you?"

"We are you, Tamara." It was the voice of the ambassador again. His dark hair whipped around his face as he stepped out of thin air and closer to her. Again, his long fingers reached out to touch her.

She ducked aside, avoiding the touch, suddenly afraid. "Who am I? What is happening to me?"

"You are we." The figure in front of her changed, flowing hair turning a ruddy color. Green eyes bored into her. "Come to us, Tamara."

"What's happening to me?" Tamara screamed at him, her voice coming out high-pitched and strained. She flew at him, suddenly flapping wings in his face, ripping at him with talons and beak, sobbing her heart out as she did. "Who *are* you?" The figure dissolved under her and she collapsed on the ground. Human once more, she wept, her body wracked by sobs.

The scream of the wind increased, filling her ears. Under the scream was a pulsating melody that continued to call and pull at her. *T-amara, Ta-mara, Tam-ara. Open to us, Tamara, open. You will never be alone. Let it out, Tamara. You know you want to.*

"No!" she screamed. *How could she? What kind of freak was she? How could she have done it?* "It's my fault, Mom." Another voice, cold and hateful. "He's dead, *he's dead!* See what kind of freak your bastard is? How could you?"

She awoke abruptly, soaked in sweat. Sunlight poured in the eastern windows. Disoriented and confused, she looked around. She was in her room on campus, her car was at … the embassy, and Mellis … she searched the room. Much to her relief, she was alone. Tamara lifted her hands to her cheeks. The crying had been so real she expected to have tear streaks on her cheeks, but they were dry. She got out of bed and made her way to the mirror. Other than heavy dark circles under her eyes, there was little sign of her night. "It's happening again." She whispered to the mirror. "Oh God!" Tears welled up in her eyes. "God, please no."

A voice came to her out of her thoughts. "They are simply very natural results of using certain parts of the brain."

"I'm not a freak?" She whispered the words to the mirror.

"I healed you." No answer, just Greg's voice.

"What am I?" she asked the mirror. "A freak? A monster? Or am I just a human with psi, like Greg said was possible?"

There was no response. Tamara looked in the mirror for a while longer, then turned away in sudden hatred for the image reflecting back at her. Could she reach out with her mind? She imagined herself calling but getting no response. Tamara pulled her hair back from her face and fastened it up in a hairclip. Where were the Azellians living on campus? She wracked her brain, trying to remember if she'd heard someone mention what dorm they were in.

She picked up her cell phone, slipping her Bluetooth device over an ear, and dialed the campus information number.

"Name?" the mechanical computer voice asked.

"Gregerin Tenricth." She decided to see if he was in the computer system yet. He probably wasn't, given the antiquated computer system. She had just entered them in the computer yesterday.

"Name unknown. Please restate your request."

Tamara tapped her front teeth as her mind raced through other options. "Uh, the Azellian Embassy."

"Dialing."

"Azellian Embassy, Kitari Derrole speaking. How may I direct your call?"

Tamara fought with herself for a moment, then said abruptly, "Uh, is Ambassador Corina in?" She could feel the blush crawl up her cheeks, but she ignored the heat of them.

"Just a moment. Let me forward you to his office."

"Ambassador Corina's office, Janille speaking. How may I help you?"

"Is the ambassador in?" Her resolve slipping away, she held on to the edge of the desk with white-knuckled tension. What was she doing, calling the ambassador of all people? He was far too busy to have anything to do with her.

"May I ask who is calling?"

"Uh, Tamara Carrington."

"Just a moment. Let me see if he's available, Ms. Carrington." Silence from the phone. They didn't even have muzak to listen to while she waited. Suddenly feeling slightly hysterical, Tamara's finger hovered over the "cancel call" button. Her urgency was fading with the remnants of her dream. After all, she would see Greg again, and she didn't need to bother the ambassador with anything.

"Tamara?" The ambassador's voice made her jump. Flushing, she lifted her finger from the cancel button. "I'm sorry about the wait. I was on another call. Did you need something?"

"I—I'm sorry. I—I shouldn't have bothered you." Tamara stammered, flushing violently. "It really isn't important. I'm really sorry." She hit the cancel button and dropped her phone onto the desk. What had she done? Shaking, she sank to the bed.

At the Azellian embassy, Merran stared at the buzzing phone. "Damn it. She had a psi episode last night and is calling me this morning? Something's up." *Greg!* He reached out and called Greg on his intimate level, calling Janille at the same time with his voice.

Janille stuck her head around the corner of the open door. "Yes, Ambassador?"

"Can you get Tamara Carrington's phone number right away?"

Mer? What's up? Greg mumbled sleepily on Merran's intimate level.

Tamara just tried to call me. I don't know why, but following last night …

"Right away, sir." Janille closed the door behind her firmly, giving him the privacy of his office.

I'm on my way. Greg responded assuredly.

The phone on his desk beeped at Merran. He touched the intercom button. "Yes, Janille?"

"I have Tamara Carrington's number and am calling her, Ambassador."

"Thank you," Merran replied and waited. An image of Tamara's face flashed across his mind—hair a bit cowlicky, like she had just woken up, blue eyes confused and somewhat panicky. Although she hadn't called in on a video phone, he still had a very strong image of what she'd looked like this morning, borne on the heels of his empathic talent. He closed his eyes to control his wandering thoughts—and sudden emotions.

❋ ❋ ❋

In Tamara's room back on campus, her cell phone trilled once, then twice. Tamara stared at it. Number unknown. Who was calling her? She hesitated, then answered the phone on the third ring. "H—hello?"

"I can't imagine you would call for no reason, Tamara. What did you need?"

Tamara flushed. Heat burned from her cheeks. "I—I was just looking for Greg's number and couldn't find it on campus. I wasn't sure if you might have it. I'm sorry, it really wasn't important enough to bother you."

"It's not a bother, Tamara. I mean that. The embassy and I are open for your questions or concerns at any time. A very large part of my job is to be there for those that need help. Even if that help is to get a hold of one of my fellow Azellians."

Tamara's blush deepened. "Ambassador—"

"Call me Merran, Tamara. We don't stand on ceremony here at the embassy and I'm not all that much older than you are. How are you feeling this morning?"

She blinked at him, taken off guard by the question. "Fine, I guess." *Frantic!* She thought back to the night before. *Did I even see him last night?* She vaguely remembered him wearing a robe—

she flushed heavily. *Did he read me last night? Can he even now? Onetwothreefourfive! Onetwothreefourfive!* "Better than last night. I was, uh, a bit overwhelmed by it all."

"I'm glad to hear it." Merran used the connection over the phone and tentatively reached out, only to be slammed into a thick barrier. The contact was a bit startling, as yesterday she had been erratically open. He could read nothing from her at all. It bothered him for a reason he didn't really want to investigate. "Did the experience make you unwilling to come back to the embassy?"

"Oh, no. Uh, not at all." It didn't sound sincere, although she was too heavily shielded to read. "When is your next get together?"

Merran clicked on the calendar on his computer. "I'm planning on having the next one when the students are back on campus. In three weeks. Three Fridays from now, actually, at seven again. Do you know any students who might be interested in coming?"

"Oh yes, I know quite a few. I'll ask if they're interested once they get back to campus. It will be early in the term, so they probably won't have that much studying to do."

"Good." Merran smiled. The phone beeped at him as Janille mentally warned him that the Director of the Earth Liaison Office was on the line for his scheduled phone meeting. "I'm sorry, Tamara, I have to take this call. I'm glad you reached out to me ... even if you did hang up on me," Merran added with a hint of teasing in his voice. "I do hope you'll contact me in the future if there is anything I might help you with."

"I will. Thank you."

"You're welcome, Tamara. I'll see you in a few weeks if I don't see you before then." With that, he ended their call and picked up the other line.

Chapter Three

MERRAN HUNG UP BEFORE Tamara remembered he hadn't given her what she'd asked for.

"Damn," she muttered. There was no way she was going to call him back, though. She'd just have to wait until she could meet up with the Azellian students again, whenever that would be. She'd very likely see Greg around campus. She could wait until then. Turning away from the phone, she went to the closet and got dressed into some clean underwear, bra, shorts, and a shirt.

She brushed her hair down and refastened it in the hairclip. *At least the shock of calling the embassy this morning jolted me out of my nightmare,* she thought to herself as she studied her face in the mirror. A sudden knock at her door jerked Tamara out of her thoughts, making her jump. Who knew she was on campus? Which of her friends was even back this early in the semester? The continuing students wouldn't be returning for at least two weeks. Walking around the bed to get to the door, she peeked through the door's peephole. There stood Greg.

She pulled the door open. "How … what … what are you doing here?"

Greg grinned at her. "Your guardian angel called me."

"My what?"

"Merran. He called me and said you called him this morning but didn't tell him why. Can I come in?"

"Yeah—yes, of course." There was something wrong with the logic of his statement, but she wasn't exactly sure what it was. "I—uh, was just looking for your number …" she trailed off. "He called me back and still didn't give it to me. I *did* tell him what I wanted, but he didn't tell you?"

"He probably hadn't called you back yet when he spoke to me. As for a phone number, he didn't give it to you because I don't have a phone yet. I'm going to sign up today. So what did you need?"

"Wait a minute. This isn't making any sense at all. You don't have a phone or a phone number?"

"Not yet."

"But you said he called you. How?"

Greg's amber eyes glinted mischievously. He walked calmly over to her desk chair and sat down, resting his forearms against his thighs as he leaned forward. He wore standard human clothing today—a pair of jeans and a t-shirt that clung to his muscular chest. Tamara blinked. He looked normal, but there was something about his air that wasn't like the usual twenty-something human. He gave her a broad smile, and she suddenly wondered if he was reading her mind. "Using those abilities you don't think exist."

She rubbed her eyes and sank down on the bed. First Merran and now Greg. Did all Azellian men like to mess with people's heads? "All right. Start over. Let's pretend I did reach you using proven means. You offered to show me about these supposed abilities. Are you still willing to do so?"

"Sure."

"When?"

"Whenever you want." Greg straightened and leaned back. He put his arm across the back of the chair. Tamara tried to ignore the way his t-shirt pulled across his chest. What was wrong with her? She was not normally so super-sensitive to guys. Greg wasn't nearly as cute as Alarin or as handsome as Merran. So why was she reacting so strongly to all the Azellian men? "Although I would suggest sooner rather than later."

Unease curled through her, settling in the pit of her stomach. "Why?"

"Why what?"

She took a deep breath. "Why soon?"

"So you are comfortable with us as quickly as possible." Greg's voice was too carefully controlled to be casual despite his effort to appear nonchalant.

The dream returned to her. The call ... the screams. *What have I done? Freak child! Let it go. You know you want to ...*

Greg leaned forward again, his eyes intent, obviously picking up something of her discomfort. "What is it, Tamara?"

She was suddenly dizzy. The bed twisted underneath her, a roller coaster ride of terror. *Onetwothreefourfive! Onetwothreefourfive!* "Can you read my mind?" *Did I just say that out loud?* she asked herself.

Greg came off the chair, kneeling in front of her, his hand resting on the bed beside her. "What did you say, Tamara?"

She cleared her throat. "Can you read my mind?" *He couldn't possibly say yes. Could he?* He said no, but not for the reason she expected. "Not at the moment. You're shielded pretty heavily right now."

"Shielded—what's that?"

His oddly colored amber eyes held hers. "It's what we call it when we block ourselves from receiving external input from other people's thoughts and emotions."

"Am I always?"

"Sometimes you are as open as any other human. You seem to be showing signs similar to what we Azellians call Awakening."

"Awakening?"

Greg leaned back on his heels, although he did not release her gaze. "That's what we call it when someone, usually a child on Azelle, is not yet able to use the energy of psi, when the mental pathways are still dormant. Awakening, the channeling of the energies of psi through those neural pathways, usually coincides with puberty and one's first sexual experience."

She jumped at that. "Always?" *Freak child! He's dead, he's dead! Onetwothreefourfive!*

"Not always. But it's the most common way." He was very still, like he was afraid she would jump up and run away. His gaze sharpened slightly and grew a little more intense. "For most Azellian children Awakening is highly sexual in nature."

"Does it ever go away once it's started?"

"Not that I've ever seen, but I suppose it's possible."

She shrugged, feeling fragile—like she might break. She looked away. *What have I done?* "Can something force it back or prevent it from being completed?"

Greg shifted forward and touched her chin, turning her face toward him. She refused to meet his eyes. "What happened, Tamara?"

She pulled away, tears welling up in her eyes. "It was an accident. Natural causes. That's what they said. I knew better." She took a deep breath and looked at Greg, willing him to tell her the truth. "Can these abilities kill?"

Greg blinked and was silent for a moment. "They can be used for that purpose, yes."

He's dead! He's dead! "Then I killed him." She closed her eyes.

Greg touched her face again. His fingers were warm—but it was the compassion in his voice that made her open her eyes again. "Tell me what happened, Tamara." He lowered his hand.

She took a deep breath. "I was seventeen, nearly eighteen. He was twenty. Mom and Dad didn't approve of him. He was totally in love with me, he said." She laughed then, a hollow sound to fill the abyss. "Don't tell me, I know. It's taken me some time, but I know that was a line. Who can be completely and totally in love in high school anyway?"

Greg said nothing, but he continued to meet her eyes steadily. No sign of the suppressed, and sometimes not so suppressed, fear and horror she'd seen from everyone else who knew. *But you don't know the whole story,* she said to him mentally, as if he could hear her. *Just wait.*

She continued the story. "It was prom night. I agreed to go back to his hotel room with him. I wasn't sure, but I knew that he wanted it and Mom had had the 'be careful lecture' with me when I started going out with him. So I knew what to do to avoid both pregnancy and disease and I thought we could chance it." She found the words coming easier, in the sympathetic atmosphere

Greg somehow managed to generate. His silence was supportive and caring—not judgmental—although what he was doing differently from anyone else who had been a part of that drama three years ago she didn't know. She'd run from the event, switched schools rather than face the rumors at the high school she'd been attending. It had made graduating a bitch, but she'd managed it. It had helped to bury herself in her studies.

"He was thrilled, of course. We had a whole evening planned— I was even somewhat excited about it. He was cute, it was my last year in high school, and all the other girls were talking about their experiences already." She took a deep breath. "I found myself really dizzy at the prom and there was all this noise … like … inside my head. People talking, voices overwhelming me. I'd had these moments previously, and they were usually followed by a horrible migraine that made me sicker than a dog and kept me in bed for a few days. Like last night, only you made it go away fast, much faster than usual." She looked at Greg. "During the prom, I was afraid that I was going to have a really bad migraine and it would end my plans for the evening. So I got Doug to bring me back to the hotel when I was still hearing voices and noises and trying not to act too crazy." She looked away. "I could tell he was really, really excited and it made me more excited. Like I couldn't quite tell the difference between my own excitement and his." She closed her eyes and struggled to continue the story. "I started to get a little scared. But I kept going. We went to the hotel room and I thought I was going to burst. Doug started to kiss me and I just exploded in my head. The next thing I knew, he was lying on the floor with his eyes rolled back in his head and I was screaming." Her hands were shaking, although this was the first time she'd ever been able to tell the story without freaking out. That oddity was enough to keep her together.

Greg continued to look at her with quiet acceptance, his amber eyes still clear of that fear she'd seen in everyone else's eyes. "What did they say killed him?"

"Cardiac arrest. He was brain dead when he got to the hospital. The coroner ruled it an accident." She took a deep breath. "My grandmother called me a freak. My parents were … caring. I hated myself for a long time. The psychologist I went to told me it was a freak accident and that my guilty feelings were normal. That there was no way I could have been responsible for his death, but that I would feel that way because I was there when he died." She stared down at Greg. "It was my fault, though, wasn't it? I did that to him. At least those horrible migraines went away. Until last night anyway."

Greg reached out to brush his fingertips against the back of her hand. "It wasn't your fault, Tamara. No more than if you threw a ball to him and it hit him in the head and killed him. It was an accident. Nothing more."

"But it's starting again, isn't it?" The brush of fingers against her hand was soothing—much more so than they should have been. Was he doing something to her? Had he been doing it all along? Was that why she was much calmer telling the whole story to him?

"Maybe, I don't know. But I'd like to help you."

"Help me? How?"

"Watch." Greg lifted a hand and extended it to the desk. She could feel his eyes on her as a pen on the surface lifted slowly above the desk and floated gently through the air toward them. Fascinated, she stared at the levitating pen, her breath catching in her throat. "Go ahead, touch it," he said gently. "It won't hurt you."

Fear, mingled with excitement, rose in her throat. "I … no.

I can't." The pen floated closer, bumping the back of her hand. She shivered at its touch, but it felt normal—like any other pen, despite its gravity- defying position. Greg's fingers gently brushed the back of her hand. Waves of calm flowed through her at the touch and nothing seemed all that frightening anymore. She touched the pen and it bounced lightly—up and down, up and down. "What happens if I pull it out of the air?"

"Try it and see."

She pulled the pen out of the air. It felt like a normal pen, heavy in her hand. She lifted it, and when she let go, it fell to the bed with a thump. "Hey!"

Greg smiled and the pen abruptly jumped up again, floating lightly in front of her face. "We call this telekinesis," he said. "All Azellians can do it to an extent, but there are some that are stronger than others, with wider ranges. I can only affect objects that I can see. Mellis, however, can affect objects she not only can't see but are many miles away."

Tamara pulled the pen out of the air and rubbed the smooth cylinder. "Are there other talents, too?"

"Oh, there are lots of Azellian psi talents. Far too many to list right now, but yes, mind reading ... we call it telepathy ... is one of them. All of us are telepathic to some extent. It's how Merran contacted me this morning to tell me you had called him looking for my number."

She shivered, remembering the night before, and, for the first time, that awful night three years ago. "But isn't it overwhelming to hear everyone's thoughts? I mean, if that's what happened to me last night, it was awful."

Greg shook his head. "No, we learn how to shield ourselves from unwanted thoughts. It's part of our training. Would you let me show you what we can do?"

Tamara studied the pen lying innocuously on her bedspread. She bit her lip. "I'm scared," she murmured.

Greg didn't touch her, but her chin lifted anyway. She met his eyes. "Am I scary?"

"No, not at all." Surprisingly, that was true. Greg was the least threatening person she'd ever met, even despite his display of non-human ability.

"Then get to know us, spend time with us. Take it one step at a time."

"Us? As in you Azellians?"

"Yes, we Azellians."

She took a deep breath and let it out slowly. "Okay," she said quietly. "Okay." She looked up at him. It was easy to trust him. The decision, once made, felt surprisingly good. "Now what?"

Greg got to his feet. "Have you gone to breakfast yet?"

She blinked at him. "Breakfast?"

"Yes, the meal beings eat in the morning? Or don't humans eat breakfast?"

"No, we eat breakfast, I was just … no I haven't gone to breakfast yet. Why?"

"Well, I'm hungry. Are you?"

"Yeah, kind of."

"Come on. Let's grab something to eat then. I'll tell you about our crew as we walk over to the cafeteria," he said as she got to her feet. "Merran's misfits we used to call ourselves. Since none of us were exactly team players, we all sort of gravitated around Merran, who's always been something of a maverick misfit himself."

Tamara blinked at him as they walked toward the door and she pulled it open. "The ambassador? You know him personally? I mean, as more than just a fellow Azellian?"

"Certainly. We're all actually very good friends. Have been for years ... since we Awakened," he said as they walked down the empty, quiet staircase toward the front door and outside.

"What kinds of things did you do?"

"Oh you know, the usual. Swimming, playing, talking, school, sex. And more sex. At least until I went into Healer training. After that I had to get creative about spending time with them. Healers are somewhat isolated from the rest of the population."

Tamara blushed furiously, hardly hearing his words about Healers, too lost in the ease with which he discussed something so taboo to humans as sex. "That's blunt. We humans don't talk about ... sex. Especially not in high school." It was hard to not feel scandalized.

Greg grinned at her. "Azellians aren't inhibited in the least. As you'll find when you spend time with us."

She had a sudden flash of visceral memory from the day before. A scent, a spicy, warm, musky scent and a surge of intense sexual attraction beyond anything she'd ever experienced. Feeling a blush crawl up her cheeks, she was suddenly very glad Greg had said he couldn't read her mind. "I'm almost afraid to find out." She glanced over at him. "Do you have a girlfriend?"

Greg laughed, then coughed. "No, no significant other. I'm a Healer," he said, as if that explained everything.

"So?"

"Healers don't form pair bonds," he explained. "It's ... not allowed. We have too much to focus on to get tied up in relationships. And honestly, most of the time I'm way too busy to think about it anyway."

"So Healers are celibate then?"

Greg laughed again. "Not if we can help it. Sex can be a great stress relief."

Confused, Tamara frowned at him. "That doesn't make any sense."

Greg gave her a strange look. "Humans always pair bond in order to have sex?"

"No, of course not." She flushed. "Although ... it's more acceptable if they do."

"Acceptable?"

"Yes ..." She trailed off, unable to explain it to him. *How do I explain our sexual morality to a culture that has a totally different set of rules?* "Never mind," she said as they approached the cafeteria.

Greg held the cafeteria door open for her. "No, go on. Now you've got me curious. So on Earth it's not okay to have sex unless it's within the confines of a pair bond?"

Tamara squirmed uncomfortably. "Well, yeah. Sort of. Except in college when it's okay to experiment. But you'd better not get pregnant or you might have to get married."

A strange look crossed Greg's face. "Merran said something about this yesterday. That he'd have to warn Justy and Alari. Are you telling me that here on Earth it's literally required to form a pair bond if you get someone pregnant?"

"Well, it's not required, but it's pretty bad if you don't. There's a lot of social pressure."

Greg whistled under his breath. "Well, I'm certainly glad I don't have to worry about that. I'd better talk to the guys, though. Reinforce Merran's warning."

Tamara frowned at him. "What do you mean? You don't have to worry about getting a woman pregnant? Is it because you're a Healer?" Something about his logic was escaping her. He'd said Healers weren't celibate, hadn't he?

"No, it's because my preferences don't run to women."

She stumbled, surprised at the relaxed ease behind his comment. "You're gay?"

He blinked at her. "I'm what?"

She blushed. "Oh, sorry. It's what most everyone calls men who like other men."

"Oh." He gave her a look. "I suppose you're going to tell me there's some human rule about that too?"

"Well, it's more okay now than it used to be. But you'll want to be careful about who you approach. Some guys are … funny about it. If they're not comfortable with their preferences, they can get … violent."

"Thanks for the warning. Although I doubt that's going to be much of an issue." He tapped his temple, presumably to indicate his telepathic abilities but didn't say anything more as they grabbed trays and scanned the hot food section. "What are those?" he asked, pointing at the food spread out in the warming pans.

"Scrambled eggs, bacon, hashbrowns, pancakes." Tamara pointed each item out as she listed it. "Are you vegetarian?" she asked as he made a face.

"Vegetarian?"

"Yes, someone who doesn't eat meat."

"Ah. Well, I don't usually eat meat so I guess that applies to me."

"Well, hashbrowns and pancakes don't have any meat in them. Neither do eggs or the cereal and milk over there."

"Is there any fruit?"

Tamara glanced at the salad bar that doubled as a fruit bar in the morning. "Yes, right over there. Probably nothing you're used to, though."

"That's okay. I don't mind trying something new." He walked over to the salad bar and picked out several pieces of different types of fruit as Tamara poured herself some cereal and milk.

Tamara rejoined Greg at the salad bar, watching the Healer as he carefully chose a thick piece of melon. "Hey guys," a new voice said, and she turned to see Mellis approaching, carrying a tray with a plate of scrambled eggs and hashbrowns on it. "Mmmm, that looks good," she said to Greg. "Can I have one of those?"

Greg handed her a slice of melon. "Good morning, Mel. How'd you sleep?"

Mellis smiled. "Good. I was so tired I managed to sleep the whole night through. How about you?"

"I slept the whole night through too. You spend the night with Justy?" he asked as they carried their trays over to one of the long tables on the outside of the food area.

"No, those beds they gave us are way too small for two people, and Justy sprawls so badly when he sleeps that he pushes you right out of bed." Mellis said, placing her tray down and climbing over the bench. "I'd never have gotten any sleep if I'd spent the night with him."

Greg picked up his fork and speared a strawberry. "Hmm. Well, I was just wondering how he was doing this morning. He was a little rattled last night. Is he calmer?"

"I have no idea. I haven't seen him since we got back from the embassy last night. Don't worry about it. You'll get a call if he's not feeling up to par." She looked at Tamara. "How are you feeling this morning?"

"Good, thanks," Tamara said. It surprised her to realize that was the truth. The residue from her nightmare was gone and she felt much better. "Thanks for seeing me up to my room last night. I don't think I would have made it there myself."

"Oh, you're so welcome! It was no trouble, really."

"Do you want me to show you around campus today? I have to work at one, but I'm available until then."

"Sure, that would be great!" Mellis replied. "Let's do it right after breakfast. Hey, Alari," she said, glancing up at the tall redhead as he placed his tray down on the table next to hers and across from Tamara. "Morning."

"Good morning, all," Alarin said, folding his long legs under the bench. His short cropped hair was darkened at the tips, dripping water down the back of his neck, his cheeks reddened from shaving. "Sleep well?" he asked Greg.

"Very well, thank you. How about you?"

"Slept the night through, although Merran woke me up at the crack of dawn this morning."

"Crack of dawn? What was he doing up that early?" Greg asked.

"Dropping Tamara's car off." Alarin leaned back, pulling the key out of his pocket. He reached across the table to Tamara, dropping it on the tabletop. "Here you go."

"The ambassador dropped my car off this morning?" Tamara stared at the long shape of her car key, looking odd all by itself without her other keys to keep it company. "Himself? I mean, he didn't send someone to drop it off?"

"Well, I don't know who else was with him, but it was certainly Merran who handed me the key and asked me to get it to you the next time I saw you. Well," he amended, "he actually told me to give your key to Greg to give to you, but since you're sitting right here I figure I'll skip a step. Your car is in the lot behind the Sports Center, by the way."

"Thanks," Tamara replied, pulling her key off the table and tucking it into a pocket.

"I'm surprised he didn't wake me up," Greg said thoughtfully.

"He tried. Said you were dead to the world so he woke me instead. Since you can sleep through anything unless there's a Call involved."

Greg grinned. "That's true enough. And I was exhausted last night."

Tamara looked at the Healer. "A call? What does that mean?"

"Healers can hear people who are in distress. They give off ... a certain vibration we're sensitive to," Greg explained. "We can't ignore it. And Alari's right. I can sleep through anything except that."

"Actually, I'm surprised you're up this early," Alarin agreed. "You were extremely difficult to rouse after we'd spent the night at the oasis back home."

Greg's grin widened. "I'm not impossible to wake. Merran managed to get me up this morning ... checking to see if we'd gotten signed up for phones yet."

Tamara could feel a blush crawl up her cheeks. She hadn't meant to wake him up when she'd called the ambassador looking for phone numbers.

"Damn, that's something else I've got to do." Alarin made a face. "So many details."

Mellis gave him a nudge. "You'd think details would come easily for you, Mr. Precision Chemical Engineer. Ida's going to be furious. A day without talking to her? She's probably having a nervous breakdown."

There was a peculiar stiffness to him as he answered. "She'll be fine."

"You sure? You did leave her to come to Earth."

"I didn't leave her. We're still together."

"With you here on Earth and her on Azelle?" Mellis raised her eyebrows. "How long do you think that's going to last?"

"As long as it needs to." Alarin stabbed his fork into a piece of bacon and chewed on it. He turned to Greg and pointedly ignored Mellis. "You want to go sign up for a phone later today?"

"We've got some first year seminar intro thing this afternoon, but we can go after," Greg replied, seemingly unconcerned with the tension in Alarin.

Mellis didn't seem to notice she was being ignored, or at least it didn't seem to bother her. "I'll go with you too, if you don't mind." She pushed away her tray. "Meanwhile, Tamara's going to show me around campus. You ready?" she asked Tamara.

Tamara nodded. "Sure." She got up and picked up her tray. "See you later?" she said to Alarin and Greg.

"Absolutely. Maybe we can all get together for dinner tonight?" Greg suggested.

"Okay," Tamara said. "See you tonight then."

"See you tonight," Alarin echoed, and she and Mellis walked away to drop off their trays.

As they walked out of the cafeteria toward the double doors at the front of the cafeteria entrance, Tamara glanced at Mellis. "Where do you want to start?"

"How about the World Center? Our seminar is there this afternoon, and it might be nice to know where it is."

Tamara smiled and pushed the doors open. "This way, then."

Mellis smiled back, her expression bright. "Let's go." As they walked down the steps of the cafeteria building, heading to the other side of campus, Mellis studied Tamara curiously, with a frank openness that was a little startling but not unpleasant. "So are you from Denver, then?" she asked.

"Yes, I was born here. My parents are both from here too. I'm sorry, but I don't remember what town on Azelle you're from."

"We're all from Azorantxl," Mellis said. "It's Azelle's capital city and the location of the main spaceport."

"Greg said you guys were all friends at home. What made you come here to study?"

"Merran. He came to us a few months ago and said he wanted us to participate in the first ever exchange between humans and Azellians. His niece Charina and Greg's sister Ida decided to stay on Azelle, but the rest of us jumped at the chance to explore a new planet."

"Ida? Is this the Ida you were just talking about with Alarin? His ... girlfriend?"

Mellis nodded. "Yes. They've been engaged since they were babies."

"Engaged? As in going to be married?"

"Yes, it's a family thing. His mother arranged it. Alari doesn't want to marry Ida, so he came to Earth. Though he's usually pretty relaxed, Alari's a Raderth. They don't take orders all that well. Since his mother is almost as stubborn as he is, they have had some huge battles, the most recent revolving around him leaving Ida to come to Earth. I'm sure that's why he didn't formally break up with her, or she and his mother would be here on Earth chasing him down, and he really doesn't want that."

Tamara blinked, trying to sort through the implications of the tangled relationship Mellis was describing. "He doesn't want to marry her so he came here?"

"He says it's because he wants to study chemical engineering. But I mean, if you were engaged to someone and wanted to be around them, would you have come all alone? Ida was willing to come, but Alari was quite insistent that she stay on Azelle. Why would you insist your sex partner stay on another planet unless you wanted to get away from them?"

Tamara shook her head, faintly scandalized by the fact they were discussing someone's personal life, but Mellis had a relaxed ease about it that made it seem complelely normal. "Wait a minute. They're engaged but Alarin doesn't want to be and they're still sleeping together?"

"Sleeping together?"

"I mean, having sex."

Her expression cleared. "Oh, yes, of course they do."

"But he doesn't want to marry her. Wouldn't that confuse the issue?"

"No, why would it? We all have sex with each other, except for those who are related to others in the group. Like Merran and Charina and Greg and Ida."

Tamara blinked, feeling as though she were speaking a foreign language. Which she supposed she was. It only sounded like English but was really Azellian. "I don't think I quite understand the dynamic of Azellian friendships." She tried to remember what word Greg had used. "Don't you form pair bonds? I mean, there is such a thing as marriage, right?" *Mellis did say Alarin is engaged, didn't she?*

"Oh yes," Mellis replied. "Of course. After we're done with the experimenting, we might choose someone to settle down with. None of Merran's misfits are nearly ready for that, which is probably one of the reasons why Alari is so resistant to marrying Ida. That and because his mother wants it."

Tamara's mind flitted on to the next implication of what Mellis was saying. "So wait a minute. You mean you've all had sex with each other? All of you?"

"Of course. Why wouldn't we? That's what it's for, isn't it? Playing and seeing who might be a good long-term fit? And we're friends, so who better to experiment with than those you already care about?"

Having trouble processing the Azellians' sexual attitude, which was obviously quite different from the human perspective, Tamara stared at Mellis. "But I thought Greg liked men."

"So?"

"So you've …. had sex with him?"

"Sure. Before we settle into our long-term preferences, all Azellians experiment with both sexes." Mellis looked at Tamara. "Don't you?"

"Uh, no." Tamara took a breath, feeling dizzy. "No, it's not like that at all. At all. Wow. Azellians are really different." She wasn't sure she could process the scope of that difference. *Did Mellis mean that Greg and Alarin …* Her brain shied away from the idea, and she suddenly realized she had a whole host of prejudices she hadn't known she possessed.

Mellis gave her a look not unlike the one Greg had given Tamara earlier when she'd confused him over human sexuality mores. "So how do humans explore their sexuality?"

Tamara could feel the blush burning on her cheeks. She lifted her head and tried to pretend she wasn't having difficulty with the conversation. "Uh, in private, actually. It's really not talked about much, unless there's a problem. And people who like the same sex or both sexes get … discriminated against … unless they conform to what's considered 'normal.' It's not so bad in a city like Denver, but people can get pretty violent about what they think is right and wrong, and quite a few still think anything that's not straight man-woman interaction is … well … wrong. It's changing in some places, but in others … not so much."

Mellis frowned, obviously having as much trouble with the concept as Tamara had with Azellian attitudes. "That doesn't make any sense to me. Why would anyone go against their natural inclinations?"

Tamara shrugged. "I'm just saying what it's like. I don't make the rules."

Mellis shook her head. "I had no idea. Well, I'll have to be careful then. I didn't realize how touchy humans can be about sex."

"It's pretty complicated," Tamara agreed. Then she frowned. "Wait a minute. I thought you and Justern were a couple?"

Mellis laughed. "Oh goodness no. Neither of us has any interest in anything exclusive."

"So you do have the concept of exclusivity?"

"Once we form a pair bond, we do tend to stick with our partner. Alari, for all his lack of interest in marrying Ida, probably will stay celibate while they're apart, at least until he formally ends it. But then, he's a Raderth and they tend to be a little more old-fashioned than the rest of the families on Azelle."

Hence the arranged marriages, Tamara thought, but she didn't verbalize the comment. *Yet, they're fine with open sex in adolescence. Wow, I just can't quite wrap my brain around it. No wonder my grandmother comes unglued about them. If my grandfather ...* She didn't really want to think about her grandfather being unfaithful, but the open, relaxed attitudes implied in Mellis's comments would be hard to resist, especially during the long stretches when her grandfather had been stationed on Azelle. It made her suddenly feel a little more charitable toward her grandmother. She cleared her throat. "This is the World Center," she said, changing the subject as they came up to a large stone building. "Your first-year seminar will be in here."

"This is a beautiful building." Mellis studied the architecture of the imposing structure designed to look like a huge cathedral. "We don't really have anything this ornate."

"There's a hall displaying flags from around the Earth inside. Do you want to go in?"

"Oh yes, please!" Mellis said, and Tamara held the door for her. Mellis's childlike wonder and awe as she walked into the building and stared around inside was alluring and sweet.

By the end of their tour, Tamara had formed a much stronger bond with Mellis than she would have expected. There was an instant connection, much as there had been with Greg, as if she'd found people she could look to for support and trust. Even Alarin and Justern, who were a little more intimidating to her, were relaxed and friendly. She had two weeks to get to know them before the continuing students and her friends arrived back on campus, and she suspected it was going to be a very interesting couple of weeks.

Chapter Four

ALMOST A FULL WEEK LATER, in his office not far away from campus, Merran studied the new trade agreement between Azelle and Earth, wondering how his friends were settling in. Although he had full confidence in their abilities to adjust, he also knew well the cultural differences that he'd tripped over when he first arrived. Sometimes he still did. Despite his daily mental contact call with Greg, he could remember the sense of distance and isolation he'd had before he got the job at the embassy.

Greg had said they were all settling in fine, the university keeping them too busy with their first-year seminars and events to notice anything like culture clash or homesickness, but it would hit them at some point—he was sure of that. *Maybe I should take a little more active role than I originally planned*, he thought, making a note with the electric stylus in the margin of the electronic pad. *Spend time with them socially, help them feel comfortable.* And then there was Tamara Carrington, the human showing flashes of psi. Greg was still feeling out that situation, getting a sense of what was going on. Their conversations about the young human had been brief this past week, Greg updating him on the progress— or lack thereof. Although Tamara had accepted the invitation to spend whatever free time they all had together with the closeknit group of Azellian friends, not much had been happening. Even though she'd been open to learning more about the Azellians and their psi, she'd been heavily shielded since the episode at the embassy party, so there was little Greg could do to tell how her psi would develop, or what they could do to help it along. That meant Merran still wasn't sure what helping her would involve, but he was rather looking forward to it. He'd never met a human psi before but had long suspected humans were as sensitive as Azellians, just in different ways. Mingling socially with his friends would be a good way to see for himself what was happening, especially if Tamara spent time with them, too.

Just as he'd made the decision to reach out to Greg to set a time to meet, the phone beeped. He reached over and touched the button. "Yes, Janille?"

"Greg Tenricth would like to meet with you, Ambassador. Do you want me to schedule him in?"

Merran glanced at the computer screen and the calendar on it. "Yes, please, that sounds great. What times do I have today?"

"You're booked until five," Janille told him after a short pause. "Tomorrow you have the lunchhour free."

"It's Friday night, isn't it? Tell him I'll meet him for drinks after work tonight. You know, you might as well invite the others too. I'd like to touch base with all of them and see how their first week has gone."

"You have an early meeting in the morning tomorrow with the Dorbin Ambassador, sir," Janille kept her tone calm, but he could hear the warning in it anyway.

A grin tugged at the edges of his lips. After six years, Janille knew him well. "I'll be in, Janille."

"Very well, sir," Janille responded and cut off the link. Merran turned to concentrate on his work again.

A few moments later, the phone beeped again. Merran answered it. "Yes?"

"You have a phone call from Azelle, Ambassador. Idara Tenricth. Are you available to take the call?"

Merran jumped a little. Why was Alarin's fiancée calling him? There was no love lost between himself and the elegant, usually arrogant, beauty. "I'll take the call."

The video phone showed him a picture of the dark-haired woman who looked ragged. It appeared she'd been crying. He blinked. Although they usually struck sparks off each other, he had known her for as long as he'd known Alarin and Greg. "What's wrong, Ida?"

"I—I'm sorry to have called you, Merran, but I didn't know what else to do. I can't reach my brother or Alarin and ... well, I'm something of a mess," Idara sniffled.

Even though he knew Idara well enough to suspect she was very likely playing up the emotional aspects to make herself look worse than she probably really felt, it was also highly unusual for her to call him over anything. "What's the matter?"

"It's Alari. I'm afraid I've lost him." Her voice caught. "He hasn't called yet—"

"Calm down, Ida. They may not even have phones yet, as the first-year seminars are designed to keep them pretty busy from the time they wake to when they go to bed. As for whether you've lost him, I have a sneaking hunch all you need to do is let him go. If he cares about you, he'll come back. Let him call you when he's ready. Present him a strong front and above all, don't pressure him. You know what he's like."

Idara sniffed and dabbed her nose. "I do and that's the problem. I'm afraid I've pressured him too much already."

Merran shook his head. The conversation had edged into the surreal. "I doubt that, Ida. He's here, isn't he? You didn't keep him from coming."

"No, but did I have much choice, really? If his mother couldn't stop him from going to Earth, I had no chance at all. Could you get me a visa to come to Earth?"

He took a moment to consider his words before he spoke. The last thing he needed was for Idara to decide to work around him. If she decided to enlist the help of Alarin's mother, she could get a visa without his help, and that would probably have the opposite effect Idara was hoping for. "I could, but I don't think you should do that. It's pressure. And Alarin's bound to react badly to that." He looked at her sympathetically. "You really are in love with him, aren't you?"

Idara laughed, a short sarcastic burst of sound. "Something like that. Do you think he's going to find someone on Earth?"

Merran shrugged. "I don't know, Ida. Look at it this way. There's nothing you can do about it if he does, so why worry about it? It's a test. And if you play it cool, you may find it all works out in the end."

Idara scrubbed at her eyes. "That doesn't help much."

"I wish I could tell you that I know what's going to happen Ida, but I can't. We just have to wait and see. I can tell you that I think he does care about you, and if you give him space, he'll realize it."

Idara sighed. "Well, that's not what I wanted to hear, but I guess I can live with it."

Something about her vulnerability was bothering him. He hadn't pegged himself as a sucker for tears, but he was certainly getting a workout. "As for calling you, he probably will once he gets his phone. If he doesn't, I'll send you his phone number myself." *Why did I just say that? The last thing I need is to be accountable to Idara Tenricth for anything,* he thought. Merran suppressed an urge to be grumpy and instead, continued to look into the camera calmly.

Idara smiled then. "Thanks, Merran. I—I know I haven't been the nicest to you. I—I appreciate you taking the time to talk to me. Really. You'll never know how much you've helped me."

Merran waved a hand. "Don't worry about the past, Ida. Just concentrate on the here and now and the future will work out." He hung up the phone and stared at it for a moment. Never, in all his years, would he have expected Idara, of all people, to thaw enough toward him to ask for help, then to thank him for it. They'd always sniped at each other, if they talked at all, and most of the time she outwardly snubbed him, despite the fact she was dating one of his best friends and was the sister of one of his other best friends. If Idara Tenricth could change that much, what else was possible? He shook his head and returned to his work.

❈ ❈ ❈

On campus, Alarin leaned against Greg's room wall. "Merran wants us to meet him tonight so we can all go out? Do you know where?"

"He's going to meet us here on campus and we'll probably walk to one of the hangouts downtown. There are quite a few, I understand." Greg bent over his bed, tucking the sheets in more tightly. Trim rows of books sorted by size and content filled the bookshelves, and all of his clothes were hung neatly behind closet doors. Alarin couldn't see them, but he knew Greg. Greg worked on remaking the bed as Alarin watched.

"When exactly?"

Greg glanced up at the clock on the desk. "In about two hours."

"Damn, I have to call Ida. I'm sure she's rather freaked out … I haven't called her since we got here. It would be easier if our abilities were strong enough to reach Azelle."

"Across light years? It's possible, but it would be a feat worthy of the *aarya*. Even you Raderths don't have that much raw power without some boosting." Greg gave the cover a final tug and sat on the bed. "She'd appreciate the call, I'm sure. Especially as it's been five or six days."

Alarin straightened and walked to the door. "Let me know when Merran gets here."

As he walked back to his room, he prepped himself carefully for the guilt trip he was certain Idara was going to lay on him. His relationship with Idara Tenricth was not one he could explain to himself, much less anyone else. He cared about her— they'd known each other for years—but there were far too many strings and baggage for him to want to declare her as his mate for the rest of his life.

As he unlocked and pushed open his room door, he braced himself for a scene. Walking to the desk and pulling out his new cell phone, he dialed the central call center on Azelle. "You have reached the central computer on Azelle. Please state the name of the person you wish to contact." *Technology … one nice thing about Earth*, Alarin thought to himself as he obeyed. Azellian technophobia made simple use of technology a pain in the ass. Not all households accepted video phones, which were unnecessary on Azelle, since everyone could communicate mentally. Only those houses that had to call interplanetarily or who liked technology had a video phone. Idara's family had one. *Thank the aarya*, Alarin thought as the connections were made. Otherwise, contacting her would be a major undertaking.

The phone was not answered until the seventh ring, and he thought he wasn't going to get through.

"Hello?" It was Idara, looking disheveled and sleepy.

Alarin did a few quick mental calculations. "I'm sorry, Ida. I woke you up."

Her face relaxed into a smile. "No, no. I just went to bed. It's all right, Alari. It's good to hear from you. How's your trip so far?"

"Interesting," Alarin replied, rather surprised at the warmth of her welcome, but still wary. "We've been here a week and already we have a human who might be going through something like our Awakening. We've also learned that their universities are not the fastest at getting anything set up, and we've been kept busy from sun up to sun up again while discovering that the wonders of Earth are quite overrated."

Idara laughed, surprising him again. "I'm sure it will improve, Alari-*alis*. It should be interesting for the future, though. A human with psi? I didn't think humans had psi."

Alarin shrugged, ignoring the affectionate ending she put on his name. "I didn't think so either. They're certainly frightened enough about the possibility that we might be able to read their minds. But this one is certainly going through something."

She smiled, but seemed a bit distracted. He could see her rub the edge of the phone. She changed the subject. "I'm really sorry,

Alari, about the way I behaved when you left. I was pressuring you and that was the last thing you needed. I know how your family is and I was very closed to you, closed to understanding your desires. I—I just want to let you know that if you want to study chemical engineering, I will support you, whatever you want."

Alarin could feel his eyebrows shoot up high. "That's quite a change of heart."

Idara half-laughed and half-choked. "I've had a lot of time to think and I spent the afternoon with your mother yesterday."

That startled a snort out of him. "That must have been pleasant."

"About as much as pulling my toenails out one by one." Idara made a face. "I realized how similar I've sounded to her. After spending an afternoon with your mother, I was more than ready to cheerfully strangle her. How have you put up with me?" She sounded rueful.

Alarin reached out and touched the screen, although he knew she couldn't feel it. "You are not always like my mother, Ida. Do you understand that my coming here had nothing to do with us?"

Idara smiled, although he could see tears hovering in her eyes. "I don't think that's entirely true, Alari. But I am willing to accept that you're there." She blinked away the tears and put a cheerful expression on her face. "And I want you to know that I've realized something else. You asked me if it ever bothered me that we were matched a long time ago, as children. It's never bothered me the way it bothered you, because I love you." She smiled again. "If you do decide to find someone else, even on Earth, I can accept it."

Alarin had his doubts about that, but he recognized her intent behind the words and the real effort she was making. "That means a lot to me, Ida. More than you'll ever understand."

She shook her head. "I know my own shortcomings, Alari. And I promise, on the *aarya's* charter with us, that next time you call I won't be nearly so depressing."

That made him laugh. "You did spend the day with Mother yesterday. It's enough to make a sunny day in the High Desert depressing."

A mischievous grin—an unusual expression for her—tugged at her mouth. "Yeah, I think she could depress the *aarya.*"

"How did you manage to escape? Mother doesn't let a sympathetic ear go very often."

"Kyla rescued me."

"That must have been interesting." Alarin's eyebrows went up again. His sister Kyla was not all that fond of Idara, mainly because of Idara's tendencies to be rather too much like their mother.

"We had a nice talk. It helped me straighten a few things out." A thoughtful expression flitted across Idara's face. "It was less weird than calling Merran."

"You called Merran?" Alarin's jaw dropped and he stared at the phone. "Did he have a cardiac arrest?"

Idara rubbed her forehead sheepishly and looked down. "No, he was actually very nice to me, considering some of the things I've said to him in the past. Very helpful."

"Why, by the grace of the *aarya*, did you call Merran?" He wasn't sure how he felt about that.

"Just trying to see if you'd arrived safely. He ended up giving me some advice. Nothing really all that important."

Just then, Alarin could feel Greg touch his mental shields and alert him to the fact that Merran was on his way. "Ida, I have to go. You've given me a lot to think about."

Idara touched the screen. "Thanks for calling, Alarin. I'll talk to you later."

"Bye, Ida." They signed off, surprising him considerably. No pressure to call her, no guilt trips, just honesty. He wondered if she could really change so much so quickly. Well, two years would definitely test them, and maybe, just maybe, a grownup Idara would be someone he could deal with on a long-term basis. Greg's touch came again, and this time Alarin acknowledged it, heading out of his room and toward the student hall.

❋ ❋ ❋

In the student lounge where they sat alone, Tamara frowned at Greg. "Are you sure you want me included in this? This is you hanging out with your friends. I'm not sure I'm feeling up to it anyway. My mother …" She choked up and fought off the tears that threatened to burst forth. She'd called Greg as soon as her mother told her to go back to campus earlier in the day. Her parents needed some time alone to deal with the aftermath of her mother's cancer diagnosis. Tamara and Greg had been able to talk only briefly during his break from class. After he got out for the day, he'd called her back and asked her to meet him in the student lounge. She'd agreed, not expecting this.

Greg gently wrapped his warm fingers around her wrist. Warmth spread up her arm and spilled down into her torso, chasing away the block of ice that gripped her heart. For the first time since her mother sat in front of her that morning and told her that, yes, the tests came back positive for cancer, she felt like she could breathe without sobbing. Her eyes burned with the aftermath of her previous crying fits, but she felt calmer. "Yes, I'm sure we want you with us. It will help get your mind off everything, Tamara. There's nothing you can do about your mother's diagnosis. You spent the morning with her and you know there's not much you can do, except continue to live your life. She wouldn't want you to bury yourself in worry about her. It's not honoring you or her to do that."

Tamara sighed and rubbed her fingers together. "She told me to go out and not stop my life, but yet I feel like I should do something. I have a hard time believing this can be happening to her. Why, Greg? Why do people get sick? We have all this wonderful technology. How is it that people still get cancer?"

Greg paused for a long moment. "There's a large psychological component to any illness, Tamara."

"Can't you do something?" Tamara asked, fighting off the urge to cry. Greg was soothing her again—she could recognize the waves of warmth now—but the urge was still strong.

"I can try, but first your mother must be willing to accept that she can be helped. Most of the recovery from cancer is in the mind and the body of the person suffering from it."

Tamara shivered, wrapping her arms around herself. "But the treatments. They'll make her sicker than the cancer!"

"It's the way you treat cancer." He did not add anything further, although Tamara thought he might. There was the faintest hint of emphasis on the "you," as if the Azellians might do something else.

She frowned at him. "Do you have another process? A different way?" She knew from the endless conversations this past week with Greg about psi and how it worked that Azellians had very sophisticated medical knowledge and an almost mystical understanding of disease. She didn't necessarily understand it, but she'd seen him Heal his fellow Azellians and even a small cut on her arm within seconds. "Azellians manipulate cells, or something like that, don't they? Couldn't you ..." She waved a hand in the air. "I don't know, Heal her?"

Greg let his breath out in an explosive puff from behind his lips. "Your mother would have to completely accept me and what I can do, Tamara. Is she even willing to let an Azellian work on her?"

Tamara frowned, thinking she might not. Her mother was not as rabid as her grandmother about being anti-Azellian, but she was not exactly open about it either. "But she could be dying! Why wouldn't she accept anything that could help her?"

"It's subconscious, to be sure, but we all choose whether to recover or to succumb. I am willing to work on her, but it must be up to her." Greg's soothing touch increased. "All you can do is support her, either way. There is nothing you can do to influence her decision ... she may not even realize she has made one."

Tamara could feel the tears slip the bounds of her control and even Greg's soothing. She wanted nothing more than to run away—to hide and pretend nothing had changed in her little world. She felt so alone. She was barely aware through her tears that Greg had moved closer to her on the couch. His arms slipped around her shoulders. Tamara turned to him and wrapped her arms around his waist, letting the quiet sobbing go. Resting her head on his shoulder, she allowed the warmth generated by his mind and her tears to cleanse away the fear and worry. He was a safety she had never felt before, completely without sexual tension, without worry about illness. Greg offered her pure support—more mothering than her mother could provide under the circumstances. "What about the others?" she managed to gasp after a few moments, remembering that Greg had told her they were on their way.

Greg smiled and brushed her hair back from her face. "They'll wait. Let go and you can start the process of healing yourself."

She obeyed.

❋ ❋ ❋

Outside the student center, Merran sat on the steps waiting for the others. Alarin was the first to join him. "What are we doing outside?" Alarin asked in Azellian. "Greg called me to say you were on the way and then told me to wait. What's up?"

"Tamara got some bad news this morning and is having trouble maintaining her composure. Greg's getting her calmed down." He closed his eyes wearily.

"Long day?"

Merran opened his eyes. "You could say that. I'm ready for a good stiff drink. Not that it will do much, but it's the idea that matters."

Alarin laughed. "You can read my mind. Regular classes haven't even started yet, but I'm ready for a month-long vacation."

"Did you have any trouble getting settled in this week?"

Alarin shook his head. "No. The bureaucracy is as bad as on Azelle, though."

"I think that's something we all suffer, human and *uma-naarya*." Merran chose the Azellian name for themselves rather than the human identification of them.

Alarin grinned, appreciating the comment. Just then, Mellis and Justern came up.

"So what's the delay?" Justern drawled. "We're cutting into our fun time here."

Merran looked up at him. "Tamara's having a bad moment, Justy. We're waiting for the all-clear from Greg."

A very strange expression flitted across Justern's face, although he remained pretty tightly shielded, so Merran couldn't catch what it meant. "Well then," was all he said. With his arms crossed, he leaned against the side of the building and stared out over the campus.

Merran and Alarin exchanged glances. Alarin's shoulders moved in the slightest up-and-down movement. Merran sighed heavily and dropped his head into his palms, rubbing his eyes. Mellis slid down beside him and touched his shielding with her mind—a suggestive slithering. "Tough day, Mer?" she asked, not touching him physically but continuing the mental caress. "Did you need some help relaxing?"

Merran looked up at her sideways. "Maybe later, Mel. Right now, I want a drink."

She took the gentle rebuff and withdrew her touch. They all sat quietly on the front steps of the student center, watching across the greenway where several students struggled with a large trunk, manhandling it toward one of the student halls. The four of them watched with a mixture of amusement and curiosity as two male students wrestled and sweated, a young woman following along behind. Merran finally gave them a small boost with his mind, almost laughing as their words floated toward them.

"Is it me, or is this thing suddenly lighter?"

"I think it's you. What the hell did you put in here, Cammy?" one asked, sounding irritated and petulant. "This is the last time I lift your crap into the dorms."

"I'm sorry, Ken," the girl said, hastily catching up. "I didn't put anything in there but books."

Both young men groaned loudly, although Merran knew it was an act. He was supporting enough of the weight himself now that neither young man could possibly be having that much trouble lifting it. He could feel Mellis, then Alarin and Justern, slide their minds in to help. "What floor do you live on?" the one named Ken asked.

"The first," the girl said, wringing her hands.

"Good thing," Merran muttered. "They're going to have to manage the indoor part themselves." The trunk and struggling students disappeared indoors, and the four Azellians pulled their minds back to themselves.

Not long after, Greg and Tamara came down. Merran jumped a little. Greg was right. He hadn't seen Tamara since the embassy party, and she was heavily shielded, so much so he couldn't tell what she was thinking. Although she looked composed, his empathic sensitivity told him she was hanging on by a thread.

Is she all right? He sent the question to Greg's intimate level.

She'll be fine. She just needs something to distract her a bit.

Did she just find out someone's dying or something? Merran asked, studying the shining shields that prevented him from reading her. Her misery leaked around those shields like a mist rising from a moist stone wall. The tone of it was familiar—too familiar.

She's shielded so tight I didn't think an aarya could read her! Greg's mind tone carried a rueful astonishment. *She's putting out a Call loud enough to deafen me, but if she hadn't told me that her mother was sick, I'd be clueless. How did you manage to know that? You're not a Healer!*

Can't you feel her leaking around those shields? It reminded me of my own experience when my father died and I had to live with my older sister. That kind of thing tends to resonate pretty intensely, if you're listening for it.

Greg was silent for a moment. *She is leaking, isn't she? Huh. It's on a different level than I usually scan during my Healing. Wow. That's weird. She's resonating on a level I'm surprised a human can reach.*

What do you mean by that?

Well, you know Azellian families have their own unique psi signature, the vibration at which they resonate, right?

Everything and everyone does, Merran sent back. *So?*

So she's resonating like an Azellian right now, which is why you picked it up and I didn't. I've been spending the entire week assuming she's a human with shields. Most of the other humans I've met this week don't resonate on the Azellian frequencies at all, so I haven't been looking for it.

Are you telling me you think she's Azellian? How? You know the workup the Council does on the people who come to Azelle ... and James Carrington had a full workup. The Carringtons are human.

No, no. I don't think she's Azellian. I just have to rework my assumptions about humans and pay attention to those frequencies I was ignoring before. I'm really glad we're inviting her to join us tonight and that she's agreed to hang out with us, though.

Why?

Because human or not, if she's actually going through something like our process of Awakening, she's going to need our support. It will be much easier for her if she trusts us before that happens. He switched to spoken words. "Hey guys," Greg said in English, his voice lighthearted and easy. Merran was sure it was for Tamara's benefit, since it didn't match his mind tone at all. "You look like you just lifted weights." He cocked his head and studied them.

Alarin grinned and got to his feet, accepting the tone Greg set. "Merran decided to help some students lift a trunk full of books. We all joined in." He put his hand on his back, pretending to be in pain. Merran wasn't sure how much of Tamara's mood Alarin picked up, but his clowning was definitely aimed at Tamara too. "What exhausting work it was."

Greg frowned. "Don't tell me you were nuts enough to handle the task physically."

Alarin winked at him as Mellis laughed. "Don't let Alari fool you, Greg. We no more helped physically than we flew," she said.

Despite feeling better than she had before, Tamara still felt disconnected from the world, lost in the fugue where heavy crying always left her. She stood quietly as the Azellians bantered, not listening to much of anything, too numb to pay attention. Several people hustled by, talking and laughing, or just being quiet as they walked, reminding her that the continuing students were coming back in a week and life was going on, despite her feeling that it should be ending. She followed the Azellians as they headed off campus toward a bar where the locals liked to hang out. Traffic whizzed by on the busy street, and Tamara was suddenly glad to be a part of a group where she didn't have to pay attention to what was going on around her.

"Are you all right?" Mellis asked, linking her arm through Tamara's as they came to a stop at the crosswalk. "You look distracted. Greg said you got some bad news. Is everything okay?"

Tamara looked over at the young woman with whom she'd spent quite a bit of time this past week—over dinner, lunch, breakfast, and the first-year student events that all four Azellians talked her into attending with them. She blinked. The benefit of having cried all day was that she didn't have any tears left to interfere as she talked about it. "My mother's sick."

"Oh, I'm so sorry to hear that." A sense of warmth not unlike Greg's, although not as intense, spilled up her arm from where Mellis gripped her upper arm. "Do you want to talk about it?"

"Not right now," Tamara said, taking a deep breath and letting it out slowly, feeling some of the fugue lift as she spoke. "I'd rather not think about it anymore. It's been a pretty stressful day."

"We can do that," Mellis said cheerfully. "Hey, Mer," she said, interrupting his conversation with Alarin, Greg, and Justern.

The ambassador dropped his conversation and turned to Mellis. "Yes, Mel?"

"Tamara needs some cheering up. Why don't you tell us a story? He's very good at telling stories," Mellis said, squeezing Tamara's arm.

Tamara could feel the hot blush crawling up her cheeks. "Oh, you can finish your conversation. We can wait until we get to the restaurant," she said hastily. Although she'd spent the past week with the four Azellian students and knew how very friendly and welcoming they all were, she hadn't spent any time with the Azellian ambassador. And though all four of the Azellian students referred to the ambassador as though he was their close friend, she didn't see him that way at all. His calm reserve was more than a little intimidating for Tamara.

The ambassador frowned at Mellis. "I think Tamara's right, Mel. We'll wait until we get inside."

Tamara fought off a sense of embarrassment as he returned to his interrupted conversation and the walk light turned white. "He's not angry, is he?" she asked Mellis in an undertone.

"Merran? Goodness, no. Why would he be angry?"

"Well, you did just interrupt him."

Mellis laughed. "Oh it takes more than interrupting him to get him angry. Hey, Mer?"

The ambassador looked over his shoulder at her. "Yes, Mel?"

Mellis grinned at him. "Nothing. Just seeing if you were paying attention."

He gave her a long look. *Is he talking to her telepathically?* Tamara wondered. Greg had said they often communicated that way, especially when they wanted to have a private conversation. Neither Azellian's body language gave anything away, though. They both remained relaxed, even as the ambassador broke his stare and turned back to the other men.

"Oh, you know you love it," Mellis said to his back, strengthening Tamara's impression that something else had happened. Mellis grinned and gave Tamara's arm another squeeze as they walked down the street toward the pub.

When they came up to the door of the pub, Tamara halted in confusion. "Wait, wait. I can't go in there. I, uh, don't have my ID on me."

The ambassador motioned to the upper floor of the building. "They have a restaurant section upstairs. No ID required. Anyone else hungry? My treat. There's a lovely balcony and everything. We don't need to leave anyone out." He gave Tamara a warm smile. Her heart skipped a beat. He was really attractive, almost intimidatingly so. Over the past week, through familiarity, she'd lost her feeling of intimidation from Justern, who reminded her of a male version of her sister Andreya, and mostly of Alarin, who had a girlfriend. The ambassador, however, was a celebrity in his own right, and it was odd seeing him as just another person.

"Talked me into it," Justern looked at the bar with a sudden, somewhat greedy interest. "Food, glorious food."

"Is that and sex all you think about, Justy?" Mellis asked, linking her other arm through Justern's so that she was sandwiched between Justern and Tamara.

Justern looked down at her. "What else is there?"

"Architecture, for one thing."

"Who cares about architecture?" Justern shrugged, although his arm snaked around her waist to pull her against him in an undeniably sexual manner. Feeling more than a little uncomfortable, Tamara stepped away. Mellis snuggled up against Justern, his hand sliding up under her shirt to rest against her bare waist. Although she'd seen a number of affectionate interactions between all four Azellians this past week, none of them had been this overtly sexual. This one was still mostly within the bounds of acceptable, but it made her jumpy, probably because she'd never before been at ground zero between a couple getting ready to be intimate.

Tamara's shields were too strong to sense what was going on in her mind, but Merran could imagine. She wasn't leaking as she had been earlier on campus, but he'd been around enough humans to recognize the tension in her body as discomfort, and he knew both humans and his friends well enough to guess where the discomfort was coming from. Before Justern and Mellis could launch into a teasing argument that almost always ended up in them wandering off to have sex somewhere, he stepped in. "Food. Right now, that's the only thing on my mind. Let's get in there. I need to unwind." He turned to the bouncer. "We're going to the restaurant upstairs," he said.

The bouncer waved them through, toward the outer edge of the crowded bar. People were amassed around the bar area, fighting for a tiny corner where they could stand. His desire to unwind would be almost impossible to realize in this frenzy. Spoken and unspoken thoughts flew through the air, forcing him to shield himself as the music blasted toward them from the interior. Behind him, Tamara stopped. Merran could sense her dismay and feel the surge of fear slip through her heavy shielding. He moved aside to let his friends pass. Justern plowed in, followed closely by Mellis, Greg, and Alarin.

Tamara stared at the crowded bar and suddenly wondered why she was here at all. The old unease in crowds moved up her throat and choked her. So loud, so many voices overwhelming her! What if they triggered another migraine? Her head throbbed a little in memory of the previous one, and she felt her stomach drop to her toes. The others did not seem to notice her hesitation.

No one noticed, that was, except for one in the group. As the ambassador held the door for her, his eyes sought hers and paused. He seemed to sense something was wrong—maybe he even knew, with his sensitivity. Without a word, he held out his hand. Tamara could feel a blush rise up her neck as her heart jumped into her throat. His hand with its long, tapered fingers stayed outstretched and steady. Tamara gave him a quick, shy smile and ducked in front of him, her head down. The noise seemed less, somehow, and she was able to enter.

Merran stepped into the bar behind her, maintaining a light shield around her. That seemed to relax Tamara, even though he couldn't tell much with her mind shielded as heavily as it was. She was certainly attractive enough in a wholesome girl-next-door way, not overdone or overly made up. Her body was attractive, too, although she was more shapely than most of the human women he tended toward, with quite generous curves. His body stirred, startling him. He knew she was attracted to him—he could hardly have avoided it during that embassy party—but he found himself watching her as he would a potential sexual partner. Despite his reputation in the human media and with his staff, he was actually quite careful about picking his sexual partners, so his body's reaction to her took him by surprise. It made him look at her differently. A human psi user? It might be interesting, especially if she were the human version of a projecting empath like he was. He'd never had the pleasure of an empathic partner himself—although the stories he'd heard about it and the reaction of his own sexual partners made him think it might be worth the experiment.

Using his body to help shield her from the people piled at the bar pressing and shoving against each other, he pushed through the crowd. She brushed against the outer edge of his aura, sending prickles through his whole body.

He rested his hand lightly in the air just above her back, feeling the sensation of her aura tingle up his arm as he guided her through the crowd. Human she might be, but she most definitely had an aura, and a much stronger one than most humans, probably because of that dormant psi. Aura play like this was foreplay to most Azellians; he had to caution himself that she had no idea what he was doing. It felt really good, though, reminding him that it had been a little while since his last sexual encounter with a psi user, so he allowed himself the indulgence.

They made their way through the crowd to the stairs leading upstairs. Only Greg and Alarin stood at the bottom of the stairs as Merran and Tamara approached. "Where are Mel and Justy?" Greg asked as Merran and Tamara joined them, his voice quite loud in an attempt to get over the noise of the crowd.

"Have no idea," Merran shouted back. "Lost in there somewhere."

Alarin shook his head. "Kids. Let's get upstairs. I think it's quieter up there. They can join us if they feel like it." He motioned for Tamara and Greg to go ahead of him.

Tamara climbed the stairs behind Greg, in front of Alarin and the ambassador, her body humming oddly as she climbed. Had the ambassador walked her through that crowd downstairs, shielding her from not only the noise but the people at the bar?

It had felt like it, and she'd been very aware of his body inches from hers as they'd made their way through the crowd. Her body tingled all over—a rather nice, if strange, feeling.

She reached the top step and moved to the side so Alarin and the ambassador could join her on the landing.

The hostess met them at the top of the stairs with a wide, welcoming smile. "Four?" she asked politely, a tall, leggy blond with skintight black jeans and a painted-on black blouse with a white vest. Tamara felt a sudden surge of jealousy as the hostess studied all three young men appraisingly, her expression quite appreciative.

The ambassador stepped forward, cocking his head and motioning downstairs. "Six, potentially, if the other two ever get free of the mob downstairs. Could we have a balcony table please?"

The hostess collected her menus. "Certainly, sir. This way please." Carrying the six menus, she walked in front of them toward a table on one of the open balconies.

Air conditioning blasted Tamara as they moved through the restaurant, making her shiver and hug her arms to herself. The shorts and top she wore might be appropriate for Denver's typical summer weather but she'd forgotten how cold restaurants kept their air conditioning.

"Cold?" the ambassador asked her as they walked.

Tamara nodded as another blast of cold air slid down the back of her neck. Greg and Alarin, who were also dressed in shorts and t-shirts, didn't seem to notice. "I forget how high everyone keeps air conditioning in the summer," she said.

He slipped off his suit jacket and dropped it over her shoulders. "Here. This should help." The jacket was quite large on her, hanging below her waist. She slipped her arms into the garment, and they hung beyond her wrists. She almost felt like a little girl wearing her father's clothes, although when she was a little girl, she'd never felt quite like this playing dress up. His jacket, still warm from his body heat and smelling like him, made her suddenly feel dizzy. She was nonetheless grateful for the added warmth. "Better?" he asked, glancing over at her.

"Yes, much. Thank you."

Merran didn't comment further when he noticed the blush spread across her cheeks.

The hostess led them to a table on the balcony. The view was phenomenal, since most of the other buildings in the area were short enough that the setting sun and the massive Front Range took center stage. Tamara had never been to a restaurant like this before—for a moment she wondered how expensive the food would be. The hostess pulled out a chair for her, then handed out menus, flipped glasses upright, and shook out napkins. "Your server tonight will be Glen. I can take your drink orders for you now, if you like. What would you like to start off with?"

Tamara settled into the chair, keeping the ambassador's suit jacket draped over her shoulders. Even though it was warmer out on the balcony where the heat of the day mingled with the intense air conditioning to create something almost comfortable, Tamara knew the sun would be setting soon. Although it was August, temperatures could drop at night. She rubbed the edge of the suit coat. The soft material was unlike anything she'd ever felt before. It was both sensuous and sensual, and very comfortable. There was something soothing and almost hypnotic about the feel of the material under her fingertips.

"Tamara, what would you like?" the ambassador asked, startling her.

She cleared her throat. "Uh, an Arnold Palmer please."

The hostess nodded and turned to Alarin. "And for you, sir?"

"Hmm. What looks good?"

"I don't know what you might like," the ambassador said. "Margaritas are tart. Daiquiris tend to be sweet."

"Tart sounds good. I'll have a margarita."

"I'll have a strawberry daiquiri," Greg said, putting aside the drink menu.

"A margarita for me as well," the ambassador said.

"Glen will be here to take your food order shortly," the hostess said with a smile. "I'll be back with your drink orders. Thank you."

The ambassador leaned back and loosened his tie, unbuttoning the top couple of buttons of his shirt, a hint of chest hair peeking through. He then unbuttoned his shirt cuffs and rolled up the bottom of his shirtsleeves, revealing more body hair. Tamara flushed and stared down at the menu, trying to pretend she hadn't noticed. "Is it me or do hostesses not normally take orders?" he asked.

"Don't ask me. This is the first restaurant I've ever been to," Alarin commented.

"Tamara?" Her name, spoken in the ambassador's voice with an Azellian lilt, populated her stomach with butterflies.

"Uh, sorry?" she asked, looking up.

"Is it usual for the hostess to take drink orders?" he asked, a smile tugging at his generous mouth. His rich brown eyes were bright with an emotion she wasn't sure how to interpret.

"Uh, no. Not usually." She coughed. "I've, uh, hostessed a few times. Usually we just seated people. It might be different here, though. Every restaurant is different."

"And it might be because of you two," Greg commented dryly, making a face at his friends. "One of these days, we're going somewhere where I get more attention than the two of you. And not as a Healer."

Alarin grinned, leaning back against the chair and stretching luxuriously. "Ah, but that doesn't work so well, does it? As we tend to garner attention in those places too."

Greg scowled. "Great, just remind me that my two best friends are just as attractive to men as they are to women."

"He's a Raderth, he can't help it. They have to be the center of attention," the ambassador said mildly. "Besides, I thought you were a Healer. And if I remember correctly, aren't Healers supposed to be primarily celibate?"

Greg snorted. "Tell that to some of my fellow Healers. There's a new one who just finished his training. He could rival you, Mer."

The ambassador glanced at Tamara. He cleared his throat. "Um, well. My reputation has been rather dramatically exaggerated."

"There's a saying," Alarin chimed in, green eyes bright, "if you go to the oasis, you find water."

"Humans say where there's smoke, there's fire," Tamara said, enjoying the teasing. It made the ambassador seem more human somehow. Although she avoided the news most of the time, even she'd heard about his exploits in the online entertainment outlets, mostly with some starlet or another. To have him here, being teased by his friends and faintly embarrassed about it all, really changed her view of him. He seemed more accessible like this—in his rolled up shirtsleeves, his tie hanging loosely off his neck, his shirt open and revealing a hint of the body underneath, with a smile hovering at the edges of his mouth.

The hostess appeared right then, preventing the ambassador from responding immediately. "An Arnold Palmer, two margaritas, and a strawberry daiquiri. Is there anything else I can help you with?"

"We're fine for the moment, thank you," the ambassador said, adding one of his blinding camera smiles. Having seen him more relaxed, Tamara abruptly realized she could tell the difference. It was subtle but there, like the difference between a painting and a photograph. The camera smile wasn't entirely real, although most people probably didn't notice. "You've been very helpful, but I think you might be needed at the front desk." He motioned to the front door, where a couple waited to be seated.

The hostess was wearing too much makeup to blush; however, her ears turned bright red. "Oh, thank you! Let me know if I can help you with anything at all."

"Thank you, we will."

"And that's probably why you have the reputation you do," Alarin commented as she walked away, stumbling over her feet and catching herself.

"Will you get off my reputation?"

Alarin grinned. "Feeling a bit self-conscious, are we?"

"Feeling jealous, are we?" the ambassador shot back.

"So what happened today that was so stressful?" Greg interrupted the good-natured bickering.

The ambassador shrugged and turned his attention to Greg. "Just some humans giving trouble about the fact that Azellians are living on Earth next to their precious daughters." He grinned at Alarin and Greg, and Tamara realized that he wasn't as upset as he'd appeared earlier. "I think it bothers them that we are actually attractive to human eyes ... myself and my reputation with the human media notwithstanding. I didn't mention the fact that they might need to worry about their sons, Greg. Humans can be a bit odd about the whole same sex attraction thing."

"Tamara warned me," Greg replied, reaching out to sip his daiquiri. "Mmm. This is tasty. What's in it?" He licked his lips. "Wow. Like a dessert. You sure it has alcohol in it?"

"I forget what's in it, but yes, it most certainly does. It contains an alcohol called rum, I believe."

"I've heard about human alcohol in what little human medical training I've had so far," Greg sipped the drink again. "It apparently causes all kinds of trouble. Mmm. I'd better watch it."

The ambassador sipped his yellow-green drink. "Oh, this is really good too. And this is why I come here. They've got really good food and drinks as well as a beautiful view. Don't worry about the alcohol content. There's only one drink that our metabolism can't burn off in seconds and that's a Geneva Slider. It still takes quite a few of those to get us drunk, but we can at least get a small buzz off one. These drinks won't do it, though. They're only flavored water to us."

Alarin sampled his margarita, his tongue touching the salt crusted on the edge of the glass before he sipped the drink. "Oh, this is refreshing … you're right."

"How's your drink, Tamara?" Greg asked. "It's a what? An Arnold Palmer, I think you called it?"

Tamara nodded. "It's half lemonade, half iced tea. No alcohol." She looked at the men's drinks. "I've had a strawberry daiquiri before, but I've never tasted a margarita. You said they are tart?"

The ambassador slid his drink over to her. "You want a taste?" he offered.

Tamara flushed but she reached for the drink, the sleeve of his suit jacket brushing the table as she picked it up. She studied the drink and the salt on the edge of the glass. "Do you taste the salt first, then drink?"

"Completely up to you. Try it both ways. See which one you prefer."

Tamara touched her tongue to the salt the way she'd seen Alarin do, then sipped the drink. A shiver raced through her as her tastebuds exploded. Tart was right. Tart and salty. She licked the salt again and took another sip, feeling the warmth of the tequila race through her stomach, spreading a delicious lassitude through her muscles. "Wow, that's good."

"Do you want one? We can always order one for you," he asked as he reclaimed his glass and took a sip of his own. A shiver moved its way down her spine. Had she just shared a drink with the Azellian ambassador? No, she'd just shared a drink with Merran Corina. It felt better saying it that way, even if he was a guy and she'd never shared a drink with a guy before.

"Actually I'm not twenty-one ... and even though the hostess didn't check IDs, the waiter might," Tamara pointed out. "I'd better not. I'm pretty hungry and I'd rather not get kicked out."

"Then you can just share mine," the ambassador—Merran— offered, shifting the drink so it sat between them in easy reach, but still close enough to his plate that it was clear it was his. "I can always order another one."

"Thanks," she said, reaching over to sip his drink again. The ritual of licking the salt, then sipping the drink was quite fascinating to her. It was half of the fun. The buzz she got from the alcohol was the rest. It helped her relax, allowing her to shed some of her shyness.

By the time the waiter showed up, she was feeling much more relaxed and a whole lot better, the lassitude and heavy feeling in her muscles quite pleasing. "Can I start you off with some appetizers?" the waiter asked as he looked around the table, his eyes coming to rest on Merran, who nodded.

"Yes, we'll start with the nacho plate. But we'll place our orders now, if you don't mind."

"Certainly," the waiter said. He looked at Tamara expectantly. "What can I get for you, Miss?"

"I'll take the, um, fajita plate, please. Chicken."

"You, sir?" he turned to Merran who was sitting to Tamara's left.

"The enchilada plate, please."

"Certainly. And you, sir?"

Alarin ordered the chicken mole.

"And you?" the waiter looked expectantly at Greg.

"Do you have any vegetarian entrees?" Greg glanced over at Tamara, giving her a wink.

"The stuffed burrito is vegetarian, as is the fajita plate without chicken. Are you vegan? The fiesta salad can be made without the cheese."

"Vegan?"

"No animal products at all. That means no cheese and no refried beans, which are cooked with lard," Tamara explained, wanting to take another sip of the addictive margarita but not daring to do so while the waiter stood there.

"Ah. I'll have the fiesta salad, but you can leave on the cheese. I'd like to try something new."

That got the waiter's attention. "You've never had cheese?"

"No. We don't have cheese where I'm from."

The waiter blinked. "Where's that, may I ask?"

"Azelle."

"Wait a minute. You're the Azellian ambassador and the Azellian exchange students, aren't you? Oh, how exciting! Welcome to Earth!" The waiter gushed, suddenly looking much more animated. "How is your stay so far?"

"Really great, thank you," Greg said, looking pleased at the attention. Tamara glanced at Merran, who shrugged, and Alarin, who grinned.

"Since you're trying new things, you have to try the guacamole dip with your nachos," the waiter continued with enthusiasm. "I'll bring you some as soon as I put in your orders."

"Thanks, that would be lovely."

"And it's just at the end of happy hour, so it's buy one get one. Would you like another of the same?" He looked around the table.

"I'll have another dairquiri, sure." Greg said.

"Another margarita for me," Alarin said.

Merran nodded. "Margarita for me, too."

"Nothing for me," Tamara said. "Thanks."

"Great, I'll be right back with your appetizer. I'm Glen, by the way. Just holler if you need anything."

They watched Glen walk away. "Well, you got your wish there, Greg," Alarin commented. "A lovely young man with eyes just for you."

Tamara reached for the drink at the same time as Merran did, his hand sliding over hers as she held the glass. His fingers were warm. "Oh sorry," she said, pulling her hand back. "Go ahead."

"You first," he replied, leaning back.

"No, it's your drink."

He gave her a smile that made her entire body tingle. It wasn't that fake camera smile he'd given the hostess, but one that lit up his whole face. "I like watching you enjoy it. Go ahead."

Her head spun. *Did he just flirt with me?* Her hand shook slightly as she reached for the drink. Fortunately, the glass was empty enough that it didn't spill. This time, as she tasted the salt and sipped the drink, she was very aware of his eyes on her. She placed the glass down on the table carefully. *Is this what being drunk feels like?* She wondered. She hadn't had that much, had she? She definitely felt different, though, so totally relaxed she didn't care that Merran had watched her mouth the entire time she'd gone through her salt-lick-drink ritual. *Did he just lick the same spot I did?* She sank into the chair and his coat as Glen came out with their new drinks. Her mind wandered momentarily as she wondered what he would taste like and whether or not he was a good kisser.

Merran leaned back too and stretched, his shirt gapping as he did. "Now this is nice. Much nicer than arguing with argumentative and anxious fathers."

Greg raised his eyebrows. "Any more alliteration you want to throw into that sentence, Mr. Poet-man?"

"I don't know if I know any other words that apply. Well, I do know one. It isn't particularly nice for mixed company, however. I'll let you fill in the blanks."

"Arrant? That's not a bad word," Tamara suggested, feeling like her brain was working underwater, muffled by a delicious sense of lethargy.

Merran grinned at her. "You're right. Although I'm not sure I would have used that one exactly," he said as Glen came out carrying a huge plate of nachos and sides.

By the end of the meal and several shared margaritas later, she was feeling very relaxed, somewhat sleepy, and completely content to just listen to the lively conversation around her. When it was suggested that they get up and walk some of the meal off, she followed, enjoying the pleasant sense of dizziness and disconnection. She didn't remember much of the next hour, grateful for the warmth of Merran's suit jacket, and then later, his arm around her as they sat on a bench listening to the rush of the Platte River, Greg on her other side and Alarin just beyond Greg.

"Is she drunk or sleeping?" a voice said just above her head, as she realized she was lying with her head on someone's shoulder and had completely lost track of the low-voiced conversation. "How much did she have?"

"Not that much. She's just exhausted," Greg replied, his voice clear and close.

Warmth spilled through her and she recognized Greg's touch. She squirmed a little. "That tickles," she mumbled.

"Wait a minute, you feel that?" Greg asked, shifting so he crouched in front of her. She realized she was lying against Merran's shoulder, his arm across her shoulders.

"Yes, shouldn't I?"

"No. Not unless your psi's active. Hmm. You're still heavily shielded. No change there." Greg ran his hands in the air over her body. She shivered, feeling the sensations quivering through her body. "But you feel what I'm doing to your aura, don't you?"

"Is that what I'm feeling?" she asked, enjoying the sensations, too relaxed to be spooked by it. "I guess so."

Greg looked up at Merran, then at Alarin. "Any suggestions?"

"How about taking her home and putting her to bed? This might or might not be an Awakening episode, but you're right, she's exhausted." Alarin joined Greg, crouching in front of her.

Merran shifted her off his shoulder and propped her up. She sat up on her own power but swayed a little. "You two will have to bring her home, since me showing up at the university with a tipsy underage girl won't do my reputation any good."

"Wait," Tamara said, pulling herself together enough to remember she still wore his jacket. "What about your coat?"

"Drop it off at the embassy later," he said, getting to his feet. "Tomorrow or Sunday would be fine. The regular staff won't be there, but I will be. This has been a lot of fun, but I've got to go." He leaned over and took her hand, kissing the back of it gallantly. "Thank you for the lovely evening, Tamara. See you later, Alarin, Greg." He strode off. She got up, Alarin and Greg stepping in on either side of her, and they started toward campus.

✳ ✳ ✳

When she woke the next morning, it was to a pounding head and dry mouth. The sun streaming in her eastern-facing windows was already making her room hot, the air conditioning insufficient to handle the load. Sitting up, she made a face at the taste in her mouth and looked around her dorm room. Although the memories were a bit fuzzy, she did clearly remember going out to eat with Alarin, Greg, and ... Merran. She felt a blush crawl up her cheeks. Had she really shared drinks with Merran? Had he really flirted with her over a margarita, or had he just been nice and she was imagining the whole thing? His jacket hung neatly over the back of her desk chair, mutely testifying to at least some of what she remembered. He had told her to return the coat today, hadn't he? Swinging her legs off the edge of the bed, she padded over to her cell phone. No text messages and no calls, but she remembered Merran telling Greg and Alarin to get her home and for her to drop off the jacket over the weekend. She also remembered him kissing her hand, which didn't answer her questions about whether he was just being nice or if he had really been flirting with her, but it made her feel better about the whole thing. She rubbed her forehead. The lingering headache this morning felt more like the remnants of a sick migraine than it did anything else. Had she really gotten drunk enough to pass out? On shared bits of two margaritas? She didn't remember much about the walk home, but exhaustion could have accounted for that.

She still hadn't answered her own question by the time she'd showered, dressed, eaten, checked in with her parents, and picked up the coat, intending to head over to the embassy to drop it off. At least the headache had disappeared. She felt much better as she walked up to the embassy gates.

The guard in the guardshack greeted her politely. "I have something to drop off for Ambassador Corina," she said, holding up the coat. "I'm Tamara Carrington."

"Let me see if he's in," the guard told her, stepping back into the booth and coming out a few moments later. "If you'd like to go on up, he'll see you, Ms Carrington."

It gave an odd little thrill to realize that the ambassador of Azelle would agree to see her personally. She kept her suddenly volatile emotions under strict control as she walked up the curved, treelined drive and the wide marble staircase that led to the front door. The last time she'd been here was for the embassy party a week ago. It had been brilliantly lit, with what had felt like thousands of people inside, although she'd been told it was closer to a hundred. The doors had popped open at her approach. Today, they did not and she had to pull the door open herself.

It opened easily, revealing the almost silent interior of the large atrium-lobby area at the entry of what had once been a very expensive, luxurious mansion. The sun lit most of the room, in-direct sunlight spilling in from the large semi-circular window high above the entry doors that highlighted the interior marble so it almost glowed. She hadn't appreciated the beauty of it last week, but she certainly did now. Elegant and stately, yet somehow inviting and peaceful, it felt oddly welcoming. She relaxed, feeling a subtle tension drain out of her body that she hadn't even been aware of earlier.

She heard voices. Looking around, she noticed one person coming down the wide stairs opposite the front door. "So we're going to need to rework some of the background on that agree-ment," Merran's voice said in English. She recognized his standard business suit and tie. "Why don't you call Janille during the week and get that set up?"

There was no answer to his comment. Frowning, she looked for a cell phone or headset or something else she might recognize, but there was nothing.

"Very good. Ah, hello Tamara. Ambassador Ki'i, may I pres-ent Tamara Carrington? Tamara, this is the Dorbin ambassador."

Even as she watched, a shimmering appeared in the air, coae-lescing into a filmy shape that hovered in the air in front of her face. She managed not to squeak and jump back, but it was an ef-fort. "Ms. Carrington. It is a pleasure to meet you," a breathy voice said, so light she could hardly hear it.

"Tamara does not have psi, Ki'i. You'll have to form more fully for her to be able to see you clearly."

"Ah, my apologies." The being solidified, looking oddly put together—as if it weren't quite sure how it should look. It also spoke more loudly, so she could hear it without straining. "It is a pleasure to meet you, Ms. Carrington." The being bowed and moved as if it didn't have joints. But then, considering it hadn't been visible the moment before, it probably didn't. "Your grandfather James was known to us. He visited Dorbin on occasion."

"I didn't realize that," Tamara said, somewhat surprised. "He never told me."

The being smiled, and it was odd, again as if it had no muscles and the image was pasted on. "Dorbin is not comfortable for non-psi. He may have not had recall of it. Well, I shall leave you with the *diarhman*, Merran."

"She's not *diarhman*, Ki'i."

"Ah, such a pity. If that should change, you will let me know? The merging would be worth much to me."

Tamara didn't understand the conversation, but she got the distinct impression she didn't want to. Merran didn't reveal any discomfort—his ambassadorial façade was quite solid this morning—but as the Dorbin ambassador left the building, his body shimmering and disappearing even as she watched, Merran turned to her and she got the strangest impression he was embarrassed. "Ah, my coat. Thanks for bringing it back, Tamara."

"Is it me or was that weird?" she asked him, staring at the spot where the Dorbin ambassador had just been.

"He's Dorbin, so they function on a totally different level than we do. Anything we define as normal goes totally out the window around them. Your grandfather must have made quite an impression on Ki'i, though. We psi can see him all the time, but for him to reveal himself to someone without psi either means he has to for a trade agreement or he likes you. Or your ancestor, anyway. Dorbin don't really distinguish between the two," Merran said, taking the coat.

Tamara frowned. "How old is he?"

"The Dorbin are immortal, or as close to it as can be, so I have no idea. He saw the fall of the Roman Empire, or so he tells me. They like to observe other planets. I met him for the first time on Azelle, when he'd come to the Temple to speak to the *aarya* about something."

"The *aarya*? The Temple?"

"Didn't your grandfather tell you about the *aarya*? Or the Temple?"

Tamara shook her head. "Not really."

Merran glanced at the clock on the wall. "I've got to grab a late breakfast before my next appointment. Join me and I'll tell you a little more about them."

"Sure," she said, following him out the front door. Rather than getting into a limo or climbing into a car, he led her to a small section of wall on the side of the building, a concealed gate that opened out onto a normal street. "Don't you watch that gate?" she asked as it swung shut behind them.

"There's no way to open that door unless you're psi," Merran replied, "and this street is mostly Azellian businesses catering to embassy workers, so it's pretty much watched all the time anyway." He held the door open to a small hole-in-the-wall restaurant. Tamara entered in front of him.

"Good morning, Merran," a woman said cheerfully as they entered and the door swung shut. "The usual?"

"Yes, Rosilyne. This is Tamara, a student from the university." He led Tamara to a booth, sliding in on one side.

"Welcome, Tamara. It's good to meet you. Welcome to the Rose Café. Can I get you some coffee or tea, perhaps?"

"Tea please. Non-caffeinated."

"Herbal tea coming right up. Do you need a menu?"

"Please," Tamara replied. The tall woman, whom she would not have picked out as Azellian, came over with a pot of hot water and a selection of teas along with a steaming cup of coffee for Merran. Tamara picked a peach tea and poured herself hot water. She ordered a bowl of fruit.

"The *aarya*?" She prompted as Rosilyne took their order and disappeared into the kitchen.

"First, how are you feeling?" Merran asked her, leaning back against his chair. "Greg says you had something very closely resembling an Azellian Awakening episode last night."

"I had a what?" Tamara stared at him.

"Did you wake up with a headache this morning?"

"Well, yes, but I thought it was the margarita." She managed not to blush, but it was only by not thinking about the flirting that had gone on around the margarita. If it had even been flirting; there certainly was no sign of it this morning.

He shook his head. "You might have been exhausted and tispy, but you weren't drunk. Not enough to account for the migraine. What do you know about Azellian history?"

"Not much. I mean, no more than any other human knows. Azellians initiated first contact fifty-some years ago and established the first embassy on Earth. My grandfather was the first human ambassador allowed to establish a return embassy on Azelle. Because of him, I know a little bit about the culture, but that's about it."

Merran picked up his mug, sipping it carefully. "Pretty standard human teaching about Azellian history. Well, here's a crash course: Azelle has several different histories, depending on the race."

"Several?"

Merran gave her a grin. "The last I checked, Earth has hundreds of histories, some of them conflicting, so don't be surprised. You knew there are three sentient species on Azelle, right?"

"Three?" Tamara frowned. "No, I didn't realize that. I mean I knew about you, of course."

"Yes, we call ourselves the *umanaarya*. Then, there are the *aarya* and the *urro*. Anyway, according to our *umanaarya* history, which is the one you probably will hear about from Greg and most of the other Azellians you meet, we have lived on Azelle for many generations, perhaps a thousand Azellian years. We aren't native to Azelle but were brought there and allowed to live there through our Charter with the *aarya*. That Charter ended a generation of bitter war and prevented us from completely annihilating ourselves. It set up our current family-driven hierarchy and established the eight High Council families, sixteen City Council families, and the three families that chose not to follow the Charter but to ally themselves with the *urro* instead." A shadow crossed his face, making her curious, but she didn't want to interrupt him, so she continued to listen quietly.

"It also placed us under the dominion of the *aarya*, who started changing our genetics, developing our psi in general and creating the Healers. That's the official *umanaarya* history of Azelle." He fell silent as Rosilyne served them their breakfast, retreating out of earshot as soon as she dropped off the food. He sipped his coffee and started up again. "What most people don't know, including most *umanaarya*, is that the Healers that were the first psi users, spontaneously erupted from our original gene pool. It was the cause of the original war that the Charter ended. The *aarya* stopped us from killing off the psi users and developed psi in all of us." He took a bite of the omlette and bacon on his plate, chewed and swallowed, and then continued his story. "The *aarya* don't live among us, at least not openly. Instead, they choose to live in temples at the center of the eight main Azellian cities, with the first and primary Temple in Azorantxl. The temples serve as refuge, meditation centers, teaching centers, and for those called to it, training centers to learn to become close to the *aarya*. Even though we venerate them and consider them guides, teachers, even deities, their perspective is so different than ours that it's uncomfortable for most *umanaarya* to spend a large amount of time around them. But there are some who are called to it, and they are welcomed as Keepers of the *aarya* version of our history."

"Do you know the *aarya* version of Azellian history?"

Merran gave her a look from under his eyebrows as he took another bite. "I never made it past acolyte. So no, I don't."

"You were an acolyte? Is that like a priest?"

"Not really, not as you define priest or minister, although there are some similarities. However, my status as an acolyte has nothing to do with Azellian Awakenings, so we're moving on."

Tamara nodded. "Okay. But I'm not sure how any of this relates to Azellian Awakenings."

"As part of our Charter with them, the *aarya* changed us, developing the psi in all of us, right?"

"Yes, I remember that part."

"Well, it doesn't kick in until puberty. It is also highly sexual in nature, which Greg probably mentioned at some point."

"He mentioned it but didn't really go into it. He said I was human so it wasn't really relevant for me and that this would likely unfold in a completely different way than it does for Azellians."

"Well, that's probably true, but it wouldn't hurt for you to know the Azellian process, either, especially if you're planning to go to Azelle to work. Azellian Awakenings are simply called that because we awaken to our psi, but it's actually a bit more complicated than that. At birth, our psi goes dormant. The energies begin to emerge again at puberty. There are typically a series of what we call 'episodes' prior to the psi energies breaking through dormancy and flowing freely through the psi channels."

She frowned at him. "What are the typical episodes?"

"They vary. Erotic dreams, migraines, flashes of talent, patchy shields appearing and disappearing, odd sensitivities and overtly sexual behavior in a child who presented none prior. These occur until the energies finally are loosened from their restraints and channeled through the body and psyche permanently."

"M—migraines?" Tamara stared at him as she suddenly realized just about everything he'd described on that list had happened to her at some point or another. *Didn't they tell me that I was open when I first met them, but now I have shields?* she wondered. She took a deep breath and spoke out loud. "But all of these types of episodes could just be coincidence, couldn't they?"

"We've all experienced Awakening for the past thousand Azellian years, Tamara. We're very familiar with what it looks like."

Tamara shook her head. "No … I mean me. I'm human. I can't Awaken." Although the idea of psi was not nearly as frightening as it had been a week ago when Greg first talked to her about it, it was still not something she was prepared to admit might be happening to her.

Merran leaned back, his expression neutral. "We don't know enough about human psi to tell what you can and can't do. For all we know, human psi develops the same way ours does."

Tamara shook her head, trying to clear it. "I don't remember what happened last night. I mean, I remember what we did, but

I don't remember anything being different ... about me. So what did happen?"

"You said you felt Greg working on you."

She bit her lip. "So? That's not ... I mean, why do you think that's significant?"

"Because non-psi can't feel Greg's touch. Most of the time, they don't even realize he's doing anything. Did you feel different last night? Sensations in your body such as tingling, prickly feelings, odd twitches, anything like that?"

She felt the blush crawl up her cheeks, a blooming heat that gave her away even as she tried not to remember the sensation of Merran standing near her, the tingling that raced through her body whenever he got near, the warmth that spread through her as she rested against him while they sat on the park bench. Then, the feelings of relaxation and expansion as Greg touched her. Had that been a moment of psi awareness?

Merran shifted in his chair. "And you developed a migraine, which is a classic symptom of any kind of Awakening episode, at least for Azellians."

She found herself fascinated and repelled at the same time as something stirred deep inside her. "It was just a headache."

Merran leaned forward and brushed his fingertips across the back of her hand, so lightly it was almost not a touch at all. She shivered at the sensation, which was making her whole body quiver. "When we're children, just prior to Awakening, we pick the partner with whom we want to unleash the Awakening energies and we play a game."

Goose bumps erupted up her arm. "What kind of game?"

A slight smile tugged at his lips. "It's a game of the senses. Close your eyes."

She closed her eyes, then opened one. "What are you going to do?"

Merran grinned at her. "It won't hurt, I promise. Just relax and let me show you what psi feels like, Tamara."

She closed her eye and sat there, both eyes tightly shut.

Merran had to suppress a grin at her tension. She looked like she didn't know if she was going to an execution or a celebration, as her whole body quivered. He brushed his mind across her fitfully flaring aura. She didn't always have one, but she'd certainly had one last night, and again today, which is how he knew he could play this game with her. Her fingertips twitched as he brushed across the back of her hand with his mind. Then he brushed against her cheek, her arm, her nose, and her forehead, carefully staying away from the areas that most Azellian children explored immediately. He didn't need to set off a full-fledged episode—if she reacted like an Azellian. From her skin twitches, he could tell she felt every single brush, as he suspected she had last night too. Flirting with her during dinner had been fun, as had the surprising but pleasant session during which she'd curled up against him and fallen asleep while they sat on the park bench listening to the river.

She slowly relaxed. "That tickles," she said as her aura began sparking under his touch.

"Good," he murmured. He focused on touching her ear and the back of her neck, making her shiver involuntarily. "It's supposed to." Her aura sparked again, and he followed it, using it to set his pace and his direction.

After a few more moments of that, she opened her eyes. "What exactly are you doing? It feels like a thousand little prickles across my entire body. It feels good but weird."

"It's called aura sparking. I stimulate your aura using my mind. Because you are able to feel it, we know you've got at least some psi sensing ability and it hasn't gone away yet. If you were Azellian, I'd say you were having another episode." He studied her. "Your aura is very strong right at the moment."

"My aura?"

"All beings have an energy field. We psi just have stronger ones that are visible to other psi." Merran glanced at the clock on the wall behind her head. Feeling uncomfortable about taking this any further with Tamara, he pushed his chair back and got to his feet. "I'm sorry, but I've got to go. I suggest that you ask Greg to continue where we left off. I really am sorry, but I've got to get back to the embassy. Are you ready? I'll take care of breakfast." He got up and put some bills on the table.

"Yeah, I'm good. Thank you," Tamara said, getting to her feet.

"Any time," Merran replied, with one of his dazzling smiles. Tamara's heart thumped hard. He gave her a little bow. She bowed back, making his smile widen further as he ushered her in front of him to the door. "I'll walk with you as far as the embassy and show you the door to get back in."

Tamara followed him out of the restaurant and back to the embassy wall. The featureless expanse of wall gave no clue as to the location of the gate, but Merran walked unerringly up to the tall obstacle and touched a spot. A wall section popped open, swinging freely.

"Telekinesis?" she asked, fascinated. She reached out to touch the freely swinging gate.

Merran grinned at her. "You got it. There's no way to open it otherwise. Without psi, you can't even find it."

"That's amazing." Tamara brushed her fingertips across the

edge of the door. Her body tingled, almost as it had when Merran had touched her hand. She suppressed a shiver. "Thank you for breakfast."

"You're welcome." Merran stepped inside the door. "See you around?"

"See you around. And thank you again."

He bowed to her, then stepped through the wall. It swung shut behind him, closing firmly. All signs of the door disappeared into the wall. She shook her head and turned toward campus.

Chapter Five

THE NEXT WEEK, Tamara spent every spare moment she could at home with her mother, but the rest of the time she organized getting her on-campus room set up, hanging out with her new Azellian friends at the on-campus new student events, and working to settle the new students into campus before the continuing students returned.

Between work, visiting her mother, and hanging out with the Azellians as a group, she didn't get a chance to talk to Greg in depth about auras, her visit with Merran, or the history of Azelle. She also didn't have any episodes of odd, possibly psi behavior, either. The entire week went along pleasantly and completely migraine free. It gave Tamara hope that those odd episodes were over.

Her cell phone buzzed as she collected her purse and computer tablet from the Registrar's Office, ready to leave work for the day. With her free hand, she pulled her phone out of a pocket in her jacket and glanced at the number. *What does Mellis want?* Tamara wondered when she saw the number. Swiping the face of the phone, she put it up to her ear and waved at Kim as she pushed the office door open with her hip.

"Hey, Mel, what's up?" she asked. After two weeks of spending most of her spare time with the Azellians, she found their nicknames coming easily to her.

"Hi Tamara!" Mellis's cheerful voice always lifted her spirits, no matter how stressed or sad she was. "We were thinking about grabbing dinner somewhere in town tonight. You want to join us?"

"Who's going?"

"Greg, me, Alari, probably. Justy's found himself a woman to seduce, so I think he'll be going out with her. Merran's got late appointments, so he's not going to make it, either."

"Well, sure. Sounds like fun. Where are you meeting?"

"Greg's room. We still have to decide where we're going. That could take hours."

Tamara laughed. She'd spent enough time around the Azellians to know they didn't make speedy decisions. "Well, Justy's not going to be there so it might take less time than that."

Mellis snorted. "Yeah, well, Justy isn't the only one who argues for the fun of it. But I have to admit Alari is less stubborn when Justy isn't around pushing his buttons."

"He always seems pretty reasonable to me."

Mellis laughed. "He hasn't shown you that side of himself yet then. See you in a few?"

"I'm on my way." Tamara hung up the phone and headed for Greg's room, feeling a little thrill that they wanted to include her. She'd never felt such a strong, almost immediate, connection with anyone before. It usually took her forever to get to know people and to make friends. Not so this time and it was a pleasant change.

The hot summer breeze hummed slightly with the background noise of traffic as she walked across campus; she jumped when a car horn blared as someone did something another driver didn't like. Shaking her head, she ducked under the shade of some trees to cool off from the fiercely shining sun. Tamara lifted her jacket off her shoulders, and she shrugged a little to get some air flow down the middle of her back before she pulled open the door to the dorm. She tucked her tablet tightly under her arm and shifted her purse as she climbed the stairs to the fifth floor.

The fifth floor seemed quiet, but when she turned the corner, several students stood in front of an open door talking about the latest seminar. She walked past them and gave a quick smile to the group as she knocked on Greg's door.

"Come in," he called, after a few moments of silence, the lock on the door clicking. She pushed the door open. All thoughts of the other students fell away as she walked in and the door thumped closed behind her. Greg lay sprawled on the bed, looking rumpled and sleepy, the sheets tangled around his waist. Tamara couldn't help noticing the smoothness of his bare, muscular chest, which was quite well defined.

She halted in confusion. "Um, I'm sorry, did I wake you up? Mel told me to meet her and Alari here..."

Greg sat up. He ran a hand through his hair and made the short blond strands stick straight up. "No, it's all right. Mel called me, too, and I was going to get up, but I must have fallen back to sleep. I was just taking a nap." He rubbed his eyes. "I'm so glad it's Friday and regular classes start next week. These past two weeks of constant events have been brutal."

Tamara sat on the edge of Greg's desk. "It's designed to increase the first-years' sense of being a class. Put them through hell together. It also keeps them from getting homesick."

"Well, it's certainly been doing something," Greg agreed, sliding his legs out from under the blankets. Tamara blushed at the glimpse of skin. Had he really been taking a nap in the nude? As he got to his feet and flashed her, she whirled, feeling the heat burning up her cheeks. Yep, he had. "I've gotten to know quite a few people, although not as many as ... you okay?" he asked.

"Just waiting for you to get dressed," Tamara said, keeping her back to him.

"Humans are really that disturbed by nudity? You can turn around now. I've got clothes on."

Tamara turned to face him, still feeling the heat in her cheeks. He wore a pair of shorts, but she could still remember that glimpse of his naked body. She blushed harder as he slipped a t-shirt over his head. He might not be interested in her sexually because of his preferences, but he was very definitely male, and an attractive male at that. She licked her suddenly dry lips. "Well, it's not like I get to see people run around nude all the time."

Greg grinned, apparently finding her discomfort amusing. "You should spend time at the oasis in the summer then. Nudity is the norm." He leaned over, tugging the blankets up to make the bed.

Tamara cleared her throat. *I'll be avoiding Azellian beaches,* she told herself.

Alarin opened the door a few seconds later and strode in. "Hey guys—" He halted and peered at Tamara. "Are you feeling okay? You look like you just swallowed a lightbulb. A red one. What happened?"

The blush, which had felt as though it might be subsiding, returned with a vengeance.

"I'm fine," she said, tossing her head. Although she had mostly gotten to a point over the past two weeks where she wasn't intimidated by Alarin as much as she had been initially, in this oddly sensitized state, she was also very aware of Alarin's lean body, although he, at least, was decently clothed. Several images, somewhat graphic—or pornographic even—raced across her mind. She hastily suppressed the images, but not before sweat broke out across her entire body. She could feel a trickle slide down her neck and side.

Greg gave her a slight smile, his amber eyes bright. He put the final touches on his bed and then sat on it. "Did you walk in with any idea of where we want to go tonight?" he asked Alarin.

Alarin turned to Greg, releasing Tamara from the intensity of his full attention. "Nope," he replied. He pulled out the desk chair and straddled it, resting his arms against the chair's back. He flexed his forearms, bracing himself against the chair. Tamara swallowed as a rush of sensation skittered up her spine. "I thought Tamara here might have some ideas. As a native of Denver, that is."

"Well, there are several—" she began, only to have Mellis interrupt when she came in.

"Hi guys. Do we know where we're going yet?" she asked, going over to Greg and joining him on the bed.

"We're asking Tamara for some good hotspots," Alarin said.

Greg rested his hand on Mellis's leg. Tamara had another uncomfortably graphic flash. She shook her head, trying to clear it. What was wrong with her? None of this was any different than it ever was—Greg was always somewhat touchy-feely with his friends. Why was it suddenly triggering a cascade of sexual images every time any of them moved?

Dizziness assailed her, and she swayed a little on her feet. "I don't know what you want to do," she said, bracing herself surreptitiously against the top of the desk. She hoped she didn't look as odd as she was feeling. "If you want to go to a club, or a dance hall, I can't go. I'm not old enough yet. There are some good ones not far from campus, though."

No one seemed to notice anything. *I must not be acting oddly*, she thought as she listened to them discuss food options not far from campus. As they talked, she was able to ignore the flashes of sexual images, and eventually they faded away.

Greg's laptop abruptly launched itself off the desk.

Using his telekinesis, Alarin grabbed it out of the air just as the tin of pens followed it. He ducked and Greg caught the pens. One of the pens shot out of the tin and danced its way toward Tamara, where it hovered at her eye level. "Uh, what's this?" she asked, staring at the hovering pen. It bobbed cheerfully in front of her.

"You've got an aura," Mellis observed.

"She sure does," Greg said. He got to his feet, placed the tin on the desk, and approached her. His hands hovered in the air just above her skin. "Do you feel that?"

She nodded. "Yes." It was actually rather pleasant, tingling through her entire body. This was different from the game Merran had shown her a week ago but not entirely unlike it. "Are you doing aura sparking?"

"No, I'm simply scanning you. I'm not even Healing you. Right now there's nothing to heal. Who taught you about aura sparking?" Greg asked, lowering his hands.

"Merran. When I returned his suit jacket to him last Saturday. He told me to ask you more about it."

"Did he?" Greg glanced at Alarin, who shrugged. "Well, it's a game children play as they're Awakening. It's designed to get them comfortable with themselves and their bodies and the new sensations that come with psi as it becomes active. After this little display, I have little doubt that you've got psi talent, probably very similar psi talent to ours." He tapped the hovering pen. "This isn't any of us."

Tamara stared at him. "*I'm* doing that?"

"Yes, unless Mel is doing it for a joke."

Mellis shook her head. "No. It's not me."

"It's not me, either," Alarin replied.

"Then you're having an episode and it's you, Tamara. The presence of your aura leads me to believe that's the case." He pulled the pen out of the air.

"It couldn't be poltergeists?"

"Polter-whats?"

"Ghosts. Beings without a physical form that throw things around?"

She meant it as a joke, but Greg took her seriously. "I suppose it could be, but I'm not sensing anything else in the room with us right now. You getting anything, Mel, Alari?"

The other two shook their heads.

Tamara made a face. "Never mind. It was meant as a joke. Are you sure that I'm doing it?" Her head pounded, threatening the migraine that always followed one of her weird moments.

"What did your scan show?" Alarin asked Greg.

Greg shrugged. "About what I would expect. Not much. But then there usually isn't much to see, at least not until the energies are ready to completely break through. She's definitely going through something, though, and the symptoms are very much like our Awakening."

"If she's Awakening like we would, would it help to have her play aura games?" Alarin asked.

"Sure," Greg replied, returning to sit on his bed. "But she's going to need another partner. I'm not going to play them with her."

Tamara swallowed and spoke up, curiosity getting the better of her. "Why not?"

"Because aura sparking is often used for foreplay," Mellis replied, "and right now, he has no one to turn to for help with the energy release if the two of you spark each other's auras and it goes too far. I'd help him, but he refuses to have sex with a woman."

Greg patted her arm. "Yes, well, it has nothing to do with you, Mel, love."

Mellis grinned at him. "I know. We tried it once and didn't like it so much. I didn't take it personally."

Greg snorted. "That's good. Nice to know I didn't scar you for life."

Mellis laughed. "Yes, well, it wasn't the women that turned you on when we were at the beach. It was pretty obvious right from the beginning." She looked up at Tamara. "I'll play, if you like."

"Uh," Tamara said, not sure how to react to the offer. *Is Mellis offering what it sounds like she's offering?*

Alarin grinned at her, a mischievous look she'd never seen on his face before. "Our friend Charina has nothing but great things to say about her abilities."

Tamara blushed, feeling the heat crawl up her cheeks. "Uh," she repeated.

"Aura sparking doesn't *have* to become foreplay," Mellis protested. "Besides, I have plenty of places to go to let off steam, if you don't want to have sex with me."

Tamara blinked at her. "I, uh, I—I don't know what to say."

"Just say thank you," Alarin said, his green eyes sparking with mischief. "I certainly would."

"Oh, you think you're the one I'd turn to? Think again, Alari." Mellis made a face at him.

Alarin leaned back, his grin undimmed by her response. "Who else is there? Justy's got his hands full for the moment and Merran's busy. You high with aura sparking … sounds like fun."

"There are plenty of humans," Mellis said, wrinkling her nose at him. "A whole city full."

Alarin laughed. "Well, there certainly are. Of course, if you'd prefer a non-psi human to me, well, then, it's your loss."

"It's no loss," Mellis shot back.

"Oh really? That's not what I remember you saying before we left Azelle."

"Well, you're the one who decided that being celibate was preferable to being chased by your fiancée," Mellis retorted.

"I thought you just said it was no loss that you'd choose someone else over me?" Alarin leaned forward, his grin widening. "Getting lost in your logic, love?"

"Oh, just shut up," Mellis grumped.

Tamara opened her mouth, then closed it, completely out of her depth. Her head throbbed.

"Oh, quit it, guys. I'm hungry," Greg said, interrupting. "Now, I'm thinking we should just order in, if Tamara's going through an episode. It will be easier if she starts throwing things around again, and after, when the migraine sets in, we won't have to carry her as far to her room. Anybody up for pizza?"

"Pizza sounds good," Alarin agreed, dropping the argument with Mellis and turning to Greg. "I think it's becoming my favorite food."

"Sounds good to me too," Mellis said as Tamara winced, trying to ignore the steadily increasing throb of her head. "Hawaiian, please. I love the combination of pineapple and ham."

"What about you?" Greg asked Alarin.

"Pepperoni sounds good, but I can go with vegetarian."

"Tamara?" Greg asked, as Tamara closed her eyes.

She opened them again. "I don't feel so hot," she admitted, sudden waves of nausea rolling through her in time to the piercing pain that stabbed at the back of her head.

"The migraine is starting," Alarin said as Greg got to his feet and came over to her. "She really is acting like an Azellian going through Awakening, isn't she?"

Greg lightly placed his hands on Tamara's arm, and she could feel the waves of warmth rush through her, chasing away the nausea. The piercing pain continued. "She is. Come on, lie down Tamara. You'll feel better." He guided her to his bed, encouraging her to lie down on it. A fleeting image of him lying naked in the bed raced across her mind, but the pain chased it away almost immediately. "I'm going to treat her like I would an Awakening Azellian," she heard him say as she lay down on the bed. Her head was spinning. "For lack of anything else. Maybe aura games would help. You willing to play them with her, Alari?"

"Not a great idea, Greg. You know the situation with Ida. I can't open that door. Not right now."

Greg's breath puffed against her cheek as he smoothed a hand over her forehead. "I guess Merran gets to finish what he started then," she thought she heard him say.

"He's going to love that," Alarin said, but she was too far out of it to tell if he was being sarcastic or straightforward. "At least he's got outlets."

Outlets for what? she wondered briefly, only to have the thought scattered by the waves of soothing warmth that spilled across her body and mind. The spinning increased, but the pain faded as he stroked her hair and she found herself slipping away, the voices merging and disappearing into nothingness.

Hours later, she woke up, confused and disoriented. The room was bright with morning light, but it wasn't the eastern sun that spilled in the windows as it did in her room. Instead, the light was indirect. The window shades angled upwards to catch the light but prevented anyone from seeing in. She blinked, sitting up as her stomach growled, reminding her that she'd missed dinner.

A pile of blankets lay on the floor, forming a mound that didn't reveal a person but was certainly big enough to cover someone. Pushing her tangled hair out of her face, she frowned. *I'm in Greg's room, aren't I? That's got to be him. There really is nowhere else for him to be sleeping but that pile.*

She swung her legs over the edge of the bed, her shirt and shorts poking uncomfortably into her skin. As she moved, the pile stirred, making something resembling a groaning noise. "Greg?" she asked uncertainly.

A head poked out of the blankets, the tousled blond hair familiar, his eyes almost gold in the early morning light. "Awake?" he asked with a scratchy voice. He sat up, pulling the blankets with him. He'd made himself a cocoon, she noticed. No pillow, just a pile of blankets.

She nodded.

"Feeling better?" he asked.

"I feel fine." She looked at the floor. "Sorry I chased you out of your bed."

"No worries," he replied. "You were sleeping so peacefully we decided not to move you."

She half remembered a discussion about that somewhere during the confused dreams she'd had most of the night, most of them heavily erotic. She flushed and chose not to mention her recollections. She swallowed and pushed her hair out of her face. "What happened?"

"You had another episode. Telekinetic one this time. Do you remember it?"

She nodded. "I remember your computer flying off your desk and the pens ..." She looked at the tin of pens, now innocuously sitting on his desk this morning. "Then pain."

"The migraine," Greg pulled the blankets around himself and got to his feet, keeping them tightly tucked as he moved to sit on the desk chair. She flushed slightly, remembering how she'd woken him up the day before. He was probably naked again. Grateful that he was obviously respecting her discomfort by staying wrapped in the blankets, she didn't ask.

"The migraine." She rubbed her temple. "I remember you saying something about me Awakening like an Azellian would?"

Greg settled himself on the chair. The blanket toga he wore was a little too bulky to be comfortable, but he managed. "It certainly appears that you are. And I really don't know what else to do for you except treat you like an Awakening Azellian."

She swallowed, her throat dry. "I talked to Merran last Saturday," she said slowly as several things clicked into place in her subconscious, bringing a wash of awareness with them. "He told me a bit about Azellian history."

"I'm glad he did. What did he say specifically?"

"Awakenings. Auras. Episodes. Aura sparking." She flushed as she remembered Mellis's comment that aura sparking could, and did, lead to foreplay. Enough so both Alarin and Greg refused to do it. And Mellis was willing—as long as she had a sexual partner waiting in the wings. "I had dreams last night," she blurted out suddenly.

"What kind of dreams?"

She bit her lip. She didn't want to admit to her dreams, but maybe Greg needed to know. "Sex … nothing specific. Just … erotic." She didn't remember them very clearly, but they had certainly been filled with indescribable physical sensation. No one in particular had starred in them, despite her sensitivity to both Alarin and Greg the night before, which made her more willing to actually admit to them.

"Really?" Greg moved, getting off the chair and coming toward her. She eyed him nervously. "I'm just going to scan you," he said as he sat next to her on the edge of the bed. "I want to see if there are any physical changes in you."

She let him run his hands above her skin. His blanket gapped, revealing that he didn't have any clothes on underneath—at least not to his waist. "Am I okay?" she asked him as he tightened the blanket around himself again and sat back.

"You're fine. No physical changes, either. But you are most certainly showing all the symptoms of Awakening. Apparently, humans Awaken the way we do."

"Do I have to?" Tamara asked, staring down at her hands.

"Have to what?"

"Awaken. Have psi. Whatever."

Greg cocked his head and looked at her. "I don't think I understand. Why wouldn't you want to?"

She ran her fingertips over the bedspread, the rough fabric catching on her skin. It sent tiny little shivers down her spine. "Because it's scary."

"What's scary about it?" he asked, scooting back so he rested against the wall, the blankets still wrapped around his body.

"It's ... different. I don't know what it will be like."

"That's part of life, Tamara. Uncertainty about where the future is going. Not having psi doesn't change that."

Tamara bit her lip. "Yes, but..." she trailed off.

"But what?"

She took a breath and let it out slowly. "Why me?"

"Why not you? Denying it won't change what's happening. It will just make it more painful."

"But I won't be me anymore."

Greg leaned forward. "Of course you will. It might be that you will become more of who you truly are, but you'll still be you. There is no way for you to lose that part of yourself that's truly you, Tamara. The only parts of you that you can let go of are the parts that aren't genuine or don't matter."

She blinked at him, her mind becoming frazzled by his words. "I don't understand."

"You don't need to. You're changing whether you want to or not, Tamara. Just let go and let it happen. Otherwise, you'll make it more difficult for yourself than it needs to be. And far more painful. Resisting Awakening never works and just creates more problems than it avoids."

She squinted at him. "I'm not Azellian," she reminded him.

"No, but there are some things that go beyond species," Greg replied. "The truth that resistance is far more painful than allowance is one of them."

"What if I just want to fight it? Because I can?"

"The choice is yours, but it's not going to get you anywhere. Your psi is breaking through whether you want it to or not. Which is why you're having these episodes. And why you're here, whether you realize it consciously or not."

There was an uncomfortable truth in what he was saying. She took a deep breath and let it out slowly. "Would you be okay if I just walked away?"

"From what? Yourself? Good luck with that. You can walk away from us if you like, but it won't change what's happening to you, and we happen to know quite a bit about it. The *aarya* have guided you to those who can help you through this, Tamara. You're not alone."

She looked up at him. "I feel alone."

Greg shrugged. "Once you open the doors to your psi, you will never be alone again. It's part of the joy of it."

She blinked at him. "Really?"

"Absolutely!"

"Even for me, a human with psi? Even though no other human I know has these abilities?"

"You'll find yourself drawn to those who resonate with you," Greg replied. "Like us. We might not be human in our upbringing, but there really aren't that many differences between us, psi or not, and you resonate with us quite well."

"I feel like I've known you guys forever. Is that what you mean?"

"It feels the same way on our end. Who knows? Maybe we knew each other in a past life?"

"Past lives? Really?"

Greg waved a hand. "Past lives, other dimensions, other experiences, on a different energy plane. Does it really matter? Don't get lost in the meanings of the words I'm using. You've brought yourself to what you've been asking for, Tamara. Friends. Most especially, friends who understand. And we're here to help you through this."

She made a face. "Why now?"

"Because it's time and you're ready?"

"Are you sure it's not because I've spent time around you Azellians?"

"Do you mean are we triggering it in you?"

"Yes. I shoved it down three years ago. Why can't I do that now?"

Greg studied her, his amber eyes compassionate. "You could," he said, "but it will very likely just pop out again. You wouldn't have been attracted to us if you weren't ready for it to come out now."

Tamara pushed herself off the bed. "I need some time," she murmured, rubbing a hand over her cheek. "Time to think about this. To get used to the idea."

"Do that," Greg said, maneuvering himself off the bed. "If you're really Awakening like an Azellian, then there are things we can do to get you prepared. We can start Monday, if you like?"

"Things like aura sparking?"

Greg smiled. "That's usually not something Healers do to help with Awakening. It's usually something Awakening partners will do with each other."

"Is it really foreplay?"

"It can be. Why?"

"Just wondering. When Merran showed me, we were in a restaurant."

"Well, it's pretty mild and doesn't reveal much to an outside observer, so it's often the way one Azellian will show another sexual interest, particularly in a public setting."

Tamara twitched. "Does that mean…"

"That Merran is sexually interested in you?" Greg asked bluntly. Tamara blushed. "I don't know. You'll have to ask him. If you were psi, you'd know pretty much right away, though. Azellians don't usually hide sexual interest from each other."

"I can't ask him," Tamara gasped, somewhat horrified by the thought.

"Why not? If he's not interested, he'll tell you. If he is, well, that's another question and one for the two of you to answer."

Tamara scrubbed her palm against her cheek, trying to rub away her embarrassment. They probably thought humans came in flaming, brilliant scarlet, considering how often she blushed in their presence.

Noticing her discomfort, Greg added, "You don't have to rush anything, Tamara. Merran's not going anywhere and neither are you." Shifting topics, he asked, "Do you want to meet on Monday? I can get you started doing some focusing and visualization exercises to help you ride out the episodes more easily."

Tamara took a deep breath and let it out slowly. "Okay, Monday. What time? I've got classes until one."

Greg made his way to his desk, waddling a little so as not to trip over the trailing blankets. He leaned over his laptop and tapped a key. The screen came up quickly. "How about two?"

"Okay, two it is." Tamara headed for the door, hesitating as she put her hand on the handle. "Greg … thank you."

"You're welcome." She didn't turn around, but pulled the door open and stepped out of his room.

154

She'd never done the walk of shame before, as the college students called the early morning sneak-back-to-your-own-dorm-room amble, but she found herself dodging other people and avoiding eye contact anyway. She and Greg had not done anything to create the shame—and honestly, never would—but it was still an odd experience to hurry back to her dorm room in the crisp morning air wearing last night's clothes, with her hair a mess.

She managed to make it back to her room without running into anyone she knew—fortunately, it was a Saturday morning and the campus was quiet. First-year seminars were over and the continuing students hadn't arrived yet, although they would be trickling in all weekend to begin classes on Monday. She got into her room without incident and gathered her clothes to shower before she had to go to work. Greg had told her to take her time, and she fully intended to, despite the meeting on Monday.

❊ ❊ ❊

A little while later, Alarin climbed the stairs to Greg's room, wondering if Tamara had left or if she was still sleeping sprawled on Greg's bed. As he came up to Greg's room, he could only sense one occupant, so he tapped at the edge of Greg's shields and entered at his friend's greeting.

"She's gone I see," he said, closing the door behind him.

Greg looked up from the computer, his blond hair still wet from the shower. "She left pretty early this morning."

"How's she doing this morning?"

"Fine. As normal as ever. There's really very little sign that she's Awakening physically, but she is sure having all the symptoms of it."

"Anything else happen after we left?" Alarin went to the bed and sat on it, resting his arms on his spread knees.

"No, but she woke up this morning and said she had Awakening dreams."

"Any unusual sexual behavior this morning?"

"No, not really, but I wouldn't expect it. She's not a thirteen-year-old adolescent who's been raised Azellian, Alari. She's human ... in her late teens or early twenties. She's quite able to suppress that particular symptom if she wants to. No, it was just the admission, which turned her the color of a very ripe tomato."

Alarin grinned. "She's really cute with that blushing she does, isn't she?"

Greg raised an eyebrow. "Not you, too."

Alarin mirrored Greg's gesture back at him. "Not me, too, what?"

"It's very interesting that Merran showed her aura sparking."

"Noticed that too, did you?" He frowned. "Are you implying that I'm sexually interested in her?"

"Are you?"

Alarin shrugged. "By the *aarya's* eyes, no. Not with Ida in the wings waiting for me to do something so she has an excuse to come to Earth. I just think it's cute that she blushes all the time. Are you thinking Merran's sexually interested in her?"

Greg turned his chair around and leaned back against it. "He certainly flirted with her enough last week when we went out to eat."

"That doesn't mean anything. Merran's a flirt."

"He reacted to her projection of sexual desire at him."

Alarin shrugged. "She's cute. Why wouldn't he react?"

"He showed her aura sparking."

Alarin grinned. "Which Mel pointed out is not always foreplay. Anything else?"

Greg threw his arms up in the air. "Well, Tamara thinks he might be."

"Ah, now, that's proof." Alarin sat up. "Why do you care?"

Greg shrugged. "I have this feeling it's going to be important. Do we encourage or discourage it?"

"If she's really Awakening the way we do, then she's going to need a sexual partner. Why not Merran? If her flash a couple of weeks ago is any indication, they share a talent."

"Do you think he'd be willing to do it?"

"He was willing to help us out, so why not?"

"This is not just doing some training and telling her about our history and psi, Alari. This is taking the brunt of her Awakening. If she does Awaken the way we do, it could get rough."

"Rough? Why?"

Greg shook his head. "There's a trauma that happened to her a few years ago. She shared a story with me about an experience she had. I don't know, but I think she may have already Awakened once, then forced it back down because of that trauma. And you know the older it happens the rougher it is. There's a reason the *aarya* have us Awaken to our psi at puberty. It never comes easier than at that time."

Alarin frowned. "Will it be dangerous?"

"While I'm training her, I can work with her through some of the trauma … get it cleared out before she Awakens fully. So I'll do what I can to mitigate it but it depends on how powerful she is. She could burn him out if she's strong enough. And if she really does react like an Azellian would, of course."

"Well, there's certainly enough evidence that she will react like one of us. As for burning him out, she'd have to be extremely powerful. Merran can channel energy like no one I've ever seen, Greg. He's had acolyte training."

Greg relaxed. "Damn, I forget that he's had *aarya* training. Okay, well let's encourage this thing between them. Do you know a subtle way to do this? You know Mer. If he thinks we want him to get involved, he'll find a million different reasons to push her away."

"Leave that to me."

"Forcing him won't stick, Alari."

"I'm not going to coerce him, Greg. I'll work around him. Believe me, with my mother, I know how to work around people. When's the next time you meet with Tamara?"

"Monday at two."

"Let me take her to the embassy. I'll arrange for Merran to give us a tour or something. That will give them a reason to spend time together, and from an angle Merran won't suspect."

"You think he is sexually interested in Tamara? You seemed to dismiss all my evidence."

Alarin grinned. "I think it's pretty certain actually. He not only flirted with her, he played her aura like it was his personal *dizvir* when we went out. And then he showed her aura sparking the next day? How much more evidence do you need? A flashing digital sign like on the Performing Arts Center?"

Greg ignored the sarcasm. "A *dizvir*? Interesting analogy ... the *aarya* use those instruments to generate vibrations during Festival."

"I know. And if you paid any attention to Tamara's resonance ... even through those shields ... he was striking quite a chord off her."

"Fine, fine. Go. Take her to the embassy, get her and Merran together, and we'll see what happens."

Alarin grinned and got to his feet. "This is going to be fun. Merran doesn't have a chance."

Greg gave him a suspicious look. "You sure you're not enjoying this a bit too much?"

"Too much?"

"You sure you're not getting him to have sex with her because you want to?"

Alarin laughed. "Yeah, that's an effective way to get a woman into my bed. Shove her at someone else. If I wanted Tamara in my bed, I'd have her there ... and not in Merran's."

"Okay, fine, just checking."

Alarin changed the subject. "You want to go to lunch?"

Greg nodded and got to his feet. "Yeah, I'm starving. You might be used to this planning of someone else's life, but I'm not and it makes me hungry."

Alarin grinned and held the door, the two of them heading out to the cafeteria.

❋ ❋ ❋

It took Alarin a day before he could get a chance to call Merran. Since he didn't want Merran to pick up on his motivations, he used the cell phone rather than mental contact. Merran was in a meeting, so Alarin settled at his desk to meditate and wait. About an hour later, his cell phone buzzed. The readout on the small screen indicated it was the embassy.

He picked up the phone and swiped a finger across it. "'Lo, Merran."

"Alari. What's up?" Merran asked in Azellian.

"Working on a Sunday?"

"Since when do Azellians observe a human religious holiday?"

"Yeah, but in a meeting?"

"Since when do the Dorbin observe a human religious holiday?" He paused. "And since when do you call to interrogate me on my activities?"

Alarin laughed. "Actually, I'm calling to see if you have some time tomorrow to guide Tamara and me around the embassy between two and four."

"Two and four? Let me see. Uh … I'd have to, um, juggle my appointments." He fell silent for a few moments. "The Atheran ambassador wants to try to talk me into something I probably don't have the authority to agree to. Then I have a meeting with the school administrators to listen to their ideas on ways to improve our program."

"That was quick. Regular classes haven't even started yet!"

"Oh, they're just bursting with ideas and can't wait to tell me about them. I could have Janille call them tomorrow and reschedule. I might be able reach the Atheran ambassador today, but not the school administrators." Merran paused. "All right, fine. I'll tell Janille to rearrange my schedule and we'll see you two tomorrow. Any reason it's going to be just the two of you?"

"She had another episode night before last. Telekinetic this time. Greg's going to start training her like an Awakening Azellian, but she's having some difficulty with the adjustment. I've seen her a few times over the past couple of days. She's a little on edge about it all. I thought she could use a change of pace."

"Greg told me about the episode. He said it was pretty typical. She's having trouble adjusting, is she? Well, you're probably right, she could use something different. We'll see you tomorrow, then?"

Alarin ended the call, smiling slightly. *It's all about management,* he thought to himself. He looked out the window at the continuing students who were just now starting to arrive on campus. Watching them struggle with heavy loads and trunks was amusing. He got to his feet. Maybe he'd go outside and offer his help. *Give me a chance to meet some new people.*

At the embassy, Merran hid his suddenly mixed feelings as he stared at the phone.

Janille poked her head around the corner of his office door. "You need to rearrange your schedule for tomorrow?"

Merran blinked at her. Even after six years of working with her, she could still take him by surprise. "I don't even want to know how you know that."

A hint of a smile twitched at the corner of her mouth. "When Alarin Raderth called earlier, he told me what he wanted."

Merran grinned and relaxed. "And here I thought precognition was one of your talents." He sobered. "Yes, I need you to reschedule the Atheran ambassador and the school administrators. As a matter of fact, let's just cancel the Atheran ambassador for now. She's going to ask me for something I can't give her anyway, and she needs to be told no once in a while or she'll start thinking I'm a pushover."

"Certainly, sir." She backed out of the room and closed the door behind her. Merran sighed and returned to his work for the day.

❋ ❋ ❋

Across campus, Tamara wandered aimlessly, her mind running over Greg's words from the day before until she became thoroughly sick of her own thoughts. She found herself standing in front of her friend Kari's dorm. Pushing her thoughts away, she entered and climbed the stairs to Kari's third floor room, wondering if her friend had gotten back on campus yet.

The door stood wide open. Inside the room, Kari was diligently pulling clothes out of a huge trunk and organizing them in the drawers of her dresser.

Tamara stepped into the doorway. "You're back!"

Kari jumped, then glanced over her shoulder and grinned. "Apparently, since I'm here. I told you I was coming back today."

"I know. That's why I ended up here. How was your summer? I haven't talked to you in months!" Tamara walked into the room and hugged her friend.

"Months? More like a week, Tam. As for my summer, it was soooooo boring, like I told you over the phone last week. You're lucky to live in Denver. You can't believe how small Allensville can seem once you've lived in Denver." Kari turned back to her trunk. "No men to speak of. Or any kind of social life. If it weren't for the occasional trips into Boston, I'd have gone nuts."

"Like we do anything in Denver anyway. How often do we leave the campus?"

"Allensville isn't even as big as this university." Kari made a face. "At least there is a city outside of the three thousand people who go here."

Tamara settled on Kari's bed, just bursting to tell her friend about her new friends. "Well, it wasn't all that exciting around here this summer, either. Until a couple of weeks ago. It's going to be a really interesting semester, Kare."

"Ohhhh, really? So what happened during the new student seminar that's going to last the *entire* semester?" Kari stopped unpacking for a moment to stare down at her friend. "I know that look. Spill it."

"Oh, there just happened to appear on campus four of the most gorgeous, sophisticated guys you ever did see." Tamara wiggled her eyebrows, a grin pulling up one side of her mouth. She exaggerated the number of guys a little bit—considering the ambassador wasn't really a student.

"Is that all? From where? I didn't think there were any sophisticated, gorgeous single men in the entire city. They're all gay, taken, or otherwise hopelessly unavailable." Kari turned back to unpacking. "Maybe Denver's not any better than Allensville after all."

Tamara bounced a little on the bed. "Did I say anything about available?"

"Then why are we having this discussion?"

"Because they're all really hot." It felt odd to be talking about them with Kari, but she knew her friend would never forgive her if she didn't tell her at least some of what had been happening. She didn't have to mention her own personal drama. "I mean it. Think Brad Pitt and Orlando Bloom. Richard Gere from twenty years ago."

Kari turned around to stare at her. "A combination?"

"No, no. Cute like them. Movie star cute, I mean."

Kari put her hands on her hips. "Movie star cute, huh? But they're here, on campus. How unavailable are they?"

That was the reaction she was looking for. "One is gay. The other one has a long-distance relationship. The other two are available, though. Sort of. One is a kid. A freshman. The other has a 120-hour-a-week job, so I don't know what kind of boyfriend he would make. He's not actually really on campus, or a student. But I tell you, they're still pretty fine."

Kari laughed and sat on the bed, giving up the attempt to unpack. "That's encouraging to know. Movie star gorgeous guys that aren't especially available. So spill it, girl. Have you met any of them? How well do you know these guys, or are they just people you just happened to see as you checked them in?"

Tamara grinned mischievously. "Well, we went out for drinks and dinner." She'd also been hanging out with them for the past two weeks, but it made a better story the other way, so she didn't tell Kari everything.

"All of you?"

"Yes." Since Justern and Mellis had never rejoined them, it really had been just her, Merran, Greg, and Alarin that night. Merran had footed the bill without any indication as to the cost of the meal, but the glimpse she'd caught had staggered her.

"Four guys and you. Hmm."

"Actually, it was only three of them. The freshman was off seducing someone else."

Kari's eyes widened. "Really?"

Tamara grinned.

"Do I get to meet them? Or are you just planning on hoarding them all to yourself?"

"Two of them have anthro studies class with us tomorrow. You'll get your chance."

Kari got to her feet and pulled another pile of clothes out of her suitcases. "Do these two happen to be one of the available ones?"

"Uh, one is."

"The freshman?"

Tamara's grin widened.

"Ah. Who's the other one?"

"The one with a long-distance relationship." It was odd describing the Azellians instead of naming them, but she felt an odd possessiveness toward them suddenly. *Where's that coming from?*

she asked herself. *I don't have a monopoly on Azellian contact with humans. Why do I want to be the only one they meet?*

A spark of interest stirred in Kari's eyes. "How attached is he?"

"Don't know."

"Well, we'll just have to find out, won't we?"

Tamara changed the subject, really not liking Kari's interest in Alarin; although, as she'd told Kari, he did have a girlfriend on Azelle. "Are you ready for diplo studies this year? Can you believe we have Professor Bennington? He's supposed to be the toughest prof on campus!"

Kari let her change the subject. She gave her an odd look. "You've never had trouble with any professor in your life, Tam. Why are you worried about it now?"

"I don't know. I just … Pam just freaked me out with her descriptions of him last year."

"Yes, well, Pam is lazy and likes to sleep her way into grades, Tam. Bennington is not about to hand out grades just because you wear short skirts to class. Unlike some of the others we won't mention."

Tamara coughed. Kari had never liked Pam, although Tamara got along with her well enough. The part about sleeping her way to grades was just a rumor, mainly because Pam did very little work in most of her classes yet mysteriously seemed to pass anyway. "Speaking of Pam, the *Azellian* embassy's supposed to have a gathering Friday. Do you think we should go?"

"Hell yeah. Especially if it gets us in good with Bennington. Despite what Pam tried to make us think last year, what I heard is that he's got a soft spot for people who are dedicated, and spending time at an embassy is definitely dedicated." Kari turned to face

Tamara. "Now what I want to know is how in hell did you manage to hear about a party at the Azellian embassy? They've got legendary parties!"

"Those four gorgeous guys? There's a small detail I didn't tell you. They're Azellian." Tamara couldn't seem to stay away from the subject, despite her best efforts.

"All of them? What about the one with a 120-hour-a-week job?"

"Him too. He's … an embassy worker. That's how I found out about the party Friday at the embassy." For more reasons she didn't quite want to analyze, she didn't tell Kari just who that "embassy worker" really was.

"Wow. Tamara's got an in with four gorgeous Azellians. You know Jenna hooked up with one of the embassy workers last year. Don't ask me how they met, or what lies she told him about her age, but she managed to go out with him for a month."

"Jenna? Holy crap. I didn't know that. What happened?"

"They are a bit funny about long-term relationships with humans, she says. This is Jen we're talking about, though. She may just think that because she was trying to hide the fact that she thought it was more than it really was and she felt stupid about it. Anyway, he broke up with her." She raised an eyebrow and grinned mischievously. "She did say it was the best sex she's ever had in her life, though, and she's been chasing it ever since. Don't tell her about these gorgeous Azellians, or you'll find yourself pestered to death with Jen trying to use you to get back into a pair of Azellian pants."

Tamara tossed her head. "If the rumors are right, she might even have a chance, but I wouldn't count on a long-term thing with any of them."

Kari gave her a long look. "Or maybe they might be more interested in you?"

"Yeah, right. Not in this lifetime." She didn't mention her suspicions that one of them might be.

"You never know." Kari dumped the now empty suitcase onto the floor. "Are you doing anything tomorrow?"

"After I get back from dinner, I'm free. They probably won't bury us in homework this first week. I do have to go home for dinner, though."

"That's kind of a pain."

"My mom was just diagnosed with cancer, so I'm trying to spend as much time as I can with her."

"Oh, I'm so sorry, Tam." Kari joined her on the edge of the bed. "Are you all right?"

"I'm fine. She's starting chemo and radiation tomorrow. From what Mom and Dad told me, they're confident the treatment will work." Tamara lifted her chin, trying to believe it. Her fears would come roaring back if she didn't.

Kari made a face. "Shit, Tam. I really am sorry."

"Let's talk about some other stuff ... please."

"Sure. Did you hear from Alice at all this summer?"

They drifted off into other realms, and Tamara was able to forget about Azellians and sick mothers for a little while, focusing instead on classes that would begin the next morning.

❋ ❋ ❋

The next day arrived too quickly. As on all first days, Tamara received lots of syllabi listing what she was to accomplish for the next three months. Her diplo studies class wasn't as bad as she'd expected—although Professor Bennington did promise to be a difficult teacher.

"You will all be expected to read three chapters and do an essay on them for the beginning of next week," he said near the end of class that day. "And if any of you get motivated and want to really learn about diplomacy, you are encouraged to visit the embassies. We have three of them located very near the campus. The Azellian, Atheran, and Dorbin embassies are all within walking distance. All offer a wonderful opportunity to expand your knowledge and practice diplomatic skills. I will also entertain the possibility of students doing an internship this semester with any one of these embassies." He scanned the room. "If any of you can manage the difficult diplomatic task of getting the Azellian or Dorbin embassies to accept you as an intern, you will get an automatic bonus to boost your final grade."

Tamara and Kari exchanged glances. That carrot was a juicy one. A boost to final grades from a difficult professor? Tamara's mind raced over the possibilities as the professor ended class and they started collecting their books.

"That's not a fair challenge," Kari groused as she collected her books at the end of class. "How in hell are we supposed to get in at either of those embassies? Ambassador Corina and Ambassador Ki'i will never accept a human intern. You know Professor Bennington and this department have been trying for years. How are we students supposed to accomplish something that even diplomats haven't managed to do so far?"

Tamara bit her lip. A tiny germ of a thought played at the back of her mind. "He's not telling us we have to, Kare. He's just dangling the possibility of extra credit out there for us to drool over."

"Drool's right. Boosting your final grade? That's pretty awesome extra credit!"

"But it's actually not a bad one. Just think about it. If one of us were able to get Ambassador Corina or Ambassador Ki'i to agree to something the whole Diplomatic Studies Department hasn't been able to do for years? It would be a diplomatic coup ... and well worth any grade." Tamara took a deep breath and dropped her voice. "Listen. Now would be the perfect time to try, at least with the Azellian ambassador. He's trying to get his exchange program off the ground. That means he's going to be more open to the idea than he ever has been in the past. It would be a wonderful experience for those of us interested in Azelle to learn more about it through an internship. Since we're invited to a party there on Friday, maybe we should feel him out then and see whether he'd be open to the idea."

Kari stared at her as they walked out into the hall. "You aren't serious!"

Tamara stopped just outside the door to the classroom. "'I'm dead serious, Kare."

"You are on enough of a friendly basis with the ambassador to actually go up to him and ask about an internship? Is he even going to *be* at the party?"

Kari's disbelief overrode Tamara's desire to hide the fact that she knew the Azellian ambassador. "That embassy worker I met before classes started? I never did tell you what his position was, did I?"

Kari stared at her—her mouth open. She snapped it shut and shook her head. "You've got to be kidding! You are telling me you met the Azellian ambassador and hung out with him? The guy with the 120-hour-a-week job? He's one of the group who wants to be friends with you?"

"He did tell me to call him Merran." Amused, but somewhat insulted by Kari's reaction, Tamara scowled at her friend. "Don't look at me like that, Kare. He's not all that much older than we are."

"Uh, you're just messing with me."

Tamara shook her head. "No, I'm not."

"I don't believe you." Kari started walking again.

"Don't believe me then. You'll see Friday." Tamara walked with her. "I may even call him before then and see what he says."

"Now I know you're not serious. You can just … pick up the phone and talk to the ambassador? Of Azelle? Yeah right."

"I did it before. I can't imagine I suddenly can't now." She kept her attitude off-handed, as though calling the Azellian ambassador were something she'd do easily, without thought, although the reality was somewhat more complex than that. "Where are you headed?"

"Azellian language studies." Kari looked at her. "Do you honestly expect me to believe some people never get to talk to the ambassador at all, yet you can call him whenever you want?"

"That's what I'm saying. Well, I don't know if I could call him *whenever* I want. He'd probably have to return my call or something. But he probably *would* return it personally."

They walked into the Azellian language classroom, getting there with a group of others. "If you're so certain you can get this internship, you should see if you can get extra credit in this class, too," hissed Kari as they settled into their chairs. Tamara nodded, liking the idea.

She was rusty after a summer of not speaking Azellian at all, despite her recent exposure to it. None of the Azellians had spoken it much in her presence, since they were all too fluent in English to make it necessary to speak Azellian to her. The class took a lot of concentration, although she did have more of a motivator to learn it than she ever had before.

After class ended, Kari watched as she went up to the professor. "Professor Madrinn?"

The pretty young woman, not much older than Tamara herself, looked up from where she was writing on a pad of paper. "Tamara. What can I do for you?"

Tamara smiled and shifted positions. "I'm—I'm really interested in learning more about the Azellian language. Would you have any suggestions for extra things I could do? I struggled with it a bit last year and I'd like to work through some of the difficulty I've had."

The woman smiled, her blue eyes warm. "Of course! One of the best things to do would be to spend time with Azellian speakers. There are four Azellian students on campus this year, you know. See if any of them will spend time with you." She pushed her pen and paper away. "Or, if you'd rather, visit the embassy. There are liaison officers there whose job it is to establish contact with humans, to foster understanding between the two cultures. Learning each other's language is the beginning of such an effort. Throughout the year, I'm planning on having my more advanced, interested students meet regularly to discuss popular Azellian fiction. It may be a bit out of your comfort level, but you are welcome to join us and listen in on our discussions … and to read the same books."

"Would an internship be a good way to learn Azellian?" Tamara asked ingeniously, trying not to seem as if she had been leading up to that.

"It could be, but I don't know that I would start with that." The professor frowned thoughtfully. "Most of the Azellian staff speaks

English quite fluently. Unless you were quite aggressive about insisting on Azellian being spoken to you, you might not find it to be so. A trip to Azelle would be the final test, of course, and once you have reached a sufficient level, that would be the optimal way to pursue it. Have you thought about participating in the return exchange?"

Tamara nodded. "Oh yes. I think that might actually be a goal in the next couple of years. I'm a diplomatic studies student."

"Perfect." The professor clapped her hands once. "I can help you with that. I believe Ambassador Corina is going to be making the choices on who goes to Azelle over the next couple of years. The Council on Azelle will be making final approvals. If you are that interested, I would be glad to sponsor you. You may have thought you were struggling last year, Tamara, but you actually have a better grasp of the fundamentals than many of your classmates. I think you would make a wonderful candidate for Azelle."

"Thank you," Tamara responded. With her new knowledge about herself, she suddenly wondered if her emerging abilities could make her more suitable as a candidate. As a native Azellian, Professor Madrinn hadn't mentioned that other abilities might be a benefit nor had she ever shown any signs that she herself might be talented psychically in any way. Maybe there were Azellians who were not as sensitive as others. Or some that were very, very good at hiding what they were, since the school might not appreciate their other talents. "When's your first meeting with your literary group?"

"Two weeks. I usually like to let the students settle in first. Let me tell you on Wednesday when exactly we'll be meeting, all right?" The professor pulled her pad and pen closer.

"Great." Tamara shifted to Azellian. "Thank you very much," she said somewhat awkwardly.

The professor smiled up at her. "You are welcome, Tamara." Her response was also in Azellian. "Until Wednesday."

Tamara nodded and turned to where Kari waited for her.

"Damn, you are a diplomat," she said as they left the classroom. "What do you have now?"

"Chemistry." Tamara made a face. "Oh joy."

"Good luck. I'm off to lunch. See you later?"

"Later."

In her next class, Tamara was rather startled to see Alarin there. She walked over to the long table where he sat pouring over his workbook. "Hi there."

Alarin glanced up. "Hi. You're in this chemistry class?"

"Yup. And a tremendous dunce I am in it, too." Tamara pulled out her books and put them on the table. "Math intimidates me."

"It's not so complicated as all that." Alarin lifted his notebook to show her some problems he had sketched out.

"You do math problems for fun?" Tamara shuddered. "Oh God."

He chuckled. "It keeps your brain limber."

"I just had an hour of Azellian language. My brain is so limber right now it'll probably slide out my ears if I try anything more."

"So you understand ..." Alarin said in Azellian, losing her after the first three words.

"I'm sorry?" she replied in the same language.

"So you understand everything I'm saying, do you?" Alarin repeated more slowly.

"Sort of," Tamara admitted in English. "The second time, anyway." She sighed. "I don't know if I'll ever get the hang of it."

"There are certain abilities that make learning a language easier, you know." Alarin leaned over. "Among other things."

Tamara flushed, aware that he was talking about her own repressed abilities. "But right at the moment, I have to muddle through the hard way."

Alarin shrugged as the professor entered. "It'll come one way or the other. It just takes time."

Tamara nodded and turned her attention to the professor as he started his usual first day speech. Like many of her other classes, this one ran late. As she was packing up to leave, she noticed that Alarin had already left. She walked out of the classroom and over to the cafeteria to grab lunch. She then headed to her room, ate her lunch, and worked on some homework until it was time to meet Greg.

She was sort of dreading their meeting. Although Greg had made it sound harmless, it made her feel somewhat grumpy. When she got to Greg's room, however, she was surprised to see Alarin sitting in one of the chairs in the lounge outside Greg's room.

"Hi." Alarin stood up and gave her a little bow, carrying it off much more gracefully than she would have in the same situation. "Greg told me to tell you he forgot he actually has a lab today at this time, so I'm taking over for today. Merran's invited us to the embassy to take a tour. You feel up to it?"

Tamara blinked. "A tour?"

"Yes. You are a diplomatic studies student, correct?"

"Yeah." She gave him an odd look. "I thought there was a party on Friday. I didn't expect there to be a guided tour today."

Alarin grinned at her. "Oh, it's not a big deal. It's really just that Merran wants to hide from his responsibilities today."

Tamara laughed. "All right, then. I guess we can't refuse someone in his time of need."

Alarin chuckled and bowed to her again. "Shall we go?" As they walked down the hallway and outside toward the embassy, Alarin asked her, "So what did you think of chemistry today?"

"It's going to be a lot of work. Three problem sets due for Wednesday. I worked on some of them before coming over and at least two of them have me stumped."

"Which ones? I got a chance to glance at them."

"The second one. How are you supposed to figure out how many grams per liter?"

"It's all about plugging in formulas from the chapter. Which units do you want on the bottom?"

"Liters."

"Then you just need to find a formula that will give you the liters on the bottom and the grams on the top."

Tamara halted in midstep and stared at him. "It can't be that easy."

"It is that easy."

"I'll try it. But if it's that easy, I'll be angry at myself."

Alarin laughed. "Most problems usually are not as complicated as they appear on the surface if you break them down into doable pieces."

"You've figured that out already? But you're in a beginning chemistry class?"

Alarin rolled his eyes. "I haven't had any formal chemistry recognized by the university so they required me to take the beginning level class. But we Azellians are not completely clueless about chemistry. It just isn't quite as developed—or formalized—on Azelle as on Earth."

"They didn't let you test out of the beginning level class? That's rude. You're going to be bored stiff in class if you are already beyond it."

Alarin sighed. "Tell me about it. I'm trying not to get bored silly already."

"You should approach the professor directly if the university won't work with you. It's a way to work around the system."

A slow smile spread across Alarin's face. "Why, thank you, I think I will."

They approached the tall entry gates of the embassy. As usual, a guard stood in the gatehouse in front of the closed portal.

Alarin said something in Azellian, too rapid for Tamara to catch anything more than his greeting.

"The ambassador is expecting you," the guard replied in smooth English, with less of an accent than any other Azellian she had met besides Merran. He added something in Azellian.

Alarin grinned but did not reply. Tamara realized somewhat uneasily that there could have been a whole subtext she did not hear, and probably was.

Alarin must not have noticed her preoccupation, or did not mention it, as they walked through the quiet gardens to the front door of the huge mansion.

The front doors opened at their approach. Merran stood at the top of the curving staircase that led up to the offices on the second floor. He wore a suit today—a navy, tailored, smooth suit jacket and a pair of navy tailored dress pants. His shirt was light blue, with an intricate tie of various shades of blue. Tamara almost didn't recognize him. His dark hair was clipped short above his ears and around his neckline, changing his looks dramatically and making him stand out from his fellow Azellians. Except for the Azellian exchange students, most Azellians wore their hair longer. It also made him look startling, disturbing, and very different from the almost feminine look he had cultivated with the long wavy hair. One could not have told the difference between him and any other human businessman walking down the sidewalk. "Welcome, Tamara, Alarin." The fluid Azellian accent sent a shiver down her spine.

"That's different," Alarin commented as Merran joined them downstairs. "Nice haircut."

Merran ran a hand through his shorn locks. "I needed a change. And I have to give a presentation to human leaders next week. I thought they might prefer someone who looks more professional ... from a human point of view. I've learned over the years that it's all in the presentation." He turned to Tamara and smiled at her. "As you'll learn soon, I'm sure. Were there any places you might like to start with to tour?"

Tamara thought for a moment, shoving away the shivery feeling that Merran was someone entirely new. His short hair really disturbed her for some reason. "How about your office? We can work our way down from there."

Merran laughed. "Starting at the top, eh? You certainly don't waste any time."

Tamara flushed. "Well, it's a place to start."

Merran grinned at her. "Indeed it is. My office is this way." He led them both up the stairs to his office, introducing them to Janille. Tamara listened carefully. Every last member of the embassy was Azellian. Each of the two hundred staff members, she was told, had been handpicked by either Merran or his predecessor. Earth was a permanent post, if one wanted it to be, and many did stay for a long time. Janille had been with the embassy for twenty years, for example, and she knew every aspect of it intimately. She handled most of the things Merran could not possibly attend to personally. Janille juggled the personnel and paperwork issues, keeping the embassy running smoothly. Her responsibility occasionally encompassed meetings with ambassadors, if Merran was otherwise occupied. Merran's bailiwick included meetings with ambassadors, all high-level negotiations, and any troubleshooting that came up. He usually orchestrated most human contact, especially in the wake of his exchange program. Tamara suddenly wondered about her ability to convince Merran to accept a human intern. No other human worked at the embassy, not even in the mail department where they sorted the electronic mail that came in. Most of the staff members processed visas and requests to go to Azelle. Surprisingly enough, quite a few people requested medical visits to Numorantxl and the hot springs there.

"Is it really the hot springs or the Healers?" Tamara asked, as Merran showed them the mailroom, watching as several staff members sorted the requests and read through them, while others sat around on the computers sorting the electronic requests that came through.

Merran smiled enigmatically. "Considering they don't know for sure about the Healers, it's the hot springs. And the therapists who work with them, of course."

"Of course."

After about an hour, Merran ended at the cafeteria. "This is everyone's favorite spot … from the top," he grinned at Tamara, "to the bottom. Would you like to join me for a refreshment?"

Alarin glanced at Tamara. She glanced at her watch. It was only three thirty. "Sure. I have to get home by five, so we have some time."

Merran led them to a round table. "What would you like, Tamara?"

"Chai, if you have it."

"Sure." Merran was silent for a moment and Tamara again got the sense she was missing something. "So, that's how the embassy works," he said a moment later, turning to Tamara. "Being ambassador means that you're the one everyone wants to talk to. The rest of the staff must sift through the requests and see who really needs to talk to you and who can be put off or handled by someone else."

Tamara took a breath as a cafeteria staff member appeared bearing their drinks. Merran must have communicated mentally, because the woman had everything right. Tamara steeled herself. It might not be the right time, but she had to at least broach the subject she'd been dying to ask. By doing it here, if she got shot down, it wouldn't be in front of her college peers. "Have you ever thought about taking on an intern to help with some of the busywork?"

Merran, who was sipping his chai, choked and set his cup down. He eyed Tamara, his dark eyes unreadable. "You wouldn't happen to be taking a class from Jason Bennington, would you?"

Tamara blushed furiously. "Uh, yes, actually. Why?"

"Because he's been trying to get me to accept a student of his as an intern for years. They've been hounding me about it since I got here." Merran cocked his head. For some reason, he was much more nervewracking with his short hair. Tamara fidgeted under his gaze. His longer hair softened his image, made him less disturbing—that was it. It had nothing to do with the fact that she found the shorter hairstyle much sexier. "He didn't, by chance, suggest to the class that he would offer a bonus if they managed to talk me into accepting an intern, did he?"

Tamara blushed even more violently. "Uh, actually he did."

Merran winced. "The *aarya* damn it. I'm going to be fielding requests from greedy students to be an intern for the next three months. He did this to me four years ago. I thought I had clarified it with him then."

Alarin sat next to Tamara, a wide grin on his face. "Of course, things are different now. We're going to have humans arriving on Azelle with the exchange program, so they are going to be exposed whether we want them to or not." Tamara sat quietly, willing Merran to agree—letting Alarin do the arguing for her. He was an unexpected ally, but she wasn't about to complain.

Merran glared at Alarin, not happy about having to face this particular issue right now. However, given the last time Bennington had popped this on him, he knew he'd better address it immediately. "But not everyone who is in Bennington's class is going to Azelle, Alari. And Azelle has managed to keep the human fear of us under control by being careful not to show them anything they don't want to see. I don't need wild rumors running all over campus about what the students see here. It's going to be bad enough if you, Greg, Mel, and Justy aren't careful," Merran replied, rubbing the back of his neck. "It's not fair to keep two hundred staff members from behaving as they do at home just so a few humans don't see us."

"You could always agree to take Tamara this semester, Mer. You already know she won't freak out about our little displays, and she will keep quiet about it. Next semester, you could choose someone from another class ... or keep Tamara for the full year. You could always insist the intern be someone who is going to Azelle anyway. You're going to be reviewing all the students before they go, aren't you?" A message came through on Merran's intimate level. *We desperately need to keep Tamara exposed to the idea of psi and to us. Greg can't do it alone, you know. I'm in at least one class with her, and if she saw you a few times a week, we could keep an eye on her. How else are you going to find the time to spend with her?*

The thought of regularly seeing her made Merran's stomach jump, but he kept himself shielded. Alarin was making uncomfortably good sense. He sighed. "Let me talk to Janille and see if we have some office work or something else Tamara could do."

Alarin's nostrils flared as he suppressed a grin. Tamara let her breath out slowly. She may have missed something, but whatever Alarin had said worked.

Merran pushed his chair back. "I have to get back to work. I'll let you know on Friday, if I don't have time to get back to you this week, Tamara."

He gave no sign that he felt pressured into it, but she rather felt like they had pushed. "Thank you. I—will you tell Professor Bennington? Or did you want me to?"

"I'll deal with it." Merran got to his feet. "Once I've talked to Janille." He shook his head. "It will be quite a triumph for the Diplomatic Studies Department. I'll have to make up a formal agreement and submit it to them."

Tamara rubbed her temple self-consciously. "He also promised the bonus if we got into the Dorbin embassy. It wasn't just here."

That made him laugh. "Oh, Ki'i will love that. But I don't think any of your students will be able to get in there. There are reasons why we don't allow humans to work in our embassies. As you know from when you met him, the Dorbin are uncomfortable for non-psi corporeal beings to be around. They also have the strangest sense of humor. Any typical human would be crazy within days of working there. As for here, well you know why we haven't allowed it."

"I do. But I can handle it. I do want to work in an embassy and go to Azelle. That means I need the exposure."

Merran's gaze caught hers, and she could feel a pressure build behind her eyes. Rather than pulling back in fear, she tried to show him how sincere she was. It was hard, but she did want this, badly. *Grandpa Jim was a diplomat,* she said in her head, hoping Merran could catch it. *He told me stories. It calls to me. Can't you hear it?*

Merran touched the edges of her aura, which flared as he touched, sending tendrils out to probe into his. Her shielding, which had been quite heavy since that first episode, thinned, and he caught the tailend of her thought accompanied by a fierce longing that drowned the fear. An imagined vista, sand dunes stretching in front of her. *It calls to me. Can't you hear it?* Then the shields returned, her aura faded, and he was left breathless.

Alarin stared at them, having caught some of the event, too. *By the aarya's eyes, she shouldn't be able to do that!*

Merran let Alarin read his reactions. *I know. Just be glad you weren't on the receiving end of it. Shit, she's a projector all right! I pity the man who receives her Awakening … if Greg's right and she Awakens the way we do.*

Or maybe it won't be much of anything at all. If she's got enough control to do that now, maybe it won't be so bad.

Her future lover is going to have his hands, and everything else, full.

She'd be wasted on a human. Can you imagine …

Merran thickened the shields between them, only letting the slightest trickle of thought through. *I thought you were in a relationship, Alari. I don't need the mental image forming with that thought, thank you. I still have work to do. You might be able to go home and imagine away, but I have to manage to concentrate for the rest of the afternoon.*

Thickening his shields around his mind, Merran bowed to the two of them. "I'll see you both Friday." He didn't wait for an answer but turned on his heel and walked away, using his training and experience to push away all the thoughts he'd rather not have.

Tamara stared after him, worried about his reaction. "Was he really angry about my wanting to be an intern?"

Alarin shook his head. "No, no." He looked at her, studying her for a moment. "Did you just try to project?"

Tamara's eyes widened. "Well, I wished really hard that he could sense my desire to be an intern and that he could see I was telling the truth. Is that what you mean? But I thought you couldn't read me."

"Normally we can't. Since you had that episode at the embassy a couple of weeks ago, you've been heavily shielded. For just a moment, though, your shields cleared and we both read your desire to go to Azelle."

"Then why did he react that way?" Tamara looked at the doorway through which Merran had left. "It was like he didn't want to be around us anymore."

Alarin laughed. "You don't just let us read, Tamara. You project whatever it is you are thinking and feeling. It can be uncomfortable for the recipient. Powerful emotion is, especially when it is not your own. For a people who can read others' emotions and thoughts easily, we are not all that comfortable with them. Or with talking about them. Come on, let's head back to campus. You've got something happening at five, right?"

"Yeah, I do." She got to her feet and followed him out of the embassy.

They walked in a companionable silence for a bit before Alarin spoke, "Do you know what that is?" He pointed at the large building towering ahead of them.

"The Botanic Gardens."

"What's that?"

"Well, they're gardens." Tamara waved a hand, trying to think of how to explain to someone who lived on a desert planet just what that large structure housed. The subject kept them occupied for a while as they walked back to campus. After a few moments of confused description, Alarin threw his hands in the air.

"I'm not sure why you'd want to put a forest in a glass structure. This would be much easier with psi, you know. You could just show me."

"It's just as easy to go. It's right there, doesn't cost much to get in, and then you could see for yourself. Form your own opinion."

Alarin grinned. "This weekend?"

"It's kind of hot in the summer. It's much better to visit the gardens in the middle of the winter, when everything outdoors is brown and cold. There's more of a contrast at that time of year."

"So that wasn't a request for a date then?"

Tamara's brain stuttered to a stop. She stared at him in shock as it spluttered and fired up again. "Uh, I mean, you have a girlfriend, don't you? A fiancée? On Azelle. I know that. I would never ..."

His grin widened. "I'm just teasing, Tamara. I would love to see this glassed forest, and I would be honored to have you escort me. As a friend."

Her cheeks cooled. His oddly archaic way of asking was actually rather flattering. "Okay. Let's plan on later in the semester. Maybe over Thanksgiving break or something."

"It's a plan." They walked up to the entrance of her dorm. Alarin bowed to her as he held open the door. "See you in class?"

She nodded. "Uh, Alarin?"

"Yeah?"

"Thanks for showing me the embassy and for the help convincing Merran to think about the internship."

He smiled. "You're welcome. Anytime. See you later."

"Bye." She went inside and headed upstairs to her room so she could get ready to head to her parents' house for dinner.

✻ ✻ ✻

After Tamara and Alarin left, Merran tried desperately to think how to broach the subject of Tamara's internship with Janille. Preoccupied as he came up the stairs, he didn't say much when he walked past her desk. He sat at his desk for a few moments, then touched her shields lightly.

She opened the door moments later. "Yes, Ambassador?"

"Janille, I need to talk to you about a rather touchy subject. Please sit down." Merran motioned to the chairs in front of his desk. With her usual unflappable composure, she settled in one of them. "How much do you know about Tamara Carrington?"

"Just that she is a human student who has access to the embassy and appears on the call accept list, sir."

Merran raked a hand through his hair. "She's a little more complicated than that." He looked at her steadily. "There must be office rumors about her." *Especially after taking her out to breakfast and sparking her aura in the middle of an Azellian-run restaurant,* he thought to himself. It had been impulsive on his part, but very enjoyable. *It has been a very long time since I've slept with another psi user. Ever since I accepted the position as ambassador, I've limited myself to humans.*

"I don't spread rumors, Ambassador."

"But you hear them. And I know a good many of them think she's going to become one more in a long string of my lovers. Reality is considerably more complicated than that. Tamara Carrington is James Carrington's granddaughter and looks to be Awakening."

Janille's expression betrayed some surprise. "Awakening? Isn't she human?"

"Yes, but apparently they have similar talents to ours, because she's promising to be a projector of some strength."

"Do humans Awaken the way we do?"

"We have no idea." He sighed. "We're assuming it's going to happen that way, if only because she's showing all the symptoms of it. She's certainly had at least one episode that's the same as the way we Awaken and probably will have more before the energies break through."

"It is a part of your job, sir, to watch over those humans who might have Azellian blood. Do you think Tamara has Azellian blood?"

"According to her records here, Tamara has not a shred of Azellian blood. So, except for the fact that I think she'll make an excellent exchange student to Azelle, I really have no jurisdiction to get involved officially."

Janille gave him a look. "That hasn't stopped you before, sir."

A smile flashed across his face. "No, it hasn't. But maybe it will explain the next few things I have to tell you. Jason Bennington has promised his class extra credit for being an intern here at the embassy."

Janille sighed, the only indication of irritation marring her perfect composure. "I'll warn the staff."

"I have a way to head it off, but I need your support to do it. Because of her potential Awakening, and because she'll probably be going to Azelle in a few years, why don't we allow her to be our intern? We don't have to hide what we are with her, as she's going to be exposed to it sooner or later. Actually, it's preferable that she starts to get a feel for our abilities now. Can you keep her busy?"

Janille's expression was unreadable, but it certainly was not neutral. Merran wished, as he did frequently, that her shielding were not quite so perfect. "I could find things for her to do."

"This is where it gets complicated: I'm going to trumpet our acceptance of an intern to the world as an example of our new openness with everyone. Tamara's possible Awakening and her abilities need to be kept quiet, as that won't help my plan any and she probably won't want them broadcasted around. I'm going to make her a junior assistant, at least for some of the meetings I have planned with the humans. It may take the teeth out of some of their accusations and their negotiations."

Janille was silent for a moment. "That could work. Although it could backfire if they found out about our and her abilities, as if we weren't actually accepting a human, but one that may turn out to be pretty much like us anyway."

Merran shrugged. "It's all part of the game."

"What about the girl herself? Is she willing to be a political pawn?"

"She's certainly going to learn some hard lessons about diplomacy." Merran leaned against his hand and rubbed his eyes with his fingers.

"And she will be your employee." Janille didn't say any more about it, but he could hear what she didn't say.

"I have no intention of making her anything more than an assistant, Janille."

"That's what has me concerned, Ambassador." Janille got to her feet. "Now, if you have nothing more to discuss, I will start to write up the agreement for the Diplomatic Studies Department."

Merran waved her away, resting his chin on his hand. Staring out the window, he tried to figure out whether he had done something bad or something *really* good.

❋ ❋ ❋

Across campus, at the dorm, Tamara headed off to her car to get home before five, then back to campus to finish her homework and sleep. Her mother was not much worse, they said, the disease having slowed its progress a little, but Tamara couldn't tell. The chemotherapy they were giving her mother made her terribly sick. It hurt Tamara to see her mother lying on the bed, weak and drained, her hair thin and brittle, her eyes bruised and puffy. Tamara managed to get through an evening of her grandmother's bitter complaints about everything and her sister's snide comments about anything Tamara said. Her father, distant and unapproachable, remained remote throughout the evening. Tamara sat with her mother for an hour after dinner, then fled back to campus and tried to do some homework. She stared at the meaningless problems, tears welling up in her eyes. She fought them for a while, then let them consume her. As she hugged her pillow to herself, Tamara lay on her bed and sobbed.

Her cell phone rang, forcing her to pull herself together. She didn't know the number that came up; it was blocked. She blew her nose and answered the phone. "Hello?" Her voice quavered a little despite her best effort to sound "normal."

"Tamara? I didn't wake you, did I?" It was Merran.

She cleared her throat and tried to mitigate the nasally sound in her voice. "No, no." It didn't work.

"Are you all right?"

"I'm fine."

"You don't sound fine. What's wrong?"

Tamara blinked rapidly, her throat choking up again. She took a deep breath as she warred with her body, which wanted to keep crying. "I went to visit my family tonight." She waved a hand, too choked up to say anything more. She struggled for composure, then collected herself as Merran waited patiently. "My mother's going through chemotherapy right now, and it's making her really sick."

"I'm sorry to hear that. It's never easy to watch someone we care about suffer."

She could sense the waves of calm emanating from the phone. The sensation was novel and odd enough that it chased away her tears. "You're projecting at me right now, aren't you?"

"You can sense that?"

"I'm just amazed you can do that over the phone." Tamara touched the edges of her cell phone. It didn't feel any different than it ever had. "How do you manage it?"

"It's not hard. Once a connection has been made, the energies are not hard to send over certain distances."

"Over any distance?" Glad to be talking about something else, Tamara leaned forward, listening intently. Her own problems with psi seemed miniscule compared to her mother's illness.

"Depends on the person. The farther the projection, the more energy it takes. It's rather hard for most of us to project to Azelle, say, even when a connection has been made first over the phone. Although if the desire is strong enough, a person could project to Azelle without the benefits of the phone first. It just takes a huge amount of energy to do it."

"I wonder how much of it is just plain the way any of us communicate emotions … in our body language, tone of voice, et cetera."

"There's more to projection than that." He sounded amused. "There's a manipulation and sensing of energies that doesn't occur unless we're in the right state of being. A very powerful projector can actively force someone to feel everything they are feeling. It can drive the recipient mad or even kill sometimes. Most of us projectors are also fairly sensitive receivers. Body language is not quite the same thing. Greg would actually be a good person to talk to about this. He's more up on the current theories about psi and the manipulation of energies. I just know that I do what I do and don't question it. Did you still want to work at the embassy as an intern?"

Tamara's breath hitched. "Yes, yes, I do."

"Janille does have some work you could do. We can work with your schedule to see what fits. She works six days a week."

Tamara's heart leaped into her throat. Her stomach twisted uncomfortably. Was she actually going to be working with Merran? "What kinds of things would I be doing?"

"This and that. Filing, sorting, scanning. Assisting me with meetings, if I can arrange it, and if you're there when I have one in the office. Possible off-location meetings, too, depending on the the subject matter." He hesitated for a moment, then continued, "This is going to be a high profile political position, Tamara. I am going to be accepting a human intern into the Azellian embassy for the first time in the fifty years Azelle has had an embassy on Earth. I am going to use this fact as a political tool in my efforts to get Earth humans and Azellians to be more open with each other."

Tamara swallowed a sudden lump in her throat. What had she gotten herself into? "Oh God."

She could hear the smile in his voice. "All part of diplomatic studies, Tamara. As an ambassador, I can't do anything without it having political repercussions, so I don't. I make everything I do have political repercussions. I'll be sending the agreement over to the Diplomatic Studies Department in the morning. You can handle it. It may sound glamorous, but actually it's more like being a babysitter to a bunch of squabbling kids."

"I wish I were as confident as you are."

"You'll see. It won't be so bad. I work my staff hard, but we have a good time while we work." He paused. "You can always say no."

"I know. I'm the one who wanted to work with the embassy, remember?" Tamara brushed her hair out of her eyes. "I'm just not used to getting what I ask for." She could feel her excitement growing. *It really will be an opportunity for me,* she thought to herself. *And extra credit with the toughest professor on campus!* "It'll be good and give me something else to think about besides my mom," she said to Merran.

"Why don't you come by a little early on Friday, before the party, and we can get your schedule worked out?"

Tamara nodded. "Thank you, Merran. See you Friday then?"

"You're very welcome, Tamara. Friday." She hung up the phone and sat back down on her bed. Hugging her pillow, her mind and emotions twirled wildly. An internship. She had an internship at the Azellian embassy! Lying back against her bed, she let that awareness—and a tiny little fantasy about the boss of the embassy—play through her mind, distracting her from the rest of her worries.

Merran hung up, wondering how the hell he was going to survive working with her. She was the most interesting mixture of insecure and fragile, occasionally showing flashes of something else far more alluring. And her projection! Suddenly jealous of

Greg and the allowances given to him as a Healer, he twisted his chair around, jumped up, and stalked into the living room. He pushed her out of his mind and went over to the television, turning on the news to see what was going on outside of Denver and his little world.

Chapter Six

EXCITEMENT CARRIED HER through Tuesday. Not even Justern's teasing could dampen her spirits, but by the time her next diplo class came around, her excitement about the internship shifted the other way. What had Merran meant when he said it was going to be a high profile position? Her family would not be at all happy with that! She found herself very nervous as she walked to her Diplomatic Studies class, wondering what Merran had said to her professor.

She suspected that she wouldn't have that long to wait—and she didn't. Professor Bennington met her at the door of the classroom. "Tamara, would you come to my office, please?"

Her stomach leaped to her throat as her heart pounded intensely. She followed him to his office. "Yes, Professor?"

The professor held up a thick sheaf of papers. "This came through to me this morning. It seems you have been accepted as intern to the Azellian embassy."

Tamara flushed. "I know. Ambassador Corina told me two nights ago."

The professor leafed through the pages. "It is a very thoroughly thought-out document. It is comprehensive ... covering almost any eventuality you might think of, from what conduct the student is expected to have to the qualifications to the grounds for termination or dismissal. When did you discuss this with the ambassador?"

"Monday."

"You managed to convince him in one day to do this? One day?"

"I had help," Tamara admitted hastily, trying to minimize her influence on the ambassador. "I'm going to declare a focus planet this year of Azelle, and I'm going to be applying to go to Azelle on the exchange program. Also, my grandfather was ambassador to Azelle for a long time. I think he thought I might adjust more easily because of my history. And I've made friends with a couple of the Azellian exchange students. One of them helped me convince the ambassador."

The professor looked at her steadily. "However you managed to get him to agree, it's not going to be an easy assignment. And he's made it quite plain that other students will not be accepted." Although somewhat impassive normally, the professor's expression grew faintly rueful. He focused on her again. "You have managed to pull off quite a diplomatic coup, Tamara. Quite worthy of your grandfather. I'm willing to offer you a percentage increase in your grade should you need it." He frowned slightly. "I do have to warn you, however. I will expect tremendous things from you this semester. You will be expected to do better than any other student in the class. Your grade may or may not reflect other things, but you and I will know that the true test will be in how well you handle the concepts I am going to be teaching."

"I am very excited about the class and the opportunity I am being given, professor."

"What's more, I am willing to endorse your application to Azelle and to sign off on a special projects course for both this semester and next, as long as you are willing to write a paper for me at the end of each term on what you are doing and learning. Ambassador Corina seems to think he's willing to offer you the opportunity to be a junior assistant, provided you do well these first few months." Professor Bennington looked at her sternly. "This is quite a singular honor, Tamara. No other student in the history of Azellian and human contact has ever been afforded the opportunity to observe Azellian activities at close hand. You will be exposed to sensitive information. Your papers will show me whether or not you are able to sort through that information and work with two conflicting sets of interests, something any ambassador must be able to do."

Tamara had to fight a sudden sense of drowning. *What have I gotten myself into?*

The professor must have noticed her expression, because he smiled. "You can handle it, Tamara. I'm confident of your ability. You will sign a contract with the embassy, as any employee would, and except for the disseminating of confidential information, it's fairly lenient. They are even willing to pay you. You can at any time decide to terminate your employment upon a two-week notice. However, I want to say that my agreement with you is that you finish out the semester for me to give you your special projects credit and for me to endorse your going to Azelle." He shifted papers around and pulled out one from the back of the pile. "Here is the contract. Read it and return it to me signed if you wish to intern with the embassy. I will get the special projects paperwork from the Registrar's Office."

Tamara took the papers with shaking hands. "Thank you. I'll return these to you by the end of today."

"No, why don't you return them to me in class on Friday? That will give you a few days to read the contract thoroughly and be sure you understand every aspect of it." The professor returned to his desk. "I'll be in class in a moment."

Tamara left, clutching her contract tightly. She walked into the classroom in a daze. Kari sat in the middle, having saved a seat for her. Most of the other students were already there, so Tamara slipped into the chair next to Kari's, placing the contract on the shared desk.

"What's this?"

"I got the internship at the Azellian embassy, Kare."

"How—what—how?"

"I asked. This is the employment contract." She shook her head. "They're even going to pay me! I don't know how much, but if it's enough, I'll quit my job in the Registrar's Office."

"So you get the extra credit. You lucky dog!"

Tamara shivered. "I don't know, Kare. I have this funny feeling I'm in way over my head. Ambassador Corina told me it's going to be a high profile position and that he is going to make my internship political. If I get on the news what are my parents going to say?" Kari could only offer a quick sympathetic look, as Professor Bennington came in at that moment and class started.

Things did not get any easier for Tamara either as she read the complete contract later that week. The terms were lenient and even generous—she would get pay that was much better than the small Registrar's Office pay she was receiving now—and the only strict item was the need for her to keep quiet regarding anything she saw or heard in the embassy that would be considered confidential. In the event of any revealing of information, she could be held legally responsible as well as instantly terminated. Not unusual, but for an intern? It was perhaps a little bit of overkill—but then, Merran had said he was creating a precedent and she wouldn't be the only intern they ever had.

By Friday night, Tamara felt no more ease about the magnitude of what she was doing, but it was done. All that remained was to set up her schedule.

She went over to the embassy right after dinner, about forty-five minutes before the party was to start, after having thrown on an outfit for the party itself. She didn't have time to mess with her hair, but fortunately the short casual style normally looked good with just a quick brushing and fluffing. She stared at her reflection in the mirror. Why she cared, she wasn't sure. Shaking her head at herself, she turned away from the mirror, left the room, and headed for the embassy.

Once again, a guard stood in the embassy gatehouse. She even recognized him from the time she and Alarin had come earlier in the week.

"Ms. Carrington," the guard greeted her with a smile as she came up to the gate. "The ambassador is expecting you." Tamara returned his smile and walked through the door he opened to the side of the main gates.

The sun, low on the horizon, cast long shadows in front of her as she made her way through the path draped in magnificent trees. She dawdled as much as she dared, wandering slowly through the leafy green shelter, but she knew she couldn't waste any more time without looking obvious, so she walked up the wide marble steps that led to the front door. It swung open silently when she approached. She took a deep breath and plunged in.

The temperature dropped inside the embassy, although it did not have the usual air-conditioned bite that most buildings did. She looked around as she entered. The entire interior of the first floor had been decorated for the party with tables clustered to the left where nametags and little party favors lay in straight rows. Soft velvet ropes swung across areas off limits to humans—the stairs and the offices to the right. To the left, though, strings of lights guided everyone to a conference room, where most of the party had been set up, including several tables of catered food. Staff members bustled about getting the food laid out for the party. None seemed to notice her. Tamara wondered if the ropes were reinforced by other means.

"They are there as a visual reminder that there are areas where students are not allowed." Merran came down the stairs wearing a formal robe that hugged his body, secured by a wide, ornate belt that swung lightly over the tips of soft, moccasin-like shoes. The long hair had made more of an impression in traditional Azellian robes than his current short cut, but his impact, as always, left her struggling to maintain her composure. His presence disturbed her in a way she couldn't name, and today he looked remote, even untouchable, as the Azellian ambassador.

"Are you including other methods of discouragement?" Tamara ignored her discomfort and touched one of the ropes. They were as soft as they looked.

Merran smiled. "Of course. No one will even think about coming upstairs or going into the offices to the right. But instead of having humans get disturbed because they've run into an unseen wall and can't move forward, we've done this so they think the ropes are responsible." He stepped around one of the barriers; the robes he wore did not permit him to step over it. He bowed to her. "However, we won't establish the mental barriers until later. In the meantime, we need to set up your schedule. Were you planning to continue working for the college?" He stepped back, motioning for her to precede him up the stairs.

Although he was being very proper, even formal with her, she felt self-conscious and nervous. Maybe it was the formality itself. "No, you were very generous with the pay. I think most interns would not expect to get anything at all. After all, we are learning from you, so you could use us for slave labor."

The smile twitched into a grin and the illusion of the remote, cold ambassador abruptly eased, if it had really ever been present. "Oh you'll be used for slave labor, all right. I just thought we might as well compensate you for some of it."

Tamara stepped onto the stairs. "Thank you for that. It certainly was a pleasant surprise. But—" She bit her lip as Merran fell in beside her. She felt a brush, almost like he'd touched her, but when she glanced down she saw that he was walking a good six inches away from her. Close, but within acceptable bounds to honor her personal space. Why then did it feel like he'd brushed her side as they walked upstairs? She was very aware of him as they walked. He was tall, and she definitely felt his height walking beside him like this. She tried to ignore her sensitivity to his presence.

Merran glanced at her out of the corner of his eye. Her aura flared strong tonight, although she was still heavily shielded and did not seem to be particularly sensitive. It glowed around her, a steady blue shine, picking up the red highlights in her hair and making her jewelry sparkle. Her short black skirt and heels made her muscular legs look longer; her blue silk shirt matched her eyes and her aura exactly, softly falling around her upper body and hinting at the shape underneath. As they walked upstairs, his aura flared, brushing the edges of hers. His breath caught as filaments of her aura reached out and slid up and around him. His whole body quivered, and he stepped a little more quickly up the stairs. Her aura did not let go easily, and he was more than a little off center when they reached his office.

Merran controlled his reactions and stepped carefully around the desk, putting some distance between them to change the dynamic completely. She seemed to be unaware of what she had done—and probably was. He had to stop and pour himself a glass of water, stalling for time to reset his internal equilibrium. "All right," he said when he returned to his desk and felt he could talk without betraying his agitation. "Let's see." He pulled out his daytimer without too much of a tremor in his fingers. "What days do you have class?"

Tamara's heart pounded steadily in her throat. If she didn't know better, she would have said her presence affected Merran. *Or by his reaction to something that had nothing to do with me,* she reminded herself sternly.

"I have class every day until noon and Tuesday I have lab in the afternoon." Did he notice the tremor in her voice?

Merran wrote steadily in the electronic daytimer, using the pen to tap out something. "The staff is here until six all week and until three on the weekends. I have written in twenty hours a week as a suggestion. Would that be too many?"

"I think I can manage it. That would be four hours a day for five days? That makes sense. I could come at one, work until five, and to make up for Tuesday when I have lab, I could come in on Saturday. Morning would probably be better since I spend afternoons with my family."

"Sounds good." Merran made more notations in the electronic daytimer. "Now, downstairs you seemed concerned about something. Do you want to talk about it?"

Tamara shook her head. "No, I just—are we ever going to be on the news?"

A frown flashed across Merran's face. "I can't say we won't. The media does enjoy us Azellians, and me in particular. Why?"

"Well, my parents aren't—uh, my grandmother." Tamara scratched at her head. "I mean my parents don't know I'm working for you. It would be … awkward for me. And when you said you would be making this high profile, I kind of worried a little."

Merran's eyebrows shot up. "Well, I can't guarantee that your working for us won't get out sometime, Tamara. An intern is not necessarily something that the media will attach to, but you know what the situation is like, and I am certainly high profile enough for them to attach to me. I could keep your working here quiet, but that would defeat some of what I'm trying to do with your internship."

Tamara shook her head. "Never mind. I'll just have to deal with it, I guess. I'm not going to be terribly popular with my family anyway. They're going to have a fit when I tell them I'm going to Azelle on an exchange program."

He didn't react to the slang she used. Maybe it was familiar to him or context told him what it meant. "It is your choice, Tamara." He leaned over the desk, his dark eyes catching hers. "I promise you, though, that if you choose to stay on this path, I will do my utmost to help you achieve your goals. Whatever they may be."

Sara L. Daigle

She took a deep breath and decided to ask the question she'd wanted to ask since he offered her the internship. "Why?"

He blinked at her. "Why what?"

"Why are you helping me? I know I'm showing all these signs of an Azellian Awakening, and Greg ... I can accept his help ... but why are you helping me?" The real question she wanted to ask—was he attracted to her—she didn't dare voice. This question tumbled out instead. "Why help me? So much that you are paying me to be an intern?"

He gave her a crooked smile, knowing she was asking about his motives as much as anything. He didn't have much of an answer to give her beyond the job answer, and somehow he didn't want to give her that one. It was his job, but that wasn't entirely why he was helping her. She hadn't picked up on his signals, apparently, which threw him off balance a bit. Most Azellian women would have figured out his interest just from the aura play alone. She hadn't. He took a breath and let it out slowly. "I didn't have it easy, either. My interest in humans and things human never sat well with my family, or with the Azellian Council. I know how hard it is to run counter to your family, to say nothing of your culture at large." It was the truth, as far as it went, but did not even begin to cover the tangled political and cultural web his birth, presence, and choices created on Azelle. He let his shields thin to the point of nonexistence, although he did not actively project at her. "Maybe I think if I can help you get there, then I will have won something, too."

Tamara blushed. "I'm sorry. I shouldn't have asked. I mean, I know it must seem as if I'm not grateful—"

"But you want to know what's motivating me. Not an unreasonable question," Merran finished for her, coming around the

202

desk. He projected at her, keeping it lowkey. "It's a very good one. We are not so different, Azellians and humans. We're all human. In some ways we are more similar to you than to any of the other native Azellian sentient species. We call ourselves the *umanaarya*, but perhaps it should just be *uman*. Family can be complicated, but one thing I have learned since I've lived here on Earth is that the family you choose ... your friends ... are as important as anything else. If you put your trust in the right people, they will be with you through thick and thin and offer you as much strength as you could ever hope to have with your birth family." He leaned against the front of his desk.

Sitting left her too vulnerable, so she stood up abruptly. At eye level, she could see his mouth and soft, generous lips. She could feel his pain, the unspoken hurt behind what he said, the bitterness shadowing his words, the sincere desire to help, to maybe make her passage easier than his. Was it her talent? Or was it something else? A sudden wild desire to kiss him, to slip her mouth against his, to feel the body behind those robes, rocketed through her.

Merran knew what shot through her mind almost immediately. Her aura flared brilliantly, and her shields shivered and wavered, her mixed emotions pouring out in waves. She had felt him, she had felt more than he intended to project. He stood still, slamming up shields around himself, not moving, not daring to move, as she balanced on the edge of a full Awakening.

Tamara stood, obviously fighting herself. The moment quivered between them, stretching into a thin, burning hot wire. From his viewpoint, Merran watched and waited as her aura snaked out pieces of itself, to be pulled back and reabsorbed. Her shields flared—thick, then thin. They remained stretched, gossamer thin across her turbulent emotions. Desire, fear, worry, excitement all careened fitfully around his shielded office and around his own shields. He held his own emotions in tight control.

"Tamara," he said finally, speaking calmly and quietly as she stood, her nostrils flaring with each heavy breath. Her eyes dilated so dark they almost swallowed the blue iris; she squeezed her hands into fists.

"What's happening?" she croaked. Her breathing quickened.

"Tamara, I want you to visualize yourself in a room. Sun is pouring in … too bright for you to see. There is a set of heavy dark curtains, Tamara. Pull those curtains across the windows. Pull and latch them tight." Merran continued shielding himself so heavily that he thought he'd momentarily gone deaf.

Merran suspected she couldn't hear him either. He knew hyperventilation would make her pass out and the episode would fade, but she could learn a lot if she were able to ride this one without losing consciousness. With his own emotions blanketed solidly under his shields, he stepped forward. "Tamara, listen to me." He hesitated for a moment, making sure his shields were tight, then his fingers closed around Tamara's shoulders.

Tamara's breath caught in a sob as his hands touched her shoulders. He could feel the waves of dizziness assailing her and the nausea rising at the back of her throat, even through the thickness of his own shields. Shudders wracked her and her knees collapsed to the floor.

Merran shifted and caught her limp body. He slowly lowered her to the floor as the terror and adrenaline raced through her and into him with their physical contact. Merran cursed to himself. He was not Greg, able to control some of her physical reaction to her fear, but he remembered something that had happened to him years ago. He'd come upon a child, lost and lonely. The child had thrown herself into his arms when he'd offered her kindness. She'd shown such relief from her terrified state that it had startled Merran and made him realize humans used touch the way Azellians used auras and mental contact. Sinking to the floor with her, he pulled her close. Stroking her hair, the way he had done to that child so many years ago, he let calm leak from his own mind. "You're safe, Tamara. Just visualize the bright sun going away. It can't hurt you. It is you, and you have thick, dark curtains. You can pull those curtains across the windows that are blinding you." Still stroking her hair, he repeated his instructions over and over. And slowly, the shields around her mind built back up and she slipped out of the episode. As he cradled her in his lap, gently stroking his hand over her hair, he made a sudden decision. Full disclosure. She needed to know about his attraction to her. It might go somewhere, it might not, but he wasn't interested in playing games with her. She was unlike anyone else he'd ever met.

The release of fear left her weak and shaking, sprawled in his arms. Merran let her sit quietly for a moment, then she felt him shift, gathering himself to lift her to the couch. She tried to protest. "I'm too heavy," Tamara managed to vocalize weakly.

He grinned down at her. "I have unfair advantages, Tamara-ala." He did something to the end of her name, giving it a purely Azellian lilt. A warm feeling curled in the bottom of her stomach. She relaxed in his hold, giving into the exhaustion that coiled through her muscles. Merran carried her to the couch and laid her down gently. He stepped away and Tamara heard the clink of glasses and water pouring.

He came back moments later carrying a glass of water. She propped herself up and sipped. "What happened to me?"

"You had another episode." Merran pulled up a chair and settled into it. "Congratulations. You managed to ride it out all by yourself."

Tamara frowned at him. "That didn't feel like an episode. I do feel a little sick, but why don't I have a migraine?"

"I don't know. But you had an episode. Maybe it's because we're in my shielded office. I was pretty heavily shielded too. You weren't getting any extraneous data to try to sort through."

"I do remember something—"

Although his skin tone did not lend well to blushing, or he had a way of controlling it, Tamara got the distinct impression Merran was embarrassed. "I may have had some responsibility in letting some information slip to you mentally. I sometimes treat you like an Azellian who's already Awakened and that probably triggered the episode. I am sorry."

Tamara exhaled, suddenly frustrated. "Greg has been working with me all week on visualization exercises. He says I'm going through the same thing an Azellian would. Why is Awakening so awkward? These episodes are going to get more and more frequent, aren't they?"

"Probably. But they may also get easier. This one wasn't so bad, was it?"

"No, this one wasn't as bad. But that's mainly because the migraine didn't come." Tamara rubbed her forehead and looked away. She leaned her head back against the couch. The leather squeaked a little as she moved. A sudden memory of wanting to kiss him flashed across her mind and she shifted uncomfortably against the couch. That had been the trigger, she knew it. No matter what Merran said about his projecting at her. "Greg tells me I can't avoid it, that my psi will break through no matter what I do.

That I can't walk away from myself." She rested her arm across her eyes, then dropped her arm and turned her head to look at Merran. "These episdoes keep happening around you, all of you. If I wanted these episodes to stop, I think I would have to stop all contact with you Azellians."

He met her gaze steadily. "And even that might not work. Tamara, you will be working in fairly close contact with me and other Azellians for the next year. If you do Awaken as we do, and it looks like that's where you're headed, it will very likely be in the next year."

Tamara sighed. "I know."

The silence stretched for a moment, then Merran shifted in his chair, his dark eyes meeting hers steadily. "Tamara, I need to tell you something." He hesitated momentarily and then continued, "I'm attracted to you."

Tamara coughed and felt the blood rush to her face. "That's certainly blunt."

"We don't usually waste words. You would have known as soon as you Awakened anyway."

She looked at him, but he was staring down at his hands. She took a breath. Maybe for the first time in her life, she wanted to say yes and mean it. It wouldn't be like the last time, she told herself. He was psi too. "I'm, uh, I'm attracted to you too."

He looked up. "We're going to be working too closely together for anything else to happen. Has Greg talked to you about what Awakening entails?"

Tamara shook her head. "Not in any detail."

Merran raked his hand through his hair. "Well, I think I told you that Azellian Awakenings are sexual. They involve bringing in and channeling energy from the outside world, from everything around the individual and channeling it through the body. Theoretically, a person could do it alone, but most of the time the channeling of energies occurs during the act of sex. Usually intercourse. Assuming you will in fact Awaken as we do, we must think about how best to help you." He took a breath. "And while I would love to be the one who channels you during your Awakening, I think someone else, like Alarin, should be the one who channels you. He might be able to keep from using sex to channel the energy. I won't be able to do that. Not only will I have to fight my own desires, I'll have to fight yours too." His eyes stared into hers intently. "And after we'd done it once, I really doubt it would only be that one time. At least not on my part."

Tamara stared at the ceiling. He was saying no, and with it came a disappointment that made her still careening emotions even more unstable. She could feel her face getting hot, and she tried to think about something else as the scalding tears built. She would not cry.

Merran watched her, cursing himself. Why had he accepted her as an intern? If he were completely honest with himself, it was partially to find this out—whether she was interested in him. Now that he knew, though, he was afraid. Afraid that if something went wrong, it would be awkward. Azellian women were fairly uncomplicated—they knew how to guard their emotions as much as he did, and any of the liaisons he had made with them had ended cleanly. He kept the human women he got involved with at a distance so they didn't develop feelings for him. Some did, and it had gotten strange. Uncomfortable. All of them, however, had had experience, and he knew they would not be hurt lastingly by his pushing them away. Tamara was another matter.

He moved, almost without volition, to kneel beside her. He reached out his hand but didn't touch her. "Tamara, I'm sorry."

Tamara fought the tears of disappointment ferociously. She swallowed the lump down with an effort. "I'm fine." She closed her eyes, the tears slipping down her cheeks. Too much to hope he hadn't noticed? They tracked across her cheek as a feather-light touch dusted them away. Opening her eyes, she saw him watching her face intently, his fingers caressing her cheek. He lifted his eyes to meet hers. The next thing she knew, he was kissing her, her head cupped between his hands.

His lips were as soft as they had promised to be, gentle and undemanding. It wasn't her first kiss, but it had been so long ago and so wrapped up in the horror of her boyfriend's death that Tamara had forgotten what it felt like. She responded shyly. The kiss deepened and changed tone. His breath came hard. He shifted, joining her on the couch. He pressed against her, the robes offering no protection from the feel of his body against hers. She hesitated a moment, overwhelmed with desire and terror.

He felt her hesitation, and it called him back to himself. She protested, but he took a shaky breath and shook his head. "No, I am not doing this." He dropped back off the couch and sat on the floor, leaning his head back and closing his eyes. "But by the *aarya*, I want to." He stared up at the ceiling. "Do you believe me now?"

Her tears gone, Tamara stared at the top of his head. "Yes," she managed to whisper. She coughed.

Merran turned to look at her. "I've managed to never have a woman for longer than a few nights of enjoyment. My staff knows that and expects it. But you? You aren't simply a few nights of enjoyment, Tamara, and I really do think it would be a mistake to start up a relationship when you are going to be working so closely with me. Besides, you know the hours I work. I'm not an easy person to have a relationship with … no ambassador is." He gave her a warm smile, quite spoiling the effect of his words and making Tamara wonder how strongly he really objected.

Tamara's desire cooled as she collected her thoughts. She sat up. "Maybe. You're probably right." *At least until I get my own head sorted on straight,* she thought to herself. "Well, should we go downstairs?" she asked him, desperate to put distance between herself and the scene that had just taken place.

Merran shifted a little. "Just give me a few minutes."

It was more like five minutes before he hauled himself to his feet, looking more composed. Tamara, too, felt less flustered. "All right. Let's get downstairs. It looks pretty bad when the ambassador throws a party and then isn't there to greet the guests."

Tamara swung her feet off the couch. "What time is it?" She tugged at her short skirt to pull it down.

Merran glanced at his watch. "It's six fifty-five. We need to get down there. The gates open at seven."

"It seems like we've been up here for much longer than that!"

Merran grinned. "Time does strange things when you're otherwise occupied." He held the door. After you."

"You just want to look at me from behind." Tamara dared the tease now that things were in the open. *How solid is he in not starting something with me? How badly do I want him to?*

Merran raised an eyebrow. "Fishing for a compliment? Hmm. I did want to mention that your outfit is quite lovely. It's … quite flattering."

Tamara swung her hips a little. "I dressed just for you."

Merran stopped. "Calm down a little, *akila*. Or I'll return the favor."

"Sorry," Tamara murmured, not very contritely, as she crossed her hands behind her and kicked at the floor. She wondered what *akila* meant.

Merran sighed, a little smile appearing on his face. "All right. One thing I want understood right here before we go downstairs. I don't want to become the focus of a thousand rumors, nor do I want my choice of you as an intern demeaned. It's hard enough to hide my interest when I work among a bunch of mind readers." He motioned with his hand and Tamara felt her chin rise, even though he didn't touch her. She met his dark eyes. "All right?"

She nodded, sobering. "All right. I understand that."

He held the door for her and let her walk in front of him. Intensely self-conscious, she walked downstairs, with Merran following behind her. As they reached the bottom of the stairs the heavy doors swung open and Greg, Alarin, Justern, and Mellis came in.

"Welcome, welcome." Merran stepped around Tamara and came forward, greeting everyone. Their greeting was muted, even subdued, but for the first time, Tamara was aware of and could almost focus on the entire level that went on beyond her hearing. It was like listening hard with a part of her mind she could just sense, but not quite. She focused on relaxing and feeling that portion of her mind.

Merran kept his shields up but had forgotten his aura as he stepped forward to greet his friends. Justern, of course, was the first to point it out. "Lovely aura you have there, Merran. Lovely shade of hazel, is it? Lots of blue? What have you been doing this past week? I didn't think you had time for that sort of thing."

Merran thought very fast. "It's not what you think. Tamara had an episode upstairs while we were settling in her schedule for the internship. Her aura's still pretty grabby. I talked her through it, and she never did develop a migraine. Does that make sense?"

He turned to Greg. *Play along, please.* He shot the thought through to Greg's intimate level.

Greg gave no sign he'd heard but he didn't contradict Merran either. "It could happen, but it's not very likely that she had an episode without the migraine. Let's go to one of the offices for a moment, if you will."

Merran frowned. "How long do you need? I've got guests coming."

"Not very long. Indulge me."

Merran looked at Alarin. "Could you make sure the guests are greeted, please?"

Alarin nodded. "Sure."

Merran and Tamara followed Greg into one of the offices. As soon as they were inside the shielded room, Greg turned to Tamara. "May I?"

Tamara nodded, looking mystified. "What's wrong?"

"I'm checking to see if Merran's right. It's very odd that you had an episode without a migraine," Greg replied, running his hand just above her torso and midsection and up again over her head. *And what's this about, Merran? There's no way Tamara's aura would be on you if you didn't have some kind of interaction with her. Are you willing to be her partner during her Awakening,* if this does unfold like an Azellian Awakening? The comment came to Merran on his intimate level.

I think it's better that Alarin handles that aspect, Greg. I don't think I can channel her, Merran replied. It was almost impossible on this level not to let some of his true feelings leak a little.

What are you talking about? If Tamara's interaction with you were stronger, then you would have more likelihood to successfully channel her.

I can't. Greg, she's working for me. I can't let anything discredit my choice of her as an intern.

Channeling does not require sex, Greg told him as he continued to sweep across Tamara's body.

Merran snorted, a little puff of sound escaping. *It will become sexual, Greg. I guarantee you that it will become sexual. I don't have the strength for it not to.*

Then just have her the once. I've seen you distance yourself from plenty of women, Merran.

I … can't. Merran repeated, emphasizing the words a little. *Don't ask me to do this. Do you know what the gossip would do to her? I can't do it, Greg. I mean it.*

Greg seemed to sense some of what Merran hinted at. *Would you rather Alarin had her? He might not be able to avoid taking it sexual either.*

I'll deal. I just can't do this, Greg. I'm … too … emotionally involved.

Something did happen between you upstairs. Greg had long ago finished with his analysis of Tamara, but he continued to pretend to scan her because Merran and he weren't done. *She certainly did have an episode, but it seems like it didn't sear out her pathways like it should have. If I hadn't seen it, I wouldn't have believed it. Yet, she's not Awake yet either. Do I need to make sure she's not going to get pregnant?*

It was just a kiss. I broke away before it went any further. I didn't think about her aura.

It's actually dormant again, but I would imagine it's got some brown in it right now, if we could see it. You certainly have enough blue in yours for just a kiss. If you want to keep the gossip down, I would suggest not doing that when your staff is in residence. Greg straightened. "You did have an episode." He spoke to Tamara then. "I wouldn't have believed it possible, but it didn't sear out your energy pathways, so it didn't cause a migraine. Maybe your Awakening will be easy."

Tamara relaxed abruptly as Greg stepped away from her. "So I'm all right?"

Greg smiled at her. "You're fine."

"What were you saying about auras?"

Merran shifted impatiently. "Are you done with me, Greg? I have to greet my guests."

Greg waved a hand. "Go." Merran didn't stay to listen to his explanation of auras or the effect sexual contact had on them. Rather, he fled the room, running from uncomfortable truths he'd discovered, to bury himself in work as usual. Fortunately, tonight he was not going to need much in the way of thought process. Tamara's presence still had him all tangled up, and he wasn't sure he had any thought processes to work with.

As soon as Merran left, Greg turned to Tamara. "Auras are energy that all psi give off in the visible spectrum, Tamara. You'll be able to see them when you've Awakened."

Tamara frowned at him. "I know what they are. But what was Justy talking about when he said Merran had a lot of blue in his aura?"

Greg shook his head. "Just that when a couple has any type of intimacy, usually physical, their auras intermingle and leave a residue. The deeper the intimacy, the deeper the intermingling."

Tamara's eyes widened. "You mean there's actual visible evidence?"

"One of the reasons there's not a whole lot of point to being coy."

"How do you hide it, then?"

"Sleep with a non-psi … or you don't. Everyone's aura is slightly different in color, so it's usually not hard to figure out who it was."

"Do I have an aura?" Tamara looked down at her arm. It looked normal enough.

Greg gently guided her arm down. "Sometimes. Usually right before you're going to have an episode. Don't try. You can't see your own aura."

"Uh … so it shows in an aura? That's not good."

Greg smiled. "Merran told me what happened, Tamara. I'm not going to say anything."

"What about the others? I don't—Merran doesn't—well, he doesn't want people to think he chose me as an intern because he just wanted to sleep with me."

"I can respect that. But it also means he doesn't feel like he can channel you, Tamara, should your Awakening progress the way we think it might. It probably would be easier if he could. Because you trust him, the Awakening process might be less traumatic for you."

"Merran said something about that upstairs. Are you telling me I have to have sex to Awaken?"

"It's not a have to, but for Azellians it usually goes there, yes."

"And Merran doesn't want to."

"I don't think it's a matter of want, Tamara. It's more like he's conflicted. From what I could see, he wants to pretty strongly."

"So why would he say that he wants someone else to get involved?"

"The person who is involved at an Azellian's Awakening doesn't usually become our permanent partner, Tamara. We channel huge amounts of energy from the planet and universe itself as the psi comes online, sharing depths of ourselves that can be uncomfortable. It's not always something you remember, either. Merran may rather wait until after you've Awakened, when you will be able to remember most of your first time with him."

She flushed at that. "Who was your Awakening partner?"

"Our friend Charina."

"A woman?"

Greg shrugged. "I wasn't expecting it. Chari was there, so I just went with what was available to me at the time. Besides, we all go through an experimental phase. Mine was pretty short, but I had one too."

Tamara studied him carefully. He made it sound offhand, but there was something in his voice that made her wonder if there was more to it than he was saying. "What about the others?"

"You'll have to ask them for their Awakening memories, Tamara."

Tamara took a deep breath and let it out slowly. "Okay, I suppose I just have to keep working with you then and not think about who's going to channel me. Or not."

A smile spread across Greg's face. "It's wonderful to hear you comfortable with the idea of Awakening, Tamara, because I truly believe your experience will be like ours, maybe even identical."

She sighed. "I'm not exactly comfortable, more like willing to see this through. If it's going to happen, it's going to happen. I might as well cooperate and make it as easy as possible."

Greg did not hug her but it almost felt like he had. He gave her a warm smile. "You're doing great, Tamara."

"Thanks. Let's go out and see who has appeared since we came in here. I have some friends coming to this tonight."

They entered the main room together. Tamara hovered on the edges of the crowd, staying near the door, until a group of three women came in talking and laughing. "Hey guys," she said, coming up behind the group.

"Tam!" Kari said, hugging her. "I managed to get most of them here, as you can see. The only one who had other plans was Pam."

"Yeah, Pam's got a hot date," Alice, the tall brunette, said. "She's too good for us now."

"Hah," replied Jenna, who—at five two and blond—was cute as a button and quite aware of it. "At least she has a date, which is more than I can say for myself." She looked around the embassy at the other people milling around. Most of the other people were human, but there were a few Azellians in the mix, including the four Azellian exchange students and Merran. "I haven't been here since Jerryn broke up with me."

"Well, have at it, girlfriend." Alice nudged Jenna. "There are plenty of Azellians here right at the moment. Mostly men, too."

"Wait a minute. Is that Kellie Darren?" Jenna hissed, staring in the direction of the door. Tamara, Kari, and Alice turned to look. "It is. Who invited her?"

"She's a diplo student too," Tamara replied mildly. Tamara didn't like Kellie either, but she wasn't quite as hostile about it as Jenna. But then, she'd never been in competition with Kellie before—or been so aware of Kellie's attention shooting across the room to stare at Merran.

"Yeah, just because she slept with the dean. It's not like she ever comes to class." Alice's tone was hardly any nicer than Jenna's.

Tamara shook her head. "They say the same thing about Pam, you know. And we know how true that is."

Kari made a face. "Well then, it must be."

Alice laughed. "Pam? Come on. Pammie's way too laid back to have the ambition to sleep her way to the top, Kare. You're just jealous that she manages to get good grades and not study."

"Hey, isn't that the ambassador? The one in the robe over there?" Jenna interrupted the argument, nudging Tamara.

Tamara glanced over. "Yes, that's him." There was a crowd of women surrounding all the Azellian men, she noticed. By far the larger proportion of humans here at the party were women, although Greg seemed to have lost his following—probably because he wasn't showing any signs of being interested in the women.

Jenna whistled between her teeth. "Wow. He showed up personally. I'm impressed."

Tamara looked at Jenna. "Of course he did. He's the one who organized the party. It would be pretty rude for him to blow us off."

"I'm still impressed." Jenna was silent for a moment. "Do you think he's looking for a girlfriend? The last time I watched Entertain.com, they said he was going out with Zarra Star."

"Zarra Star?" Tamara turned to stare at Jenna. Merran's words echoed in her head. *He said he is attracted to me—but did he say he wasn't involved with anyone else? No, he didn't.* She didn't voice her sudden fear. "The actress who just won a Golden Globe for her part in *Three Lives Apart*?"

"That's what they said. You'd think she'd be here if he was seeing her, though, wouldn't you?"

Tamara could vividly recall the little interlude between her and Merran not an hour ago in his office. "Uh. You'd think." He wouldn't have kissed her if he had a girlfriend, would he? It occurred to her that she'd never asked if he had one or not.

Kari nudged Tamara. "Well, attached or not, it looks like Kellie's making a beeline toward him."

Tamara's stomach clenched as the beautiful woman cornered Merran. He certainly was polite, giving her a bow and listening intently to whatever it was she was saying. "Excuse me for a moment, will you?" she asked her friends.

"What are you going to do?" Jenna asked, staring at Tamara.

Tamara shrugged. "Oh nothing. I just have a question to ask the ambassador about my new internship."

"Wait a minute. What internship?" Alice demanded.

"Kari will tell you," Tamara said and headed over to talk to Merran. The awareness that he might actually have a girlfriend and not have told her made her nervous. She also knew Kellie would proposition him anyway, attached or not. The idea disturbed her far more than she wanted to admit.

"It won't be a problem, Ms. Darren," Merran was saying as she came up to them. "I will have—"

"Ambassador," she interrupted as Kellie glared daggers at her. "May I have a moment?"

He took her interruption in stride, looking up at her politely. For a moment she wondered what she was doing, approaching the Azellian ambassador while he was talking to someone. "Certainly, Tamara. What can I do for you?"

"I need to ask you about the internship. Could I speak to you privately for just a moment?" Tamara asked.

Merran bowed to Kellie. "If you'll excuse me, Ms. Darren. Thank you for the information. Come," he said to Tamara, motioning her into a small office just off the conference room. Kellie stalked off, muttering to herself.

As soon as the door closed behind them, Tamara shrugged, holding onto the door handle, her back against the door. "I really didn't have anything to say. I just thought Kellie was getting a bit too predatory and you might need rescuing."

Merran turned to her with a broad smile. He stepped close, pressing his body against hers and kissing her so thoroughly that she gasped, breathless. "Don't you have cameras?" She fought to catch her breath when he finally released her. "What about your aura?"

"The cameras are for humans, not for Azellians." He kissed her again. "As for your aura, you don't have one at the moment. Mine's already blue from earlier." He grinned but did not release her. "Thank you for rescuing me." He nuzzled her hair. "I like it when you're jealous."

Tamara pushed at him, almost serious. "I am not jealous. Who is Zarra Star? Is she your girlfriend?"

"Fine. I like it when you're watching out for me." Merran kissed her neck. She shuddered at the sensations that spilled through her. "Who's Zarra Star?"

"Zarra's supposed to be the starlet you're dating."

He hugged her tighter. "Oh, you mean that story Ecom ran on me? I talked to Ms. Star all of ten minutes one night and they've plastered the rumor all over the planet that I'm seeing her. I don't have a girlfriend at the moment. Unless we count you." He kissed her neck. "Hmm. You smell very good."

"How is this behaving? How is this avoiding gossip?" Tamara

protested faintly, not really wanting him to quit, but a little miffed that he could tease her while she wasn't allowed to tease him. The sense of relief at his information was enough to make her lightheaded. Or maybe that was just the feel of his mouth on her neck.

He kissed her neck one more time, then pulled away. "All right, we've been in here long enough." He looked at her critically. "Not a hair out of place. Although you do look like someone just kissed you pretty thoroughly."

She returned the favor. "Hey, it's not fair. You don't look like that. You look perfect."

"I know," Merran grinned. "One of the benefits of my abilities."

Tamara made a face. "So, how do we explain my mouth?"

"There's a bathroom through there. We go out separately." She could tell he was enjoying this thoroughly.

"I thought you didn't want to sleep with me." She didn't quite understand his behavior.

"That's not true. I certainly do, quite badly. But I can't."

"So what's this? Not that I mind, but aren't we going to drive each other nuts?"

"Probably. I thought I could stay away completely, but I'm realizing that might not really be possible." Merran sobered. He lifted his hand and brushed it down her cheek, his expression becoming very gentle. "I may not be allowed the whole thing, *akila*, but at least allow us this."

"If you can stand it, I guess I can too. I must admit, I did enjoy it," Tamara replied. It was kind of exciting and at the same time liberating to know they were going so far but no further.

"Good." Merran gave her one last kiss and left the room. Tamara went to the bathroom, leaving by the back door, and stared at herself in the mirror. Her eyes wide and dilated, her lips just a little bit swollen, she looked like someone had just done to her exactly what he'd done—kissed her fully. No red mark colored her neck, thank God, despite his attention to it. She splashed cold water on her face and thought about Merran's kisses.

Kari came in as she stared at the mirror, water dripping off her face. "I was wondering where you were. The ambassador came back ages ago."

Kari had come in too soon. Tamara's face had not quite calmed down, and she was still thinking way too much about him.

Kari stared at her. "What happened to you? You look like someone just … I don't know, kissed the life out of you or something."

"Nothing happened." She managed to sound mostly normal, bending over to splash more cold water on her face, hoping it explained the reddening of her cheeks and chin. "I just had to go to the bathroom."

Kari walked over, locked the bathroom door, peered under the stalls, and leaned up against the washbasin. She scrutinized Tamara's face more closely. "Beard burn on your cheeks and chin, too. Or just too much cold water." She grabbed Tamara's upper arms. "The ambassador didn't do that to you, did he?!"

Tamara snorted. "The ambassador? You must be dreaming, Kare. Like I should be so lucky. Did you see him? Why would any gorgeous guy like that be after little ol' me?" There must have been enough conviction in her voice to convince Kari, because she moved on, successfully diverted.

Kari took her by the shoulders. "Then who was it? I didn't see you go off with anyone else. Who was it? One of the other Azellians?"

"A guy. I don't want to jinx it, Kare, so please don't tell anyone."

"Who was it?"

"I told you, I don't want to jinx it."

"Then I was right, you did get kissed?" Kari wriggled a little, vicariously enjoying Tamara's conquest.

She ducked her head. "Yeah."

"How was it?" Kari leaned forward hungrily.

"Pretty intense. Oh God, is he hot."

"Are you going to sleep with him?"

"No, we're taking it easy."

"Easy? Being kissed like that? You'll be sleeping with him in two or three days if he keeps going like that. Exactly how did he kiss you?"

Tamara touched her mouth, remembering. "As I said, it was pretty intense."

"Was he pressed up against you?"

Tamara grinned. "I was pinned against the door actually."

Kari sighed, putting her hand to her throat. "Feel anything?"

Tamara giggled. "Hell, yeah."

"Circumcised?"

Tamara stared at her in shock, choking on laughter. "I don't know that … I couldn't tell by feel. I wasn't exactly touching it, you know. It was more just this hard area pressing against my stomach."

"Why not?"

"Because we weren't exactly going to take it any further in the hallway!"

Kari laughed. "Two weeks. If it's that intense, I give you guys two weeks and you'll be in each other's pants."

Tamara couldn't fully argue with her, but she didn't know what Merran's strength of will might be. She shook her head. "We'll see."

"You have to tell me. Please? Promise me."

"All right, you voyeur. I'll at least tell you if it happens. I don't promise details, though."

Kari sighed again. "God, would I love to have one of those Azellian men kiss me like that. Can you imagine the redhead? Ooo, would I like to have those long fingers on my breast."

Tamara hit her friend. "Oh God, you're disgusting. They're actually friends of mine, Kare. I don't need to be thinking of them that way. Besides, Alarin has a girlfriend on Azelle. He's the one with the long distance relationship, remember?"

"Damn. What about the dark one? The one who is not the ambassador?"

"I wouldn't get too involved with him. He's pretty young. But if you want to have a story to tell posterity, then that's the one I'd go for. Justern's just your speed, too."

"Is the blond one gay or something? He's spent the whole evening dodging us women."

"Yup. So don't even try."

"You're serious? He's gay? Oh damn." Kari sighed. "And the ambassador's unattainable. Maybe involved with Zarra Star. Pity. I think he's one of the most gorgeous of the lot. He's certainly got power and influence. God, are you a lucky duck! Are you sure you want to keep going with this guy if you're going to be working with the ambassador? Your new guy might get jealous."

"Oh, I don't think this guy's going to be too worried about it."

Kari shook her head. "Damn. Waste of a perfectly good man to have a girlfriend. Kellie certainly was hoping to move in on the ambassador before you broke in and interrupted. She was pretty hot about it, you know."

Tamara shrugged. "I had a question to ask the ambassador about my internship and thought she looked a little predatory. So I figured then was a good time to offer it."

"You did do it on purpose, didn't you?" Kari stared at Tamara. "Oh my God, you broke in on Kellie on purpose." She grinned. "That's awesome! You go girl!" She lifted her right hand.

Tamara slapped it. "She deserves it. It's disgusting how she moves in like that. I think I'm ready to go. Let's go back out."

"Sure." The two women left the bathroom and went out to continue socializing.

Not much else happened the rest of the night, even though Tamara kept an eye out. Merran managed not to get himself trapped in any more conversations with predatory human women, and the other Azellian men proved to be even more slippery. Even Justern, which surprised Tamara somewhat, although Jenna certainly tried hard enough to tempt him.

Kari came up to her after a few more hours had gone by. "I'm not getting anywhere with the guys. Alice is going to bail, Jen is making moves and has no interest in anything but closing her deal, and it's getting pretty late. Do you want to head out?"

"Yeah, sounds good. I'm getting tired." *And getting nowhere with Merran.* He was too much of a polished ambassador playing host to take any more time out to whisk her into another room. Although she found herself somewhat disappointed by this, it was probably a good thing, or rumors might have started that very night. "Let's go find our host and tell him we're leaving."

Tamara walked over to where Merran stood talking to a group, Kari trailing behind. "Excuse us, Ambassador. We are going to be heading home now. Thank you for inviting us."

He turned to them. Tamara's heart skipped a beat. He didn't give her any particular indication of anything, but the sudden image of him kissing her and talking in her ear afterwards took her breath away. Something in his smile made her wonder if he knew what had just run through her head. "Thank you, Tamara, Kari. It was wonderful to have you visit us. Please, come back soon." He bowed to Kari.

She smiled at him, a coy look, but such an unconscious one that Tamara couldn't blame her. Merran brought that out in a lot of people apparently. "When is your next party, Ambassador?"

"I'm not sure yet. Maybe in a month or so. But students who are interested in traveling to Azelle one day are welcome to make an appointment to come and see us at any time. And Tamara, we will see you at one o'clock on Monday?"

Tamara nodded. "Monday." She would have liked to add more, but someone came up just then and pulled Merran's attention away.

The two of them left, Tamara's mind quite happily away from the present, thinking about dark eyes and thick, dark, soft hair.

❀ ❀ ❀

It was not until very late that the rest of the group left. Merran stepped around the room, carrying a plastic bag and using a combination of mind and hand to pick up the used cups and plates. The movement gave him the chance he needed to think about Tamara and his lack of control earlier. It hadn't been all that long since his last dalliance, but with Tamara it felt different. Wilder, better. And it was apparent she was most likely psi. *What would it be like after she Awakened? What would an Awakened human be like?* A tickle at the edge of his shields warned him that he was not alone.

"Doing manual labor?" Alarin stuck his head around the corner. He spoke in Azellian.

"Not gone yet?" Merran retorted in the same language. "Did you care to help?"

Alarin grinned and stepped into the room. "If you need it."

"I can always use the help in cleaning up," Merran replied as two more cups danced off the edge of the table into the bag. His method of cleaning consisted of holding the bag open and sweeping the table top clean with his mind. Alarin grabbed the bag and held the other side, helping with the boost.

"Don't you have house cleaners for this?"

"Of course. But they don't usually come Friday night. I don't like leaving the leftovers of a party for the work crew the next day." He whistled a fragment of a song through his teeth.

"That mood have anything to do with the blue in your aura?"

Merran did not answer, continuing to whistle.

"You're not fooling any of us, you realize. It will take quite a bit more discretion on your part to fool any of your staff too."

Merran continued to sweep the cups and plates into the bag, using his hand this time and still not answering.

"I'm just saying. You going to be her partner?" Alarin went on.

"I'm not going to channel her at all, Alarin."

Alarin raised his eyebrow. "Why not? You'd have the most chance at making it successful. As I presume the interest is returned."

"But there's absolutely no way I could avoid having sex with her," Merran replied, dropping the garbage bag and turning one of the tables on its side. He folded a leg in. Alarin stepped over to do the same on the other side.

"Why would you want to avoid it? She's pretty, she's smart, she's very likely psi."

"She's five years younger than I am, by human standards, she's a college student, and she works for me. All very good reasons to leave her alone."

"Oh please. You're not talking about permanently mating her." Alarin helped flip over another table. "As for her working with you, why does that matter?"

Merran gave Alarin a look. "And have the Councils of both worlds start screaming about my partiality? I can't get involved with anyone who is going to participate in the program, Alarin. It would invalidate everything I'm trying to do."

Alarin stared at him. "She's very likely Awakening, Mer. She's not necessarily even going to remember the whole experience. It's just once. We've all gone through it. As for the humans, they don't need to know."

"But I will. Besides, you know Tamara. Do you think she's a just once kind of woman?"

Alarin stared at him. "You *are* talking about mating her."

Merran shook his head. "No, not really. But I am talking about a relationship. I can't start one with her or I'll make my whole exchange program a joke, to say nothing about this internship."

Alarin sighed, sobering. "To say nothing about your family. Maybe you're right. But you've already opened the doors to something, Mer. You don't have a hazel aura because you restrained yourself. And you disappeared with her for a good five minutes tonight. You think we didn't notice that?"

Merran swore. "I'm not having a very easy time of staying away from her." He raked a hand through his hair. "As for disappearing with her, she was rescuing me from that *aarya-kal.* Kellie, I think her name was. It was technically to discuss her internship."

"And how much talking did you actually do?"

"Not a whole lot." He raked a hand through his hair again. "See why I can't channel her? I'd have sex with her. After that, I know I'd do it again. And probably again and again. You're going to have to channel her."

"Me? She doesn't trust me the way she does you, Mer. And if I tried, you do realize I might not be able to avoid using sex as an outlet either? If I have to defuse the energies immediately, I may need that particular outlet. I may not be able to avoid it. Are you going to deal with that?"

Merran shrugged, carefully casual. "It's better than the alternative."

"Oh really? You're telling me with words that you have to stay away from her, but you're not doing that. You don't have a hazel aura because you stayed away from her. You didn't drag her off tonight because you were staying away from her. You didn't show her aura sparking and play with her aura all night long because you're staying away from her. You know as well as I do that sex is an external expression of other things. And you are already emotionally involved with her."

"But the external expression is what the Councils might discover. I know I can't hide forever, but maybe if I can manage to wait a few months it won't look like I chose her because she's my lover." Merran tugged at the hair on his forehead.

"All right, all right. Do me a favor though?"

Merran raised an eyebrow.

"Keep getting her used to the idea of psi. The more she's comfortable with it, the easier it will be, no matter who channels her." He looked around the room. "Is it clear enough in here?"

Merran nodded. "I think so. Alarin … thanks."

Alarin bowed. Merran watched him go, praying briefly as Alarin left that he could maintain his life with some simplicity rather than the complications that threatened to overwhelm him. And that Tamara would not prove to be something far more than any of them expected.

Chapter Seven

HER FIRST DAY OF WORK at the embassy several days later knitted Tamara's emotions into knots. The guard at the gates let her in with only one instruction. "Ms. Carrington. Please use this path and enter the door on your left. It will take you to Ambassador Corina's office. They are expecting you."

Tamara obeyed. The path wound around and led her to one of the side doors to the left of the front doors. As usually happened with the front doors, the side door popped open at her approach. The effect never ceased to freak her out; it felt like ghosts were opening the door for her. She looked back to see the door close itself as silently as it had opened. She walked up the metal stairs to the door at the top. This one opened for her too. She stepped through and found herself to the left of a large desk.

"Come in." Janille, the older woman sitting at the desk, whom Tamara had met once only briefly, looked up and motioned to Tamara. "Please, have a seat and I'll be with you in a moment." She turned back to the phone. "No, sir. I'm sorry. The ambassador is in a very important meeting and cannot be disturbed. Yes, I can give him a message. I assure you, sir, he will call as soon as he gets out of his meeting. All right. Have a nice day."

She tapped a button on the phone and looked up at Tamara. "I'm Janille, as you probably remember from your tour."

Tamara nodded, more nervous than she expected to be. "I think I've spoken to you on the phone too."

"I believe we have." Janille pushed her chair back. "I do have quite a bit of scanning and filing for you to start on. It's a place to start and it will give you a good idea of what embassy work really is. The files are back here." She stepped into a room set off from the office. "This is the incoming box. Incoming mail comes in here and needs to be scanned and filed. Each file, once it is complete, is tagged in the computer and given to the ambassador or one of the liaison officers for review. An appointment is set up once the requisite paperwork is reviewed and the request is considered."

Tamara blinked. The pile of mail towered almost to head height. "Is this what you do?"

The faintest smile tugged at Janille's lips. "Much of it. My job is perhaps one of the most important, although one of the least glamorous." She pulled out one of the papers. "Step one. Every piece of mail has a name on it somewhere, usually at the top. Mail that is not identified is thrown away." She showed Tamara where the individual had entered their name. "Step two. You do a name search on the computer and pull up the citizen's record." She spoke in the name from the top of the sheet of paper, which was a request for a visa to go to Azelle. "Each request has a par- ticular form number here in the corner, or it is correspondence." She typed in the number and the computer popped up the appropriate form. "The rest of this form is for the ambassador to complete, so we don't need to do anything with the form but scan it into the computer and put in the file. Step three. Scan the mail into the computer. The scanner is here." She motioned toward a flat computer screen. Placing the form face down on a pad next to the screen, she tapped a button at the bottom of it. The computer hummed, then flashed at her, and a picture of the scanned form appeared on the screen. "I take care of sorting the computer files into the appropriate places for the ambassador or one of the liaison officers. Step four. File the paperwork. Allen Martin probably has completed several other requests, as quite a few apply more than once before being accepted to go to Azelle. His file is in here." She stepped over to the bank of files and pulled one out. "Put the paper away in file order, the most current request on the top. Step five is to see if the file is complete. For visa requests, there are a number of items we require from other government agencies. Until you get familiar with what is necessary for a complete file, I will simply have you bring the file to me and we will process the letter requesting further information. For the last hour of your work time, we will send out requests for more information."

"Thank you." Janille's brisk, competent attitude put her at ease, although Tamara was a little overwhelmed by the sheer volume. "It's hard to believe people still fill out paper requests. If you did online only, we'd have a quarter of the work." She stared down at the mound of paperwork.

The flicker of a smile on Janille's face was almost undetectable. "It wouldn't cut it down by much, as you will see. Most of the requests are submitted online. It's the backup documentation that is making up most of that pile. The backup requirements for a visa to go to Azelle are pretty complex. But they are just as important as the requests themselves. It's how the ambassador and liaison officers make their choices."

"Oh," Tamara flushed. "I'll stop asking questions and get to work now."

"Not at all." This time, Janille's smile made a real appearance. It also made her look much less forbidding. "If you don't ask questions, you won't learn. I'll be outside should you have any more." Janille turned on her heel and marched back to the outer office.

Tamara made herself comfortable and jumped into the pile of paperwork.

The work was not hard, and she had to keep herself from reading the requests and taking too much time to do them. Time flew as she figured out where everything went, scanned, pulled files, filed, then put the files away. After three hours, she had managed to get through the entire pile. She went out front to tell Janille she had finished.

Merran's door was still closed when she went up to Janille's desk. It remained that way through the last hour when Janille introduced her to the complications and joys of completing other governmental request forms. Each visa required two sponsors, medical and legal records, and a partridge in a pear tree. The requirements were strict and harsh, and Tamara wondered how anyone got to Azelle at all. Janille made no editorial comments about them, however, so she didn't say anything either.

Five minutes before she was supposed to leave, Janille bent over one of her drawers and pulled out a form. "You are being paid as per Earth rules, so I need some forms from you before you leave."

She handed Tamara a very familiar standard work request form to complete, telling the embassy how much money to withhold from her check.

Tamara completed the form quickly, but though the completion of her payroll forms took longer than she'd expected, Merran's door had not opened by the time she left.

* * *

That week and the week following, she saw him only a few times, usually on the run to a meeting or as someone came in for a meeting. Each day as she walked to work she wondered if she would see Merran at all. Most days she didn't.

She complained vociferously to Kari, although she limited what she could say. It was better than suffering alone; she had no idea how much Alarin and Greg actually knew.

"So how's the boyfriend going?" Kari asked one evening, stopping by to gossip after three weeks of this frustrating strain at work.

Tamara sprawled on her bed. She snorted. "Not. We see each other during the day, briefly, but nothing has happened. Usually he's running off somewhere."

Kari settled cross-legged at the end of the bed. "What about at night?"

"Haven't heard from him. I've even tried to call. Nothing." She didn't mention that she'd always hung up before leaving a message. He didn't need her mooning over him.

"He's probably cheating on you. It's a new relationship. How is he so busy he doesn't have time to see you? No college guy is so busy he doesn't have time for a new relationship. I don't care how academically inclined he is!"

Tamara's stomach dropped to her toes. She didn't even want to think about that, although they didn't really have anything going on to call a relationship. Besides, hadn't Merran told her he didn't have a girlfriend, that if anyone qualified, she did? She stared down at her fingers. "I have a confession. He's not a—uh, college student." She wanted Kari's input, but with Kari too unaware of whom Tamara really was—or wasn't—dating, she couldn't be of much help.

Kari stared at her. "What do you mean, not a college student? Where have you met a non-college student?" A thought came to her. "The embassy? My God, you're dating an Azellian?"

Tamara thought frantically. "Well, yes, I met someone right before classes started. He wants to keep it quiet. I do, too. My family ... well, they wouldn't be too happy about it."

"And that night you were kissed, that night in the hallway, he was there, right?"

Tamara nodded. Blend truth enough and one has a plausible lie. And she might even be able to share some of her real concerns.

"There weren't that many men at the party. Mostly the ambassador, the new exchange students, and a couple of other embassy workers." Kari frowned, biting her lip. "What does he look like?"

"Dark hair, dark eyes." That described about three-quarters of the Azellians at the embassy. Merran's coloring was not unusual. "Tall, well-built. Gorgeous."

Kari uncrossed her legs and hugged her knees to her chest. "I didn't see anyone there like that. Except the ambassador, of course."

Oops. She'd forgotten that detail. "He didn't really show up at the party for that long. Just long enough to tell me he was there and to lure me outside," Tamara said hastily and couldn't repress a smile at the memory. "But since then, it's been nothing. I see him every day at work, but as I said, it's like he's running off somewhere ... or I am."

"How does he look naked?"

Used to her friend's obsessions—Kari had been actively looking for a boyfriend for a year now and spent quite a bit of time vicariously enjoying her other friends' conquests—Tamara shouldn't have been irritated by the question, but it set her temper off anyway. "How am I supposed to know? I haven't gotten the opportunity to find out!"

Kari held up a hand. "Whoa, girl, calm down. I think you need to get laid."

"At the rate this is going it's going to be, like, four years from now!"

"It's all right. Just calm down, Tam. "

She pulled on her hair. "What if he is cheating on me, Kare?"

"Don't borrow trouble, Tam. Why do you think he is?"

Tamara stared at her friend. "Uh, I don't know, maybe because you just said he might be."

"When I said that, I thought he was an immature college student, not a mature productive member of society. And I thought he was human."

"Do you think humans hold the only cheating card? Have you met Justern Memaxthal?"

Kari laughed. "Justern falls into the immature college student category. Your new guy's probably just waiting for an opportunity, Tam. Is he blowing you off?"

"No, not exactly. He's just not giving me the encouragement I want." Tamara scowled. She bounced impatiently on the bed. "I want opportunity to knock tomorrow." Even if it would set off her Awakening. The tension she was feeling needed an outlet, badly, and right now she didn't care what the consequences might be.

Kari laughed. "Don't we all? Be patient, Tam. Just think, Jenna would drool to be in your shoes."

"I'm starting to understand her obsessions."

It was the end of the fourth week before opportunity knocked. That he'd been busy, she knew, because he hadn't spent any off-embassy-time with the Azellians, nor had he contacted anyone at all. It was the only reason she didn't run screaming, certain that he was not interested anymore. She'd had three Awakening episodes, all of them relatively easy, most of them as she slept, and most of them starring Merran in a rather provocative role. Greg told her it was because as she slept she was more open to psi and less likely to panic, but as she didn't tell him who the star of her dreams was, he didn't say anything on that particular subject. She still showed no sign of a full Awakening. The stress and confusion of everything she'd been juggling finally caught up to her, though, and she ended up with a nasty cold.

Dragging herself to work that Friday was hell. Grumpy and tired, sniffling and blowing her red, raw nose, feeling as though she'd been run over by a truck, she struggled to stay awake and focus. As she bent over a file while trying to keep her nose from dripping onto it, she felt someone behind her.

She turned to see Merran standing there. Wearing one of his dark suits, with his tie loosened and top button opened, he was quite as gorgeous—and disturbing—as always. Dark circles ringed his dark eyes and his hair hung scraggly and long over his forehead, falling onto his eyelids. He blinked and tossed the offending hair back. "Hi."

Tamara sniffed. "Hi, stranger. You've been busy."

Merran smiled and leaned against the doorjamb, folding his arms across his chest. The suit jacket pulled. "I've been desperately trying to get the Dorbin to agree to trade some of their psych-sensitive plantlife to us. They've insisted on a certain level of time and commitment from me to substantiate our reasons for wanting it. It appears the Dorbin are rather attached to their plants." He sighed and rested his head on the doorjamb. "They've been training me on how to care for them. I think I've had an hour or two of sleep per night for the past three weeks."

"Did you pass?" Tamara swabbed her nose, wincing as the tissue rubbed it raw again.

"I know more about Dorbin plantlife than I think I will ever need to know. But I did manage to get them to agree to sell them to us as long as they get to train whoever will be in charge of plant care and harvesting." Merran took a deep breath.

"What's so special about the plants?"

"They're useful for Healers." Merran looked at her more closely. "You, I see, are suffering from a cold. What are you doing here? You should be in bed resting."

Tamara sniffed again. "You sound like Greg. I'm fine."

"Colds are our bodies' way of telling us to take it easy. Among other things. Come on, I'll take you home."

She scowled. "I'm fine." She blew her nose again. "Oh this stupid nose."

Merran grinned, his expression making him look years younger and much less tired. "I'll take you home, Tamara. Don't be stubborn."

"I don't want to go home." Tamara could feel herself pouting, but since that was how she felt she didn't try to change her expression. "I don't want to lie in a bed staring at the ceiling. I hate being sick. Besides, I have work to do." She pointed at the partially finished files.

"Janille can finish them. I'll help you bring them out."

Tamara set her jaw and crossed her arms. "Janille didn't say I could go."

Merran cocked his head and looked at her from under his long eyelashes. "I'm the boss, remember?"

"But I don't want her to think I can't do my job."

Merran made an exasperated sound. "She doesn't want you dripping all over the files either." He collected the files. "You have proven yourself plenty in the past four weeks, Tamara. You've made quite a name for yourself with your speed and accuracy. I have heard nothing but praise for our intern. You can certainly afford to take a day off and take care of yourself. What's more, you aren't coming in tomorrow."

Tamara watched him gather the files. "Are you always this bossy?"

He laughed. As he stood up, he brushed his hand against her cheek. Even though she felt terrible, the touch made her skin tingle and her stomach jump. "Usually I'm worse. Just ask anyone in the office." He turned away from her and walked into the office, with Tamara trailing behind.

Janille looked up as soon as Merran and Tamara entered. "You managed to get her to leave, I see."

Merran grinned. "I'm going to have to make sure she actually makes it home, though. Even though Greg prefers to let us suffer our folly when we work ourselves hard enough to get a cold, I think I'm going to see if I can talk him into giving her something. Would you finish these, please, Janille? "

"Certainly, Ambassador. Shall I call a cab?"

"Thank you," Merran replied, although he hesitated for a moment. Tamara heard the pause and wondered again if she'd missed something. "Shall we?"

Tamara nodded and followed him downstairs. It was not until they got outside that she ventured to say anything. Merran shook his head and held up a hand as he led her to a small door at the back of the property through the employee parking lot that led to the alley behind the embassy. The cab waited at the corner and they got in. Merran gave the cabbie the address to the campus.

"What happened?" Tamara demanded as soon as the cab pulled away from the curb. "I think I missed something. We could have walked. Or don't you have a car at your disposal?"

A grin teased the edge of his mouth. "There are lots of cars at my disposal. But a cab is far more discreet."

"Discreet?" Tamara's eyes widened as she looked at the cabbie who was either ignoring them or deaf. He didn't appear to notice them at all. "What do you mean by that? Can't he hear us?"

"No, I'm shielding us."

"You mean you can prevent humans from hearing something?" Tamara hissed, staring at him.

Merran lowered his voice. "It's not easy, and I couldn't do it if he weren't concentrating on the traffic more than on us. The cab company Janille called usually sends out pretty close-mouthed cabbies as a rule. We do a lot of business with them. I wouldn't call his attention to us, though. Unlike Alarin or Greg, I couldn't make him forget what he heard or saw."

"They can actually make someone forget?" Tamara spoke in an incredulous whisper. "They never told me that!"

"It's a very grey area of ethics, of course. At least what Alarin can do. Greg's version of it is even more effective, but he's bound not to unless requested by the person whose memory he is changing. Have they been working with you?"

Tamara sniffed, her head aching a little "Every damn day. But obviously, they aren't telling me everything."

"We should probably discuss this later." Merran motioned with his eyes to the oblivious cabbie and leaned his head back against the seat.

The cab driver pulled up to the curb on the main street that ran through the center of campus. Suddenly not wanting to get out of the car and end their little private interlude, Tamara hesitated. She doubted Merran would see her to her room—it was too public. "Are you going to just drop me off into Greg's untender care?"

A slow smile spread across Merran's face. "I was going to see what I could talk him into. But other arrangements could be made, if you prefer."

A sudden sense of shyness gripped her. "I would like that." A sneeze tickled her nose, making her question her decision, but she hung in there, hoping whatever he planned wouldn't be too energetic. She did feel better than she had when she was staring at files and feeling miserable, but the cold still had her in its grip.

Merran leaned forward and gave the driver another address. The cab driver obeyed, pulling free of the curb. The cab driver pulled up to a tall skyscraper that wasn't far from either the embassy or campus— although it would be something of a long walk from the university. Instead of dropping them out front, he pulled into the underground gated parking garage entrance, which was sheltered from the street outside. Pausing only briefly to speak to the guard at the gate, he pulled up to the curb just around the corner from the gates. Merran discreetly handed him a large wad of money and got out of the car, extending a hand to help Tamara get out. She crawled out of the cab and looked around as the cab zipped away. The area was quiet, not visible from the street out front. Glass sliding doors, slightly mirrored so no one could see in, protected the entrance. The glass doors slid back as they approached, but whether or not they used the usual human technology or the weird Azellian technology Tamara couldn't tell. They didn't startle her as badly as the doors at the embassy—she was used to sliding doors opening automatically. No human guard stood in the lobby, but cameras watched from every nook and cranny. She could count ten cameras from where she stood. The lobby was quiet, an almost library hush to it.

Tamara looked around as Merran led her to a middle set of elevators. "Aren't we going to be obvious?" The elevator door opened immediately, which startled her. Elevators never opened immediately!

He stood back to let her go first. "Like I told you before, cameras are for humans."

"You distracted me after that," Tamara sniffed. "So, what? Are you telling me cameras can't register an Azellian?"

Merran looked up at the camera in the elevator, then placed his finger on a pad and tapped in a code. The elevator doors whooshed closed. It gave a little jerk, but the sensation of movement was minimal. "Projection onto a digital media is something we all can do, more or less."

"So what are the cameras looking at right now?"

"Blurs."

"What do the physical eyes that see this think about those blurs?"

"They aren't using the cameras anyway, except to catch humans entering this building, or in case we need proof for prosecution. No humans live here. All of the guards watching are Azellian, and they knew who I was the moment I entered the building." Despite his assurances that they were not being observed, he didn't make any moves on her, something she thought a little odd considering he was taking her up to what she assumed was his apartment. *Going to visit Merran's living quarters.* The thought made butterflies wiggle a bit in her stomach. She suppressed a sneeze. She did wish she felt better.

The elevator doors slid open to reveal the most breathtaking apartment she'd ever seen. It was huge! Based on the panoramic view out the windows, it had to cover most, if not all, of the top floor. "Oh my God," she said, staring around. Huge windows looked out over the mountains. The skyscraper loomed tall enough that no other building blocked its view of the whole front range from Long's Peak in the north to Pike's Peak, barely visible in the distance to the south. The sun poured in the window, but some kind of polarization must have been on the windows because the temperature of the room was pleasant. The open floor plan held a large, circular, sectional leather couch that formed a semi-circle around a large stone table. A flat screen television was on the ceiling. How one could watch it she had no idea.

Merran walked past the couch to the open kitchen. "I have some herbal teas that will help your cold." He turned on the water, filled the kettle, and put it on the stove.

Tamara stared around the room. To the left of the kitchen was something resembling an alcove, too open to be a bedroom, but definitely another "room." A huge mahogany desk dominated most of the space. A large bay window with a balcony provided the backdrop. The window faced south, not west, revealing more of the city, although the mountains were visible to the southwest. Gray-and-black metal and tile formed the décor—very formal, very cold, and very clean. Two doors framed the metal elevator doors, one on either side of the elevator. One led to a bathroom that she could see from where she stood. The other door, firmly closed, probably was his bedroom. She sniffed and wandered toward the bathroom. The room itself was small, only a half-bath, with a black toilet, black sink, and white carpet.

When she came back out, Merran stood in the kitchen, watching her. "How do you like it here?"

"It's overwhelming."

"It's what ambassadors are expected to live in, though. And entertain in. Not that I have the time to entertain. I personally prefer my little house in Azorantxl." He motioned to the couch. "Did you want to sit? Your tea is done. I'll bring it to you."

Tamara went over to the couch and perched on it. It squeaked as she sat, the leather talking in soft tones. She sank down and it folded itself around her. The couch was much more comfortable than she'd expected.

Merran brought over the tea and placed it on the coffee table in front of the couch. The tea cut through her stuffy nose and smelled wonderful. She reached forward and picked it up. "What do you do in this mausoleum if you don't entertain?"

Merran leaned over and pulled a remote out of a cleverly designed door in the arm of the couch. He touched a button. The flat screen on the ceiling slowly dropped down and came on.

Tamara stared at it and blinked. "Damn. That's scary."

He smiled and handed her the remote. "Relax for a moment. I want to get into something more comfortable than this suit."

Tamara kicked off her shoes and curled her feet under her, watching him as he walked across the near-white carpet. At the moment, he was definitely more interesting than the television. Merran opened the door to what she'd assumed correctly to be his bedroom. She caught a glimpse of a room very similar to the rest of the apartment. A huge, four-poster bed with gauzy curtains draped around it dominated the room. When he didn't close the door behind him, she got to her feet and padded across the floor. "This tea is really good. I do feel better."

"Good," Merran's reply came back muffled. "Greg would rather have us suffer because it forces us to slow down for a while. But, since I have to manage to work anyway, I have managed to brow beat some very good remedies out of him."

Tamara hovered at the edge of the open door, suddenly feeling awkward at seeing this, Merran's inner sanctum.

"Come in, I want to show you something." Merran emerged from the depths of a huge walk-in closet. "I have a duplicate of it in my office, but since the view from the office is much nicer than this view, I don't use this one much."

Clinging to her cup, Tamara stepped across the threshold. Wearing a pair of loose shorts and a t-shirt that had some intricate Azellian lettering on the front, Merran walked barefoot over to the bedside table and touched something. His outfit made him look different, and much younger, than when he wore his usual suits. The bank of darkened windows facing east lightened and showed one of the most breathtaking scenes Tamara had ever seen. An alien sun danced over the red sand and threw rainbow sparkles into the air, making the shadows in the room jump. Far to the left, a sparkle of blue, then a spattering of green caught the eye, and made her seek to catch the tiny rainbows with her eyes. Each rainbow danced away as she looked at it. She stepped closer, her eyes riveted to the scene. She lifted her hand to touch it, then lowered her hand again.

Merran stepped up behind her and slid his arms around her waist. She craned her neck to look up at him. "It's beautiful. What is it?"

"It's Azelle." He dropped to kiss her neck, his warm breath caressing her skin. "At sunset."

"How can you tell?" She sneezed.

She could feel his chuckle vibrate through his chest. "It said so on the controller. I also commissioned the picture to be taken at sunset. Then and at dawn are the only two times the rainbow phenomenon is visible. I was pleased with how it came out actually, although like I said, the other picture I have at my office is more dramatic."

She sneezed again, a little more violently. Merran guided her to the bed and padded toward what appeared to be a huge master bathroom to get some tissue. He returned, handing the tissue to her and rescuing her tea. He placed it on the bedside table beside her. "Do you have other views?" she asked between sneezes.

He motioned across the bed. The picture changed. A twilight view with a tremendous sunset. "I have four—sunset, the rainbow, full day, and night. I'd like to add dawn but I haven't found the right one yet." He leaned across the bed and lay on his side, resting his head on his hand.

"You just used your psi, didn't you?"

Merran smiled. "Yes. I could have done without the gesture, but I wanted you to notice."

"How far away does it work?"

"Depends on the strength of your ability."

"What's yours?"

"Unless I'm really familiar with an area, I usually have to see something to manipulate it telekinetically. Visual range is my limit."

Tamara was silent a moment as she digested this information. Greg had talked to her about their talents before, and all the Azellians had used them in her presence—Alarin made an effort to use psi as often as he could when they were in private—but she was more curious about Merran, since he was so reserved and distant most of the time. Her eyes wandered to the lettering on his shirt. The letters were Azellian and she could make out most of the words, but the sentence didn't make any sense to her. "What does it say on your shirt?" Tamara reached out and touched the slightly raised lettering. Merran's breath caught a little as she traced the letters.

"It's just a saying that we have. That to see the rainbow is to experience the ultimate in beauty. It's referring to the phenomenon I just showed you."

"How do you say it in Azellian?"

He spoke a phrase, much shorter than she expected. His voice was deeper somehow when he spoke Azellian. She closed her eyes to listen, and a shiver slid up her spine. "How do you stand being away from it for so long?" She opened her eyes.

"Earth has its beauty, too. Azelle doesn't just represent the planet either. There are times when being light-years away from my relatives is a good thing."

She leaned back against the headboard of the bed. "Do you have any brothers and sisters?"

"Both. One brother and one sister. Half-siblings, actually. After Junian and Alerra'a mother died, father took up with my mother."

Something about the way he said it made her ask, "They weren't married?"

Merran shook his head. His expression was flat and neutral, as was his tone. "My mother was a Liporinn. There was no way Father's family would let him marry her. It didn't win me friends when I was growing up."

Tamara remembered something from class, something that had startled her when she'd heard it in passing. For a planet renowned for its individualism, Azelle also had its archaic remnants. "Azelle has a formal class hierarchy, doesn't it?"

"I wouldn't say it is formal, but there is a pretty strong sense of family, yes. We're not as structured as say your historical monarchy. But there are definitely families to belong to and others that create more of a problem. Corina is High Council. Liporinn is not one of the families that followed the *aarya*, so they have been ostracized. My father taking up with a Liporinn was not exactly acceptable to the other members of the family. It's been one of the reasons I've enjoyed Earth so much. Here rank is held more in your job status than in your family name."

"That's primarily because of the history of where we live. What used to be the Old West was pretty damn egalitarian. Might and ability were more important than name because life was hard here." Tamara sniffed again, dabbing her nose. "It's certainly not the case across the world. There are areas of the world that are more or less hierarchical than others. Money talks, of course, across the board." She sipped her tea again, enjoying Merran's unusual openness. "Do you get along with your siblings?"

"Now that I live on Earth most of the time? Sure." He closed one eye, thinking. "Alerra's never been difficult, actually. She's pretty easygoing. My niece is not a whole lot younger than I am and she's quite friendly. She decided not to come to Earth with Alarin, Greg, Mellis, and Justern, but she's part of the crew anyway." Merran turned over, dropped his head onto the pillow, and linked his hands across his chest. "Junian, well there's such an age gap. When I was born, Junian had just moved out of the house. Alerra married her husband and moved out when I was five. Junian never did forgive Father for his liaison with my mother. Alerra treats me like her child—I lived with her for a while once my parents died, before I struck out on my own."

"I'm sorry." Tamara turned her head to see his expression.

He smiled. "Don't be. It's over now. How's your family?"

Tamara shrugged. "My parents are all right, but Andreya and I don't get along at all. She spends most of her time certain that I'm getting something she's not. My grandmother has been on an extended visit with my family and is not all that fond of me. She's got something against me, but I don't know exactly what it is. I was actually born two years before my parents were married, so I think it has something to do with that, although I suspect there's more to the story than me being born out of wedlock. Andreya likes to remind me of the timing of my birth whenever she wants to feel superior. So ... I kind of know how you feel." She slid down the headboard to lie next to him. "It used to bother me, like I was a mistake or something. My grandmother has on occasion called me the bastard. She's almost downright vicious at times." Her grandmother's words still hurt ... much more than Andreya's thin attempts to belittle her.

It was Merran's turn to search out her expression. He rolled over on his side, reaching out his hand and gently tracing the side of her cheek. "People only have power over us if we let them." He leaned over and kissed her very gently. It was not a passionate kiss but a sweet one. His mouth moved and traced across her cheek. Tamara closed her eyes, letting the feelings sweep through her. Somehow Merran did make some of the old pain go away, at least for now.

She lay on his bed in his bedroom and for the first time in her life trusted someone else enough to let herself totally relax in his presence. The only problem was that she fell asleep. She didn't mean to, but the combination of the tea, her cold, and lying on his bed created such a state of relaxation that she fell asleep before she even realized she was tired.

She woke sometime later, disoriented and confused, and cold. Memory returned slowly as she looked around. The windows that had shown a scene of Azelle were once again dark. A soft light spilled into the bedroom from the other room, providing her with the ability to see more of her surroundings. To her right, Merran lay sprawled on the bed, appearing much younger and more vulnerable in sleep than she'd ever seen him look while awake. His dark lashes lay against his cheek, his mouth slightly open as he slept. Still wearing his shirt and shorts, with one hand up against the headboard and the other down at his side, he snored softly.

Tamara stifled her cough as she slid off the bed. She shivered, her body drenched in sweat. The cold had finally broken. Rubbing her eyes, her cheeks, and her sinuses, she padded over to the bathroom and closed the door softly behind her before flipping on the light.

She blinked and stared with her mouth open as she took in the room that lay revealed in the stark light. The master bathroom was almost as large as the room behind her. A window dominated the far wall, revealing the glow of the lights of Denver glittering across a dark tapestry. Below the window, a huge black Jacuzzi tub with gold fixtures beckoned invitingly and she wondered if Merran ever used it. Next to the tub was a large black-and-gold stall shower made of clear glass, with two gold showerheads. The toilet on the other side of the shower stall was black, just like the one in the smaller bathroom. Tamara used it, flushed, and then sampled some of the lavendar hand soap on the edge of the sink.

Of all the rooms in his apartment, this was the one place she actually saw Merran's personal effects and not just some decorator's idea of modern chic. Shaving supplies lay scattered on the black sink. An electric toothbrush rested in its recharger and toothpaste lay beside it. Tamara used the towel hanging from the gold towel rack to wipe her hands. Curiosity prompted her to pull open the glass-and-metal frame of the medicine cabinet. Minor ailment remedies, a first aid kit, and other miscellaneous items lay scattered inside the cabinet. She turned out the lights and opened the door, waiting as her eyes adjusted to the dimmer light of the master bedroom.

Merran still slept soundly, so she padded out to the kitchen area where she finally found a clock. Three o'clock in the morning—she realized she had been asleep for a long time, since she had fallen asleep at about six in the evening. It took her opening three different black metal cabinet doors before she finally found the glasses and poured herself a glass of water.

She brought the water back with her to the bed. It was not time to get up, even though she wasn't nearly as tired as she had been. If she'd been at home, she would have gone downstairs to watch television, but she didn't even want to try to figure out how to work the setup Merran had, nor did she want to wake him. She stood at the bedside, still soaked from the broken fever, so she pulled her shirt and shorts off and slipped under the covers in her underwear. The sheets were a cool satin and felt wonderful against her skin. She didn't think she would sleep again, but she was out within minutes.

When she woke for the second time, the sunlight poured in through the windows. Merran's body cupped hers, his arm across her stomach. She didn't know if he was awake or not; as she moved slightly, he shifted, sighing and turning over onto his back. Her eyes swept down his body and hastily back up. Either his body was reacting to her or to something else, but the shorts he wore weren't hiding much.

Under her scrutiny, he opened his eyes and looked over at her. "Morning. How do you feel this morning?"

Tamara flushed but she smiled. "Much better. I think my cold broke last night." She took a deep breath through her nose. "See? Clear."

Merran stretched. The cloth across his legs and lower abdomen stretched too. Tamara worked very hard not to look. "That's good."

She would have sat up but remembered at the last moment that she was only wearing her bra and panties. She stayed under the covers, holding them up to her chin. "Did you sleep well?"

"Extremely." Merran yawned, stretching again. He didn't seem at all self-conscious.

"When did I fall asleep?"

"Early. I got up and did some work for a while, then joined you. You were sleeping so hard I didn't want to wake you by getting you under the covers." He grinned. "And I didn't know how you'd take me undressing you."

"I did that myself last night. I woke up at three and was soaked from the cold breaking, so I took off my shirt and shorts and got under the covers. I hope you don't mind." Tamara tried to control the fidgets, but she was far too nervous. "I've never woken up in a guy's bed before." *Except Greg, who doesn't count*, she thought to herself, but didn't mention out loud.

Merran turned over again onto his stomach, hiding that part of him she really didn't want to be aware of right now. "Not at all." He shifted so that he was partially on top of her, which didn't improve matters because she could now feel what she had merely seen before. She had thought anything would be preferable to seeing him, but she quickly revised that opinion. Her stomach tensed and weird things happened to her nether regions at the feel of him pressed against her. "It is certainly making waking up in the morning much more enjoyable." He lowered his head and kissed her.

Maybe it was the unreality of waking up in a strange bed, but Tamara gave herself over to the kiss, responding to him wholeheartedly. Her arms went around his neck, her hands sliding down under his shirt. His skin was soft and warm and it twitched where she touched. She pressed against him. The covers slipped and his hands bared her shoulders and back, with only the fabric of her bra between them.

He broke the kiss and lay stiffly on her, breathing hard. Tamara tried to slide out from under him, but he held her close, pressing his weight on top of her. "Don't move." His voice was barely audible.

Her ardor cooled in the wake of his behavior and she lay still. His breathing slowed as he lifted his head. His eyes were dilated and huge, the dark brown almost indistinguishable from the black.

"I, uh, don't think sleeping together is a great idea when we aren't going to be doing anything else. This is going to drive us both nuts."

Merran lowered his head again and breathed deeply. "It already is. The *aarya* help me."

She held herself still. They both quivered on the edge of what might come next. If either of them moved, the sexual tension would surely knock them both over. "What would happen if we did? Just theoretically."

"Beyond the almost certain chance that we would trigger your Awakening? We're almost past the point when people would be certain to say that I gave you the job of intern because I wanted to sleep with you. But not completely."

Tamara suddenly knew that if she pushed it, he would give in. It was in his voice, in the tension in his body. And maybe in his mind. Something—an instinct, an inner awareness, something—told her that he was holding on by only a thread of control. Unfortunately, the first reason was enough to cure her of the desire to push it. She'd been told sex would most likely trigger her Awakening and she wasn't quite ready for that yet.

He must have read some of what was running through her thoughts, or otherwise shared it, because he rolled off her and got into a sitting position.

Suddenly irritable and cold, she rubbed her bare shoulders and sat up too. "I don't care what anyone else might or might not think. The only thing keeping me from you this morning is the possibility of triggering my Awakening. I'm not quite ready for that yet. After it's over, though, we are reevaluating ... and don't think I'm going to take my internship as a way to put me off. If we're still in this state, don't even think I'm going to stop just because you are worried about what other people will think. We'll deal with it and them as it happens." She leaned over and kissed him. "Do you mind if I use your shower and borrow some clothes? Mine are really nasty." She crawled out from under the covers, not caring that she only wore a pair of panties and a bra. "Do you have any clean towels?" Climbing out his side of the bed, she slid off and looked at him. "Hello? Merran?"

Merran shook his head, breaking out of whatever spell held him. "Yes, I have clean towels. As for clothes, I don't know if I have anything that will fit you."

"Let's look." Tamara felt better than she had in a really long time and more herself since the semester had begun. She headed for the closet.

Merran joined her in his huge walk-in closet. The search for clothes turned into a silly wrestling match that had them both back to where they had started earlier that morning. Tamara groaned as they split apart again. "We've got to stop this."

"And you've got to stop running around here in your under-wear." Merran snapped the back strap on her bra. "Although I'm not sure you running around in my clothes is going to be any easier on me. Go take a shower. Clean towels are in the closet in the bathroom. Shampoo and soap are in the shower."

Tamara squealed and jumped away from him. "Be nice or I'll make you join me."

"Be nice or I will. Go."

As she obeyed, he went out to his desk. He sat down and lis-tened to the small sounds as she moved around in the bathroom. He didn't think he could resist her, not if she pressed the issue. He was quickly losing his desire to resist her. Janille had all but given him her blessing when she had offered to call him a cab yes-terday—as much of a blessing as she would ever give. The rest of his Azellian staff was closeknit and loyal, and a relationship could always be hidden from the media and the Council for a while. He thought about waking up next to Tamara. He had never let anyone get close enough to find out about his history or his fam-ily before. The Azellian women he'd slept with already knew and didn't care, or they wouldn't have dallied with him at all, and the human women hadn't been important enough to be told. The feel of her against him this morning— he had to stop thinking about it or he was going to find himself in a lot of pain. He took a few deep breaths.

His personal cell phone beeped at him. Looking down at the number, Merran frowned. It was not a number he recognized. Who knew his personal phone number other than his friends? "Hello?"

"Ambassador Corina?" Greg's voice sounded strained. He spoke slowly and clearly in English. He had never called Merran ambassador in his life. "I don't mean to disturb you, but we have something of a crisis here."

"What's wrong?"

"It's Justern. He's been arrested. I'm down at the precinct head-quarters now. They're not letting me in to see him." Through the connection on the phone and his intimate level came the news. *They've drugged him with something that has him completely out of it. I can't get through to him at all. The aarya-cursed-stone-head standing behind me is listening to everything I say. I think we need the ambassador right about now.* "Would you come down?"

Merran scowled. "I'll be there in five minutes. Which precinct are you at?" He didn't really need to be told—he could have followed Greg's mind, but he knew it really would not be a good idea to spook the police. Not when they'd drugged Justern.

"The third. The one not far from campus."

"I'll be there momentarily." Merran hung up. He grabbed his clothes and knocked on the bathroom door. "Tamara, are you done? I have to get in there to get dressed."

Tamara opened the door, dressed in his t-shirt and shorts. Somehow she'd tied the waist, and although the t-shirt hung large on her, she looked good—wet hair and all. "What's wrong?"

"Justern's been arrested." He stepped into the bathroom.

"Justem? For what?"

"I don't know. Greg just called me." Merran stripped off his clothes, ignoring that she stood there, his attention completely on what he was doing.

She turned her back as he got dressed. "Why didn't Justern call you? He gets one call."

"They've drugged him. A nasty little habit the cops have when dealing with Azellians." Merran pulled on a clean pair of boxer shorts, his pants, and a shirt. "They also have a tendency to ignore the civil rights humans take for granted."

"You've done this before?"

"A few times. It's not pleasant, and the longer Justern's in there the worse it's going to be. Cops don't like beings who are rumored to have dangerous built-in abilities. They tend to shoot first and ask questions later." Using the mirror, Merran pulled his tie over his head and tied it. Tamara turned to watch him finish dressing, but her expression indicated that she was listening more to what he was saying than paying attention to what he was doing. "I've got to get over there and remind them that Justern does indeed have a supporter." He walked out of the bathroom, slipping the suit coat on as he walked.

Tamara followed him, grabbing the clothes she'd left in a pile on the floor beside the bed. "Do you have an attorney? An Azellian lawyer who knows human law?"

"Not per se. The embassy has one, but she's a corporate lawyer. In the cases before now, we've used the public defender."

They walked toward the elevator. "A public defender? For an Azellian? I'll ask my dad to recommend one. He's an attorney. I'll call him as soon as I get back to my room."

Merran tapped the elevator call button. "That would help tremendously, Tamara. Come downstairs with me or you won't be able to leave until I get back. Can you get back to campus your-self?" Tamara grabbed her shoes from beside the couch and joined him at the elevator. They entered together.

She balanced herself against the elevator wall, slipping her shoes on as the elevator dropped. "I'll be fine. Don't worry about me. I hope he's all right."

"Me too. They're treating him like a dangerous criminal. Not the best start." He frowned, trying not to worry too much, but he knew human police far too well. If Justern survived—he pushed the thoughts away and stared at the elevator wall, the memory of the last Azellian the police had tried to hold far too strong in his mind for comfort. Tylin Serryn, accused of having killed a hu-man—fortunately by mundane means—hadn't done well at all after being released by the police. The damage had been exten-sive, and if Tylin had been from one of the High Council families, like Justern, and innocent to boot, Merran would have had an in-terplanetary incident on his hands. Fortunately, Tylin's guilt had been quite obvious, and the damage to his psi and brain had been deemed suitable punishment by the Council. Justern, however—Merran pushed the thoughts away and tried to let his worry go.

As soon as they parted ways, Tamara made her way back to campus, glad that her cold had broken. When she reached her room, instead of calling home, she changed quickly—her father would not approve of her showing up in some man's clothing, she was sure—and drove home.

Luck smiled on her. Her father was home, but her sister was not. Tamara stopped in to say hi to her mother, who didn't seem to notice, slipped past her grandmother, and made her way to her father's office. She knocked quietly on the door.

"Come in."

She opened the door. "Hi Dad. Do you have a moment?"

Her father looked up and smiled, although the expression did not convey his usual relaxed state. The stress of the recent family tensions was etched into his eyes and his face. "Hi Tammy. We didn't expect to see you until tonight. Is everything all right?"

Tamara settled down in the armchair in front of her father's desk, folding her hands across her stomach. "Actually, uh, no. I have a … legal question for you. A friend of mine got arrested last night. Do you know a good defense attorney?"

Peter Carrington eyed his daughter, his expression shifting to what Tamara called his usual lawyer look. His voice tightened just slightly. "What did she or he get arrested for?"

"I don't know. I just found out this morning that he was arrested at all. A criminal charge, I think, because the cops are holding him. He's probably going to be assigned a public defender, if they let him exercise his rights at all."

Peter frowned. "Why wouldn't they? How could they keep—" He stopped. "There was a news event this morning. It seemed one of the Azellian students was arrested for the rape of a human student." His voice took on a funny tone.

Tamara went pale. "Oh God. If that's what he was arrested for, he didn't do it, Dad. I'm sure he didn't." *Rape? Justern has been arrested for rape?* she thought, trying to wrap her brain around it. *He doesn't need to force himself on anyone. Justern is good-looking enough to get any woman he wants. And there's no way Merran would have allowed a rapist to come to Earth, is there?*

Peter Carrington watched the emotions play across her face. "Was this the friend you were referring to?"

Tamara suddenly realized she shouldn't have known the Azellian students, much less express friendship with them. She could imagine his reaction if he knew where she woke up this morning, but she ignored the implications and pretended she hadn't said anything out of the ordinary. "I'm sure he didn't do it, Dad. The ambassador went over there this morning to work through it."

Peter raised an eyebrow. "The embassy has attorneys, Tammy, dear. Very good ones, as a matter of fact. I'm sure they'll be able to handle this case quite well on their own."

She shook her head. "They have a corporate attorney, not a criminal attorney. You know as well as I do it's completely different law. I know you wouldn't want to defend him, but do you know someone who could? Who wouldn't care that he isn't human?"

Peter stared out the window for a moment, then turned to look at her again. "It's going to be ugly, sweetheart. You know that. Any rape is the man's word against the woman's, unless there's physical evidence or witnesses to the contrary. If there was consensual sex and it becomes a date rape case, it usually goes to the one who gives a better show in court. Anyone taking a case against a woman in a rape case had better be a damned good attorney. The courts tend to be rather overprotective. It also depends on the judge you get. In a case against a non-human, when fear's involved, he'll be lucky to just get deportation if he's found guilty."

Tamara didn't know how he felt about the Azellian arrival, not really. She looked down at his desk, unable to hold his gaze anymore.

Peter turned his chair and jumped out of it, pacing back and forth restlessly. "This is going to be a political show too. Anyone who defends him is going to become a media star." He stopped at the window and stared out once again, then his shoulders straightened. He seemed to come to some internal decision and turned to face Tamara. "Let's hope your grandmother is struck deaf. What's this young man's name?"

"J—Justern Memaxthal."

"Memaxthal?" A strange expression crossed Peter's face.

"Do you know him?"

Peter shook his head. "No, no. It's nothing. Just a thought. You said the ambassador's there?"

Tamara nodded.

"Defending his project, eh?"

"Yeah, probably."

Peter didn't seem to have heard her. "The political ramifications are going to be overwhelming, you can be sure of that. Especially when a Memaxthal is involved."

Tamara bit her tongue. She was sure her father's behavior was more than just politically motivated, but if she wanted to be included, she knew she'd better keep quiet.

Peter returned to his chair. "If you're wrapped up enough in the Azellian happenings to know that the ambassador is helping this young man out of his difficulties, I suppose you have contacts at the embassy?"

Tamara blushed and looked down at her hands. "I'm an intern there. I work for the embassy."

Peter looked less surprised than she'd expected, but he did shake his head. "When you declared a diplomatic studies major, I was rather expecting this." He sighed. "I'd hoped—but there isn't much I can do about it. You're an adult, quite capable of declaring yourself and making decisions on your own. You do realize it will be open war when we go down to the station?"

Tamara knew what he meant. "Grandmother."

"There's more to it than that," Peter told her. "There are things you don't know about, honey. Things that will come out if we do this. Things that might ruin your chance to go to Azelle, if that is indeed in your plans."

Tamara stared at her father. What was he talking about? She decided to leave his comments alone for the moment and focus on Justern. "We can't leave him in there, Dad. Not if we can do something about it. No matter the consequences."

Peter got to his feet again. "I just wanted to be sure you were committed." He waved her on. "After you. Let's go beard the lion in its den."

They didn't say much on their way out. Peter told his mother that they were on their way to work and asked if she could watch Jeanine for a while. She grumbled and scowled but gave in, probably secretly thrilled at the chance to have them indebted to her. Tamara and Peter were at the police precinct within ten minutes.

Merran and Greg were nowhere to be seen when Tamara and Peter arrived. As they entered, Peter motioned to a bank of chairs. "Wait here, Tammy. I'll find out what's happening." Only one duty officer sat at the front desk—everyone else who normally should have been sitting at desks working on cases was gone.

Tamara sat on the benches in front of the desk. Peter went up to the desk, said something to the officer behind it, and was allowed into the back area. She wished suddenly that her psi was active and she could have communicated with Merran and Greg, wherever they were. The quiet hum of the fans rotating overhead made the room seem oddly hushed, as if the room were holding its breath. Or maybe the lack of people created the unnatural hush. She wondered what was going on.

Merran appeared at the low door leading to the bench area. Even without being Awakened, Tamara could see that he was agitated. She jumped to her feet and went up to him. "Merran, is everything all right? What's wrong? Where's Greg?"

Merran lifted his hand and ran it through his hair. He glanced at the duty officer and went over to sit on the bench. Tamara settled near him as he spoke in a very low voice, using presumably the same sheltering he had in the cab. "Greg's working on Justy and has been since I managed to get through to them that if they didn't let us back there to take care of him they were going to precipitate an interplanetary incident."

She stared at him. "Is he all right?" Her voice went up and Merran hushed her.

"I can't shield us if you aren't quiet. He'll live. The police, especially here in Denver, know how to keep us chained up. It takes drugs because there are no human prisons that can hold one of us. But we metabolize drugs very quickly. There are only a few sedatives that work at all to block our abilities, and those have to be given in massive doses. They were keeping him unconscious, and it depressed his physical functions so badly he started to go into respiratory failure and cardiac arrest. Greg got him breathing again and has managed to burn the drugs out of his system enough so that his autonomous functions are working again." He shook his head. "There may be permanent damage—we don't know yet whether the sedatives and oxygen deprivation harmed his psi or his higher brain function."

Tamara gaped at him. "Oh my God. Oh my God. Weren't they even going to call an ambulance? What if there hadn't been a Healer here?"

"They would have called an ambulance," Merran replied grimly, "but he would have been in critical condition for a long, long time, until he could manage to fight off the sedatives himself.

He might have died, depending on his will to fight and how quickly they noticed his distress. He certainly had enough sedatives in him to knock out a horse. Greg and I could sense him starting to fail before he showed physical signs of it, which is when I threatened the police. They let us in, finally."

"Where is everyone? It's the middle of the day."

"Those who are not out on the street are watching Greg work. Not that there's much to see, but it's giving everyone quite a show. And more ammunition against us." Merran sounded terribly tired. "I have to get a major PR campaign going. I suppose my effort to get Azellians and humans more comfortable with each other was going to cause a clash like this at some point. I do wish Healers weren't the ones who were the focus of attention, though."

"Healers are the ones who have the least threatening and the most beneficial abilities." Tamara longed to reach out to comfort him, but she didn't dare. Not in public, and especially not with her father in the next room. He seemed to be handling her internship and interest in Azelle really well, but she didn't want to know how he'd react to her having a relationship with an Azellian. Especially not this particular Azellian. "You probably will want to focus on their ethical code too. Are you going to work through the media?"

Merran nodded, his dark eyes distant. "I will have to come up with a method to help Justern and talk about our softer abilities at the same time."

"What's he been arrested for?" She was afraid she already knew that answer.

"Rape." Merran rubbed his cheek. "The girl is quite hysterical, I'm told. Also happens to be the daughter of a trustee."

Her stomach sank. "Does Justern know what happened?"

Merran shook his head. "He's too far gone right now. Greg's completely focused on saving his life, not anything else right now. I just hope his memory is still intact when he recovers, or we're going to have one fine time trying to prove anything at all. Especially without forcing the girl to tell the truth ... and that probably wouldn't be allowed in a courtroom."

A weird sort of relief washed through her. She didn't think he'd done it, but she didn't know Justern that well. "You don't think he did it."

"No. He's not violent, he doesn't have any particular issues with dominance, and he's never forced himself on any woman in his entire life. He may be sarcastic and childish, but he's a telepath and not sadistic. I can't imagine maintaining desire, much less forcing someone when their pain and fear is rebounding back on you, unless you get off on that sort of thing."

"What do you think happened? Why would someone claim rape when it really wasn't?"

"I don't know what happened. I just know Justern. I can't see him raping anyone."

"Could you find out from her what really happened?"

"If she were maliciously accusing Justern of rape, we'd be able to tell she was lying. But finding out what really happened? Alarin could literally force her to tell the truth, or any one of us could read her memories. But that's not admissible in court and won't help Justern in the court case. That's if she's being malicious. If she seriously thinks she was raped, either because she regretted her decision to sleep with Justern or because she was drunk at the time, there isn't much we can do either."

"Could you get her to drop the case? If someone went and talked to her? She doesn't know what you can and can't do."

Merran smiled at her. "I appreciate the effort, Tamara, but I think we'll take the advice of counsel on this one. This is going to go political, so we have to be squeaky clean in how we react to this."

"Do you have rapes on Azelle?"

"No date rape, no." Merran shook his head. "It's all pretty clearcut, mainly because we don't have the issues with sexuality that humans do. The rape that does occur can be worse, far worse than the sexual assault humans call rape, though. There are criminals who use their minds to strip people of anything resembling sanity. Sometimes sex is involved, sometimes not. It's hard to hide when your aura leaves a visible trail on your victim, though, and their aura marks yours. It doesn't happen very often. The person doing it is usually pretty sick and our justice system tends to react quickly and harshly."

Just then, Peter stepped out of the back with Greg beside him. The Healer looked exhausted, grey-skinned, and cadaverous. Dark circles ringed his bloodshot amber eyes, making them look like black pits in his face. He shook like he had palsy. It seemed as if he might pass out at any moment. Merran leaped to his feet but did not touch Greg. Tamara could not sense what was going on between the Healer and the ambassador, but she knew something was.

He'll live, Greg's thought barely reached Merran in response to Merran's query. *I have no idea if there'll be anything left when he wakes up, but he'll live. I need to sleep.*

I'll get you home. When will he regain consciousness? Merran asked, supporting Greg with his telekinesis. Greg sagged, then caught himself with an effort.

In about three hours. Get them to let him out of here. He's not going to run away. He's probably barely going to be able to walk when he wakes up. Or do anything else for a long time. Greg sounded disgusted, his indignation the only thing fueling his ability to walk. Behind Greg and Peter stood a knot of more than twenty people who stared at Greg in a combination of fear and fascination.

I'll work on it. Merran helped him to the embassy car that waited outside. "Take the Healer back to the embassy and put him in my office," he told the driver in Azellian. "I want him in a shielded environment until he wakes up." He sent a brief mental call to Janille, who returned an immediate confirmation.

The driver stood at attention. "Yes, Ambassador. Shall I come back?"

"No, if I need you I'll call. I'm going to be with the attorney for a while."

"Very good, sir." The driver started the car and drove off.

Merran watched the car drive away and turned to Tamara and her father, his eyes sweeping over the two of them. She certainly looked like Peter Carrington's daughter in the shape of her jaw and chin and the cant of her face. Peter's eyes were an ice blue, not the softer grey-blue of Tamara's, with a dark ring around the edges of his pupils. Although his hair was peppered with gray, Tamara did resemble her father enough to tell they were related. He stepped forward to speak to Peter, his hand outstretched.

As Merran extended a hand in a traditional human greeting, Peter offered a low, formalized bow instead. Tamara stared at her father. "Ambassador Corina. It is an honor to meet you," he said in clear, fluid Azellian.

"I thank you for the honor you accord me, Mr. Carrington, but I assure you, you do not need to offer me that level of respect," Merran replied in the same language, eyebrows high. "You are not Azellian, not that any Azellian would offer me that particular bow either."

Peter smiled as he straightened. "I have not seen a Healer at work in twenty years. It was an honor to watch." He continued in Azellian, proving that he did indeed speak the language quite fluently. "Will the Healer be all right?"

"After he gets some sleep, he should be fine." Merran switched back to English. Tamara was grateful for the shift. She had been having a hard time keeping up with the Azellian.

Peter did the same. "And how is Justern? I have my car around the corner. Shall we go to my office? I think we've got some talking to do."

Merran followed Tamara and her father toward Peter's car. "Justern will be awake in a few hours. Whether or not he is able to answer any questions, we will have to wait and see."

Peter frowned at him as he got into the car. "What do you mean?"

Tamara climbed into the back seat, listening intently.

Merran didn't answer until they were in the car with the doors closed. "The police had him drugged enough that he almost died. What kind of brain damage there might be, we don't know yet."

"Do—does he have a family to fight for compensation?" Did her father sound odd?

Merran shrugged. "His mother died in an accident and his father disowned him. Right now, he's living with my sister and her husband, his uncle. If I choose to pursue something, they'll probably join me, but I don't know if they will be willing to contribute anything more than moral support."

The odd note in her father's voice suddenly made itself very apparent. "Would his mother's family be willing to do anything? They are High Council, aren't they?"

Merran didn't seem to notice anything amiss. "Yes. Uzorantxl Dorvath, actually. No, since Jasmian Mennak Dorvath died, they really haven't had anything to do with Justern either."

Peter choked and settled into a fit of coughing as they stopped at the entrance to the parking lot of the large house that served as his law offices.

Tamara leaned forward. "All you all right, Dad? What's wrong?"

"Nothing. I just swallowed the wrong way. I'm fine, I'm fine." He recovered, pulled the car into a parking stall, and cleared his throat. "All right, Ambassador. Let's go inside and figure out what we're going to do." He seemed to pull himself together, leaving Tamara to trail along behind him in confusion. Her father's odd behavior had something to do with the fact that he could speak Azellian and seemed to know more about Azelle than she did. It had to be related, didn't it? She'd never thought her father was particularly fond of Azellians. She'd thought the whole family shared her grandmother's vociferous, vicious opinions about them. To find that her father spoke Azellian—better than she—was a shock. There had to be a reason. She followed Merran and her father into his offices and wondered what he was going to say.

Chapter Eight

AS THEY STEPPED into the office, Peter motioned for Merran to sit across from him. Tamara settled into a chair next to Merran. "Before anything else, I think we should discuss my fee."

Merran leaned back to pull a thin wallet out of his front pocket. He pulled out a card and handed it to Peter. "I am prepared to cover whatever's necessary for Justern's defense. As I mentioned in the car, I'm probably the only one of Justern's relatives and acquaintances who is willing to contribute to his defense."

Peter stared at the card on his desk. "It will be from your private pocket. If I remember correctly, Azelle does not provide for its off-planet citizens should they get in trouble with the law."

Merran smiled. "That hasn't changed."

Peter sniffed and slid the card back at Merran. "Well, I'm willing to take Justern's case for one-quarter my normal fee."

Merran stared at Peter, momentarily speechless. "I can cover whatever is required."

Peter shook his head. "No. In memory of his mother, I will take Justern's case for one-quarter of my normal fee."

Something clicked in the back of Merran's mind. A story. The Dorvath-Memaxthal fiasco. This man's surprising awareness of Azellian and the elaborate language of bows. Justern's hushed-up, tragic history. Justern's father disowning him immediately upon the death of his mother. "This wouldn't be because of twenty years ago, would it?"

Peter's eyes flicked to Tamara, and he looked nervous. Merran could sense the waves of suppressed guilt, worry, fear, and anger that leaked around his up-until-now calm veneer. "Something like that."

Merran leaned toward Tamara. "Tamara, would you mind stepping outside for a moment? I need to ask your father a question I think he would be more comfortable answering in private."

She got up, and though he could sense that she was somewhat irritated by the dismissal, she left.

Merran turned back to Peter as soon as Tamara left and spoke more bluntly than was his normal wont with humans. "Are you Justern's father?"

Peter stared down at his desk. "No."

"But you were the human that nearly upset the entire Uzorantxl Dorvath-Izorantxl Memaxthal clan plans," Merran said, not really framing it as a question. "The young man who was banished from Azelle for having fallen in love with an Azellian."

Peter sighed heavily. "It was a long time ago. When did she die?"

"About ten human years ago."

Peter closed his eyes, his face pale. "I made her life a misery. I didn't mean to, but … we didn't intend on it going as far as it did. We met during Festival."

Merran raised his eyebrows. "That shouldn't have caused a problem. We all know what Festival is like." Although it did surprise him that Peter had been exposed to Festival—most humans were strictly kept away from it—there were a few who could hear the Song that were allowed to participate. A few humans showed up at the embassy doors every year, drawn by the Song and the call to gather, unaware of why they'd been called or what they were doing. They were let in, quietly, and then ushered out, quietly, remaining on the very fringes of the Festival fervor that took all the psi Azellians. Peter had some shielding, and probably some level of psi himself, and from his attitude, obviously knew much more about Festival than Merran would have expected.

"Continuing the relationship after Festival was a problem. For six glorious months we were together. Then her pregnancy started to show and it couldn't be hidden anymore."

"Pregnancy?" Merran frowned. Justern was just a little too young for it to have been him, and Peter had said Justern wasn't his son anyway. "Azellian women don't get pregnant unless they want to."

"She did want to." Peter sighed, opening his eyes. "I tried to talk her out of it, but she said what we had couldn't last and she wanted something of me to remember. So she got pregnant."

"Tamara." Merran rested his fingers on his forehead, everything suddenly becoming clear. "It's Tamara, isn't it? She's half-Azellian."

Peter stared at his hands. "She doesn't know. Jasmian didn't get to keep the baby, although she begged and pleaded. Her family took Tamara away and sent us both back to Earth. Jasmi was married off to a Memaxthal and last I heard was pregnant again within the year. With Justern, I assume."

"You have to tell Tamara."

"The woman who raised her is dying and you tell me I have to tell my daughter that her mother is not who she thinks she is?" Peter's temper flared, overwhelming his shields. "No. I've kept the secret this long. I can keep it longer. I don't care if she finds out that I had a lover before she was born, or that I lived on Azelle, but I will not destroy her view of her mother."

"You are aware of our abilities, I assume, since you know about Festival and you had an Azellian lover?"

"Of course. But they hit at puberty, and Tamara showed no signs of it when she turned thirteen. Nor did she throughout her teen years. I watched her. I'm not without a little talent myself, you know. Enough to hear the Song and enough to—" He stopped and flushed.

Having had both human and Azellian lovers, Merran knew what he had been about to say. "Then you got lucky. However, your luck has run out. Based on what you've just told me, I can assure you that Tamara is Awakening, at twenty, unaware of who she really is or why this is happening to her. She's showing all the symptoms, and we've all been trying to figure out where it's coming from and how to help her."

Peter stared at Merran, going pale. "You're not serious."

"I'm deadly serious. She's been having the flashes of talent, aura flashes, the dreams, and especially the migraines. You have to tell her. It may help her make a smoother transition to being psi. As it is right now, we've been treating her like an Azellian, mainly because we didn't know what else to do, but if she really is … she needs to be told, Peter. And soon."

Peter lifted a shaking hand to his neck. "I don't—how do you tell your daughter she's not who she thought she was?"

"It may be a shock to her, but I think she'll be glad you told her. She's going to be relieved that she's not different, or a freak, that the reason for her Awakening is simply because she's inherited abilities that all Azellians have. She's pretty sharp, and she'll probably figure it out eventually on her own … regardless. But you telling Tamara now will help her come to terms with Awakening that much sooner and help us support her." He paused for a moment, glancing down at his phone. "I'm sorry to have to step out for a moment, but I need to check in with the embassy. We can discuss the battle plan when I get back." Merran got to his feet.

"Can you send Tamara in?"

"Certainly." Merran walked to the door and stepped outside. The look Tamara gave him as he came out of the office spoke volumes about her opinion of his rather high-handed dismissal earlier. He came over to her. "Your father has something he'd like to tell you, Tamara." He left it at that, not at all sure she would be able to listen to an apology. He walked over to the secretary's empty desk, lifting his cell phone and sliding his finger over the screen. As he passed Tamara, he brushed her shoulder with his hand but did not follow it up with anything more.

Tamara, still quite irritated at having been kicked out of the office—she felt like a child who couldn't be told some big secret—ignored him. She got up and went into her father's office.

Her father stood at the window, staring out onto the street. He turned slightly as Tamara came in. "Hi sweetheart. Please, sit."

He was acting so strangely, Tamara felt her anger evaporate. "Dad, what is it?"

"There's something you need to know, honey. It's not easy for me to talk about, so please bear with me. It's been twenty years, but some memories still cut deep." Peter turned back to the window. "Twenty-one years ago, as you probably already have figured out by now, I went to Azelle with my father. I was about your age, and I went against the express wishes of my mother."

Tamara remained silent, sensing that she was about to learn some very big secrets. A tiny part of her exalted in the awareness that Andreya could not possibly break into this conversation. She sat on the chair, watching him intently.

Peter stared out the window as he spoke. "I loved Azelle. The planet, the people, the city. It seemed like nothing could stop me. I refused to listen to my father, who warned me that if I didn't calm down, the Azellians were going to find a reason to eject me. What did he know? I was a nineteen-year-old carefree human whom nothing could stop." Peter turned around to look at Tamara. He looked haunted. "Azelle was beautiful and very free in certain ways that I enjoyed. There was—" He cleared his throat and came to sit on the chair beside her. "There was always a … a woman. Or two. Sometimes more, depending on the night or the party."

Tamara could hardly believe her ears. Her father? Solid, dependable Peter Carrington who she could never imagine being that wild. He had been with her mother so long she couldn't even imagine him having any other girlfriends or lovers.

"It was … intoxicating. Then came the most incredible experience of my life. I don't imagine you've learned of it in school because Azellians tend to keep it pretty quiet, but I ignored my father's orders, as always, to be off planet during that time. It's called Festival, and it's the yearly mating season for the *aarya*, Azelle's other sentient species. That's a very dry explanation for the actual event." Peter paused.

"I've heard about the yearly *aarya* mating season," Tamara put in as he hesitated. "Don't they sing for mates? It seems pretty normal."

Peter smiled. "Yes, they do. But that doesn't even come close to describing what happens." He took a deep breath. "The *aarya* project their mating at every other being on the planet. Those lucky enough to have some psi talent, as all adult Azellians do, and a few humans as well ... no matter what our scientists say ... can hear their song. It absorbs and controls you. Anyone with any psi talent gets pulled into the mating dance."

Tamara shook her head, her mind balking at the idea. It took a rather dramatic effort to bring her brain back on line to listen to his story without reacting to it.

"It's the absolute capstone of Azellian freedom. I wasn't supposed to be on the planet at all, much less participating in Festival. I don't have much psi myself, but I could hear the incredible song. It had ... it had an intense effect on me. I was ... lost in it. So lost I forgot about everything. Everything. It was better than the drugs I tried as a college student. So alluring." Tamara controlled her reaction to that revelation, too, as her father continued, his eyes focused on something far away. She could almost feel the sorrow he had at having lost it too. "A beautiful girl about my age was visiting relatives during that time and we hooked up." He stopped, got to his feet, and went to the little black fridge in the corner, pulling out bottled water. "Do you want some?"

Tamara extended a hand to take the water from her father. She didn't say anything, afraid to break the spell.

"After we recovered our senses, we realized that we had quite a bit in common. We spent all of our spare time together, since I was rather footloose at that time of my life. Her name was—" He stopped again and sipped his water. "Jasmian Mennak Dorvath." He swallowed and Tamara could see the pain etched in his features, a pain she'd seen before but never really understood. "She was supposed to be marrying some man she didn't know from another town. She wasn't happy about it, but there wasn't much she could do to change things. In some ways, Azelle has some archaic remnants."

Something clicked. "Jasmian? Wasn't that Justern's mother's name?"

Peter didn't seem to hear her, but she knew he was talking about the same person. It felt true, like an awareness she'd carried around for years without knowing it. "Well, as we got to know each other better and we got closer, we decided that Jasmian couldn't possibly marry Benaren Memaxthal. We loved each other too much. We were full of plans to run away, to come to Earth. If you think it's hard now to get a visa, back then, it was virtually impossible for someone not connected to the embassy itself to get a visa to come to Earth or vice versa. My father was the only reason I made it to Azelle at all." He folded his arms across his chest and frowned. "I tried to get her a visa, but it didn't work. Short of stowing away, she was not going to get off the planet. I even went to my father, who advised me to stop seeing her. Azellians and humans never succeed, he told me, because our cultures are too radically different and there were far too many pressures from families for it to ever work." He sighed. "Jasmian knew we couldn't last. She told me she wanted to get pregnant, so she could have something of mine forever."

Tamara stared at him, not quite sure she wanted to process what he was saying. Why that would make Justern—it wasn't possible. He couldn't be her half-brother. He certainly looked nothing like her father, although he did bear some resemblance to herself, now that she thought about it.

"I loved her too much to argue with her, so I agreed. I don't know how she did it, but she hid the pregnancy from everyone around us until she started really showing at six months, when it became very obvious. Our relationship came out, and everything we feared would happen, did." Peter closed his eyes and swallowed again. He continued the story with his eyes closed. "Her family went wild. If abortion had been an option at that point, I think they would have forced her to do it. But, as it was not an option, she was allowed to carry to term. She wanted to keep the baby and begged to be allowed to raise it. I was pretty much confined to the embassy at that point. Guards actually watched the doors to be sure I didn't leave. Somehow, though, she managed to get messages to me and that's how I knew what was happening. Her family wouldn't hear of her keeping the baby; she was to go to Benaren Memaxthal as soon as the baby was born, and it would all be hushed up. I went to my father and told him what had happened. Father went to the families involved and the Azellian Council and managed to get them to agree to send me home as long as I took my daughter with me."

Tamara was listening so hard to the story that she almost missed the import of his words. "Your daughter?" She grabbed the chair arm so hard she lost the feeling her hands. "I have a sister?"

Peter shook his head. He uncrossed his arms and crouched down in front of her. "No, sweetheart." His voice was soft and gentle. "The baby was you. If you had been named according to Azellian custom, you would have been called Tamara Dorvath Carrington. Instead of getting something of mine to keep forever, I got something of hers. And that young man in jail is your half-brother."

Tamara swallowed hard. "You—I—I'm half-Azellian?"

"I would have told you sooner, but ... I didn't know how. I met your mo—stepmother when you were two. We agreed that the fact you weren't her biological daughter was irrelevant. When you went through puberty without showing any signs of Awakening, I thought I had gotten away with it and my secret would remain an irrelevant piece of information lying around the family history somewhere. But the ambassador just told me that it appears you are Awakening, that you haven't understood why, and that I needed to tell you the truth."

Tamara closed her eyes, her breath coming fast and hard. *Do not hyperventilate*, a little voice said in her head. *Do not—need to slow down. Take deep breaths. Justern is my half-brother, just not as I thought. We share a mother, not a father.* The thought almost made her giggle. Or cry. *The man—boy—who has been accused of rape, who almost died from his treatment by the cops, is my brother. A year younger than I am. Andreya is my half-sister. And Dad, who I thought had only ever loved my moth—stepmother, actually loved someone else enough to agree to get her pregnant so she would have something to remember him by, but only to lose me anyway.* She could feel the tears build. One thought dashed across her mind as she wrenched her mind away from the frenzied circling. *I am not a freak. I have psi because ... I am Azellian. I am Azellian. I am not a freak. I am Azellian.*

Her father had not moved as these thoughts bolted across her mind, as she sat there trying not to throw up, or cry, or laugh, trying to assimilate everything she'd been told.

The world settled into an unreal place. "Thank you for telling me, Dad." She stood up a little unsteadily. "I think I need to go see Mom for a while. Does she ... know? Who I am, I mean?"

Peter shook his head. "Only that I had a daughter when we

met. Not who your mother was. My mother knew, though. I'm sorry, Tammy. I thought maybe she'd learn in time to forgive and to forget. I'd hoped that maybe with exposure—"

Tamara shook her head, holding her hand up. "I need to think. Let me know what you and the ambassador decide to do with Justern. I need to process ... everything."

Peter stood up, giving her space. "Do you need a ride back to campus?"

"No. I want to walk. It's not far." Tamara gave him a smile, almost afraid she was going to break somewhere between the door and the street. "I'll send the ambassador back in." She looked at her watch. "We only have an hour before Justern is supposed to wake up." She knew her father watched her as she left, but she pulled the door closed quietly behind her and didn't look back.

Merran leaned against her father's secretary's desk. He studied Tamara as she came out of the room. "You are strong enough for this, *akila-ala*. If you need someone to talk to, call the embassy. Janille will be able to find me no matter where I am, and I'll come."

A ghost of a smile pulled Tamara's lips up as she headed for the door. "Thank you, Merran." He straightened and started to walk toward her father's office door. "Oh, Merran?"

"Hmm?" He turned, his hand on the doorknob.

"What do you keep calling me? *Akila?* What does *akila-ala* mean?"

He smiled. "I'll tell you later when we have more time."

She had to be content with that. It wasn't hard, given how many other things she had to think about already.

✻ ✻ ✻

Tamara wandered around the streets of Denver for an hour, intending to head back toward campus, but not quite getting there. She walked by the embassy and stared up at the beautiful mansion. She was Tamara. Who was that? Not the unwanted, bastard girl who was born before her parents were married—although technically, she was still a bastard, since she didn't think her father had married her mother before she was born. But there was no question that she had been wanted. Desperately. Her mother—it felt alien to call someone else that, other than the woman who had raised her—had wanted her so badly she was willing to defy everything she knew to have a child. Only her mother didn't get to have her. What did that make her, Tamara? She was half-Azellian. She was Awakening. She was the sister of an Azellian. She was psi. She was in love with an Azellian. That last thought made her stop in her tracks. Well, maybe that one was jumping the gun a bit. She *could* be in love with an Azellian. Azelle certainly seemed to dominate her life even though she had never been there—that she could remember, she amended. She had been born there apparently. Tamara shivered, wrapping her arms around herself as she started to walk away from the embassy.

"Tamara?" The voice was familiar. Tamara turned to see Alarin coming out of the gates. "Are you headed back toward campus?" He joined her.

"Eventually. Were you visiting the embassy?"

Alarin looked tired, although she couldn't pinpoint exactly what it was about his demeanor that made her think that. He looked the same as he always did. "Checking on Greg."

"How is he?"

"Still sleeping. After healing that deeply, he's probably going to sleep for a week."

She stared at him, suddenly not sure if he was joking or not. Nothing seemed quite normal at the moment. "You're kidding, right?"

Alarin shook his head. "No. Normally the kind of healing Greg did is handled by two or three Healers, not just one. He depleted his energy reserves almost completely to Heal Justy. He also did something very dangerous. To siphon the drugs out of Justern, he absorbed them into himself. I don't expect he'll do much more than sleep for the next week or so. We're probably going to have to move him to Merran's apartment tonight, since I don't think the embassy can have its ambassador's office taken up by a snoring bulk, Healer or not."

Tamara fell in beside him as he headed toward campus. Something about Alarin's presence was relaxing, maybe because she could think of something else other than her world ending and her sense of identity shifting. "Why those two places?" she asked, very aware that he'd mentioned them for a reason.

Alarin glanced over at her. He was slightly shorter than Merran, she suddenly noticed, but because he was thinner than Merran it felt as though he was just as tall. "Because they're shielded and Greg doesn't have the energy to shield himself right now. He's pretty vulnerable."

"What happens if he isn't shielded?"

"He goes psi blind or dies from overload." Alarin's voice remained unemotional and flat, but goose bumps crawled over her skin.

"What about Justern, then? Is he going to need a shielded place, too?"

"And then some. After what he went through, Justern is going to be lucky if he has any psi left at all."

Tamara fell silent, musing over that statement as they walked. It reminded her of her own situation and her new relationship with Justern, and she suddenly wanted to share it with someone. Over the past couple of months, Alarin had become something of a friend, somewhat less threatening than Merran, maybe because they weren't involved with each other. There had been small hints over the past few months when they studied together of a subtle attraction, but he'd never pushed those moments and an odd sort of trust had begun to develop. She took a deep breath. Telling him might put it into perspective. "Alarin? Have you ever found out something that turns your world upside down? Like finding out you're not who you thought you were?"

He seemed to snap out of his mood. His glance was curious. "No, I can't say as I have. What do you mean? Did you learn something about yourself?"

"Yeah. I'm—I'm uh, I'm half-Azellian." Tamara blurted it out. It made her pause and think to herself. *That feels so weird to say. Like I'm not really ... and that Dad's just going to laugh and tell me he's kidding. Of course, I'm my mother's daughter. But then, where would this frustrating Awakening have come from if not because I'm actually Azellian?*

Alarin said nothing, stopping in the street to study her. She couldn't feel his mind against hers, but she had the sudden impression he was somehow using those psi abilities. She stood under his scrutiny until she couldn't stand it anymore. Feeling jittery, she started to walk again. He followed her. "It certainly explains a lot. Did you just find this out?"

"Yes. And there's more. Justern is my half-brother." She had to say the rest of it. *How many impossible things can you believe before breakfast?* She spoke to Alarin silently, suppressing a slightly hysterical giggle. *Of course, it's not breakfast, so maybe they're more believable.* She pushed the irrelevant thoughts out of her mind.

"Well, is that so?"

"My father is going to be his attorney." She couldn't seem to stop the startling thoughts. *Maybe it is breakfast. I'm certainly being asked to believe the unbelievable.*

That made him raise both eyebrows. "Really. I assume you share a mother, since Justern is most definitely a Memaxthal?"

"Yeah. Can you believe it?"

Alarin shook his head, but the motion seemed more as though he were trying to clear his head than respond to her question. "Are you going to tell him?"

"Justern?" At his nod, she shrugged. "I don't know. Should I?"

"Would you want to know?"

"Yeah ... yeah, I guess I would."

Alarin spread his hands in a "see?" gesture.

"But how?" Tamara started walking again. "How do I go up to someone I don't really know all that well? I've been spending hours and hours with you and Greg and Merran and Mellis, but Justern ... I really don't know him well ... except that he makes snide comments in anthro studies class that make the whole class laugh. Do I say to him, 'Oh by the way, you're my brother? Do you want to go get a sandwich?'"

Alarin laughed. "Sure. Tell him in that way. He might get a kick out of it."

"What way? Oh, I don't know you, but you're my brother?"

Alarin's grin widened. "Don't forget the sandwich part."

Tamara sighed, but a smile edged in. "All right. You're right. I guess it doesn't have to be that complicated."

Alarin reached out and brushed his fingertips gently across the back of her hand. "Look at it this way. What does you being

Azellian really change, except your outer view of yourself? You're still you, even if that doesn't quite feel the way it did before. The inner self hasn't changed any, and neither has the outer self really. You're Awakening ... we know that now for certain ... and now you have a genetic reason for it. And knowing that makes Greg's and my job to train you much easier, as there is a certain predictability to how your psi will react. You're still an intern at the embassy. What has really changed?"

Tamara sighed again, liking his perspective, but not really accepting it yet. "Yeah, but my mother ... my stepmother actually ... isn't who I thought she was."

Alarin cocked his head and shrugged. "Does that change the love she gave you? Or the love you have for her? Who says the only ones we can love have to be genetically related to us? It would be an extremely inbred universe if that were so."

That startled a laugh out of her.

"Instead of looking at what you've lost, look at what you've gained. You just gained a brother ... something I remember you somewhat wistfully remarking that you would have liked to have when you were talking to me about your sister last week. You've gained the truth about your past, and with that, you can begin to deal with it. You've grown, changed, taken steps toward maturity."

Tamara gave him a wry look. "I'm not sure I want to grow. Even if it does mean I now have a brother."

Alarin smiled, then said thoughtfully, his mind obviously miles away, "You're High Council on your mother's side."

"And this means?"

Alarin ran his fingers along his jaw line. "Not much, except that you're occupying a place very similar to Merran. High Council on one side, not High Council on the other." He shook himself. "Never mind. It doesn't matter."

Tamara suspected there was more to his comment, but she also knew how close-mouthed Alarin could be when he didn't want to talk about something. She'd learned that much about him over the past two months.

They reached her dorm. "Look. I gotta go," he said." I've got a class to catch. See you later?"

"Alarin, wait."

He glanced over his shoulder at her.

"Thanks."

"You're welcome." He strode away. Tamara went into the building and headed up to her room.

Her phone buzzed at her as she walked into her room, telling her she had a message. Frowning, she pulled the cell phone out of her pocket.

It was her father. "Tamara, Merran and I are at the hospital. Justern has been moved to Room 504. If you want to come down, we are at Denver Mercy. He will be kept here for observation for a few days, then released on bail until his court case." Tamara smiled to herself. How odd that her father had called her with the information. It was almost as though the whole universe was telling her that she should tell Justern. The least she could do was go down there and see how he was doing.

She found Room 504 with a little difficulty. The room occupied a wing away from the other rooms and was guarded.

A uniformed policewoman sat at a small table at the entrance to the wing. "Room number?" she asked as Tamara came forward.

"504."

The officer looked down at the list in front of her. "Name?"

"Tamara Carrington to see Justern Memaxthal." Tamara felt her pulse speed up, especially as she could see yet another pair of guards by the door that must be 504. They were treating Justern like he was a dangerous criminal.

"You aren't on the list." The guard looked back up at Tamara, her expression cold. As she spoke, Tamara looked down the hall, hoping her father or Merran would come out. Suddenly, the door between the two guards opened and Merran stepped out. The guards twitched and did not relax even slightly as Merran came out of the room.

Tamara took a deep breath, hoping Merran would notice her. He did, turning and walking toward where she stood. Tamara spoke to the policewoman. "Peter Carrington and Ambassador Corina asked me to come. The ambassador is right there."

The guard shook her head, a line appearing between her brows. "He did not announce any visitors, and I don't have you on the list, Ms. Carrington. Unless you have been authorized, I cannot let you in."

Merran came up behind the policewoman. "I'll vouch for her. We did ask her to come."

The guard scowled up at Merran. "You need to announce any visitors, Ambassador. Or make sure you clear her on the list."

Merran smiled down at her. "I apologize, Officer," he said in a smooth, polished tone Tamara was beginning to associate with the Ambassador of Azelle. He offered her a bow. "I am very sorry for the confusion. I am not used to your conventions. I will be certain to announce visitors or clear them first in the future."

The policewoman eyed him like she thought he might be making fun of her, but after a moment, she waved them through, taking refuge in her irritability, yet unable to find offense in his behavior.

Tamara didn't say anything as they walked down the hall toward the other two guards standing completely still at the door. The guards stared straight ahead as the two of them entered the room. She would have said something once Merran closed the door behind them, but the figure lying on the bed immediately drew Tamara's eyes away from him. Far paler than she'd ever seen any Azellian or human before, Justern lay under a sheet with eyes closed, his eyes bruised looking and his lips white and dry, obviously beginning to peel. A bag of fluid and a tube attached to his arm dripped the fluid slowly into his bloodstream. Tubes ran up his nose; Tamara traced the tubes to a tank of what must be oxygen. His skin had an unhealthy yellow tinge—*is he really out of the woods?* she wondered. Peter sat at a table not far from the bed, surrounded by papers.

She turned and left the room hastily, unable to stay inside. Silently, Merran followed her, leading her to a bench a little way down the hall away from the guards at the door. She sat and stared at the floor, trying to process what she'd just seen. "How is he? Really?" Tamara asked after a few moments of silence. "He looks about three steps away from death."

Merran shrugged and managed a slight smile. "He looks about one hundred percent better than he did last night. Greg says he will be fine. Physically anyway."

Tamara glanced at the guards and lowered her voice to a whisper. "What about his, you know? Any brain damage?"

Merran shook his head. "Don't know yet. He opened his eyes an hour ago when he was first transferred, but he hasn't said anything."

"So we don't know? What about, you know?"

"He's shielded, heavily, which is a very good sign, but I can't tell for sure. He could be shielding the way you do, subconsciously, and it's all gone latent. We don't know how much he remembers either. I'm pretty sure he's awake in there, but he's refusing to interact in any way. Based on that, I suspect he remembers quite a bit. Justern's pretty sensitive. I don't know how he's going to react to an accusation of rape." He ran a hand through his hair. "I wish Greg were functional."

"What could Greg do?"

"There are certain things a Healer can tell without having the patient's acquiescence. Like whether or not his brain has been physically damaged. It won't help us with any psychological damage, of course, but at least we'd be able to start somewhere." Merran brushed his hand through his hair again, a gesture Tamara was starting to realize was an exasperated or nervous one on his part.

An idea popped into her head, a feeling. If she were in Justern's boat, she'd want to know that there was support for her, that someone cared. Maybe that was all he needed. "Let me talk to him."

"I don't know if Justern can handle any new information right now." Merran looked down at her, his dark eyes studying her. "He's got enough to deal with and memories of his mother are not going to help. There's just too much pain right now."

Tamara scowled. "He's got no one, Merran. No one at all. He probably feels more alone right now than he ever has in his entire life. It can't hurt to tell him I do care, no matter the reason for it."

Merran got to his feet abruptly. "Well, it's better than him lying there like a lump. All right, if you can get him to open up, then be my guest." Tamara followed him over to the door. He held the door open for her and walked in behind her. Merran went up to her father and leaned down to say something to him.

Peter looked up and frowned. Tamara just looked at him, pleading with her eyes. Peter looked from Merran to Tamara and back again and finally nodded. Without a word, he got up and followed Merran from the room.

Tamara walked closer and stared at the young man lying on the bed. Dark hair hung limp around his dirty, sweat-soaked face. Dark lashes lay against his pale cheek. She pulled a chair closer and sat beside him. "Hi, Justern. It's Tamara. You don't have to wake up. I don't mind. I just came to see how you're doing." She was silent for a moment, studying him carefully, thinking about the tone she wanted to take. Although her psi wasn't online, something told her that Justern was indeed aware of what she was saying. She snorted. "Well, if I go by appearances, you're not doing all that great, I'd say. You're lying in a hospital bed with tubes stuck up you. If I were in your position, I don't think I'd be too happy either." She couldn't help but grin. "Of course, there are worse places they could have stuck the tubes." Her eyes wandered down the bed. "Unless they did that too. Ugh. I'm told it hurts like hell."

A small noise made her jump. Her eyes flew back to his face. His blue eyes were open and focused on her. When he spoke, it was a hoarse whisper. "It does."

Tamara leaned closer, resting her arms on the bed. "Really? How bad?" *He's talking. This is good, right?* she asked herself.

"Like someone stuck a burning match up my penis." He coughed a little, cleared his throat, and sounded a little stronger. "But then it just matches the burning in my head. And my throat. And everywhere else. Come to think of it, maybe it's not so bad."

Tamara grinned, relaxing against the back of her chair. "What, didn't you want to participate in the torture session known as the hospital?"

"I think the next time I'll pass." Justern turned his head a little, as far as the tubes up his nose would allow. "What are you doing here?"

"Visiting. Checking to see if you need me to bring you your homework assignments next week."

Justern's face spasmed at that. He closed his eyes. "Thank you, but I don't know that I'm going to be needing those."

Tamara thought frantically, *What is he referring to? The accusation against him? Or that he doesn't think he is going to live?* "This will be over in no time, Justy. I can help you keep up."

Justern opened his eyes again. She suddenly realized that it was like looking in a mirror. So similar to her own. Changeable, blue-grey eyes, a ring of dark on the outer edge of the iris. Were her own eyes the inheritance of that mother she'd never known? She suddenly was desperate to spend as much time as she could with Justern. He was her only connection to a woman who had helped form her, who had given her what? Eyes? Psi talents? What else? "Why would you do that?" He turned away. "If I'm lucky, I'm going to get my ass kicked right back to Azelle."

He did remember. "Justy, my father is a defense attorney. He's going to be representing you. You've only been accused, not convicted."

Those eyes, so similar to her own, met hers with a force she didn't expect. A faint frown ghosted between his eyebrows. "That's as good as a conviction, Tamara."

Tamara picked up his limp hand. "Not if you didn't do it. And I know you didn't, so you don't have anything to worry about. I mean that."

His fingers twitched in hers. "I already know that society decides long before courts get in there, and what society judges, stands."

"We can still fight it, Justy. And we will. Especially if you remember what happened and we can counter her claims." Tamara squeezed his hand. "Please don't give up."

"I remember." Justern pulled his hand away. "The little *sheei* did everything she could to throw herself at my head. For weeks. I knew what she was. I knew. So I avoided her, told her no. Slept with her friends, but not her."

"You didn't sleep with her at all? How did she manage to get an accusation in against you? Enough that the cops really thought you were the one?"

"I was stupid. I got drunk." Justern closed his eyes. Tamara gasped, horrified to see tears leaking out the corners of his eyes.

"I thought Azellians couldn't get drunk." She reached for his hand again, unable not to touch him. He seemed to need it so badly.

"Oh, we can. It takes a fucking lot of it, but we can." Justern opened his eyes. Despite the moisture at the edges of his eyes, he looked calm enough. "She came at me. I didn't resist. I don't remember it that clearly. I know that I wasn't particularly functional, but she did manage to get enough out of me that I'm sure she has plenty of evidence."

"Oh my God. You didn't rape her ... she raped you." Tamara lifted a shaking hand and brushed his hair out of his face.

That made him cough. "I suppose. But it's hard to make that accusation when I was drunk off my ass and I didn't say no. Of course, it didn't stop her from doing to me what she's apparently accusing me of doing to her."

"Then the cops came and pumped you full of sedatives. Oh God, Justern, no wonder you almost died!" Tamara held his hand up against her face, tears running down her cheeks. "And no wonder you look like someone ran over you with a truck." She hugged his hand to her.

Justern turned to look at her, a strange expression on his face. "If I didn't know you had it bad for Merran, I'd think you were actually coming on to me."

Tamara shook her head, wiping her tears away and releasing his hand. "Haven't you ever had anyone care what happened to you who didn't want to sleep with you?"

"No." Justern looked away.

"What about your ... mother? You can't tell me she wanted to sleep with you."

"My mother died when I was ten," Justern replied flatly. "And with it went everyone who cared about me."

No wonder Merran had said there was pain there. What he hadn't said was the depth of the pain. Tamara could see it in every breath he took. "No other siblings? Father? No one?"

"My parents fought too much to ever have any more children after me." Justern still sounded flat and uninterested. "My father decided I was the cause of my mother's death and abandoned me. No other siblings. Although—"

"Although what?" Tamara breathed, prompting him. Had their mother told Justern about her? Or had she hurt too much to tell him anything?

"My mother used to pretend with me. Pretend that I did have a sister. An older sister who would be there when I needed her, who would rescue me from whatever mess I made for myself. Sometimes Mother would cry and tell me that she pretended she had a daughter too."

Tamara's eyes welled up again, although she couldn't stop the tiny frisson from crawling up her spine. *My mother. Justern is talking about my mother,* she said to herself, a sense of wonder spilling through her.

"What was she like?" Tamara couldn't help herself from asking—for herself as well as for him. Memories of his ... their ... mother seemed to relax him a little, despite what Merran had said.

"Gentle ... loving. She would have done anything for me. She did do everything for me. I was the only reason in the world she continued fighting. One of the reasons my father abandoned me after her death, I think. Because she loved me, not him." Justern didn't notice Tamara's tears as he continued in a dreamy tone. "She had brown hair and grey eyes like mine. She was sad most of the time. She told me once about a man she had loved, a man who had to go away, and it broke her heart. She didn't love my father and he knew it. It took me a long, long time to understand it myself, although I'm glad she had some happiness in her life." His eyes cleared and he continued in a different tone. "Once she died, I was alone."

Tamara shook her head. Her nose was running, but she didn't want to break the spell. "You're not alone, Justern."

"You believe friends are family? Spoken by someone who has family. It's not quite the same thing." His voice sounded brittle.

"I'm not talking about that," she said quietly, making the decision to tell him. Alarin had been right. "My father told me a story today. About how he went to Azelle and fell in love with a woman. They had a baby and she was forced to give her daughter up, because her family wanted her to marry someone else." Tamara met his eyes steadily. "That daughter was me. What if the story your mother always told you was not pretend, but true?"

Justern stared at her. His breathing became rapid, as if he were gasping for breath. He coughed and writhed in pain for a moment. "You can't be serious."

"I'm Awakening. You tell me. Do I look like her?"

Justern studied her face. The scrutiny was intense and uncomfortable. "I don't know." He closed his eyes. Tears spilled from the corners of them again. "Please, leave me alone."

Tamara did as he asked, getting to her feet, her own tears streaming down her face. She wiped her nose on her hand and left the room.

Merran and her father were standing not far outside the door. Both of them saw her and nearly dropped their coffees. "Tamara, are you all right?" The alarm and worry in Peter's voice made her smile. Justern was right. She was very glad she had her father—and her stepmother—and even though she was a royal pain, her sister as well. Merran would have reached her, but because he held back for a split second, her father got there first. "Is Justern all right? Merran told me you were talking, so we stayed out here. What happened?"

Tamara sniffed and wiped at her nose again. "He's awake and he remembers everything."

"That's not why you're crying, honey. Or is it?" Peter put an arm around her shoulders as Merran came up and handed her the handkerchief he pulled from somewhere. Tamara blew her nose.

"Justern is innocent," she said as she tucked the handkerchief in a pocket. "She'd been pursuing him, he refused her, then she got to him when he was drunk. She was the aggressor in the whole thing, Dad."

Peter slipped back into attorney mode. "Any witnesses to that effect? Is he ready to talk about it?"

"I don't know. I also don't know if he's going to want to talk to you. I, uh, told him who I was. Who you are is going to be pretty obvious." Tamara bit her lip. "We were talking about his mother, and it came out."

Peter didn't say anything, his gaze riveted to the door. Tamara looked at Merran, suddenly wondering if he was mad at her. There was a look she was starting to recognize, a slightly distracted look that told Tamara he was hearing something Peter and Tamara could not.

His eyes cleared after a moment. "Justern would like to see you, Peter. Alone."

Tamara watched as her father squared his shoulders and put his hand on the door. When he went in, his chin was high and his shoulders back. Tamara never did know how much it cost Peter to walk into that room to face the son of his rival.

"Are you mad at me?" Tamara asked in a small voice when her father had been gone for a few moments. She was shaking, she realized with some surprise. Had she just made a terrible mistake?

Merran shook his head and smiled at her. "No, *akila*. I just think the timing could have been better. Justern's gone through quite a bit already."

"And he needed to know he's not alone. He's feeling pretty beat up." She sounded more confident than she felt.

"You could have done that as a friend too." Merran cocked his head and looked at her. "Why did you choose now, Tamara? Was it really for Justern's sake?"

Tamara shivered, her stomach clenched. "I don't want to lose my only connection with a mother I never knew." She closed her eyes as the awareness filtered in through her. *It wasn't only for Justern's sake. Have I done a horrible thing? I hope not.*

Merran touched her shoulder gently but did nothing else. "It's all right, Tamara. The words have been said and cannot be unsaid. It remains to be seen if Justern is going to be pleased or not that he has a sister, or if he's willing to accept anything from his mother's lover, but at least you know why you did it."

Tamara shivered. "That's pretty cold comfort if I just ruined his life some more."

"Sometimes that's all we have. I don't think you did just ruin his life, if that makes you feel any better. If it were me, I would want to know. You are his family and he's always thought he had none."

"How's it going in there?"

He gave her an arch look. "Do you think we Azellians aren't taught any better than that? Would I eavesdrop?"

Tamara shrugged. "I would if I could."

Merran smiled slightly. "Justern's shielding within an inch of his life and your father's always hard to read."

"So you would too, if you could?" Tamara pounced on his phrasing. "Speaking of Justern, how is he really? You know, deep in his head?"

"Fine as far as I could tell. In pain, but clear enough. Greg will be pleased to hear that. Once he wakes up."

Tamara looked up at him. "Alarin told me you were going to have to move Greg to your apartment."

Merran leaned slightly toward her, a smile tugging at his mouth. "Probably."

"That's going to curtail nights like last night." Tamara blinked at him coyly. He was standing far enough away from her that she didn't think anyone would notice the change in their conversation.

"Unless you want the Azellian ambassador showing up at your dorm room and titillating all the young girls. My face is a little too well known."

"Now that we know for certain, maybe when Greg recovers we should just get this over with and trigger my Awakening." Tamara dropped her eyes to his stomach, where the belt cinched his dress pants to his waist. She followed a crease on his shirt up his tie to his neck.

She watched his breath catch. He was not unmoved by her deliberate teasing, which made her feel good. "The reasons I wanted Alarin to do it are still valid."

"I don't think Alarin's the one who can trigger it. I like him, but he's a friend." She met his eyes. They were slightly dilated and very, very dark. "I'm not just talking about Awakening here, you realize."

Merran closed his eyes. "I know." His voice sounded strangled. "Tamara, I—I don't know. I want to, more than you can imagine, but I never would have let it go so far as last night if I'd known Justern was going to get arrested." He took a deep breath and visibly pulled himself together. "Let's deal with things one at a time, shall we? Because of the political nature of this case, I suspect Justern is going to be on trial soon. Depending on how the case turns out, we may all be recalled to Azelle. I don't—I don't want to start something with you that I might not be able to finish, and my dream to have an exchange might very well be dust."

Tamara stared at him as the import of what he said sank in. "No, no, no." She could feel the blood drain from her face and her head begin to spin. "No, no, no. You can't go. The students might be sent back, but not you too. We've had an embassy here for fifty years! Why would they recall all of you?"

"It depends on the outcome of the court case, Tamara. If Just-ern's falsely accused and the courts uphold that accusation, then the Council is going to be mightily insulted. I suspect a dramatic gesture is going to be their choice. This isn't the first time things like this have happened, but the Council may decide it's the last." Merran clenched his fist. "I'm going to argue with them, but they do have the final say."

Tamara touched the wall to brace herself. "If they withdraw their embassy, they're also going to refuse any visa requests, aren't they?"

"Oh, they're definitely going to do that, at least temporarily. The embassy withdrawal is iffier. Considering they'll have us to replace if they decide to open up relations with Earth again."

"So I won't be able to see you again?"

"If I got reassigned to another planet, say Ather, for instance, we could work around the restrictions. But there are too many variables. I don't want to tie you up and prevent you from enjoy-ing your life, Tamara. If the embassy is withdrawn, we can't have a relationship. It's going to be complicated enough if we're not re-called. You're not just a one night fling, Tamara." One side of his mouth pulled up. "So as I said, let's see what happens, shall we? I do agree that we need to trigger your Awakening as soon as Greg feels well enough, but let's see when that is and where we're at. The Council may be more reasonable than I expect, and none of this may come to pass. One step at a time, okay?"

Tamara could feel tears threatening and she didn't want to break down again. Not in front of Merran and not with her father ready to come out of the room at any second. "Fine." She looked down at the ground and worked frantically to find something else to think about. *The lecture from class yesterday. Don't remember last night. Don't remember Justern. Don't remember my mother—either one of them. The lecture from class yesterday.* Focusing on her professor's droning voice did help, and she pulled herself together.

Her father walked out of Justern's room just as Tamara straightened up and pushed her hair back. Peter looked tired.

"What happened, Dad?" Tamara brushed past Merran, who did not move.

Peter blew his breath out in a sigh. "Well, he's going to work with me. Unfortunately, this is not going to be easy. The girl is the daughter of a very influential trustee, and she does have physical evidence that they had intercourse. So I'm going to have to say it was consensual. No witnesses, his word against hers. Apparently, the times she came on to him and he refused her, he doesn't remember any witnesses being around. I don't know that I can prove she was the aggressor, so I'm going to have to say she agreed to it. The level of alcohol in Justern's system when the cops came was pretty high—toxic to any human—but the blood test for that is probably going to be thrown out of court because the sedatives the police shot him up with are very similar and invalidate the blood test. It comes down to his word against hers, and in cases like this, I'm afraid the judge and jury are going to be heavily biased in her favor. I'll try to work the jury the best I can, but a pretty young thing who can turn on waterworks in court is going to have most of the court on her side." Peter looked at Merran. "What's your government going to do if this case goes against Justern?"

"I'd rather discuss this in the car or at your office. Justy's asleep, so why don't we take it outside?"

Peter nodded, and the three of them walked downstairs. No one said anything until they reached the car, each lost in their individual thoughts.

Once they'd gotten into the car, Merran turned to face Peter. "I have talked to the Council liaison for the embassy. The Council wants to know the truth in this. If Justern did rape her, they are willing to let this go with whatever punishment is afforded to him. If he did not, they want a formal apology from the girl and her father. How far this will go depends on human reaction."

Peter made a face. "I know of the girl's father. No matter what he believes privately, he will support his daughter. I doubt we will get an apology out of them unless it is proven in court that Justern didn't do it. And I have a feeling that's not going to happen, unless Justern puts on a better show than she does." He sighed. "I know enough of Azellian law to know that the Council will not accept the court's decision as the decider of truth in this. How did they say they want you to determine the truth?"

"You probably already know the answer to that. They want me to get both their memories of the event, if I have to rip it out of them. Justern's won't be a problem even though it's alcohol hazed, but the girl's? I can't see it happening."

"Not unless it's court ordered, and as the courts don't accept your abilities in the first place, I think we're pretty safe in thinking it's not going to happen." Peter thumped his hand on the wheel. "What then?"

"The Council will make a decision based on Justern's memories of the event alone. I highly doubt Justern is lying about any of this. He knows what the Council does to establish guilt, and all of us learn very young how to keep things as clear as possible. The cloudier the memory, the more likely the Council is to decide that the whole thing has been rewritten and determine that the memories are lies."

"Who will read his memories?"

"Probably one of my staff. I'm too closely related to Justern in this case. He's my sister's nephew. If they feel this is big enough, the Council will send someone. That part isn't the problem. It's the near-death drugging that they just might take as a colossal insult. They'll recall all of us, the embassy included, and close down all visas to or from Azelle."

Peter shook his head. "It can't get that far, even if the case against Justern does go badly. I doubt humans will let it. Too many humans are going to want access to Healers, after what the whole precinct watched the Healer do. As afraid of possible Azellian talents as we humans are, we're also jealous of them, and I know the medical community would drool to get ahold of a Healer." He rubbed his chin, leaning his arm against the steering wheel. "All right, we go after the police then. Suspected criminal or not, Justern should never have been treated that way. The state he was in when we found him? The Healer had to deal with some physical abuses as well as the drugged state. After Justern was stabilized, I took pictures of the physical injuries, before the Healer healed them. It will be easier to convince the Council it wasn't all humans, especially if you work on the media. They're already watching the case because Justern's an Azellian. We can do some damage control and make sure the Council doesn't recall the whole embassy, or the other Azellian students. I will file a lawsuit with the courts against the police. Maybe we can even get the police to stop drugging Azellians."

Merran shook his head, an odd kind of relief washing through him at the thought there might be a compromise position. "There is unfortunately not a whole lot humans can do to restrain us. But we might be able to work something out. I just hate the idea that Justern is going to be a casualty."

"Let's take things one step at a time. We might yet win this. When Justern is released, I'm going to offer my house as a place he can stay. They won't allow the embassy because it's not human property, and I think he needs to stay away from campus for a while. I'll get a request for bail to be set first thing Monday morning. You handle the PR, and I'll get the paperwork ready to file a case against the police. Tamara, did you want to go back to campus or home?"

"Campus. As much as I hate to remember, I do have homework. And the others are going to want to know what happened." She took a breath. "Dad, what about Grandma?"

Peter turned on the car. "I think maybe it's time for Grandma to go home for a while."

Tamara hardly dared breathe. Her grandmother did not live with them normally—she had just never left after her mother got sick. Would her father stand up to her? He never had before, at least not overtly.

"Don't worry about it, Tammy. I'll take care of it tonight. I don't think she's going to want to be around when the house is full of Azellians." Peter backed the car out of the parking stall.

"What about Mom?"

Peter glanced at Merran.

Merran studied him for a moment. "Maybe once Greg's feeling better, he can have a look at her. If you'd like."

Peter nodded once. "That would not be refused."

The drive back to campus and the embassy was not far. Peter dropped Tamara off first. She got out of the car, wanting to say something to Merran, but in the presence of her father and not knowing what she might say that would be helpful, she remained silent. She watched them drive off, praying briefly that things would turn out all right.

She made her way to Alarin's room first, figuring they would want to know.

Alarin answered the door on the first knock. "See, Mel, it is Tamara." His greeting was actually a comment to Mellis, who was sitting behind him. "I bet she was visiting with Justern and her father." He stood back to let her in.

Tamara stepped into the room. Mellis was sprawled on Alarin's bed, her face and eyes red. She looked at Tamara and got to her knees. "Have you seen him?"

Tamara nodded. "He's all right."

Mellis fell back on the bed. "Oh the *aarya* help me, when Greg told us he was near death—" She shivered, sinking into sobs.

Alarin closed the door behind Tamara and walked over to Mellis. He slipped an arm around her shoulders, and Mellis turned into his chest, sobbing. He soothed her for a moment, then asked Tamara, "Was he awake?"

"I talked to him for a while. He's fine and he does remember everything that happened." She didn't mention what Merran or her father had said about the consequences. "He didn't do it."

"Of course not!" Mellis flared, turning to Tamara. "He would never force someone against their will!"

"Hush, Mel, she just said that." Alarin looked up at Tamara again. "How is his psi?"

"Merran said he was in a lot of pain, but he was clear. Justern confirmed to me that he was in quite a bit of pain, but I imagine that will go away soon."

Mellis lifted her head and sniffed. "Where is he going to be? I want to see him. They wouldn't tell us anything."

"If he makes bail, he'll be out on Monday and be free to see anyone."

Mellis glared at her, the only human in the room for her to lash out at. She and Tamara were friends, but they'd only been friends for a few weeks. Justern and Mellis had been friends for most of her life. Mellis couldn't fathom the ordeal Justern would have to face because of certain humans. "What's bail?"

"He has to pay the court money and agree not to leave the area, but he'll be free to move around within the city itself."

Mellis's face went very red. "But he's innocent! Why don't they just let him go?"

"Because humans can't read memories or the truth, Mel. Don't yell at Tamara here. She didn't make human laws, and the day we arrived on this planet we agreed to abide by them," Alarin interrupted. "Calm down." There was a sharp note to his voice that Tamara had never heard before.

Mellis quivered on the bed for a brief moment before she relaxed and took a deep breath. "I'm sorry." She directed the comment at Tamara. "I—Justy ... I just can't believe they're treating him like this. I hate to see him in this situation."

"It's okay. If it's any consolation, I hate it too. I really do wish we could read memories and dig out the truth, but we can't."

Alarin added a comment before Mellis could go on. "So Justern goes to trial in a human court?"

Tamara nodded. "My father is defending him. He'll do what he can."

"Well, I think we should all go have dinner. There isn't much we can do about this right now." Alarin slid off the bed. "I, for one, am hungry. Would you like to join us, Tamara?"

"Okay. I was going to do my homework, but I think I'm too distracted." Tamara followed Alarin to the door.

The idea of dinner turned out not to be such a good one after all. Shortly after Mellis, Alarin, and Tamara got plates of food and settled down at a table, a group of young women took seats at the other end.

"God, how did you survive it, Joely?" one of them asked. "It must have been horrible!"

The young woman named Joely shuddered. "It was." Tears filled her eyes, making her eyelashes spiky. "I don't know if I'll ever be able to trust anyone again."

"I can't believe it," one of the others said. "When I slept with him, I never imagined he would hit someone or do those awful things. It makes me sick!"

"Do you think he's going to come back on campus? Do you think he might try to come after us?" a third said. "Maybe get his Azellian friends to come after us, too?"

"After my father's done with him, I don't think he will dare show his face on campus again," Joely tossed her long, blond hair over a shoulder. "And if he did, I'd just slap a restraining order on him. As for the others, they won't dare do anything."

"How did you get away to call the police?" one of the others asked her. Obviously loving to be the center of attention, Joely launched into her story again.

Mellis trembled beside Tamara as they all realized who the girls were talking about. Tamara's stomach wrapped itself into one hard knot.

"Alarin," Mellis hissed.

"I hear," Alarin said coldly. He stood up, leaving his tray, and headed for the end of the table. "Good evening," he said, interrupting the conversation between the girls. They looked up at him, their mouths gaping open. He stopped behind Joely, slightly off to the side, not quite looming over her but letting her feel his presence. "I hope you're having a pleasant conversation, because what I can hear of it down the table I would prefer not to."

Tamara and Mellis joined Alarin on the other side of Joely. Joely twisted to see who was standing near her and went pale.

"Among us Azellians, there is nothing worse than spreading rumors. Do you know how we know when someone is spreading untrue rumors?" Alarin leaned over, resting his hands on the table beside her. He did not touch Joely, or even come close enough to be in her space. All he did was meet her eyes directly. "Did you set up Justern, Joely?" There was that note in his voice again, that echoing whiplash, much stronger now, too strong to be denied.

Joely struggled not to answer. Fear slowly grew in her eyes. *Fear of what?* Tamara wondered. She knew Alarin knew why Joely was afraid. Beside her, so did Mellis. Tamara stared at Joely too, willing herself to hear whatever it was Alarin and Mellis did. And she did hear it, abruptly, in an overwhelming wash of emotions. Fear—no, terror—pulsed through every heartbeat, every breath. *What is she afraid of? Those green eyes boring into hers?* Tamara thought, in the middle of the deluge of emotions washing through her.

The voices held her, gripped her in coils that squeezed tighter and tighter. Confused images. A body, warm skin. Justern, eyes wide, laughing at her. Other students laughing. Embarrassment. Justern's refusal, at first gentle, then increasingly acerbic. His humiliation of her in front of other students. Another rejection from someone else. Justern's face tangled in with another's. Eric, her ex, dark-haired, physically similar to Justern. Fury. Anger. Twisted hate. Images. Images of a strong, wiry young body wrapped around hers. Eric's or Justern's? Did it matter? Then, clearly Justern, snoring loudly in drunken stupor. Getting the evidence, forcing it. Pain, the hard length of the footboard as she slammed it into her own stomach to make it look as though he'd hit her. Finally, and the most damning, Justern asking blearily behind her what she was doing before passing out again. *I will make him pay*, Tamara heard with that part of her mind that had just come awake. *Justern hurt me, and he will pay. He will pay for every humiliation I have suffered. Being deported in disgrace is about perfect. How dare this jerk standing in front of me question me? There is no way I am going to say yes.*

But she would. There was an irresistible urge to say it. *I can't lie. Not with those eyes staring at me.*

Tamara had had enough, especially realizing that the images were of her brother. She gagged and almost went to her knees. Once turned on, however, her damned abilities could not be stopped, threatening to overwhelm her. The other girls around Joely, all of them in various stages of fear, near belief, and titillated sensibilities, radiated enough emotion to drive her to her knees. Alarin's cold anger, Mellis's indignation and fury, her own disgust and anger, other students discussing this, the big event on campus, the rumors flying despite anyone's best attempt to stop them, the sudden sharp curiosity as it appeared that they were going to witness a fainting spell. Tamara fought it all, trying not to collapse.

Alarin released Joely from his will just in time to see Tamara go grey and sway on her feet, radiating freely. *Mellis, she's going to be sick. We've got to get her out of here!* He ignored Joely and came around to Tamara, completely dismissing the girls. He threw a shield up around Tamara as Mellis helped her walk out, supporting her with telekinesis so it appeared that Tamara was walking on her own.

They managed to get Tamara back to Alarin's room. Although it seemed she was close to it, she did not get sick. She did develop the migraine, though. Her head pounded, her eyes watered, and she thought her brain was going to swell out the top of her head.

Alarin's touch soothed. It chased back some of the pain. Not as much as Greg's Healing, but enough that she could function. She lay on his bed with a wet cloth on her forehead and eyes, two painkillers in her stomach.

"Tamara, can you hear me?"

Tamara opened her eyes and squinted at him from under the cloth. He crouched by her head, his hand still lightly touching her forehead. Mellis was nowhere to be seen. "What are you doing?" Tamara asked.

"Shunting your migraine a bit. I can't heal it, but I can take some of it so you're not feeling the whole thing."

"So you're feeling my migraine right now?" Tamara closed her eyes again. It hurt too much to open them.

"Yes." Alarin stroked her hair.

Tamara moved her head. "Stop that. You don't need to suffer an episode with me."

"Hush," Alarin ordered and somehow that order could not be disobeyed. His hand returned to her hair. "I need to know what you saw, Tamara. As unpleasant as it was."

"Don't you know?" Tamara coughed a little, then froze as her head pounded. "Ow."

"I knew she was lying and that she would have said yes if I had pushed her a little harder, but she was fighting pretty hard. It took most of my concentration to keep her docile."

Tamara turned her head restlessly, then stilled as the movement sent shards of pain flying through her brain. "Didn't Mellis see it? Please, don't let me be the only one who saw into the cesspool that's her brain. Ow!"

"That girl has some formidable defenses. Mellis only caught the whiff of lying, not any of the details. You've got a migraine, which means you had another episode, didn't you? Did you see anything?"

"Ow. Yes. Not a damned bit of it is going to be admissible in court, Alarin. From what I saw, Justy's telling the truth. He was too drunk to rape anyone." She coughed, fighting back her nausea. "Ow. God, don't make me relive it. He's my brother, Alarin. I didn't want to see what I saw. Could Greg get rid of my memories of it?"

"It may not be admissible in human court, Tamara, but the Council will need to see it. Justern is not only going to be on trial here but at home too." Alarin continued to stroke her hair and her nausea abated. He rested his chin on the bed. "And if he doesn't win the court case here, he's going to need the truth on his side when he gets home, or he might as well move to Ather. And yes, Greg can blur what you remember once he reads your memories of it for the Council."

Although her stupid abilities were once more locked safely behind walls, she suddenly knew Alarin was well aware of what this court case might lead to, including the larger possible political repercussions. "Why did you force Joely tonight? You know how touchy this situation is. What if she calls rape on you? Or tries to say you assaulted her?"

Alarin's hand stilled. "I lost my temper. I do that sometimes. To hear her telling everyone that Justern hit her ... I wanted her to know some of us know the truth and could force it out of her if we wanted."

Tamara shrugged and winced. "Ow. God damned headache. I guess we have more than we started with, as much as I hate the fact that it's lodged in my brain."

Alarin surprised her by leaning forward and kissing her lightly on the cheek. "Even if we do all get sent home, Tamara, I'm very glad we've had the opportunity to know you. It will have been worth everything." He stood up.

Tamara smiled, feeling the brush of his lips on her cheeks long after she should have. "Thank you, Alarin. That may even make the memory I'm holding bearable. Where's Mel?"

"We can't reach Merran, so she went to the embassy to find him." Alarin moved to sit on his desk. "Why don't you sleep? The pain will be gone in the morning."

"Not in your bed," Tamara protested faintly. She moved and her migraine threatened to explode again.

"I don't have the energy tonight to carry you home, Tamara. You need to sleep or the migraine will be back. I'll be fine. Sleep."

Again, that whiplash of command. Tamara found herself drifting off, despite her intentions. Of all the talents she had seen the Azellians display, this one had to be the most terrifying, she thought, with a sudden surge of sympathy for Joely. *What would it have it been like to resist that force of mind, that irresistible command? Not pleasant,* she thought. But then she remembered the confused cesspool she'd been forced to watch and she was suddenly glad. Pleasant wasn't something Joely deserved. Tamara fell asleep hoping the other girl had nightmares.

Chapter Nine

TAMARA WOKE THE NEXT morning almost as disoriented as the day before. Blinking up at the ceiling, her kinetic sense off balance, she told herself that waking up in strange beds would have to stop. As her memory slowly returned, she turned her head to look for Alarin. Other than a pile of blankets on the floor, she saw no sign of him. As she stretched and yawned, Tamara glanced over at the clock. *It's only seven. Where did he go?* She rubbed her eyes and sat up.

The door opened then and Alarin walked in, wearing a pair of shorts. The smooth spread of his chest, with only a thin line of red-gold hair that ran down the middle of it and his belly to the line of his shorts, contrasted dramatically with the rippled muscles of his abdomen. His wide shoulders narrowed to a slender waist, much more obvious without his shirt. A light dusting of red-gold hair also covered his lower arms, standing out against his bronze skin. The tan spread over his entire upper body, and she had a moment of sudden curiosity as to how far down the color went. She curbed that thought hastily, tearing her eyes away and pushing the covers back. "Thanks for letting me sleep here, Alarin. But I'd, uh, better get back to my room. Unless you want to start rumors of your own."

He grinned. "I'm strong enough to handle it. Speaking of, Merran woke me up about ten minutes ago looking for you. He wants me to tell you that Greg's awake and ready to read the memory you have."

Tamara shuddered. "You told him? Good, I don't have to. I'm just glad I didn't dream about it last night." She stood up. "Uh, Merran wasn't bothered or anything, was he?"

Alarin raised an eyebrow. His nostrils flared, but he seemed to be very relaxed, unlike yesterday. "Why would he be?"

"Well … I uh … sort of spent the night at his place the night before last." Tamara flushed and walked gingerly past the bed. "We … uh … I—I'm not exactly sure where we stand, but I don't want to upset him."

He laughed. "At his place, eh? My, my. Night before last in Merran's bed, last night in mine. Even a night in Greg's. You are taking the Azellian thing quite seriously, I see."

"Oh stop it." Tamara grabbed the towel hanging over the edge of his bedpost and threw it at him. "You're just teasing me. You know as well as I do that I slept alone in the bed last night. You slept on the floor." *Unlike the night I spent with Merran*, she thought but didn't say it out loud.

Alarin's grin widened as he caught the towel. "It's a little awkward to sleep two to a twin bed. Especially when a certain person seems to like to talk and move around in her sleep."

Tamara flushed, feeling the heat crawl up her cheeks. She had always been a restless sleeper. Merran's kingsize bed had minimized that little difficulty. "I thought Justern was the only one who teased about that sort of thing," she said, tossing her head and trying to change the subject.

Alarin laughed and stretched, reaching his long arms up and linking his hands above his head. The move drew attention immediately to his stomach, which undoubtedly was the point. "We all do at times. Don't expect Justern to quit teasing you, either, just because he's your brother."

Tamara shuddered, trying to keep her eyes away from his chest and stomach muscles. "Do you tease your sister?" She stared at the floor, trying not to look at him.

Alarin laughed. "She'd remove my head if I tried." His tone made Tamara look up at him. Those green eyes twinkled brightly. "But then Justern didn't grow up around you, and you're really cute. Especially when you blush. Besides, he's Justern. Flirting is his life's blood."

Tamara blushed violently, not sure what to make of Alarin's behavior. Didn't he have a girlfriend on Azelle? "I'm leaving. See you later." She walked quite firmly toward the door.

"Tamara," he said soberly as she lifted a hand to turn the latch. Something in his tone made her stop. "Seriously. I do have one question before you leave. At the risk of raising memories you'd rather forget, when you had your episode last night, what triggered it?"

She turned to face him. It was unnerving to talk to him in his half-dressed state, but she ignored it as best she could. She pressed against the door, squeezing the handle behind her back. "I don't know. I just wanted to know really badly what she was thinking.

To hear like you guys do. And I did. I just couldn't stop again when I wanted to." Tamara wrapped her arms around herself and shuddered. "And I learned more than I wanted to know. Ever."

He stood up, pushing himself away from the desk. "I'm sorry. I was partially to blame for why you got hit with it so badly. I was forcing Joely to remember what happened so Mel or I could pick it up."

Tamara frowned. "All you were doing was asking her a simple question. Why would that bring back all those thoughts?"

"No one ever has a simple answer to anything, especially not if they're guilty." Alarin gave her a look, one she couldn't read. "Here's one. Did you have sex with Merran Friday night?"

The question called up an immediate progression of vivid memories—seeing Merran lying on the bed, dark against the light covers, kissing him, wrestling with him in the closet. It brought back her blush, too, and she was suddenly glad Alarin couldn't read her mind. Given his recent behavior, she wasn't sure she wanted him to see those memories. "All right, all right, I see what you mean. How did you do that? Are you forcing me?"

Alarin cocked his head to the side. "No, not at all. It's a simple response. You have to remember what I'm asking about in order to give me an answer, whether you're lying or telling the truth, unless you're prepared beforehand. If I'd been forcing you, you would have answered me immediately and not just seen the images in your head. The only trick is in knowing the question to ask. If she'd been Azellian, that would not have worked. I would only have had an answer ... truthful, but no details. We can shield those particular association memories."

Her curiosity peaked. Alarin seemed to be in teacher mode, so she let herself be carried with it. "So when you are walking among humans you get bombarded by these thoughts all the time?"

"Yep. Unless I spend my days shielded, which I usually do. Even then, when the human is thinking some particularly strong thought … at highly emotional times, say … I pick up the most interesting details."

"Ugh. No wonder I've refused to Awaken."

Alarin frowned. "Your rejection of your Awakening probably did save your sanity, especially if you've had to struggle with all of this on your own." He stepped closer, his green eyes catching hers. "Last night was a huge accomplishment, Tamara. I think Greg's going to insist you spend your nights either watched over by one of us to maintain a shield, or you are going to have to spend your nights in a shielded area. If you are starting to gain conscious control over the shields that are blocking your psi and holding back your full Awakening, you're going to be very vulnerable at night. I suspected as much last night, which is one reason I made sure you stayed here."

Tamara stared at him, an odd feeling passing through her, a cross between excitement and fear. "Have I reached another stage, then?"

"Maybe. Greg's going to have to see if he can tell. It's definitely getting closer. You're using the pathways more and more, and the more you use them the easier it will to be to access them. Your fear is fading and with it your shields that have been blocking your full Awakening." Alarin saw her expression and continued, "Don't worry, you didn't have another episode in your sleep last night."

The door handled rattled slightly as her hand shook. "How awful is this Awakening going to be, Alarin? Tell me the truth, please."

Alarin walked over to where she stood. He reached out and brushed the air just above her cheek. It felt like a gentle caress, although he didn't touch her. "Maybe not bad at all, Tamara. The more of these little episodes you have and the better you deal with them, you may find Awakening to be very simple after all. As easy as waking up one morning able to hear thoughts."

"How was yours?" Tamara shivered at the kinesthetic sense of his hands near her, although she told herself it was because of the nerves about Awakening. "If that's not too personal."

He withdrew, moving to sit on the bed. "That's about as personal as you can get, considering it's usually closely connected with our first sexual experience."

"Never mind," Tamara sighed, releasing her grip of the doorknob. "I didn't mean to pry. Maybe I'll ask Merran about his."

"It was ... intense." Alarin scooted back against the wall. He focused on a spot somewhere above her head. "I don't remember it clearly, but I do remember the constant dreams off and on for what seemed like forever, waking up sticky in the morning." His eyes cleared and he looked at Tamara. "One aspect of adolescence I don't miss at all." Then he continued, "During the days, off and on throughout, I could hear conversations in my head. I could even hear the animals communicating. I got the most hideous migraines."

"Animals? Is that common?"

"Only if you're sensitive enough to pick up their level. They don't communicate on the same level as we do, and to hear it you have to be pretty sensitive." Alarin shifted position. "Mellis, Justern, and Greg can't. Merran and I can."

"So you had these migraines, too?"

"Oh yeah. Every day off and on for a month. It was awful. At night, it was the dreams and during the day, one migraine after the other. I knew what was happening, but that didn't seem to stop any of it." Alarin's eyes reflected the pain Tamara knew well. "I made it harder on myself, of course, because I refused to accept that it was happening. I did everything I could think of. Even masturbating before I went to bed did nothing. I wore myself out and still had the dreams. I started waking up with migraines. My sister tried to tell me to stop fighting it. She was in Healer training, and I should have listened, but I was stubborn."

"What finally stopped it?" Tamara asked, suspecting there was more to the story than he was telling her, but also guessing she wouldn't hear it from him.

"I met Mellis. She was just starting to Awaken too, and she was ... uncomplicated." It was an odd choice of words, but one that revealed more of the story, if she could piece the clues. "One afternoon we were sunning ourselves at the beach and sharing migraine horror stories, when it occurred to us we were attracted to each other. I don't remember which one of us started it, but by the time we were done, I was Awake. Looking back on it, I wasn't too bright about it, especially considering how powerful I am, but it worked and I didn't burn her or myself out in the process." Alarin focused on her. "Everyone is different. There are two rules, though, that never fail. The more you resist and the more sensitive you are, the worse it is. I don't believe Mellis really had much of an Awakening at all, although she did have a few migraines. Through her, I met the others. Justern, who was living with his cousin Charina, and Merran, Charina's uncle."

"What about Greg?"

His expression closed down. "I met Greg through his sister Idara. Greg started spending more time with us after he finished his Healer training, right before Merran left for Earth."

Idara, where have I heard that name before? Dropped in some conversation? Alarin's girlfriend at home, she remembered abruptly. Something told her there was a story there, too, but she let it drop. "Thanks for sharing that with me, Alarin. Even though I have a feeling it was partially meant as a lecture."

Alarin's expression cleared and he grinned. "Now why would you get that impression?"

"Maybe because it was?"

He chuckled. "I think you'd better get going, my dear, because I'm getting communications from Merran and Greg that tell me they're getting antsy. Merran has another press interview today and he has to get moving."

"All right, all right. Tell them I'm coming."

"Or you will be." Alarin grinned wickedly. "Lucky Merran."

She grabbed a book from the bookcase by the door and threw it at him. He caught it telekinetically before it had gone halfway across the room. "See you later, Tamara."

She put her hand on the door and turned to him. "Oh, Alarin, can I ask you one more question? What does *ala* mean? I can't find it in my dictionary."

"It's an affectionate diminutive, equivalent to saying love or sometimes beloved when used between lovers. Why?"

"I heard someone use it and wondered what it meant." Tamara shrugged, trying to seem casual, but her heart leaped to her throat. "It seemed odd to change a person's name that way. I heard someone at the embassy talking to someone else. What do women say to men?"

"*-alis.*"

"Thanks. I'll see you later." Tamara opened the door and went out, her heart still pounding at the thought that Merran had been calling her love without her knowing it. *It may mean nothing* she told herself. *There are plenty of humans who run around calling each other love all the time. But he didn't tell me what it means, did he? And the other translation, beloved, is not casual at all.* As she walked over to her room to change and call Merran to see where he and Greg were, she decided that no matter what Merran said, he was going to be the one who initiated her into her adulthood. *I want an Awakening memory like Alarin's. Haven't I seen Alarin's affection for Mellis even now?* She suspected, though, that she could trigger herself into her psi Awakening without sex involved. *I did it yesterday, didn't I? What if I trigger it when it's quiet, like the time I went in to set up my intern schedule in Merran's office and I had an episode without a migraine? That seems so long ago. The key seems to be not losing control ... and not to panic.*

What if I Awaken first, then sleep with him? The thought of that sent a shiver down her spine. *Being able to feel him inside me, in my mind as well as my body—mmm, what would that be like? I can do it. I can Awaken without sex. I really want to, because I don't ever want to hurt Merran.* For the first time since it happened, she let herself remember the climb, the sucking in of energy that had burned along every nerve, the burning of her first sexual experience, and the horror as she realized he was dead, his heart stopped and his brain erased by what the doctors had called a freak electrical accident. *But it was me. It was my Awakening and my Awakening alone that killed Doug. Didn't Greg confirm it when I told him? I would never, could never, hurt Merran like that.* Logic told her calmly that Merran was easily as strong as she and could fend for himself, but fear ruled. Fear kept her shackled. *Can I let go of being so afraid?*

As she walked home, her cell phone buzzed in her pocket. She jumped and answered it.

"Hello?"

Merran sounded irritated. "Tamara, you need to come to my place now so I can let you in. I have to go to an interview in an hour and I want to see this memory you have before I go."

She pulled open the door to her dorm and walked up the stairs as she talked. "I'm on my way. Can I change first? I'll even be nice and won't ask for a shower. You'll just have to put up with the sleep slime."

She could hear the slight grin in his voice. "Sleep slime? Sounds like fun. Very slippery."

Tamara scowled as she opened the door to her room. "What's up with you Azellians in the morning? You're all disgusting. I'm on my way." She hung up and pulled out clothes as fast as she could. Maybe she could shower there. Thinking a bit ahead, she pulled a duffel bag out of the closet. She decided she'd better pack a change of underwear and her homework. If they really wanted her to spend the night shielded, she might as well stay at Merran's. Later, remembering all that transpired, she wondered if she'd had a flash of foresight.

✳ ✳ ✳

It took her fifteen more minutes before she walked up to the large blue-glassed skyscraper that housed Merran's apartment. She stood outside the main doors of the building and touched the pad for his apartment.

"Corina." Merran's voice sounded curt and oddly mechanical through the speaker.

"It's me."

"Come up." The door buzzed and she entered, heading for the only elevator that actually went to the top floor. The trip up in the elevator seemed to take forever.

As she stepped off the elevator into Merran's living room, Alarin lay sprawled on the couch, wearing a pair of jeans and a loose button-down shirt. Tamara stared at him. "How did you manage to get here so fast?"

He grinned. "I have my talents."

"You do not. Don't tell me instantaneous transportation is an Azellian talent."

"It is." Alarin made his mouth and eyes into perfect o's.

"Which he doesn't have. Stop teasing her, Alari," Greg broke in. "He just didn't ... pack?" He stared at her duffel bag. "What did you bring over?"

Tamara shrugged, swinging the duffel to the ground. "Since Merran wouldn't let me have a shower at home, I thought I'd bring some clothes over so I could have one before I change."

Greg raised an eyebrow. "Oookay."

"How do we want to do this?" Merran stalked into the room from his desk in the back of the apartment. Looming like an annoyed boss, he commented, "You aren't strong enough to breach her shields, Greg."

"I'd like to try to let you in," Tamara walked over to the couch, stepping over the duffel bag. "Alarin told you yesterday that I was able to lower my shields on purpose, right? Well, I'd like to try that again."

Alarin grinned at her proudly, patting the couch next to him. "We can help."

"You were right, Alari. She's definitely reached a new stage." Merran leaned against the arm of the couch as Tamara settled in between the end of the couch and Alarin.

Greg nodded slowly, kneeling in front of the couch. He waved his hand in front of Tamara's eyes. She focused on his fingers, then shifted to look at his eyes. "All right. Are you sure you can do this, Tamara? Alarin told me the memory was a difficult one for you. My reading of the memory is going to bring it back again. Are you sure you can hold your shields down? It's going to be somewhat dangerous for me if they slam back up while I'm in there."

Merran shifted restlessly on his perch. "Are we going to trigger her Awakening with this? Maybe we'd better do this later, after my meeting."

Greg stared into Tamara's eyes. "I don't think so. It will trigger an episode, I'm sure, but I doubt she's going to stay open. She should be having steady dreams at night if that were the case. I won't be able to Heal the migraine, though. I'm still pretty drained from Healing Justy."

Alarin spoke from his position beside her. "I'll split the pain with her. Unless she's Awakened, the painkillers will work if I do that."

"What kind of dreams?" Tamara touched Greg's hand. She flushed a little. "I haven't had sexual ones lately, if that's what you mean. But I have been having quite a few dreams where I'm flying."

Greg raised an eyebrow and glanced up at Merran and over at Alarin. "Flying dreams. Unless that's a new Awakening warning, I'd say we're safe."

Alarin shrugged. "It's worth a try."

"I would like to try," Tamara said shyly. "The worst that can happen is I'll fail."

"I'm game. I know I'm not up to reading her while she's shielded." Greg straightened and moved back to sit on the coffee table.

Merran tapped a hand on the arm of the chair. "I don't think I've ever heard of flying dreams being Awakening precursors." He straightened and scratched behind his ear. "If Tamara wants to make the effort to try to lower her shields, let's get to it. I'd better warn Janille." He strode over to his desk.

"Relax, Tamara," Greg told her. "All right. You remember all those visualization exercises I've had you do endlessly?"

Tamara settled back into the leather couch. Greg shifted forward and picked up her hand. Alarin relaxed back against the couch within touching distance—a warm, supportive presence. She let herself drift, closing her eyes and imagining the walls around her mind. Slowly, she took bricks out of the walls, her mental hands shaking only a little. When she was done, she sat quietly, not sure anything had changed.

Very, very good. Open your eyes, Tamara. The voice echoed in her head, the timbre like, but at the same time, unlike his speaking voice. Her heart pounded in her throat as she opened her eyes. Greg crouched in front of her, surrounded by a beautiful amber gold light. It was not so much a halo as a nimbus, surrounding his whole body. She frowned. "Is that your aura?"

Greg winced. *Gently, Tamara. Gently. You're open, don't forget. Anything you say will also be projected by your mind.* His mouth didn't move, but the voice was definitely his. It didn't have quite the resonance of his spoken voice, but it came connected with a strong, calm personality. *You're a really powerful projector.*

Sorry. Tamara could almost feel her thoughts flying out from her. She imagined pulling them back.

Greg smiled, pleased. *Good. Now, I want you to very slowly remember Joely yesterday. Did you see her memories?*

Just as Alarin's question this morning had evoked memories, so did this one. At Greg's gentle prompting, Tamara imagined herself watching a movie, able to leave at any time. This time, the memories lost the immediacy of yesterday—she was able to close her eyes at the parts she didn't want to see and ignore the fact that they involved a real person she knew. *Just actors on a screen*, Greg's voice whispered to her in her deepest levels. *Just actors.* He was doing something to her; she could feel it as he adjusted and moved in her mind. The feeling was alien but not unpleasant as he sorted the memories for her, digging up a few she hadn't known she'd seen, filtering through her perceptions.

He withdrew, leaving her with a warm feeling. *Very, very good, Tamara. How do you feel?*

Okay. Tamara again imagined the words leaving her slowly, softly. If she took the time to think in words, they didn't go flying out quite so fast.

You're absolutely right, Tamara. You're controlling this very well. Like an expert. Greg's mind tone stayed calm and quiet despite the approval woven through it.

Tamara stared at his aura; the golden light drew her attention like a magnet. She lifted her hand to reach out, but pulled back, biting her lip.

Go ahead, you can touch it. Greg answered her unspoken thought.

She reached out and brushed her hand through the golden light surrounding him. A tingling sensation quivered through her as she touched the light, then pulled away, startled. She'd felt this before, on the receiving end when Merran and Greg touched her sometimes, but never so strongly—Alarin moved into her vision, startling her. The thought that flew through her mind dissipated with a shower of sparks. His aura shone emerald green, kicking highlights off his red hair and flaring bright enough that she had to blink. She could read nothing from his mind, but his glow drew her eyes.

Get her shielded again Greg ... before she sees Merran. She's free associating right now, and if she starts thinking sexually, she's going to open those channels. See them? They've hardly been touched, even with all her episodes. Alarin spoke to Greg on his intimate level, carefully not touching her.

You're right, Alari. Greg betrayed some alarm. *By the* aarya, *she's strong! She hasn't even touched her full potential! Merran, you stay there!*

Tamara heard the sharp command and turned to see, her mind wondering what Merran's aura looked like. An invisible force distracted her, though, holding her face. She frowned and imagined herself pulling the invisible fingers from her face.

Alarin grunted. "Tamara, don't fight me." When he spoke, it was with a weird double echo. Like Greg, his mental voice lacked the resonance of his physical voice, but the feel attached to his voice was strongly his. She relaxed a little against his restraint, accepting his guidance.

"Why can't I look?" She spoke out loud, imagining that she was holding her breath as she spoke to try to prevent her thoughts from flying out away from her. "Does everyone have differently colored auras?"

"Yes," Greg answered. "All right, Tamara, concentrate. I'm going to have you shield again. Do you think you can do that?"

Tamara nodded, looking at Greg. "I don't want to, though. Is this how you see everyone?"

"Azellians, yes."

"How do you get used to it?" Tamara shifted her gaze to Alarin. "It's beautiful but weird. What color is mine?"

"Blue." Alarin looked at her directly. "Concentrate, Tamara." He tried to capture her eyes with his, to help her focus, but he moved too close and brushed her aura with his.

Tamara jumped as the tingling sensation, far stronger than before, skittered up her body, settling somewhere in the vicinity of her stomach. Her breath caught in her throat as she turned to see him crouched next to her on the couch. His aura hovered inches off hers. She lifted a hand to trail her finger through his aura the way she had done to Greg.

She didn't expect his reaction at all. He gasped and scrambled back from her, his eyes wide and nostrils flared.

"Did I hurt you? Oh God, I'm sorry, Alarin." Tamara managed just in time to remember not to project at him.

"You didn't hurt him," Greg assured her. "Just concentrate."

"What did I do?" Tamara turned to Greg, too worried to focus. "Please tell me."

"I'll tell you when your shielding is back up, Tamara," Greg told her. "Focus."

She tried, but her concentration seemed to have scattered. Warmth curled out from her stomach and wound fragile tentacles around her torso and head, destroying what concentration she had left. She ran her fingers over her forearm, her skin twitching at the touch.

Are you all right, Alarin? Merran asked from his position in his office as Tamara lost herself in the physical sensations. He watched, trying not to interfere as they struggled to control what was promising to turn into a full Awakening.

I've gone way too long without sex, Alarin's mind tone snapped back grumpily. *I don't know if I can channel her without sex, Merran. I think she's too strong for me to dissipate the energies without it, not when I'm this wound up myself.*

Do what you have to. Just get her through this. Merran kept his mind heavily shielded, so as not to add to the stimulation flowing around the room.

Alarin returned his attention to Tamara, snapping at her with his telekinesis. "Tamara, listen to me." She turned to look at him. "You are very close to Awakening."

Tamara blinked. "This isn't Awakening?"

"Not all of it. There's a large portion of your potential still not tapped. You're almost in a hypnotic state right now, very susceptible to suggestion. We're trying to keep you from making associations that will open those pathways. But it seems like you are headed that way no matter what we do. So I offer you an option. Greg and I can help you get there. Or we can try to put this back in its box."

Tamara's eyes glowed with wonder. "I don't want to lose this new vision. I want to Awaken."

Alarin and Greg exchanged glances. "All right, Tamara," Greg said hesitantly. "I'm too injured to Heal … if any of you need it. But I'm going to have Alarin guide you and try to help open your channels."

"How?" Tamara stared at Greg, wide-eyed.

Alarin lifted his hand. "Just lay back and listen to Greg."

Tamara obeyed. She rested her head on the couch and closed her eyes, listening to Greg's quiet voice. "Visualize, Tamara. Imagine your mind. There are layers upon layers in your mind. All you've really done is open the upper levels. There are many, many more. The further down you go, you will find still more levels. I want you to open them up one by one. Feel the energy start to flow through those levels, like a flowing river circulating and cleaning the moss from the rocks of a stream."

She obeyed. To her surprise, she could almost feel the currents of energy like that stream Greg was talking about. She sank deeper, listening to Greg's voice.

A tingling started in her left arm, racing up to her shoulder and twirling around her stomach, spreading rapidly across her body and out her right hand. The currents of energy she was feeling swirled faster and faster. She almost felt as though if she opened her eyes, she would see it flowing in and out of her body, a thin trickle at first, a stronger and stronger flow as she opened more and more.

She listened to Greg's voice, and not much else, as the energy continued to build. She opened layer after layer, going deeper and deeper. The river of energy flowed through her, spreading warmth, clearing cobwebs out of her brain, dispersing a delicious feeling through her limbs.

Merran watched, thinking they might actually be successful. Tamara obeyed and opened up layer after layer of her mind, listening only to Greg's voice. In the shielded apartment, nothing else offered her excess energy to suck up, so the flow was smooth. Alarin stroked his fingers through her aura, leaving little green trails, keeping the energy flow moving smoothly through her mind, using the very mild sexual stimulation to help her relax and open the rest of the channels. These levels seemed to have been opened once, so it was not nearly as hard as they had thought it was going to be, given her age.

The controlled, careful Awakening continued.

Abruptly, everything changed. Tamara screamed, grabbing her head. The last layer, the last channel in her mind, stayed obdurately fused shut. Fear and horror, self-loathing and guilt all swirled in an impossible morass. She sat, feeling horribly, terribly naked in front of Greg and Alarin—and *Merran*. She could feel Merran, not touching, but just behind them, watching. *How can they know my terrible secret?* Everything was forgotten, that she was half-Azellian, that it had been an accident, that they already knew.

Merran could see the energy start to build. It jammed up against the walls, sliding back over her mind. He could sense her agony, the terrible words that echoed in her mind. *Freak, you killed him!* Alarin fought her, struggling to keep the shields open, trying to filter the energy through himself at the same time, while Greg watched helplessly.

Damn it, we're so close. It's going to hurt her if she tries to shut it down now, possibly permanently, Greg shot to Alarin, but Merran could hear it, too.

The damned energy is still building. She's still sucking energy in but not letting it back out again! Alarin's mind tone strained, almost in pain. *She's going to burn herself out and take me with her.*

Merran got up and walked into the room. He came around the front of the couch, squatting in front of her. "Tamara."

Merran's voice pulled her up out of the nightmare. *No, he can't know!* But there was a reason she couldn't shut down. Something, someone held her open. She struggled.

Tamara. Listen to me. We all have our ghosts that we must make our peace with. We all have them. Do you hear me? You are not the first person who has accidentally been part of the death of someone, nor will you be the last. But you will be responsible for the death of yourself if you don't stay open now. Open up that last layer, Tamara. Let the energy cleanse it, too. She could feel his hands touch her face.

The physical touch of his aura against hers, of his skin against her skin, made her gasp. She relaxed, listening to his soothing voice. Was this Merran's true voice? She felt his lips touch her brow and travel down her face. *Open, Tamara. Let me help.*

She could feel the energy building, that huge mixture of burning pleasure and pain. *I don't know how!*

Let me in, Tamara. Merran's lips touched her mouth. A new sensation spread through her, a pulse. He kissed her, darting touches of his tongue encouraging her to open her mouth. She did, shyly, nervously.

Merran responded to that shy beginning. He deepened the kiss, a part of his mind still monitoring what they were all doing. Pretty thoroughly distracted, she writhed on the couch, having completely forgotten about Greg and Alarin. Merran's monitoring mind noted that Greg sat in the kitchen, pressed up against the cold of the refrigerator to give himself space from the events in the other room. As he opened himself to Tamara, Merran could feel the sluggish, swollen channels of Greg's psi, injured from the heavy Healing he had done on Justern, throbbing painfully in the energy currents that pulsed through the room. "My room," he murmured in Greg's general direction. "Extra shielding." Greg attempted to make his way to the bedroom, his channels pounding as he did so.

Merran's monitoring mind returned to Tamara as he observed that about halfway up, the walls covering the outflow stopped their slow upward grind, but the energy still jammed against them. Alarin shunted as much of it as he could, but hampered by the uneven walls and his own attempts not to react to Tamara's projected excitement, he was not being terribly successful. She moaned as Merran's hands joined his mouth, exploring her. His hands touched her neck and her shoulders, then tugged insistently at her blouse. He felt it when she let herself go, writhing against him in response. She pulled his shirt up, sliding her fingers between the buttons and trailing her fingers across the hair on his chest.

The touch of her hands on his skin made him gasp and move closer to her, pulling his shirt and tie over his head. He pressed her into the couch, his bare skin rubbing against her shirt. She made a sound low in her throat and pulled her mouth away from his. For a wild moment, Merran wondered if she was going to try to stop what was happening, but she just shifted her attention to his chest, licking at the hair on it, sucking on his nipples. They hardened, and for a moment, he lost control. He pushed against her, a moan escaping him. Somewhere, he could feel Alarin, harsh breathing attesting to his difficulties, channeling as fast as he could. Merran sensed that Alarin was shunting energy through himself as quickly as he could. *Now that his energy is mixing with the sexual energy we're generating, he's probably going to ride the whole thing with us,* Merran suddenly thought.

As Merran moved against her, Tamara started matching his movements, rubbing against him through her clothes and his. Merran arched back, his own excitement climbing. She reached down for his belt, her breath coming hard and fast through her nostrils. He pulled her mouth back up to his and kissed her ferociously, his hands helping her to unbuckle his belt and unbutton his pants.

Is she ready enough that she can ignore the presence of Alarin? Not that Alarin will care, but human-raised Tamara certainly will. Merran made sure the thoughts were hidden behind the shields around his inner self. *To get my pants and her clothes off, it's going to require me to pull away a little. Neither Alarin nor Greg will care ... this is a necessary part of Awakening, useful to free the channels. And after Festival, this is nothing, anyway.* Merran shoved his thoughts away and kissed Tamara again, moving his mouth down her body. He pulled her shirt off. She still wore her bra, and he teased her through it as he continued to kiss her. She moaned and wriggled under him, which nearly set him off, but he managed to hang on. Barely. The monitoring portion of his mind was only vaguely aware of anything at all. He did notice that she sucked in more energy—*where the hell is it coming from?* He didn't care anymore whether Tamara cared or not, or who else was in the room. He pulled his pants off forcefully, with an urgency that would have surprised him if he'd had the attention to spare.

Tamara didn't think she could feel anything more strongly than what was already coursing through her, but the feel of Merran's body against her was almost enough to make her peak. His soft skin, his hard, muscular body so different from her own. With his help, she scrambled out of her own pants and underwear.

The leather slid under her as he kissed her again. If she didn't release soon, she knew she would explode. She reached up to him.

Merran could feel that final mental wall give as he entered her. What he didn't expect was that it was already full of damned-up passion and energy. When the wall around it went, washing away in a deluge the nightmares that had surrounded all that trapped emotion, she screamed with a mixture of pain and pleasure. The energy flashed up through her, into him, and back through Alarin, searing along all their nerves and tumbling both Merran and Alarin over the edge, Merran's body expelling so violently he thought he was going to die. He could hear Alarin's moans—he didn't sound much better. Pleasure and pain faded to a burning, throbbing agony that made him roll off Tamara and lay panting on the couch next to her. She passed out, and he fought not to do the same.

He must have, though, because the next thing he knew, calm warmth spread through him. He opened his eyes, the migraine pounding through his head. "Are we all still alive?" His voice didn't want to work and it came out as a croak.

"Barely." Greg knelt in front of him. "I have never in my life seen an Awakening where the one Awakening took not only herself, but two other adult, mature psi over the edge with her. If I hadn't been in your bedroom, she would have taken me, too." He motioned down at himself. "As unattracted to women as I am, I would have reacted exactly as you two did."

"Is she Awakened?" Merran didn't dare move for fear of triggering the throbbing in his head, despite the fact that he was uncomfortably sticky.

"Yes. All levels fully open, shunting energy the way they should. But they're badly inflamed. That was a lot of energy you three handled. She came damned close to burning all three of you out. Since I can't Heal you right now, you're going to be incapacitated for a while. None of you are allowed to leave this apartment for a week, at the least." Greg leaned back against his heels. "Healer's orders."

At that, Merran struggled to sit up. Greg held him down. "Don't move. You're going to hurt if you move."

"I can't stay in this apartment, Greg. I have work to do. I have an interview today."

"Do you want to keep your psi? You will stay in this shielded environment for a week, or you will find yourself on your back for a month, or six months, or a year. You won't be able to shield yourself adequately to move around in public for at least a week. You should be confined to this apartment for three weeks, but I know I'll never get you to agree to that. If your channels try to handle anything more, you will burn them out and do permanent damage."

Merran closed his eyes. "What about Justern's trial?"

"It won't be handled in the next week. Beyond that, if you take this week off, you might, and I stress might, be able to go back to work. I'm sure Tamara's father can handle some of the PR stuff, or you can interview from this apartment over the phone. He's going to need to know that his daughter's Awakened anyway. I doubt you're going to feel up to answering questions in ten minutes, but you can try, as long as it's a phone interview."

Merran managed to sit up. He looked down at himself. "I can't interview like this."

Greg motioned to his clothes lying scattered across the floor. "Those aren't going to work either. They're a little wrinkled."

Merran put his hand to his head. "The *aarya* help me, I think my head is going to come off. Call Janille and tell her I need to get the interview postponed an hour, no make that two hours, and switched to a video interview."

Greg nodded and got to his feet, going over to do as Merran asked. Merran himself swung his feet over the edge of the couch. Tamara lay pale and still, her eyes tightly closed. He couldn't sense her, not with his psi the way it was, but she breathed at least.

Alarin lay on the floor not far from them, propped against the couch. He opened his eyes when Merran moved. "Damn," he moaned. "Am I alive?"

Merran managed a smile. It was about the only thing that didn't hurt. "Don't ask me, I'm not in any better shape."

"Is she all right?" Alarin didn't move, obviously in some pain himself.

"Greg says she's Awake and functioning, but hurt like we are. She's still unconscious." Merran looked back at her. "What I'm more worried about are her sensibilities when she wakes up."

"Ahhh." Alarin crawled to a sitting position and looked down at himself. "Do you mind if I borrow some clothes? I think I'm going to need a shower. We don't need to tell her, do we?"

"It's going to be pretty obvious from your psi and your aura that you shared what we went through." Merran raised an eyebrow.

"She doesn't need to know how much of it I shared, does she?" Alarin made a face. "I think you're right. She's going to be pretty upset as it is. She doesn't need to know what I shared with you. It will embarrass her terribly. She asked me to tell her about my Awakening experience today, you know."

"You told her?"

"I gave her an edited version."

Greg came into the room. "Janille's handling it. Good, you're functional."

Alarin winced. "If you can call it that."

"Greg, are you feeling strong enough to get Tamara into my room, so she wakes up covered and in some privacy?" Merran glanced down at Tamara, who stirred slightly. "Otherwise, we're going to have some fast explaining to do. I don't think she's going to remember much of anything, but she's pretty vulnerable right now."

Greg nodded. "Yes. Go, Alarin. Take a shower first. I'll get Tamara into bed. You get yourself into bed, too, Mer. Waking up next to you won't traumatize her, and if you're in the same state as she is, she might not feel so vulnerable. I'll clean up in here and call Mellis to bring Alarin a change of clothes and some painkillers for Tamara, although I doubt they'll work now that she's fully Awake."

Merran nodded. He got up, though the effort nearly made him pass out again. Alarin looked as unsteady as he felt, using the wall for support.

Merran got himself to the closet, found Alarin a change of clothes, and dropped them in the bathroom where Alarin was showering, then tottered to where Tamara lay on the bed. He stood for a moment gazing down at her. She looked as though she were in normal sleep, her color coming back a little. Greg had tucked the covers around her. Merran climbed into bed beside her.

It felt wonderful to be lying in bed, although he knew he did have a phone interview shortly. *I will just close my eyes briefly*, he told himself. *Just for a little while.*

Tamara came back to awareness slowly, feeling very strange. Her head ached but not in the same way as it did when she had a migraine. Instead, it felt like someone had taken a red hot poker and shoved it into her brain. She moved slightly and found herself sore elsewhere too. Between her legs was another poker, burning and sore. What had happened? The last thing she remembered was this deliciously warm feeling as she held her walls open and listened to Greg's voice. She decided to risk opening her eyes. She was lying in Merran's bed, she realized, under a sheet. She moved and the sheets slid against her skin in a way she'd never felt before. She realized with a start that she was naked under the covers. Moments later, she realized that Merran was sprawled, snoring slightly, in the bed beside her. She flushed. Had they? They must have. He glowed light brown, blue and green swirled through it so thoroughly that the effect was really more of a hazel tone, telling her as well that she must be Awake. There were some sounds from the other room; she decided to try to listen.

She gasped and had to blink away tears as her head throbbed, a sharp shooting pain lancing through her. Curling up into a fetal position, she tried to ride the pain.

Merran woke up with a start to Tamara's little moans of pain. He propped himself on an arm. "Tamara? Greg! She's awake!" He yelled the words, rather than use his mind, something that didn't really impress on her right away.

But which Awake does he mean? The thought shot across Tamara's mind somewhere underneath the pains. Not long after, a soothing warmth slid through her, dulling the pain just a little. She uncurled and opened her eyes.

Greg ran his hands up and down her body, although he didn't touch her. "How are you feeling, Tamara?"

She moaned. "Squashed. Like someone just ran me over with a boulder. Twice."

Greg smiled and perched on the side of the bed. "Congratulations. You've successfully Awakened. I'm sorry you're in so much pain, but I can't Heal you."

Tamara kept the covers up to her chin. "What happened? The last time I remember anything I was drifting quite pleasantly and listening to your voice." She frowned, "then—"

"The old trauma you had was still there, Tamara. Under all the mental layers." Greg motioned to Merran. "You tensed up and blocked the energy flow out, creating a backlog. You would have done some serious damage to yourself had Merran not stepped in at that point. Your attraction to him allowed you to focus on something else. The rest, well, I suspect you know that part."

Tamara flushed. So they had done what it felt like they had done. All she remembered was building energy, sharp and painful, and maybe pleasurable. Maybe.

"You might want to be sure she won't get pregnant, Greg. I don't know that I was thinking clearly enough to have done it myself," Merran interjected, propping himself against the pillows and leaning back. Tamara had a sudden very sensual image of kissing his chest—she blushed and clenched the covers over herself.

Greg lifted a hand, hovering over her abdomen. She felt a warmth in her uterus and a weird clenching. "What are you doing?" She wanted to scramble away, but her state of undress held her firm. Although she suspected neither of the young men in the room would care, she did.

"I'm killing the sperm, and forcing you to ovulate early so I can kill the egg right away. It's something you can learn for yourself, once you've healed enough to use the psi you now have access to," Greg replied. "Azellian women do not get pregnant by mistake. And I suspect in the future, your Azellian partner will not be quite so distracted and be sure his sperm are dead before they leave his body."

Tamara shot a glance at Merran and flushed. He didn't tease her, for which she was profoundly grateful.

Greg stood up. "I think you look pretty good for someone who just Awakened rather violently. Your psi channels are still pretty inflamed, but they are considerably less than they were, and I think you'll be up and about in about a week."

"A week? I have classes!"

Greg shook his head. "Healer's orders. You are confined to these quarters, which are shielded and will prevent any more stimulus getting into your mind than you can handle."

"But how—what do I tell my professors? I can't be out for a week!" Tamara started to shake her head, then thought the better of it. "What about Justern?"

"That's what I told him," Merran said dryly from the other side of her. "But he didn't listen to me either."

"You deserve each other." He glared at them both. "You both are confined to this apartment, and I mean that. There will be no arguments. Not this Monday, but next Monday morning, if everything goes well, you can return to your normal routines. As for Justern, I suspect there won't be much you can do for him in the next week except make sure you don't burn yourself out and finish what you started." He leaned over and looked Tamara in the eye. "You have Awakened and are now going to heal, but I want you to know, Tamara, that you very nearly burned yourself, Merran, and Alarin out. All three of you will remain in this apartment to heal. Is that understood?"

She blinked at his intensity.

"Good. When I'm feeling better myself, I'll be able to speed some of the process along. A week is not that long." Greg straightened and included Merran in the comment. "No complaining about it, as I'm going to be stuck here with the three of you, understood?" He turned. "Now, do as you will, but I am going back out into the living room to try and relax. We've had a very busy morning." He walked out of the room, leaving Merran and Tamara alone, closing the door behind him much more gently than Tamara expected from his obviously exasperated state.

That left her alone with Merran, a state she found herself much more nervous about than she'd expected. "I, uh, are you all right?"

"I'm sore," he replied. "But I'm fine." He cocked his head and looked at her. "But I suspect you're more sore than I am."

She flushed. *Does he mean what I think he does?* "I'm okay."

"I'm sorry. I know I was a little rough, but things were getting a bit—we were running out of time and I didn't have time to be as gentle as I'd have liked. Awakenings are not always pleasant memories." He pulled his knees up to his chest, the sheet preventing her from seeing anything.

Yup, he does. She could feel herself turning redder. "I can't remember it actually. I have patchy flashes every now and then, but I can't recall it in any detail."

"You're lucky. I remember mine far more clearly than I'd have liked."

Tamara frowned. "Alarin's seemed to be pleasant enough."

Merran closed his eyes. "Mine was hell." He opened them again. "I also suspect Alarin's version was edited. Awakening is not pleasant because it's not always easy, not for psi as strong as we are, especially if we resist our Awakenings."

Tamara took his hesitancy as her cue to state what was going through her mind. "It just feels strange. Unlike what I expected. To be Awake, to suddenly not be a virgin anymore, but to not really remember it ... I feel awkward, strange. And sore." She smiled at him. "I didn't have time to get used to the idea that I am half-Azellian, and now I have to be an adult too. You know what I would like?"

Merran looked at her quizzically.

"For you to just hold me." She looked back at him from across the gulf that had opened between them. "I'm weirded out by all this and I just want to lie still for a while." It was also going to be an experience, touching him without any clothes on.

Merran smiled and moved, opening his arms. He had a layer of hair across his chest running down toward the sheets and to the regions she didn't remember. She was a bit too shy to really look, but she shifted herself so she was resting against him. His arms came around her stomach and he rested his chin on her hair. Her bare back on his chest felt nice—warm, cozy, and as if he could hold all the horrors of the world away. Tamara held his arm against her stomach, wrapping her fingers around his muscular forearm. "Azellians aren't normally as physical outside of sex as humans," he murmured into her hair. "I could definitely get used to it, though."

They lay like that for a while. She rested there, almost dozing, and sensed that he was too, when a knock on the door startled them both.

"Yes?" Merran's voice vibrated through his chest.

"I don't want to disturb you, but did you intend to have your interview, Mer, or would you rather put it off until tomorrow? Janille's on the phone. You are supposed to be on in twenty minutes." Greg's voice.

"Shit!" Merran tensed. "No, I'm coming. Tell Janille I'll be ready."

Tamara shifted to look up at him. "Is this about Justern?"

He nodded. "One of the PR handlings I have to do." He sighed. The sheet slipped off her chest, and his eyes drifted down. He lifted a hand and gently traced down her chest, following his fingers with his eyes. His eyelids drooped, making him look almost sleepy. The look made her stomach clench and the parts of her she would have sworn were too sore to do anything at all react. "I'd much rather stay here and hold you. By the grace of the *aarya*, you are beautiful, *akila*." He lowered his head and kissed her.

The kiss was meant to be short but turned into something else quickly. Merran didn't think he would have it in himself to react to her again so soon, but he did. Her response, shy but growing more confident, drove him wild. She fell back and he followed.

He drew away gasping, his heart racing wildly. "Whoa! We have to stop or I won't be able to, and twenty minutes is way too short to do what I want to do."

A part of her was sorry, but there was another part of her that was glad. She was a little too sore to really continue what they were doing. It felt good, though, and the pressure of him through the sheets was very exciting. She reached down and touched. "I don't want to be a tease. Can you stop now?"

"Not if you do that." Merran pulled himself free and rolled off her. "As for being a tease, I started it." He stood up, fully naked. Tamara found herself watching him intently. There was something incredible in the feeling that she'd caused this kind of reaction. Merran also had an ease about being naked that she envied. He walked into the bathroom.

"Are you taking a shower?" Tamara asked, not quite confident enough herself to follow. *Topless is one thing. The rest is something else entirely.*

"No, just washing off from our earlier exertions. I don't have time for a full shower." Merran appeared in the doorway, holding a washcloth. "You may want to take one, though." He washed himself unselfconsciously as Tamara watched, then disappeared into the bathroom again. When he came back, he had a folded towel that he handed to her as he walked to the closet. "Greg told me Mellis was headed over with a change of clothes. You can borrow some of mine until she gets here."

"How is she going to get into my room?" Tamara asked, still watching him and not reminding him that she'd brought a change of clothes over already.

Merran stuck his head around the closet door. "You have just Awakened, haven't you? Locked doors are not all that difficult to get into if you need to."

She made a face at him. "All right, all right, rub it in."

He came out of the closet fully dressed and walked over to her. He leaned down and placed his hands on either side of her on the bed. "I'll show you a few applications of our abilities, if you like."

She looked at his eyes, only inches away from her face. "Is that a promise?"

He kissed her. This time he didn't let it get too far. "Yes. And as for the rest, we'll see if we're up to it later."

She smiled. "It's a date. What about Alarin and Greg in the other room?"

He straightened. "What about them? The room's shielded. If we don't make any noise, they won't hear us. Unless you want them to join in?"

She flushed. "Uh—"

He laughed and kissed the top of her head. "I'm kidding."

"Ugh!" She pulled the sheets up and watched him leave, closing the door behind him. She wondered suddenly if Azellians had more than one partner at a time regularly, then shook her head and banished the thought. She got up and went to take her shower.

When she came out of the bedroom, she elected to wear nothing but one of Merran's t-shirts that fell to her knees. He was quite a bit taller than she was, but the t-shirt must have been huge on him, too, because it made a passable dress on her. She'd scrounged up her bra and a clean pair of underwear from her duffle—she actually had a change of clothes in there, but she wanted to wear his shirt. She'd also found a belt, and cinched it around her waist. The t-shirt covered everything it should and didn't even look that odd.

Greg was perched on the couch watching some program on the flat screen, now suspended from the ceiling. Alarin walked in from the kitchen, carrying a plate of some kind of fruit as she stood shyly by the door.

"Feeling better?" he asked her. Surrounded by a brilliant turquoise glow, his hair gleamed in the dimness of the room. Green with lovely blue and even a few brown streaks, creating a hazel overtone, he joined Greg on the couch. "Come, join us. Greg's watching some medical show. It's very gory. Just what I want to watch while I'm snacking."

Greg growled something in response.

She frowned as she looked at him. "Isn't your aura usually green? Or am I remembering that wrong?"

Alarin nodded. "Normally, yes."

"Then what's all that blue in it? And brown?" she asked, suddenly remembering a conversation she'd had with Greg on the subject. Merran's aura was hazel—normally brown—but add her blue, and some green, and you got hazel. Her own was probably hazel, too. From Merran. Right?

Alarin shrugged. "Side effect of helping you Awaken." He walked to the couch. "I managed to find some fruit. Let's get Mel to do some food shopping too, shall we? I'm going to starve staying here." He looked back at Tamara. "Are you joining us?"

Tamara thought quickly back to her talk with Greg. *Auras intermingle whenever a couple has any type of intimacy, usually physical. I don't remember the sexual part of my Awakening. Actually, I do remember dark hair. Merran, then? But do I remember Alarin? I remember him from earlier, but where did he go when Merran stepped in? I don't remember.*

"Tamara?" Greg poked his head over the couch, either sensing her unease or knowing her well enough to know what she was thinking. "Stop freaking out about it. It's not really all that complex. It took the two of them to channel you, especially as Merran was doing all the physical part. If I'd been able, I would have helped with the mental part, too. The channeling left Alarin with both your and Merran's auras on him. The effect will fade. Now will you come and sit down?"

Greg's matter-of-fact tone and Alarin's casual behavior made her relax somewhat. She walked into the living room, hearing Merran's voice coming from his office as she passed. He looked relaxed, but his fingers off-screen rubbed a pencil, speaking of internal tension. She walked the rest of the way into the living room.

"Sit, before I hit him with that plate." Greg patted a spot between himself and Alarin. Alarin grinned at Greg. "Try some fruit. You're going to be hungrier than usual the next couple of days."

Tamara settled down between them and looked up to see some bizarre, bloody mass of pink tissue on the screen. "Ugh. What is that?"

Greg stared intently at the screen. "They're doing a liver transplant."

"And you want me to eat something while watching this?" Tamara demanded. "Gross."

"Thank you," Alarin chimed in. "I vote for another channel."

"Me too," Tamara added. "Anything else, please."

"Fine." Greg changed the channel to a tall, dark man talking earnestly about making a fine Italian dinner. The slab of meat on his plate looked way too much like the liver they'd just seen.

"That's awful!" Tamara and Alarin said simultaneously. "Anything else, go, go, go, before he gets a plate of fruit between his eyes," Tamara added.

Greg grinned and changed the channel again. This time it was to watch a man stick his hands up a horse and help it give birth.

"What in the name of the *aarya* do humans make shows about?" Alarin demanded. "Isn't there anything on that doesn't turn your stomach?"

Tamara glared at Greg. "He's doing it on purpose, choosing the channels he knows will gross us out." She moved a little too quickly and tried to grab the remote. The effort left her dizzy and her head pounding, as Greg held the remote out and away from himself. "Give me that!" She reached up his arm.

Greg looked at her, then licked her nose.

"Eewww." Tamara returned to her own spot, rubbing her nose. "That was gross."

"He has an unfair advantage, you realize," Alarin told her solemnly, his eyes bright and spoiling the solemn note in his voice. "He's not in as bad of shape as we are. And he knows it. Just wait until my psi comes back on line, Gregerin Tenricth."

"All right, fine." Greg flipped to something innocuous. The good-natured teasing and playing continued, and Tamara managed, for a short time, to forget the world outside that apartment. It was a time in her life she would remember later as being one of the happiest.

Chapter Ten

INDEED, THE REAL WORLD intruded itself within the next hour. Merran came into the living room looking tired. He loosened his tie and discarded the suit coat.

Alarin looked up from the movie they had finally compromised to watch together. "Finished?"

"I don't know that it will ever be completely finished," Merran retorted, running a hand through his dark hair. "But yes, that interview is over."

"How did it go?" Greg hit the mute button as he and Tamara moved to make room.

"Better than I expected, not as well as I'd hoped. They spent most of the interview demanding to know about you, Healer." Merran settled down on the couch in the spot between Tamara and Greg. He rested his head in his hands. "And now that headache that was nagging me earlier has become a full-fledged nuisance."

349

Greg ran his hands lightly through Merran's aura. Tamara suddenly noticed there were little eddies in his aura, roils in the hazel. They soothed as Greg touched them, smoothing into an even, fine flow.

She stared, fascinated. "Is that Healing?"

Greg shook his head. "Not really. This is something anyone can do. I can't Heal, so I'm just soothing his aura. It won't help except to calm him down a little and maybe allow him to ride out the pain better."

Merran laid his head back and closed his eyes. "It's very relaxing, which does help the headache."

Alarin leaned over to look at Merran. "Did they try to find out about any of our other talents?"

"Not really. They were more fascinated with the Healing and grilled me at length about it." Merran opened one eye and looked behind Tamara's head to meet Alarin's eyes. "No hostility at least. They are having a hard time reconciling their idea of the world with Greg's activities. It's only a matter of time, though, before they start asking me some pretty blunt questions about the rest of us."

Greg continued his ministrations until Merran's aura evened out. Then he pulled his hands away. "We expected this when we agreed to come here. I do wish I didn't have to reveal my abilities, but as the choice was between Justern's life and revealing our abilities, well, I made the choice."

"So did I." Merran turned to regard Greg. "I gave you the go ahead. The Council was none too happy with me."

"Would they have preferred that you let Justern die?" Alarin sounded indignant.

Merran turned again and winced, putting a hand to his head. "Not really. Which is why they weren't happy, but there wasn't a lot to be said about it. They've left me to sort out the minefield myself. They haven't made any kind of formal statement yet, either supporting or chastising me for the decision."

"Ohhh ... they're going to see which way this goes, then." He fixed his gaze on Merran. "And disengage or support you at that point," Alarin added.

Merran nodded. "Damage control. We're hanging out here alone at the moment. I don't have any doubt that should it prove politically expedient, they'll withdraw completely."

"And recall us?"

Merran shrugged. "It's possible. Very possible, if we can't handle the firestorm."

Alarin sighed. "We're in for a long week."

"The interviewers think I've been called out of town, although I haven't been too specific on that point. Janille's going to be swamped with phone calls." Merran closed his eyes again. "This week's going to be one interview after the other, I suspect. I just hope I get to air some of the unfairness about Justern's case in between the buzz of Greg's abilities."

A beeping noise from the other room made them all jump. Greg got up and answered it. He came back moments later. "It's Tamara's father looking for you, Mer. Janille's got him on hold through the embassy lines."

"I'm coming." Merran leaned forward and got to his feet. "He's going to want to talk to you, Tamara."

She nodded and got up too. "Did you want to talk to him first?"

"Come back with me, but stay off camera. I'm going to tell him you're here, but I'll leave it to you to tell him the rest," Merran replied.

"He's going to know what Awakening entailed, won't he?" Tamara clicked her fingers together nervously.

"He spent a year on Azelle. I'm sure he's aware of it," Merran responded as he scratched the back of his neck. "I don't know that you need to tell him who was involved, though."

Tamara gave him a look. "Who else would it be? I'm in your apartment and Greg's too injured. I think he'll figure it out."

Merran made a face and blew air out his lips with a short puff. "Let's get this over with." He led her to the office area and settled in the chair in front of the computer. "Janille? Patch him through. Thank you."

Peter Carrington's face appeared on the screen. "Merran? Is everything all right? I got a call from the embassy telling me that you were called away from town and you would only be available through video or phone interviews. What happened? Did the interview go all right?"

Merran nodded. "Everything's fine. This issue is becoming a Healer issue. We are in danger of losing media coverage on Justern's case completely."

Peter looked grim. "I know, and that's not the tack I need. If it gets buried under the much more sensational revelation of Greg we aren't going to get what we need from this case. It gives her far too much ammunition to try to pretend Justern forced her mentally, rousing whispers about what each one of you can and cannot do. Would Greg be willing to do any interviews?"

"I might be able to convince him, once he's ready to face the world again. I do have Joely's memories of the event." He tapped his fingers on the desk.

"How did you manage to get those?" Peter demanded, his eyes widening. "You didn't do anything she could bring against you, did you?"

Merran shook his head. "Nothing provable. Alarin, Mellis, and Tamara ran into her spreading rumors at dinner the other night. Alarin stopped and asked her if she'd set up Justern. The question prompted her to remember everything. We got a visual on the memories, and it appears Justern was unable to force anyone, even himself. He was pretty drunk and passed out. She definitely set him up." He sighed. "For some reason, she's got it out for him and developed quite an emotional reaction to him as a result. The memories weren't all that clear, but I suspect he's a stalking horse for someone who hurt her badly. Or he himself hurt her badly. It wasn't clear if he'd had a relationship with her or not, but the night she's claiming was rape was not."

Peter rubbed his chin. "Hmm, this could work. We could carefully reveal Greg's abilities and say that he can read memories. If the court will allow the information, we could set it up in court to have him supposedly read them both and get interpretations."

"If they accept the word of a friend of Justern's. Is it worth revealing our mind-reading abilities just to get told it's still inadmissible?"

"That could and probably would start a panic that might hurt our case. Damn. Have you read Justern's memories at all?"

Merran shook his head. "No. Actually, Peter, you're going to have to wing it a bit, for the next week at least. I wasn't really called out of town. I'm still at my apartment downtown and am stuck here until Greg gives me the all clear to leave."

"What happened? Are you all right?"

"I'm fine, just confined to quarters for a little while," Merran assured him. "I'm going to be running the PR end of things from here, as if I were out of town. There is more news, though. I have someone here who would like to talk to you." He got out of the chair and waved Tamara over.

"Hi Dad." Tamara settled into the chair.

"Tamara? Honey, is something wrong?" Peter leaned forward. "Are you at the ambassador's right now?"

Tamara nodded. "I'm fine, Dad. I—I'm kind of stuck here, too. Healer's orders."

Peter reached out. "What happened? Oh my God, Tamara, what's wrong? I want to see you. Where does the ambassador live?"

"I'm okay Dad. Don't worry. I just Awakened, that's all. No big deal," Tamara said hastily as he grew more and more agitated. "I'm fine. Really, I am." She glanced up at Merran, who stood off screen. Merran turned into the living room and waved Greg over.

"No big deal? Tamara, I know enough about Azellian Awakenings to know that you don't get confined to quarters after you Awaken. Tell me where you are!" His voice inched higher and louder. Merran waved his hands and nodded silently at Tamara.

"All right, Dad. You can visit, but Greg wants to talk to you first." Tamara tried to interpret Merran's motions and gestures as she attempted to calm her father.

Peter took a deep, slow breath. "I want to talk to him too."

Greg stepped into view. "Mr. Carrington."

"How is she?" he demanded. "Tell me the truth."

"She's fine. Your daughter inherited a very sensitive ability to project and receive emotion, Mr. Carrington. You know that the later the Awakening, the more trouble it can be, right?" Greg asked. Peter nodded, keeping his eyes glued to the monitor. "Well, she's very powerful and her Awakening was a little rough. She's fine now ... and functioning very normally ... but there was some trauma involved that related to her having suppressed her psi due to that incident in high school. She was able to release those bottled-up emotions and memories during her Awakening and initate healing around it. I've confined her to these shielded quarters so she doesn't irritate the already inflamed channels further or do permanent damage. It's merely a preventative measure really ... nothing more. She's in perfect health and came through the Awakening quite well. The channels are clear, and as soon as they heal, she will be a fully functioning, projecting empath. You can see her now, but I want you to know that you will need to keep your emotions shielded. You do know how to do that?"

Peter took another deep breath and nodded.

"It can be dangerous for her to receive right now, so you have to promise that you will be calm when you arrive. Tamara is fine, in perfect health, and there is no reason to be upset," Greg emphasized.

Peter's expression was calm—and attorney perfect. "I will be calm, Healer. I would very much like to see her, though. Just to reassure myself."

Greg smiled. "Understandable. When would you like to come by?"

"Now, if possible. I'm at my offices right now. Where is the ambassador's apartment?"

Greg gave him the address and stepped back.

"I know where that is, sweetheart. I'll be there momentarily," Peter said to Tamara and cut the connection.

Tamara's hand shook as she sat back. "God, that was harder than I expected."

Merran came over and gave her a little hug. "Your father's just worried about you, Tamara."

"I know, and it bothers me to do that to him. I wish I could have warned him or something."

"He knew you were Awakening. I told him a few days ago, so he knew." Merran led her back to the living room. She was so nervous about what had just transpired, that she didn't even notice Alarin disappear. "Just relax. It will be fine."

Just the same, when the buzzer sounded from downstairs, she jumped nervously. Greg reached out and ran his hands lightly over the surface of her skin. "Shhh," he said gently. "You're fine, Tamara."

Tingles ran up her arm and down to her stomach, where they settled and swirled. They were certainly distracting and strangely calming at the same time. Tension drained out of her.

The sound of the elevator as it stopped made her get to her feet. Greg released her.

The doors opened soundlessly and Peter stepped out. "Tamara."

Seeing her father standing there made her blink away tears hastily. "Dad." She went over to him and hugged him tightly. True to his word, not a hint of emotion seeped into her mind, despite the touch. His eyes were red and suspiciously moist as he pulled away after a few moments and looked down at her.

He lifted her chin and studied her face, turning it. "You look so much like Jasmian right at this moment. I never expected you'd inherit the psi, honey. I'm so sorry I didn't tell you sooner. It might have made your Awakening easier."

Tamara shook her head, tears quivering at the edge of her lashes. "It's all right Dad. I'm fine now, and I will be fine. I have people here who know how to deal with it and who have been training me from the day they arrived. Maybe it's better that it happened while they were around."

Peter let her chin go, but did not drop his arm from her shoulders. He looked up at Merran, who stood back against the elevator wall, then over at Greg, who sat on the couch watching. "Thank you both." He gave Tamara another hug and then let her go. He walked over to Merran. "May I talk to you? In private."

Tamara could see the expression on Merran's face clearly, although she could not see her father's. Diplomatically blank, he bowed, a very low, elaborate gesture, and waved Peter into the office.

Merran controlled his stomach's nervous roiling with an effort that left his head pounding. His hamstrung psi made it much harder to maintain an even demeanor, but years of habit helped. The two men faced each other.

"I'm aware of what the process of Awakening involves," her father began. "And Tamara is twenty, an adult, and more than capable of taking care of herself. You're older than she is, and we both know your experience is considerably greater in all ways. I'm not going to ask you what your intentions are. All I ask is that you think carefully before you decide where to go from here. Don't hurt her."

Merran bowed again, using the most submissive bow in the complex sublanguage he knew. Peter accepted the bow with a nod of the head and turned away. Merran stayed in the office, calming down his pounding heart and taking a few deep breaths.

"I need to get back to your mom, sweetheart," Peter said to Tamara as Merran came into the room. "Take care of yourself ... and be careful." He hugged her again. "Grandma's gone, so when you're better, come home."

Tamara returned the hug. "Thanks, Dad."

Peter stepped onto the elevator and exited.

Alarin came out of the bedroom as soon as the elevator doors whooshed closed.

"What happened to you?" Merran asked, scowling at him.

"I thought there might be just a few too many people here to make her father comfortable, so I made myself scarce." Alarin walked over to the couch and settled down on it. "Let's watch a movie, shall we? It's going to be a long week if all we get to do is sit around and stare at each other."

Tamara came around and joined Alarin on the couch. "The movie we were watching is over, right?"

"Long over," Alarin mused, touching the menu button on the remote and calling up the movie listing. "Hmm, how about this one? Nice love story for Greg, the gore hound."

"Hey, I gave in and let you watch what you wanted to, didn't I?" Greg protested.

They squabbled for a few moments more, as Tamara glanced back to see Merran standing in the kitchen. He seemed distant, a little cut off from the good-natured raillery.

She got up, leaving Alarin and Greg to continue their argument, and went over to him. "What is it?"

Merran focused on her. "Nothing you can help me with." His eyes traveled down her body and back up. "Nice use for that shirt."

Tamara struck a pose. "Like it? My fashion sense isn't always on the mark, but this shirt just screamed dress."

That got a grin out of him. "Funny … that. It never screamed anything when I wore it, much less dress."

She tugged at the hem of the shirt that landed somewhere below her knee. "This must come down to your mid-thigh."

Merran nodded. She could see him relaxing a little. He shifted his stance. "It does. I like it because it's cooler than an Azellian robe but very reminiscent of one."

"So what do Azellians wear under their robes?" Tamara asked, looking up at him and batting her eyelashes. "And the rest of the question ... what does a newly Awakened half-Azellian wear under her shirt dress?"

The smile was slow, curling up one side of his mouth. "I don't know what's under a shirt dress, but an Azellian robe includes very little, unless we need the support." He cocked his head and looked down at her. The expression on his face made her breath catch. "I could imagine what's under the shirt dress, though."

It was Merran's turn to have his breath catch. Her coy, shy smile just about undid him. Despite his desire to keep it slow. And despite her father's warning. He straightened and controlled his reaction with an effort. "That would be interesting," she said, her voice taking on a husky tone, daring him to reply while Greg and Alarin were sitting not far away.

His eyes took on a mischievous glint. He leaned over so his mouth was not far from her ear. Tamara froze when he spoke in her ear—his breath puffing against her neck as he told her in somewhat graphic terms just what he imagined was beneath her shirt dress. Her heart pounded, her cheeks burned, and she jumped back. "All right, all right. You win." She glanced over at Alarin and Greg, who seemed oblivious to the whole thing.

"They aren't, you realize." Merran crossed his arms, a little smile playing at the corners of his mouth.

"They aren't what?"

"Oblivious. They are ignoring us, yes, but they are very much aware of what's going on over here."

Tamara glared at him. "Did you read me just then?"

He grinned. "Guilty as charged."

She made a face at him. "That's not fair."

He laughed. "You started it, *akila*."

"What does that mean?" Tamara asked, grumpy that he was right.

"Find out," Merran invited. She could sense, somewhat fuzzily, that he was open, inviting her to reach out to him.

"How?" Her anger faded as she focused on him. Her head pounded a little, but she discovered she could do it. She imagined reaching out to touch another pair of hands. As the two hands came into contact, she could read his intention behind the word, although the word was not translated. It was an affectionate pet name and carried almost childhood connotations with it. She pulled her mental hands back quickly. "Whoa. How did you do that?"

"I didn't. You did. It's one of the secrets of psi. With that technique, you will be able to pick up the meanings of the words I use without translation and without having to know what I'm saying."

Tamara extended her hands again. "Say something in Azellian."

A good portion of Azellian is psionic, Merran sent mentally and continued out loud in Azellian, "It is the way we have worked for years. Maybe the only reason we use spoken language anymore is to communicate with children. They need the physical speech. And for communication with other cultures, of course."

Tamara found she could follow what he said clearly and easily. It was not precisely that she understood the words themselves, but the intent behind them. Before he even finished talking, his intention was already clear to her. She opened her mouth to speak

Azellian back. "But—" the words didn't come any easier than they ever had. "I still am not speaking very well."

"That takes practice," Merran replied in English. "Practice and time. Psi helps with understanding, but not speaking, because this particular talent is simply that you are hearing my intentions and giving form to the words after you already know what I'm going to say. There are ways to enhance the speaking ability, but they are far more intense and require a form of teaching that involves sharing knowledge and minds." He grinned at her. "They're cheating, really."

"Is that how you learned English?"

"No. I learned it the hard way."

"Which is probably why he won't use the other way," Alarin interjected from his position on the couch. "He doesn't know how."

Merran raised both eyebrows. "Speak for yourself, *syyada*." The word didn't translate.

"Hey," Tamara protested. "It didn't work that time."

"That's because we don't want to start teaching you bad language before you've even had a chance to learn the right stuff," Greg commented.

"I know better than you do, *kiitir*," Alarin shot back, using another word that didn't translate.

"Oh, is that how you learned English?" Merran retorted.

Alarin grinned and leaned back, lacing his fingers behind his head. "I learned a lot of things that way."

Merran snorted. "*Syyada*."

"Look who's talking, *kiitir*." Alarin blew air through his lips. "Do you two lovebirds want to join us for the movie?"

"What did you finally agree to watch?" Merran walked into the living room.

"Red Sun," Alarin replied. "It sounds pretty funny."

"It's supposed to be about Azelle, actually," Tamara followed him into the living room. "I've heard it's okay. Not really great but somewhat entertaining. One of the reviews said it's supposed to be titillatingly spooky."

"Titillatingly spooky. How does that translate?" Merran looked over at her and grinned.

Tamara spread her hands. "I'm not entirely sure the reviewer even knew."

"Sit." Alarin tapped the couch. Merran stepped over the back of the couch and settled down beside him. Tamara elected to go around. Alarin made room for her between himself and Merran. "Let's watch our titillatingly spooky movie, shall we?"

The movie turned out to be primarily about humans' fears of Azellians. The three Azellians found it rather funny and kept up a running commentary throughout most of it. They paused the movie when one or the other had to go to the bathroom and when Mellis showed up with clothes and dinner. So she could join them, they ran over each other to describe what had happened up to that point and then started the movie again.

"I don't know, Alari. Do you ever run around trying to kill someone because you're dangerously low on some mysterious vitamin complex that humans have never heard of?" Merran asked after the movie was over, eyeing Alarin like he thought it might happen in the next three minutes. "Has anyone you've ever known run dangerously low on anything?"

"It could happen," Greg said, his eyes twinkling brightly."You never know. Any one of us could snap."

"I might." Alarin eyed Merran, Tamara, Greg, and Mellis. "I would command the lightning bolts to fry you as you sit." He gave an evil laugh.

Mellis got to her feet. "And I would dance around in my underwear chanting spells." She obliged, swinging her hips and kicking up her feet.

Tamara could barely stop giggling. "How did they consider that titillatingly spooky in any way? Stupendously stupid is more like it."

Merran rolled his eyes and put his hand against his forehead. "But it's about those titillatingly spooky Azellians, you know." He lifted his head and glared, managing to look more dead than spooky, showing nothing but the whites of his eyes. Tamara grabbed her stomach, bending in half and gasping for air. "And we can command the heavens to do as we please." He lifted a hand and pointed. "Kneel, mortal!"

Tamara fell over, leaning against him. "Enough!"

"Where do they come up with some of those ideas?" Mellis wondered, picking up her plate. "That movie was the strangest mix of fear and rumor I've ever seen. It's like someone took their idea of evil gods and stuck them into a movie, then had to cut them down to size."

Tamara caught her breath and straightened out. "That's probably what they did. The writer of that movie certainly has never met any actual Azellians."

"Although he has certainly heard enough about our openness to portray us all as oversexed orgy fanatics. How many orgies have you participated in?" Greg asked. "Do you know how long it's been since I slept with anyone at all, much less participated in an orgy?"

"Speak for yourself." Alarin sniffed and held his hand up. "I'm an orgy connoisseur."

"Really?" Mellis sidled over to him. "Can you invite me to one sometime? I don't seem to be on anyone's list."

"I don't think I've ever seen an orgy quite the way they tried to portray one," Merran commented thoughtfully. "Did you want to try?" He gave a wide, clenched tooth smile.

"Complete with the lightning bolts?" Greg asked. "Can't do it without those lightning bolts."

"Or the ZX-20 in those delicious bananas," Alarin added. "It might become dangerous without those bananas. Why does a mysterious vitamin complex appear in bananas anyway? How did we ever survive without humans and their bananas?"

"And the sinister music playing. Maybe we didn't exist before humans discovered us. And provided us with bananas," Mellis commented as she made a face. "We're just *aarya* who became *uman*." She heaved herself off the couch and turned to Tamara. "Congratulations, Tamara. I'm so glad you're really one of us now." Tamara could feel a light brush against her mind, the sensation traveling through her entire body, as if Mellis had given her a big hug. It felt warm and wonderfully welcoming.

"Me, too," Tamara replied and got to her feet, giving Mellis a physical hug, since she didn't think she could manage a mental one with her psi so hamstrung. Mellis planted a kiss on her cheek and tightened her arms around Tamara, the physical embrace echoing her mental embrace beautifully.

After a few moments, Mellis stepped away from the hug and turned to the others. "Well, guys, it's been fun, but I have to get back. You all are lazy bums for a week, but I have class tomorrow." She blew Alarin, Merran, and Greg a kiss as she walked over to the elevator. "Any of you decide to have an orgy, please invite me."

"We promise, although I don't think we'll be up for it until we've healed a little more." Alarin crossed his fingers over his chest. "Those lightning bolts take energy, you know." Mellis laughed and got on the elevator.

Merran got up, too. "You and Greg can fight over who gets the couch and who gets the air mattress on the floor in the office." Tamara's stomach clenched when the hilarity disappeared with Mellis's departure, at least for her. Alarin and Greg certainly seemed to be in high spirits as Merran dragged an air mattress, extra pillows, and blankets into the room.

Should I just follow Merran into the bedroom? she asked herself. He hadn't asked her, and though she'd spent last night and a couple of nights ago in his bed, this was completely different. Their relationship had changed, for one thing, and this wasn't a suddenly-they-found-themselves-in-bed situation. For another, Greg and Alarin were going to be sleeping in the very next room, and that thought made her oddly nervous.

Merran dropped the last of the pillows on the couch. He looked over at Tamara. "I'm going to bed. Would you care to join me?"

Tamara blushed furiously and didn't know what to say.

Alarin and Greg grinned. "Don't demur on our account," Greg told her. "Good night."

"Good night," Alarin added. He winked at her. "Sleep well."

Merran was standing at the door of the room when Tamara gathered enough of her courage to follow him. She entered and he closed the door behind her.

She stood with her back against the door as he walked into the bathroom, did what he had to, and came back out.

"I'm not going to bite," Merran told her, seeing her still standing against the door. "You can come in."

Tamara ducked her head, her hair falling toward her face, suddenly feeling very shy.

A wash of an emotion he didn't immediately recognize spread through him. He walked over to her and reached out to cup her chin. He lifted it, brushing the hair away from her face with his other hand. Merran bent his head and kissed her, offering a gentle, exploratory kiss.

It took her a few moments to lose her tension, but she wrapped her arms around his neck and responded. The kiss deepened, and he lifted her, carrying her to the bed, his hands exploring and caressing.

Merran knew what he was doing—places he touched made her gasp and writhe. His focus was entirely on her—it was unnerving to be the focus of that much attention. She tried to touch him too, but he stopped her. "Not yet," he whispered, kissing her neck. "First you." As he built the tension in her body and mind to a feverish pitch, she lost every sense of anything else but the overwhelming feeling starting to peak. Somewhere in the back of her mind, she remembered she had to be quiet, so she held her breath and made noises under her breath. Her hands touched skin—when had he taken off his clothes? His skin was so hot; she could feel him press against her. She moved, welcoming him. His body moved above her as she wrapped her legs around him and moved with him.

As she moved, Merran lost his detachment, his desire to give her pleasure beyond himself taking over. He could feel her slipping in under his shields—what thin ones he could maintain, as injured as he was. The sensation was not what he was used to—it made him spasm. He felt her reach her peak and it sent him spiraling after her, his mind wrapped around hers in an incredibly intimate way he had never experienced before. It was a tight spiral, the orgasm spreading out, then back in, through the two of them and … into someone else. Merran became aware there was a shadow, almost like another being was wrapped with them, a mind entwined through Tamara's. It had a familiar flavor to it. Merran tried to chase down that thin presence, but his injured psi defeated him and he had to let it go.

Tamara felt Merran tense, then relax, still breathing hard. He dropped down onto her, his weight pressing into her body. Their breathing slowed together. "Is that what it's always like?" She was a bit sore again but not nearly as bad as she had been earlier.

Merran rolled off her, still holding her close. "No. I wasn't intending for it to end that … quickly. You rather tipped me over the edge."

"Sorry."

He chuckled and she felt it rumble through his chest. "That's quite all right." He kissed her hair. "I certainly enjoyed it."

She lay relaxed against him. Her mind told him she was drifting off slowly. Far from relaxed himself, Merran looked down at her. An ache stretched the back of his throat and he closed his eyes in pain. Her father's warning echoed in his head. *What are my intentions? How can I balance a job that demands all of my time with someone who needs to have my time, too? To say nothing about the complications of her history and my own family?* Lying there, his mind whirled for a long time after Tamara fell into the deeper patterns of sleep.

The next morning, Merran woke much earlier than Tamara. His clock told him it was early—almost five. Tamara lay sprawled across the bed, the glow trailing from the bathroom nightlight revealed her face relaxed in sleep. Even asleep, she moved him.

Why is she so attractive to me? She is a distraction, after all, one I can't afford right now, not with Justern's trial looming close and Azellian fates on Earth hanging in the balance. What if I am recalled? Given who her father is, and how picky the Council is about allowing people to go to the planet, getting her to Azelle is going to be a fight I'm really not sure I can win, although a stint on Azelle is probably essential for her development. She works with me ... we really shouldn't be doing this. Unless I cut her out of my life completely, though, I'm not going to be able to stay away from her. He scowled at the canopy above and swung his legs over the edge of the bed to get up. Tamara stirred and he froze in place, waiting until she drifted back into sleep again.

In deference to Greg and Alarin, he got a robe out and pulled it on, although they probably wouldn't care. *She's already changing me,* he thought to himself, belting the robe loosely around his waist and opening and closing the door stealthily.

The lights of Denver kept the living room from being shrouded in complete darkness. Merran could sense—and hear—Greg snoring softly on the couch. Alarin was a dark figure on the air mattress in his office. Merran couldn't make out his features in the dark but sensed he was asleep as well.

There wasn't much he could do without waking up at least Alarin, but Merran made his way to the kitchen and turned on the light over the stove. He pulled out a teapot and set water to boiling.

"Can't sleep?" Alarin's voice, speaking in Azellian, made him jump and turn around. He sat on the edge of the air mattress, green eyes far more alert than Merran expected.

He rubbed a hand over his eyes. "You could say that," he answered in the same language.

"Restless night for all of us." Alarin sighed and slipped onto one of the stools in front of the kitchen island. "This week is one of those periods in life that are turning points. There are momentous changes going on."

Merran reached up, pulling out two cups. "Momentous is right." He sighed and put the cups on the counter. He leaned over the counter and rested his arms, his head hanging down below his shoulder blades. He looked up after a moment. "How do we control the flow of our lives? To prevent what should not be?"

"And accept what should?" Alarin finished. "*Alawahea*, Merran. What is, was, and will be."

Merran poured tea for both of them. "*Alawahea* is for those who lack the strength to fight. I will not be overwhelmed by anyone. I've spent too much of my life fighting for what I have." He handed Alarin the cup.

Alarin accepted the cup and was silent for a while. "It's not a sacrifice when made for someone we care about."

"It's still a sacrifice. Maybe one we willingly accept, but it is still a sacrifice when there is no room for it."

"It's worth it. What are the chances of finding it again? We aren't talking about an abstraction here. We're talking about a living, breathing person who is adrift and completely alone. An alien among her people because we appeared in her life. We have a duty to her."

"What do you mean by that?" Merran knew his tone bordered on belligerent, but he did nothing to soften it. Under his belligerence, though, he sensed something—something Alarin did not say.

Alarin did not answer. His eyes watched Merran over the rim of his teacup.

Merran hissed in irritation. "You don't know what you are asking. She's—"

"Not full-blooded High Council," Alarin finished, an odd edge to his voice.

Merran scowled. "That has nothing to do with it."

"Then what does?" Alarin leaned forward, far more intense than he should have been.

"I'm working with her. She's just a student. She's too young. This thing with Justern is going to blow up in all of our faces. The Council would never approve her visa. Her family doesn't approve of Azellians. Mine won't approve of her human side. What about the Council? Do you think they would let me even start a relationship with a human? I'm the ambassador of Azelle, damn it. I don't have time for a relationship, much less one that threatens to take over my whole life."

Alarin just looked at him.

Merran paced the kitchen. "The *aarya* damn it all."

Alarin watched him pace. "It will work out, Merran. What others say doesn't matter. You know that. They're not the ones you have to face at the end of the day. It's yourself."

Merran stopped. "What do you know about it? You've never had to deal with the whispers, the snide comments, the constant struggle to prove that even though you don't have the name on both sides, you still can get things accomplished." He glared at Alarin. "You don't even have to worry about the woman you love meeting up to the acceptance and approval of everyone else."

Alarin did not react immediately, but Merran could tell he had hit a nerve. The Raderth temper flared. "No, I just have to accept that I have no choice in the matter at all. You think you've had it hard, Merran? You don't know hard. You've managed to accomplish everything you set out to do. Everything! When we were younger, you told me that you were going to become ambassador. Did you let the Council stop you then? You fought and managed to get us here. Did the Council stop you? Justern may be found guilty, and if you want it badly enough, you won't let the Council recall all of us, much less the embassy. You think the Council thinks any less of you because you're not pure High Council? Wake up, Merran! You have managed to accomplish more than your last four predecessors and you know it. Greg has been brought out into the open. Do you know what kind of bargaining tool this is? Humans will be drooling to give us whatever we want, just so long as we let our Healers walk among their sick. You could probably end this farce of a trial tomorrow if you wanted. But you don't, do you? You're going to let this trial rip you and her apart. Why? Not because you are really afraid of the Council or of your family or hers, but because *you're* afraid. *Of her.* Of the feelings she's bringing out in you. Tell me you don't love her. Tell me you aren't in love with her. Tell me you aren't terrified that she might be the one woman in the universe who you could be with forever."

Merran leaned against the counter, his hands pushed against the smooth hard surface, his arms locked against awareness, with his head down once more. He didn't say anything.

Alarin continued after a moment. "She's innocent and falling in love with you, the *aarya* know why. If you hurt her, Merran, because you're too selfish to see what's in front of your face, I swear, I will never speak to you again." Merran could sense the strongly restrained emotion. Alarin, who never leaked, was leaking all over right now.

Suspicions clicked. Merran stared at Alarin with his mouth open. "You're in love with her, too."

Alarin made a noise between a groan and a growl. "Not that it matters how I feel. For whatever reason, she's chosen you. So I warn you, if you hurt her—" He took a deep breath and with some effort calmed himself down. "Tamara's very special, Merran. She's a wonderful, very sweet girl who I would snap up in a moment were circumstances different. Don't screw it up."

Merran didn't say anything for a long moment. "What about Ida?"

"I don't know. I just don't know," he repeated in a tired, almost defeated tone. "I came to Earth looking for solutions and found complications."

"Join the club," Merran snorted, running his hand through his hair. He said nothing for a few moments. "So how do I manage to integrate everything?"

Alarin quickly returned to his usual calm state, shields hiding his emotions quite thoroughly. "I have to figure out my own mess. How am I supposed to know the solution to yours?"

Merran put his cup in the sink. "We didn't come out of that Awakening unchanged, did we?"

"No, we didn't."

"Are you going to be all right?"

"*Alawahea*, Merran. All we can do is see what life hands us and work with what we have." Alarin sighed. "She doesn't need to know, all right? It's my problem, not hers." He managed a weak smile. "Side effect of the Awakening and sharing far more than I should have. Chalk it up to the fact I'm not a Healer."

Merran studied him for a long moment. The turquoise streaks in his aura were stronger today, more vivid. "You rode it with us last night, didn't you?"

Alarin sighed, rubbing his eyebrows. "That's something else

she doesn't need to know. Another side effect of the Awakening, I assume, and the fact that my aura is still entwined with hers."

"We'll abstain for the rest of the week."

Alarin looked at him sideways. "What will you tell her?"

Merran made a face. "Ah, that'll be tricky, as I've already told her you two don't care."

"Don't tell her anything."

Merran raised an eyebrow. "And this helps how?"

"Don't abstain. Not on my account. If it bothers you, go ahead, stay away from her. But don't worry about me." There was definitely an odd note in his voice.

"Keep—you can't possibly mean it. To ride her orgasms with me? You'll be wild by the end of the week. Or insane."

Alarin sighed. "Let that be my problem. I—what if this effect doesn't fade? You can't stay away from her just because I'm around. I may as well get used to it."

Merran stared at him. "Alarin—" He shook his head. "She's sensitive enough to figure it out eventually."

"I was there for her first time, so she has nothing to compare it to if I'm there for later times, too."

"Don't you think this is complicated enough as it is?" Merran folded his arms across his chest.

Alarin shrugged. "Probably." A grin touched the edges of his mouth. "But I can't do anything simply."

"What about Greg?" Merran looked over to the couch. "He's stuck here too."

Alarin grinned. "Poor Greg."

"You're damned right, poor Greg." The voice came from the couch. Greg sat up, his hair tousled. "It's not just you who's going to be wild by the end of the week, given that these two might as well be *aarya* in mating season."

"And a good morning to you," Merran said with feigned cheerfulness as he walked out of the kitchen, followed by Alarin. "What's your opinion about this little situation we seem to find ourselves in?"

Greg rubbed his eyes. "Well, for one thing, you're probably right about it being a side effect of her Awakening. At least the physical part is."

Merran leaned against the couch arm. "And the mental part?"

Greg yawned. "Is the *aarya* playing a joke on us?"

"So will the effect fade?" Alarin asked from shields as tight as they could be, considering. Merran couldn't tell if he was happy or sad about it.

"I have no idea." Greg looked at Alarin out of grave, amber eyes. "I've never seen this particular complication before." He frowned. "Have you thought about how difficult it would be to try to carry on your normal life with her there all the time? Right now, you're riding her orgasms. If this is a two-way thing, she'll ride yours too, and that's going to be something to try to explain to her."

Merran looked at Greg. "So he's not sharing with me, then?"

Greg's eyebrows shot up. "He could be. But considering that it was Tamara he was entwined with, I suspect not. If this is a permanent side effect, it's going to play hell with your sex life, Alarin. I doubt Ida, or any other woman for that matter, will want to share you with Tamara, and there's really no way you can hide it. Not if it's leaving tracks like that in your aura."

Alarin sagged, looking tired. "I know."

Greg looked sideways at Merran. "And how about you? How do you feel about sharing Tamara?"

Merran was silent for a long moment. "I don't know, actually," he said finally. "It has ... possibilities. What about me? Am I tied to her that way, too?"

"Maybe. It's possible. The only way to test it is to have her sleep with someone else and see if you ride her orgasm too. It's too difficult to tell when you're actually with her." Greg spread his hands. "I don't think she'd go for that just for curiosity's sake. Of course, should you both agree to share her, it would certainly be one solution."

Alarin made a noise. "A human? Half-Azellian she might be, but she's purely human in her upbringing."

Greg grinned suddenly. "It certainly would be an unorthodox arrangement, but not unheard of."

Merran rolled his eyes. "Ah yes, the infamous Darvyne sisters and their husband."

"It's actually more common than that story might lead you to believe," Greg said, his eyes twinkling. "You'd be surprised what we Healers see."

Alarin sighed. "Either way, Ida's not going to be happy."

Greg sobered and shook his head. "No, she's not. Of course, if you return to Azelle, you might find distance makes the effect weaker. But that means you'll have to stay planets apart." He looked at Alarin intensely. "But then, you weren't really expecting your relationship with Ida to survive the separation anyway, were you?"

Alarin sank down at the end of the couch. "I care about her, Greg, and she's surprised me while I've been here on Earth these past few months with her attempts to be patient and understanding, but she's too entrenched in the future my mother wants me to live. I can't share with her the way I did ... do ... with Tamara.

And after having shared that much with Tamara, I can't go back to the guarded relationship I have with her. Even if I never have Tamara, I can't go back to Ida. I know she's your sister, but I won't make her happy if I'm miserable. Psi couples can't live that way. Look at Justern's parents."

Greg studied him for a moment. "No couple can live that way, human or Azellian." He seemed to be about to say more, then shook his head. "As long as you three find a way to be as happy as possible, I'll be happy too." He made a face. "If I survive the week and the spillover, that is."

Merran looked toward his bedroom door. "I think the *aarya* have got it out for me. Just when I thought my life was complicated enough, it gets more complicated." He sighed and straightened. "I think I'm going back to bed." He looked at Alarin. "I'd ask you to join us, but I think Tamara might get suspicious."

Alarin grinned. "I doubt she'd be suspicious for the right reason." He shook his head, sobering. "She may figure it all out eventually, but I don't know that we need to tell her right now. This is a new world for us, too."

Merran shook his head. "I agree with you there. We'll tell her later. Good night." He headed for the bedroom, leaving Alarin and Greg to discuss the situation further, if they chose.

Tamara was still breathing softly in sleep when he came in. He stopped by the side of the bed and studied her for a moment. *Alarin is right. My feelings for her scare me to death. Alarin's presence in this little relationship is nothing compared to that. I knew her Awakening would change things between us, but that it would be like this?* He thought about what the results would have been if Alarin alone had channeled her and he shivered.

"A sense of humor?" he muttered to himself. "Or a streak of sadism?"

Tamara stirred, a frown etching across her brow. Merran dropped his robe and climbed back into bed. Tamara moved again, murmured something, and turned over. Merran lay on his back, looking up at the canopy overhead. *A streak of sadism. The aarya don't have a sense of humor. They have a streak of sadism. To have tied three people together like this …* "Alawahea," he whispered into the early morning light beginning to spill in through the curtains and partially darkened windows. Although it was a philosophy he'd been taught long ago during his training as an acolyte, he had never really accepted it as a philosophy. *Maybe it's time I tried.* He turned over on his side and wrapped his arm around Tamara. She moved in her sleep, cuddling up against him. Although Azellians were not typically demonstrative physically, her warmth against him was soothing and stimulating at the same time. He took a deep breath and let it out slowly. *I simply don't have the time to be with her as much as I want—my time is not my own. Maybe the aarya are offering me a solution, not a sadistic trick. Can I share Tamara? Will she accept the solution?* He didn't know. A feeling of peace crept through him. *Maybe it's not time to worry about it right now.* He drifted off to sleep, his mind going still.

Chapter Eleven

THE REST OF THE WEEK passed much like it had the first day. The journalists, just as Merran had feared, clamored for more information about Greg's talents. Justern's plight and the abuses he'd suffered in jail were lost in the excitement and speculation about Azellian talents. Walking a thin line, Merran juggled the various reporters with a deftness that took every last erg of his energy and ability. Greg was unusual, he pointed out. Not all Azellians shared his talents, he emphasized. Greg's talents were useful but bound by a strict moral code. Yes, when Greg recovered from saving Justern's life, he would be willing to speak to the media. No, he did not know when that would be. Healing of any type took time, and Greg's abilities had been strained to the limit.

The dynamic between him, Tamara, and Alarin was pushed to the back burner—Merran was far too exhausted by nightfall to do much more than fall into bed. He spent every spare moment, when he wasn't talking to journalists, with the Azellian Council in an attempt to calm them down about the revelation of the presence of Healers. Far from happy, they resisted as Merran talked very fast to keep them from immediately recalling all the students home.

Tamara watched Merran struggle through the week with a sense of awe for what he had to deal with and accomplish. On top of the media attention, there was the usual paperwork to be done and phone meetings with the Dorbin ambassador, who was curious to see what Merran would do and how he felt about the current situation, as well as the Atheran ambassador, who hoped to gain some kind of leverage during this time to get access to Azellian resources too.

"God, how does he do it?" Tamara asked later in the week, staring over to where Merran sat at his desk arguing in Azellian with someone at the other end of the video phone. It sounded like an argument, although she couldn't sense any of the real emotions behind Merran's rapidly recovering shielding.

Greg glanced over at Merran. "It's what he does. And what you would have to do if you wanted to become an ambassador."

"Not all ambassadors are as ... intense as Merran," Alarin disagreed. He sat sprawled on the couch beside Tamara, helping to train her by providing jabs whenever he felt she wasn't concentrating hard enough. "They don't accomplish nearly as much as he has either. His refusal to give up has gotten him to where he is ... as young as he is."

Tamara shook her head. "It takes up all of his time and energy, though. Is it worth it?"

Greg shrugged. "He thinks so."

"It makes things difficult when a relationship is involved," Alarin said softly. Tamara looked over at him. Deep inside her mind something stirred. Since her Awakening, he'd been in her head far more than he should have been. *He shares a spot oddly entwined with my feelings for Merran.* She pushed the thought back and buried it deep, using Greg's training to hide it. *I am with Merran, not Alarin, and that is that.* Wayward feelings for someone who had helped with her Awakening—she did remember his calm, cool depths clearly before the muddled mess that apparently had been the moment she had blocked off, when the strongest level had broken free—were not acceptable and would not be allowed expression.

That Alarin himself might share her feelings was the farthest thing from her mind as she shook her head. "You have to accept your partner in full for who they are. I've known Merran is busy as ambassador. I need to have the space to grow too. I'm still learning so many things, and Merran's giving me that space." She glanced over at the other room. "It's actually a good thing."

Greg tapped her hand. "Don't lie, Tamara, *akila.* You're leaking too much to lie."

Tamara tightened her shielding up. "All right, all right. It does bother me that I play second fiddle to his work. But it takes time to build a relationship and I want to give it time."

"Not bad," Greg replied, surveying her shields. She felt a sharp jab against them and held far more tightly than she had been able to do even a few days before this incessant training started. Nothing. She could feel something brush across her aura, but she was too controlled to let it affect her.

"You're right." Alarin leaned forward. "I'm impressed. For someone as sensitive as you are to have shielding that strong bodes well."

Tamara looked over at him. "You and Merran have shielding just as strong."

"That's one of the reasons I insisted you stay in this shielded environment until we could get a sense of how good your shields are," Greg told her. "If you tried to go outside unshielded, you'd probably pass out. Here on Earth there's far too much energy running around to ever go completely unshielded. In fact, I'd suggest that you spend nights here, or we set up a minor level of shielding on your room, at least until your shields become second nature. Shields tend to relax when you're sleeping. You also have to learn not to project or completely relax your shields during sex, or you're going to have lots of very uncomfortable people around you."

Tamara blushed furiously. Not that she and Merran had done much since the first couple of nights, but had they sensed those first few nights?

Greg reached over and made a few passes over her aura. She could feel the calm radiating outward from his motion. "Don't worry about it. Alarin and I expected it and were prepared."

But did that mean they'd heard or not? She was suddenly terribly self-conscious. Greg tapped her arm, making her look up at him. "Very good. The only reason I know you're embarrassed, beyond the fact that I know you pretty well, is because you're blushing. But you're not leaking at all. "

She could remember swallowing her moans, trying so hard not to project. *Oh God, did I project anyway?* "How do I avoid it?"

"You're doing well right now," Greg told her. "There'll come a time when you learn to separate out your different areas, to shield partially, letting some thoughts flow through and keeping other thoughts hidden. Polite behavior on Azelle is to let the surface thoughts show but to keep the rest hidden away. Like Alarin's doing right now."

Tamara thinned her shields enough to sense Alarin sitting beside her. Beyond a faint amusement at her blush, she could read nothing. She touched his surface thoughts, skimming over them. Beyond the amusement was a much stronger emotion. He was proud of her, proud of the speed at which she was picking this up, glad to be able to help. She touched the edge of that emotion, savoring it. He let her, as he let her read some of his memories about her learning, showing her how fast she had advanced. His view of her drew her attention, and she watched in amazement at herself from someone else's eyes.

The contact could not have lasted very long, but she flailed, suddenly enmeshed at a much deeper level than she had meant to be. The memories took on more depth, not just flashes, and the emotion coloring them deepened. His mind tangled around hers, sliding against her in an intimate way she had never felt with anyone other than Merran. She thickened her shields abruptly, pulling away fast. She swayed on the couch as she severed contact, feeling the blood leave her face and seeing the world go dark.

"What happened?" were the first words she heard as she fought off the black at the corner of her vision. She focused on Greg who leaned forward. "Tamara, Alarin, are you all right?"

Alarin looked calm, in control, but a tremor in his hand as he lifted it to brush away a lock of hair from his eyes betrayed that whatever had happened, he'd felt it too. "I'm fine. We just cut off contact a bit too fast and it made me dizzy."

Greg frowned. "Cut off—" he stopped. "All right," he continued after a few moments. "Just lay down, Tamara. You just found out what happens when you cut off contact too fast. You'll be fine in a few moments. The disorientation will pass."

What in hell happened over there? Merran sent to Alarin on his intimate mode. Merran hung up the phone as he replayed his memory. Like a low noise in the background, Tamara's training normally didn't disturb him, but the stark fear and pain that had just shot through the ether slammed against his shields.

Alarin took a moment to answer. When he finally did, Merran understood why. Pain throbbed through the link between himself and Merran. *Tamara was reading my surface thoughts and slipped in under my shields. We meshed without meaning to, and she panicked, ending contact too fast. It made us dizzy. Fuck, that hurt. Damn it! She's strong. How the hell do you survive lovemaking with her?*

Merran projected amusement at Alarin. *Don't ask me. Maybe you can tell me someday. Why did she panic so badly at meshing with you?*

I don't know. I'm rather glad she did. I couldn't have hidden what I need to if she hadn't panicked and slammed the door shut on me. Nowhere near centered, Alarin's thought trailed off in a series of swears.

Merran didn't answer that. He got to his feet and came into the living room.

Tamara flushed as Merran came in. Off center, aching with some nameless feeling she didn't dare examine too closely, she laid her head back against the couch. Alarin's cool depths beckoned to her, but she closed her eyes and locked that particular thought away with the others that were far too disturbing to look at closely.

"Are you all right?" Merran asked her solicitously. "I heard the aftermath from the other room."

"I'm fine," Tamara struggled to sit up, wishing desperately to be somewhere else. *All this closeness to everyone is getting difficult.*

That's all it was, she rationalized. *We've worked pretty closely this past week, so we've built a rapport. That's all. A result of our working together.* Her shields high and tight around her, she kept the turmoil buried deep. "How are things going with the embassy?"

Merran sighed and made his way around the couch. "Unfortunately, I'm going to have to go back to Azelle as soon as Greg gives me the all clear."

"What's happening?" Alarin asked.

Tamara's stomach dropped to her feet.

Merran seemed not to notice anything amiss. He gave Tamara a light caress by brushing against her aura and put his head back against the couch. "The Council is not at all happy about Greg's revelation. They want to go over my battle plan in person with me."

Alarin made a face. "They want to rake you over the coals, you mean."

Merran nodded. "As much as I hate to admit it, yes, they probably want me to strip for them."

"Strip?" Tamara couldn't help asking. "Wh—what?"

Merran laughed as Greg and Alarin looked at each other. "It's what we call it whenever someone wants to do a deep probe. The sensation is similar to being forced to remove all your clothing while another sits there fully clothed." Merran turned his head and winked at her. "Not that I've had the experience."

"I thought you were comfortable with nakedness," Tamara said, confused.

Merran spread his hands. "We are. But being forced to be mentally vulnerable when the other is not isn't the most pleasant thing in the world. It's totally different to choose to be naked than to have it all ripped away." He stretched. "I have no intention of letting them read anything personal." He yawned. "But it's not going to be enjoyable, and the media's going to have a fit that I'm leaving ... again ... since they think I've been gone this past week already."

"For how long?" Tamara shivered, hugging herself miserably.

"Depends on how fast they get answers out of me. Maybe a week. Maybe three. Not more than a month. I need to be back for Justern's trial." Merran turned to her.

Greg got to his feet. "You want to order a pizza, Alari?"

Alarin jumped up too, moving a bit stiffly. "Tonight? Nah, I think we need something different. Indian maybe?" They moved to the kitchen, still talking.

Tamara didn't let her disappointment show. "All right. That will give me time to get caught up on my classes, at least."

"*Akila-ala.*" Merran seemed to know what she was feeling, although she'd tested the edges of her own shields to make sure she wasn't leaking and found them solid. "I don't want to go away this soon in our relationship either, but I have to get this sorted out, or you'll never manage to get to Azelle and all of us might end up recalled."

"I know." Tamara met his eyes. "I'm all right with it. Really. You've got a whole bunch of people depending on you. Did you want me to continue working?"

Merran nodded. "They haven't told me I can't have an intern, so you'll go to work like you normally would."

"Good." It didn't feel totally like he was going to be out of her life, then. A whole month? Maybe only a week. She kept her shields up and strong and even managed to be lighthearted, joking with all of them that evening. Instead of working as he had for the past four days, Merran spent the evening with them. Later that evening, he wrapped his mind around hers as they made love, which afterward made her think about what had happened earlier. Despite a very conscious attempt to screen her orgasm from the other room, she almost felt as though Alarin's mind was wrapped in hers, entwined around and through her, an unusual but strong counterpoint to Merran. Again, Merran seemed to notice nothing amiss, and they fell asleep like they normally did, still partially entwined.

That night, though, Tamara dreamed. All through her dreams, green eyes and brown chased her, cool depths and fiery warmth, as she tried to hide—to get some space to think. She woke the next morning unrested and exhausted and not sure she could handle another day locked in this place with these—men. Azellians. Aliens. She felt alien in her own body, in her spirit. She wanted to talk to Kari, to share with someone different, to get away from the constant presence of herself. She lingered in the shower for a long time that morning, avoiding everyone.

When she finally came out, bracing herself to have to deal with more training, another day of Merran working, and Alarin and Greg assaulting her, she got a rather big surprise. Alarin was nowhere to be found in the apartment. Merran stood at his desk, wearing a suit and obviously ready to leave. Greg finished up something, running his hands up Merran's aura and back down again—his amber aura flaring an angelic gold.

Tamara walked over to Greg and Merran. "What's happening?"

"Greg's decided to let us out of prison a day early, because he got his abilities back and can finish our Healing immediately." Merran turned to her. "Which is good, because the interview I have this afternoon is demanding I meet with him."

Greg made a face as he stepped away from Merran. "Just don't push it too hard." He turned to Tamara, his expression requesting her permission. She spread her hands and let him run his hands over her aura.

His touch did quite a bit to calm her down, and the nagging headache she'd woken up with cleared. It didn't help her troubled mind, but it did wonders for how she felt.

"All done. You were pretty well Healed anyway." Greg stepped back from her. "Are you ready for the great outdoors?"

Tamara took a deep breath. "I think so."

"I would suggest maintaining a pretty thick shield for a while and sleeping in a shielded area tonight," Greg added. He glanced at Merran, then backed away.

"You're welcome to stay here," Merran told her.

Tamara shrugged, feeling awkward for some reason she didn't really want to explore. "Uh, I don't want to impose."

A slight frown touched his brow. "It's not an imposition, *aki-la-ala*. I would … miss having you here. And I'm leaving tomorrow. I'd like to see you tonight."

"All right." Tamara wanted to hug him suddenly. She gave in to the desire. Merran wrapped his arms around her and kissed her lightly. "I'd miss you too," she whispered to him. "I'm going to miss you."

Merran held her tight, breathing against her neck. He murmured something in Azellian, then pulled away a little and looked down at her. "I know I'm not the easiest person in the world to have a relationship with, Tamara, and it's hard for me to express how I feel. But I do care."

Tamara blinked away a sudden desire to cry. She didn't say anything, but they parted and joined Greg.

The elevator trip down was not anything different, so Tamara wasn't quite prepared for the outdoors. She apparently wasn't shielded enough, and the cacophony that assaulted her as she stepped into the bright sunlight almost overwhelmed her. She stopped, shading her eyes and thickening her shielding.

"I'll see you tonight," Merran's voice made her jump. "Greg, will you make sure she gets to campus all right?"

"Of course." Greg waited silently as Merran walked off. Tamara thinned her shields just a bit, allowing the noise to come through, sorting as best she could the various sounds. Birds talked incessantly, yelling about boundaries, nests, and seduction, squirrels chittered about acorns and raced in fear, anger, or in sheer joy around the trees in the nearby park. A pair of human lovers emoted all over the place as they passed arm in arm. A man and a dog on a leash ran by, the man's mind all but blank as he pushed his body to its utmost. The dog focused on happy thoughts about running and loving his master. Greg touched her shoulder, bringing his mind suddenly in contact with hers. *You could stand here all day and not sense all of it. Thicken your shielding, Tamara. It's not good to be too open. It may be heady, but if there were any really powerful emotions around right now, you'd be hurting, like someone was shouting in your ear.*

Tamara obeyed, even though listening to the tiny thoughts of the birds relaxed her. *How often do Azellians talk like this?* She let the words form in her head and move through her shielding, her more private areas still protected.

More often than you think. Most of our communication is sharing impressions, Greg replied, demonstrating.

Communication with Greg was different than the meshing with Alarin. She picked up a quick impression of his pleasure at being out in the open, able to Heal and whole again. She practiced returning the communication, her own mind revealing her happiness to be able to see her family and her other friends after being away for the week.

Speaking of your family, Greg sent to her. *Your mother. I would like to take a look at her now that I'm better. And Justy's there.*

How do you know Justern's out of the hospital? Tamara queried, projecting a hint of confusion.

I asked him. I contacted him when we left the apartment. Since he's with your father, I am going to do two things at once, before I have to deal with the media this afternoon.

Tamara sighed, disgusted with herself. *When will I ever learn to do that?*

You will. One day, psi will become second nature. Greg smiled at her. "Don't worry about it, Tamara."

They walked in companionable silence, Tamara sharing her opinions and new impressions with Greg as they walked through the streets to campus. Tamara picked up her car and drove the two of them to her parents' house.

The house had an odd hush to it, as if it were holding its breath, waiting for something. Andreya came out of her bedroom when Tamara and Greg walked into the house.

"Hey," Tamara said, feeling odd around her sister for the first time. She'd changed so much in the past couple of weeks that nothing seemed the same. Her light mental touch confirmed that her half-sister felt the same. "Is Dad home?"

Andreya nodded, for once with no rancor. Her attitude had changed dramatically, or had Tamara just gained the ability to read it, not needing to react so badly to it? "He's in his office."

"Thanks," Tamara replied. She turned to Greg. "Andreya, this is Greg. Greg, this is Andreya, my sister." She could sense Andreya's hesitant, anxious question about Greg's identity. Tamara suppressed a smile. She could just imagine how Andreya felt when Peter had shown up with Justern in tow. "Greg's a Healer."

Andreya looked at him wide-eyed. Tamara did not look at Greg, but shot a comment to him mentally. *What did Justy do to her? Damn, she's positively overawed.*

I didn't do anything. The voice came from one of the rooms, sounding irritable but strong. *Is it my fault if she sneaks into the room at night and things just start flying around the room? I'm sound asleep.*

Justern! Greg's mind tone was chastising. He added something Tamara didn't hear. *You've got your psi back, then?*

Not as good as I want it, Justern replied, *but enough to frighten away the sister of my half-sister.*

God, you're as bad as she is, Tamara scolded.

She received a strong impression of amusement. *No, I'm worse.*

Good to hear you're feeling better, Justy. How have you survived the past couple of days? Greg continued the conversation as they walked through to Peter's office, Andreya trailing along behind.

Tamara knocked on her father's study door. "Dad? I'm here with Greg."

"Come in," Peter called. As Tamara stepped into her father's inner sanctum, he looked up and smiled at Tamara. "You look good, honey. It seems they treated you well. How are you feeling?"

Limited because Andreya stood behind her, Tamara nodded. "Great. I feel wonderful."

Peter smiled and turned his attention to Greg. "How can I help you, Healer?"

"I am here to check up on my fellow Azellian and on your wife." Greg bowed. "If you still wish me to look at her."

Peter nodded. "More than ever. She seems to have slipped a bit in the past week."

Greg inclined his head. "Then I would be happy to." He bowed again. "May I?"

Peter returned the bow. "As you will."

While Greg worked on Justern, Tamara went into her step-mother's room. It felt strange to think of her that way, even if it was true. A sweet, rotten odor greeted her at the door, and she had to close her eyes for a moment. Her mother lay on the bed, apparently asleep. On her wasted body the greenish yellow skin sank between the bones, except on her hands, where skin stretched taught over swollen tissues, giving her hand a false impression of youth. Tamara could feel the tears build as she went to sit by the hospital bed. "Hi, Mom," she whispered. Feeling suddenly terribly guilty about not having been around for the past week, she reached out slowly and tentatively to touch her mother's hand. *Even though Jeanine Carrington may not have given birth to me, she's been my mother for as long as I can remember,* she thought as she sat down on the chair.

Jeanine opened her eyes. A ghost of a smile crossed her face. "Tamara." The word was barely audible. Tamara had to blink quickly to keep back her tears. "Your father tells me you have been sick. Are you okay?"

Tamara took a deep breath. "I'm fine, Mom. I just had a little bug."

"Good." Jeanine closed her eyes again. Her hand rested in Tamara's.

Tamara sat like that, with her head bowed, trying not to cry, until Greg came in radiating soothing calm. He didn't say a word, just sat down on a chair beside Tamara and bowed his head.

Jeanine didn't open her eyes, not even when Greg stood and extended his hands to run them lightly above her body. He rested his hand lightly on her head, then withdrew his touch from her head and turned to leave. Tamara followed.

Greg stopped outside the door. He touched Tamara lightly on the shoulder. "I'm sorry. There's not much I can do. She's made her choice."

"You could manipulate cells. There's got to be something you can do."

Greg shook his head, his hands playing in the air just above her neck. Warmth and calm spread down her body. "Any disease is a choice, Tamara. Your mother has chosen to move on to the next stage. If I had seen her three months ago when she was still fighting, maybe there would have been something I could have done. But she's riddled with the cancer now, and there's not much I can do. She doesn't have long to live."

But it's not fair! I just learned something about her, and now I am not going to have the chance to learn about her in this new way? I lost my birth mother before I even knew her. How can I lose another one? Tamara screamed in her mind, the warmth of his touch disappearing with the wash of pain.

She could feel Greg's touch trying to soothe her, but she ran away. Away from the bearer of the news she didn't want to hear, away from the gibbering thing she wanted to be. And away from the one person in the world who had always been shelter for her, but who was now the cause, not the solution.

She walked outside for a long time before a presence behind her made her stop pacing. She stared sightlessly at one of the young locust trees her mother had planted just last summer. Justern was a cool breeze, a blue-grey glow at the corner of her eye.

"It sucks, doesn't it?" he spoke in a low voice, pain threaded through his whole mind. "Losing a parent makes you question everything."

Tamara breathed steadily in through her nose and out again. Steady breaths.

"Especially one that you feel like you never really knew," Justern continued. No comfort poured around the edges of his shields, only understanding. It lifted her spirits. "Learning what I did when I was in the hospital … I've been thinking that I didn't know her at all. My mother. I thought I did … but she had this whole life I knew nothing about. She wasn't who I thought she was."

Tamara bowed her head. "I don't even know myself. How can I presume to know anyone else?" She glanced at the door.

"Andreya's not listening," Justern told her, reading the concern there. "She's listening to Greg and Peter and deciding her world is coming to an end."

Tamara lifted her head. "It is, after all."

They both sat on the bench under a tree. "It is what? Coming to an end? No. It may feel like it, but it's not. You do survive death, Tamara. Even the death of someone you didn't think you could survive losing." He looked up at her from the corner of his eye. "Then you discover that you have connections you never knew you had, and you begin to dream again. Even to live again."

Tamara took the tendril he offered her and slipped behind the first level of his shields. Justern offered up memories to her, which she read and soaked up eagerly, of a brown-haired, blue-eyed woman who smelled of jasmine and lily, who always spoke gently, who loved her son to distraction. And who always missed her daughter. Justern and Tamara shared memories of their mother's sadness, the constant sorrow that dogged her. At the time Justern had not known about Tamara, but now, looking back, it was obvious that Jasmian Dorvath had wanted very badly to know her daughter.

When Tamara came back to her own mind, tears slid down her cheeks freely. Wordlessly, she thanked him for the gift he had given her. He pulled his hand across his wet face and sniffed, smiling at her and returning the communication in the same way. Tamara laughed and handed him a piece of tissue.

Justern blew his nose. He gave her a watery grin and offered the tissue back to her.

"No thanks." Tamara made a face.

Justern stuffed the tissue in his pocket. "I know that doesn't help with what you're going through now, but just so you know you're not alone. That was something I would have appreciated nine years ago."

"That means a lot to me. Justy ... I'm sorry. I wish ... I wish things were different with this whole stupid thing with Joely."

Justern shrugged, his shields thickening between them smoothly, cutting off even the small awareness they shared. "It was my own stupid fault for not watching to make sure I didn't give her the opportunity."

"I got her side of it, you know. I played the memory for Greg, and he's given it to Merran so you aren't castigated on Azelle, so there is some sort of truth, no matter what happens to you at the trial, or if you are sent home."

Justern gave her a one-sided smile. "I know. Greg told me you had done that. Thank you. Having both memories to judge really makes a difference, and I wasn't … functional. There was always a chance the Council wouldn't support me if my memories weren't clear enough. As terrorized as it made you, it will save me on Azelle."

Tamara shuddered. "Watching what is basically a rape, all because she was determined to make others as miserable as herself. Greg faded the memory for me, thank God. It's like I watched a movie years ago. Just disjointed images."

Justern touched her shoulder lightly, but he didn't say anything. Tamara was silent too, thinking about what had followed the memory replaying for Merran and Greg. Her Awakening came hard on the heels of that, and it had changed her life. *For the better*, she thought, glancing over at the person who was also her half-brother, *as he can share with me memories of a mother I never knew. And for the worse, as it's making me question everything.* She pushed her thoughts back, not wanting to dwell on them. Getting to her feet, she extended her hand to Justern. He grinned, kissed the back of it with exaggerated gallantry, and got to his feet. They went into the house.

Greg looked up as they came in. His touch reached out, and this time Tamara let him soothe down her aura. Warmth spread through her from the contact and made her feel a little more coherent. Peter came over and put his arm around her, which also helped. "How much longer does she have?"

"Her liver's starting to lose its ability to function. I would say maybe a week or two," Greg said somberly. "But it depends on your mother and when she chooses to let go."

Tamara could feel tears building again. "Great timing," she said, with a sarcastic little laugh. "I have midterms in two weeks. I'd rather just spend the next two weeks with her."

"The professors will surely let you take makeup exams if you need to," Greg told her.

Peter's grip on her shoulders tightened. "And if you have one not-so-good semester, honey, it's not the end of the world either."

Tamara swiped her hand across her face. "I'll get through it, Dad." She gently disengaged. "I'd like to sleep at home for the next two weeks, though."

"Certainly," Peter told her. "You know you can anytime." Tamara, shaking a little, excused herself then, as Peter asked Greg some questions.

She called the embassy from her cell phone in her room.

"Ambassador Corina's office. May I help you?" Janille answered the phone on the fifth ring.

"Janille, it's Tamara. Is the ambassador available for a quick call?" Tamara asked, hoping she could get through the call without crying. *Maybe I shouldn't have used the video call feature.*

Janille glanced up at something. "Let me check, Tamara." She gave Tamara a small smile. "You are looking good."

"Thank you," Tamara replied, swallowing the lump in her throat. She tapped on the edge of the phone impatiently.

When the contact came, it was not through the phone. She was still on hold, but suddenly Merran's presence seeped through her mind. *What is it, akila? Is everything all right? Janille says you need to talk to me.*

I just wanted to tell you that Greg saw my mother today, and she's— Tamara lost the ability to form her thoughts into words. She let him read the memory instead. *I ... want to spend the next nights until ... well, I want to spend the next few nights with her. Is that all right?*

Of course, was Merran's instant response. *You didn't even need to ask, akila.* He wrapped his mind around hers, making her feel as though he had just given her a hug. *I'll keep my trip as short as I can. I'll contact you when I arrive on Azelle.*

Tamara didn't say anything, but she let him read her gratitude. He severed the connection, and Janille came back on the phone. "He's in the middle of a very important meeting, Tamara. Can I take a message?"

"No, that's all right." The second part of the conversation was for the benefit of other ears, should anyone be listening. Tamara was sure of that. Janille must have known Merran had talked to her, but she didn't reveal that she knew. "I'll try again later. Bye."

Janille nodded. "Goodbye."

Tamara turned away from the phone, feeling suddenly lonely. *The next two weeks are going to be hell.*

They ended up being worse than she'd imagined, in a way she could not have foreseen. Jeanine slipped badly after that day, sliding into a delirium. Her father ran himself ragged taking care of her and juggling Justern's case at the same time. Tamara dragged herself to class with barely enough energy to care how she did. Her professors knew what was happening and were sympathetic, but Tamara insisted on continuing forward anyway, even though the quality of her work suffered. Everything faded from her mind but her mother. She spent long hours alone, struggling with her thoughts and fears and watching as her mother slipped further away. The fact that Jeanine Carrington had not borne her became irrelevant and meaningless. Tamara loved her anyway, and that was all it took for the intense pain to set in as she helplessly watched her mother's decline. Greg helped some, as did an almost daily conversation with Justern and Mellis—and, oddly enough, Alarin.

Tamara lay on her bed almost a week later, having managed to get through classes that week. She had just talked to Merran and was missing him terribly when the doorbell rang. She shivered. Too busy being miserable to rouse herself to get up and answer the door, she sank back into the dark gloom that surrounded her.

A knock on her bedroom door made her jump. "Who is it?"

A mind brushed her shields, making her quiver with sudden, nameless emotion. Tamara scrambled back on the bed, pulling her legs up to her chest, and gave him permission to enter.

Alarin walked in, his mind open and calm. He closed the door behind him. "Hello, Tamara."

"Hi." Tamara's heart pounded a little, causing some of the depression that pressed down on her to lift slightly.

There wasn't much of a place to sit in her tiny bedroom other than on the bed with her. He settled on the edge of it. "I wanted to make sure you are all right." His spoken words seemed almost meaningless, absent any emotion. The offer in his mind, however, shone brightly—his shields were wide open and invited her to touch minds with him without pressuring her.

Tamara's bottom lip quivered. *A moment to get away from the hell in my mind,* she thought. Dangerous to her sense of self, but strong, his mind offered support and blessed escape. Merran expected to be on Azelle for another week at least, with little to offer but words in the meantime. Too enmeshed in his own upheaval,

Justern could not truly help her either. The emerald green of Alarin's aura glowed beside her, as he patiently sat saying nothing, only offering.

She reached out tentatively. Tendrils of his aura curled around hers, sensuous and soothing at the same time. Cool green water slid silkily around her. The pain eased, lessened, and flowed, until she breathed freely. As the relaxation spread through her, she caught her breath in a sob. She collapsed on her bed, still entwined with Alarin, curling up into a ball and letting go for the first time since she had learned of her mother's impending death.

She felt him move in her mind before he touched her. Warmth pressed against her back and she cuddled close, still wracked by sobs. He let her cry, absorbing rather than soothing. She poured herself into his depths, pain cascading through and out, until she had nothing left. She obliterated herself in his mind, burying herself in the depths.

When she came to herself again, she lay prone on her bed. Her body felt unreal, as if drugged, but her storm of emotion was gone. She could sense the cool pool that had absorbed all her pain—terror and sorrow still spread beneath her, still open and inviting. Turning her head, she met his eyes.

"How did you do that?" She coughed, trying to clear the thickness out of her throat.

Alarin tightened his grip around her and smiled. He lifted a hand to brush a tendril of hair away from her face. "It's a little trick I learned from my Healer sister."

"Greg can't do that," Tamara protested, too exhausted to do more than lie there.

"He knows the technique. It's just a rather drastic one, used only in very special cases." The cool green pool radiated warmth, comfort, and gentle support.

"Can everyone do it?" Tamara asked him, testing the edges of her new serenity. His presence, enmeshed with hers, made it hard to know whose calm she was experiencing.

"No. Healers are the ones who know it and a few of us others who know Healers. There are some requirements before it's usuable, though." Alarin did not elaborate, and his mind, so open before, pulled a thin veil over its depths. He did not fully disengage, but the depths grew murky over an awareness—a forbidden awareness. The withdrawal made her cold. She didn't want to let him go, yet she didn't want the return of the real world. Tamara pressed against him, both physically and mentally, feeling like a child bumping for the comfort of a bottle or a mother's breast.

When the childlike feeling transmuted into something else, she was never quite sure. She pressed against him. A slow tension broke through her comfort, a slowly growing awareness that disrupted the solace, as warmth spread upward from that murky depth. His touch changed from soothing to caressing. She lay against him, feeling the tension wash through her. Still entwined with him, she could feel his heart speed up and hear his breathing catch as blood raced through his veins. A pressure pumped against her thigh as his body moved slightly closer to her. She turned her head to meet his eyes and saw recognition in them. There was no lying. There could be no pretending, not wrapped around each other as they were. Her own breathing went ragged as they looked at each other, warmth flaring into heat.

Which one kissed the other first, she didn't know. But Alarin met her with tongue and lips as his arms pulled her close. A noise escaped her mouth and he shifted against her, his breath coming hard through his nose. His hands explored where his mouth did not, and he pressed harder against her body, his legs trapping her beneath him.

He broke the kiss first, holding himself above her. The length of his body hovered just above, their auras mingling slightly at the edge. Currents flashed between them. "Tamara, wait. Do you want this?"

It was hard to clear the smog of desire from her brain. The aching of both their bodies called to her, a clamor almost too loud to ignore. Tamara struggled to sit up, brushing against him as she moved. His muscles quivered as he pulled back. His jeans did nothing to hide the physical evidence she noticed when she lay back down. Still wrapped up in his mind, she didn't know what she wanted. His desire tugged at her as images flashed through her mind—Alarin nearly naked as she woke up in his bed, Alarin showering in Merran's bedroom as she sat joking with Greg outside, the oddly familiar feel of his mind as he entwined his aura with hers. "God," she whispered. "Yes, I do. But ..." Confusion danced wildly through her.

Alarin withdrew from her mind gently, pulling shields up between them to spare her the awareness of his discomfort. He swung his legs over the edge of the bed.

Afraid he was going to leave, Tamara shook her head. "Don't go ... I ... please."

"I'm not," Alarin assured her. "I'm just trying to get a little more comfortable." He sat with his back against the headboard of her bed, one knee pulled up while the other leg stretched out in front of him.

"I just—I'm sorry, Alarin. I—I don't know what this means." Tamara lifted a shaking hand to her temple, finally managing to sit up herself. "How—how can I feel this way about you when I still feel the way I do about Merran? I don't understand. Is this normal?"

"Your Awakening changed us all, Tamara." He lifted his head and looked at her steadily. "It's not unheard of on Azelle, although I wouldn't say it's common."

Tamara rubbed her cheek, not really hearing him. "I don't want to cheat on Merran. We have an understanding, I think, and I don't want to betray that trust."

"Merran called me and told me to make sure you were all right. He knows how I feel, Tamara." Alarin took a deep breath through his nose. "He may not realize you share it, but he knows there's a good chance you do. We couldn't have done what we did at your Awakening and not have been left with some kind of effect." He took another deep breath. "Our people have a saying. *Alawahea*. The literal meaning is *what is, what was, what will be*. In this case, it means that we need to accept what has happened, that the reason doesn't matter. We have what we have." Tamara stayed silent, struggling with alien concepts, trying to understand what he meant. He shielded from her. Reaching out a tendril of his mind, he brushed across her aura. "Don't worry about it right now, Tamara. You have more than enough on your mind as it is, and this particular issue can wait for Merran's return."

"You can't mean—" Tamara took a deep breath. Some huge awareness hovered at the edge of her senses, something she didn't want to know or acknowledge. *Too much to process*, she thought. "What's—what do you mean, it's not unheard of? That you're attracted to me? That I'm attracted to you? That Merran knows?"

Alarin raised his eyebrow. "There's more to it than that, Tamara, and you know it. Your Awakening tied all three of us together. What we are going to do about it needs to include Merran."

That was it. What she felt about Alarin was not simple, and far from casual. She had determined to keep it buried, because like it or not, she was with Merran. But to know Alarin shared it—for what seemed like the hundredth time in the past few weeks Tamara felt as though her world was shaking, twisting on its axis, and collapsing around her.

Alarin brushed across her aura again. "Don't. Tamara. Give yourself time. I'm not going anywhere, you're not going anywhere. Let it go for now. I'm not going to pressure you or make you uncomfortable."

"But you're talking about a three-way relationship—" Tamara stopped herself mid-sentence. She found that saying it made it sound absolutely awful.

He put his hand up. "I'm not talking about anything at all. Not at all. I'm talking about not thinking about it until later." His voice did not quite have the crack of command she knew it could, but it was close. He did not want to discuss it now. And God knew she was far too confused to disagree with him.

"You're right." She thought about the peace he'd given her just a few moments earlier, a release she had rarely felt in her life. "Merran doesn't know how to do that trick, does he?"

Alarin shook his head. "No, although he might want to. Not even all Healers can achieve the necessary state of mind to accomplish it."

"Would it be pushing too hard to ask if sometimes over the next few weeks I could empty my stress and relieve my pain with you?" She couldn't quite look at him, feeling guilty and embarrassed for asking. "I don't want to ... bring up anything neither of us is ready to handle."

He shifted on the bed, resting his legs off the edge. "It may be." He was silent for a moment. "My ability to offer you this comfort comes from my—those issues we'd rather not discuss and shouldn't be discussed until Merran returns." He took a breath and she could feel him look over at her. "But I can also see the relief it gave you, and I think I am enough of a friend that I can offer you this. My depths are yours, Tamara."

Startled, she met his eyes. The awareness in his eyes, the pressure of his feeling for her, and the echo of her own unwanted emotions tugged at her. She closed her eyes against acceptance and felt him brush her lips with a kiss. Her eyes flew open, but he'd moved and was off the bed, so she almost thought she must have imagined it.

A mischievous smile touched the corners of his mouth as he looked down at her. "Of course, I can't guarantee that you're going to like what you see in my mind, but I can guarantee it is yours whenever you want."

Tamara frowned at him, picking up the lightening of his attitude. "That's an awfully generous offer. Should I be suspicious about your motivations?" She tried for playful and managed frightened.

"My motivations are for you to read, my dear Tamara. Whenever you are ready for them, that is." Alarin sobered and shook himself. "As it stands now, I'll leave you alone. Besides, I need a cold shower."

Tamara flushed. The depression that had lifted with his arrival threatened to return, as did the aching loneliness. Putting her hand out, she touched his wrist. "I—I don't want to be alone. Do you think it will push us too far if you just hold me?"

Alarin took a deep breath that shook just a little. He looked down at her fingers. With his other hand, he unlaced her digits from his wrist and linked his fingers through hers. A fine trembling carried down his arm and into her hand. "The temptation is strong, Tamara, but I think it's not a good idea. Maybe once I have my equilibrium back, but right now I'm not that sure of my control. I don't have it in me to pull back as I did earlier. I'm not certain I can manage it twice in one night. You're very vulnerable right now, and I'd be taking advantage of that."

She shivered a convulsive shudder. "Right now I almost don't care. I'm scared and lonely, and I just want comfort."

He smiled at her and brushed her aura with his. "I may be able to offer a temporary escape, Tamara, but you will still need to deal with the emotions that you're generating. Hiding behind a relationship with me or with Merran is not going to change the basic fact that your world is changing. If you still feel the same way in another month, when all the things around us have calmed down, I will gladly join you in that bed or in any other you choose." He disengaged his hand. "What I can do now, however, is sit over here and keep you company for a while longer." He settled on her desk.

It wasn't until later, when she thought it over, that Tamara realized how hard he worked at dispelling the vibes between them. She never did know for sure what it cost him to spend the evening with her, ignoring what must have been a terrible temptation to him. The next morning as she lay in her bed staring at the ceiling, she appreciated his restraint, but at the same time it made it harder to dismiss him from her thoughts. Her feelings for Alarin jumbled together in one fine mess, a chaotic nightmare that didn't sort out any as her mother continued to slip toward death, as her exams approached and Justern's trial loomed, and even once Merran returned.

✳ ✳ ✳

She anticipated and dreaded Merran's return to Earth at the same time. She'd survived her midterms wondering if she would, and once they were over, she'd gathered a little breathing space, if only briefly. Merran's shuttle landed at the spaceport at noon after the last day of exams, and Tamara found herself torn between visiting her mother and meeting him at the port. He solved the dilemma for her by contacting her mentally. *Stay with your mother,* he told her, slipping his mind through hers. *I need to consult with your father anyway, so I'll just come by there when I arrive. I missed you.*

I missed you too. Simple truth, Tamara realized, despite Alarin's disturbing presence. His touch on her shields made her realize just how much she had missed him. *So what does that mean about my feelings for Alarin? Can I love more than one person at a time?* She came no closer to an answer by the time Merran appeared at the door of her family's house. He greeted her casually, warm only mentally, and promptly disappeared with Peter for an hour.

He strode out of Peter's home office an hour later. Tamara sat with Andreya on the couch watching some movie, most of her attention on Merran rather than the movie.

"I'm headed back over to the embassy," Merran told her as he walked through the living room on the way out. "Did you need a ride to work?" His aura snaked out and slipped suggestive tendrils around hers. Tamara's breath caught.

"Sure. Let me get my coat." She got to her feet, stuck her head into her father's office, and grabbed her jacket from the hook. "Dad, I'm going to work for an hour or so. Be back by dinner."

Peter responded with some distracted comment, but she didn't catch it. Hoping she didn't look too eager, she joined Merran demurely in the car. Both of them maintained a correct distance from each other, Tamara heavily shielded as they drove to the embassy and walked up to Merran's office. As soon as they stepped into the main office, and it appeared that Janille wasn't there, Merran turned and kissed her.

"Oh by the *aarya*, I missed you," he murmured as his hands searched and found their way under her shirt. She met his kiss with one of her own, then broke off, panting. "This is a little public, don't you think?"

Merran laughed and pulled her into his shielded office. The door was hardly closed before he kissed her again, drawing her to the leather couch and pulling clothes off as they stumbled along. As he kissed her hungrily, she could feel Alarin not so much between them as with them, sharing the explosive release when it arrived.

Later, when they lay quietly satiated, Merran studied her shields. In the two weeks he'd been gone, her shielding had improved so much that she now leaked as little as Alarin. He had an advantage, though—he could slip underneath her shields and he already knew what was bothering her.

"She's having trouble with her feelings for us, Merran," Alarin had told him as he got off the shuttle earlier that evening. "She won't let me in."

"But you did go to her?" Merran asked, slinging his luggage over a shoulder. "You've got knowledge I don't and the feelings to give her some true support. Was she able to get benefit out of that?"

Alarin spread his hands. "When she accepted it, yes. The first time I took her emotion for her, she let me, and we even got somewhere. Of course we reacted to it the way you might expect, but I backed off because I sensed she might have a violent reaction to it. Since then, I haven't been able to get nearly close enough. She's too guarded to give me her emotion, too afraid of your reaction, of betraying the agreement she thinks the two of you have."

Merran frowned at him. "I would never prevent her seeking solace from somewhere or someone else. That would be selfish and cruel. To say nothing about threatening our relationship because I'm being unreasonable. I've thought a lot about this over these past two weeks. I can't give her the part of me that belongs to Azelle, so why should I demand a promise out of her that makes her limit herself, too? This seems to offer a perfect solution, especially if she cares about you."

"I know that," Alarin replied, his frustration leaking a little, indicating the depth of his emotion. "You know that. Tamara doesn't seem to have that attitude. She won't talk to me about it, either."

Some hours later, Merran looked down at her, remembering that conversation. Her shields glowed stonily at him. "*Akila-ala.* Is something wrong?"

Tamara jumped, startled at his perception. Adrenaline rushed through her. "No." She curled inward, pulling her knees up to her chin.

Merran pushed himself up on one elbow, his skin sliding against hers as he moved. She moved slightly, just enough that they no longer touched. He traced a finger down her side. "I know better than that, Tamara. You're shielding so heavily at the moment I don't think an *aarya* on the attack could get through. Considering that I'm the only one in the room to shield against, I think that means something's bothering you."

Tamara's breath caught in a sob and she turned over. "I—I— something happened when you were gone. Something really bad. I—I didn't mean it. I ..."

She sounded so miserable that Merran could hardly believe Alarin's earlier account was accurate. "What happened?"

Tamara could feel tension build in his legs and body, and she lay there, miserably certain their relationship was over but wanting the misery to end. "I—" She swallowed hard. "I—God, I feel so guilty. Alarin—I—we—I kissed Alarin. Only once, and we didn't go any further," she said in a rush.

Merran relaxed with an explosive snort. "Is that all? *Akila*, I thought you had killed someone or something."

Tamara stared at him. "What?"

"I asked Alarin to go to you and take your emotion." Merran rested his hand on her stomach and played with her aura. "I knew you were suffering, and as I don't have the knowledge or the ability but knew Alarin did *and* I also knew that he has the feelings for you to make it work, I told him to offer. I've known full well that if you shared his feelings, the two of you might end up sleeping together. Your Awakening left marks on all three of us, Tamara. It would be terribly selfish of me to demand that you put Alarin out of your mind when he can offer you things I can't. This time I was called away from Earth for two weeks. Next time it might be a month, or six months. I go where Azelle tells me. There is a large part of me that is and always will be Azelle's. I can't change that, and I can't ask you to limit yourself because of me either. Just because you love your mother, does that mean you don't love your father? Or because you love one grandparent, you can't love another? I also care about Alarin too much to ask him to torture himself by preventing him access to someone he cares about as much as he does you. Does your feeling for Alarin mean you don't care about me?"

Tamara shook her head vehemently. "No, not at all."

"Well, then, why would your feeling for me mean you don't care about Alarin? The human heart has a vast capacity to care, Tamara." Merran stroked his hand lightly up her bare stomach. Her skin twitched. "And life is too short to throw away something genuine just because it doesn't happen to fit what we think life should be. The *aarya* sometimes like to stretch our views of the world, and they are doing that to you."

"You don't mind?" A hysterical little laugh bubbled through her. "You wouldn't care, for example, if I were with Alarin, too?"

Merran grinned and slid his body next to her. "It could be interesting to be on the other end for a change."

Tamara frowned at him. "Other end?"

Merran tapped her nose with his finger. "Don't tell me you haven't sensed Alarin riding our lovemaking with us."

Tamara's eyes widened and she scrambled to a sitting position, pulling her knees up and staring at him. "You—I—I thought I was just imagining it, that it was my preoccupation with him that made me feel like he's there. Do you mean to tell me he actually has been?"

"Every time since the first." Merran leaned back against the couch. "Calm down, *akila*. It wasn't on purpose. Your Awakening tied us all together that first time. Since then, I don't think Alarin could have avoided it if he wanted. You are very strong in the throes of passion, my Tamara, and you suck energy in like a vacuum. It makes sex with you an incredible rush, but it also means that you are pulling Alarin in too."

She cradled her legs and rocked back and forth. "Oh God. I thought—oh God. It is all my fault. My Awakening, my passion—"

Merran touched her chin. "Tamara, it doesn't bother me and it doesn't bother Alarin. Why is it bothering you?"

She shook her head and pulled her chin out of his grasp, burying her head in her knees. "I don't know. It just seems like … well, like I should be happy with one, that there's something wrong that I feel for both of you." She looked up at him. "It just seems wrong … I don't know. If, for example, I arranged to see you one night and Alarin the next. It feels like I'd be betraying our … my and your … relationship."

Merran pulled himself up too. He took her shoulders in his hands. "Tamara, the only way you can cheat on me is if you break a trust between us. Isn't it a bigger betrayal of trust if I expect you to give up pieces of yourself to adjust to me?"

He could sense her reluctant understanding, but she fought against the alien thinking he was offering. "So the concept of cheating on a husband or wife doesn't exist on Azelle?"

"Of course it does. The basic premise of trusting a husband or wife is the same, and we aren't perfect. It's almost impossible to hide, of course, because of the effect on our auras and the fact we can read emotions. But this is different, Tamara. Alarin and you are not engaging in an activity I don't know anything about, for one thing. For another, I cannot give you everything you deserve or need. My job is an exacting mistress. Our trust, our agreement, is not the same as between two people who don't have jobs that demand quite so much from them."

"But wouldn't it make it easier to just—?" Tamara waved a hand to finish her sentence.

"Have flings whenever? I think you'll have your hands full with Alarin and me."

"What about you? You are willing to share me with each other, but I don't think I could do the same. The thought of you with another woman …" Tamara's nostrils flared.

Merran shrugged. "I have more than enough with my job and you. The last thing I need is to complicate my life any more than it already is. As for Alarin, I would suggest you do with him what we're doing. Make an agreement." He put a hand under her chin and kissed her lingeringly. "I care about you, Tamara Carrington. But any relationship needs work, and just because we have an unorthodox one, don't think it won't be the same. I do want to continue to spend time with you, as much as I can spare from here." He grinned as he pulled back. "This could be fun, you know."

Tamara could read something about the source of his amusement. "Oh God. When we—today— did you warn Alarin?"

Merran's grin widened. "Nope."

She reached out toward Alarin, touched his mind deep in her own, and received a rather rueful reply. They had definitely caught him unawares, although not in too bad a compromising position.

She withdrew and frowned at Merran. "He was talking to Greg. Fortunately, Greg understood and left him alone for the duration."

Merran laughed a full-throated chuckle. "He'll have fun getting me back, I'm sure."

Tamara scowled at him and shoved at his shoulder. "No getting to each other through me."

The shove degenerated quickly into a wrestling match that led to more. This time, Tamara could feel Alarin clearly, and she rather shyly welcomed him. Although Merran seemed to be fine with the whole thing, she was still not sure about everything. She knew she and Alarin needed to talk too. It was not a conversation Tamara was sure she was ready to have.

They lay with minds semi-entangled after, relaxing together.

"How did your trip to Azelle go?" she asked, playing with his chest hair.

"I managed to prevent them from recalling all of us immediately." Merran leaned his head back with his hand resting lightly on her hip as she spooned against him. "Which is better than I expected to do. They're not happy that although there is strong evidence for Justern's innocence, the prevailing doubt still surrounds and necessitates his trial. At the same time, they don't want me to reveal any of our talents except through Healers and Greg. I've been implying that only Healers can do what most of us can, just so it becomes an isolated case, and the Council agrees with me. It's going to be a long, hard road to get them to allow any more humans on Azelle, though."

"But doesn't the mere fact that Healers exist give Azelle more bargaining power? Greg's already besieged by requests for help. He can barely move around without the media tracking him everywhere he goes. He's been reduced to disguises for most of his movement around town. The fact that the media has been blocked from campus is the only thing that makes his life at all bearable right now."

"I know." Merran heaved a sigh. "And yes, it does give us some bargaining room when it comes to treaties we're trying to establish. It doesn't help Justern, though, unless the leaders of Earth are willing to get involved and speak for him, which it appears they aren't willing to do at this time. The Council is willing to release a statement supporting Justern according to our justice system, but my hands are tied from influencing things here unless the director, or even the president himself, is willing to do anything to shape the outcome."

"What's the president's opinion? I would think you could get him to support Justern easily. Just to get you and the Council to agree to let humans access Healers?"

"It's not as easy as that. Your conservative side is terrified of Healers and Azellians and anything we represent. As often as I insist that Healers are special, we've opened a can of worms with their abilities. Justern's situation is fanning fears of beings who can read minds and take advantage of helpless young college students." Merran shifted against her and sat up. "I'm trying to minimize that feeling, but the political powers are staying out of it until they see which way the wind blows. Politics and careers are always a larger motivating factor than poor innocent Azellians."

Tamara moved too, so she could sit against the couch. He got to his feet and started collecting their scattered clothing. "It's so unfair. If we could just show people what happened, let people know—"

"Your father doubts that any such evidence will be acceptable, especially not with this information being so new. But you can be sure we're going to try." Merran walked over to the little bathroom in the corner, wetted down a towel, and wiped himself off. He wetted another towel and handed it to Tamara, then pulled on his clothes.

She used the towel and dressed. "Is this ever going to be over?"

"For Justern, it's likely. As soon as the trial takes place, and if he is found guilty, I will do what I can to get him sent home. Then it will be over for him, but probably not for me. I'm going to be handling the consequences of this for a very long time, both in how our exchange continues and in influencing the Council to not take any retaliatory action." Merran brushed a hand down his suit. He looked up at her, his eyes twinkling mischievously. "Did you actually want to get some work in today?"

She laughed. "It's not required. It's midterm break, remember? My schedule runs with the semester."

Merran kissed her lightly. "Then go home and be with your family. I'm going to get some work in, probably until late tonight, so don't worry about coming over."

She hugged him mentally and physically. "All right. Until later." With that, she walked out of the embassy, a little sore from their exertions and a bit shaky, but also feeling more relaxed than she had in a while. As she walked, she wondered when the personal trials that had scooped her up at the beginning of the semester would see fit to let her be.

Chapter Twelve

AS SHE WALKED HOME, Tamara had every intention to speak to Alarin as soon as possible, but her mother took a bad turn and she didn't feel she could leave her side. She called Greg in desperation, who told them that her mother was not likely to survive the night. He was able to dull her pain, but he could do little else. With her father and Andreya beside her, Tamara sat in vigil around her mother's bedside that evening.

Lost in a dream world, her mother lay insensible and unreachable for hours. Tamara fought off waves of despair as Jeanine Carrington moaned monotonously in a low voice. *Let her die*, she prayed to any deity that might be listening. *Let her be free.*

Jeanine gave up the fight at three o'clock the following morning, answering Tamara's prayers with the dark of the night. Dull with exhaustion and adrenaline, Tamara made her way into the living room. Andreya trailed after her, looking lost and forlorn, and Tamara could sense her need for some kind of comfort. Too lost in her own emotions, however, she could offer nothing.

Greg was sprawled on the couch, facedown with his head pillowed against the cushions. Somewhere through the thick strands of emotional cotton that surrounded her, Tamara touched his mind with hers, and he woke immediately, flipping over and sitting up at the same time in a graceful move that made Tamara vaguely jealous. "It's over?"

Tamara nodded, too numb to respond in any other way.

Greg touched her mind. *Are you all right?*

I will be eventually. I think I need to sleep, but I don't know if I can.

Try. It will be the best thing for you. There isn't much we can do now. It's too early in the morning. His mind brushed up against hers and she could feel his compassion.

Her father came out of the bedroom, his eyes red-rimmed. "I'm going to call the funeral home. Why don't you girls try to get some sleep? We're going to have a long day tomor—today."

Andreya looked more miserable than ever.

All right, I'll try. Would you work with Andreya, please? Tamara sent the request to Greg on his intimate level, although she sometimes still had difficulty aiming at that level.

Of course, he answered, as he walked over to Andreya.

"I don't know how much sleep I'll get, but I'll try." Tamara told her father. "Dad—"

Her father hugged her tightly, opening his arms to Andreya too. He held them tightly. Tamara could sense the tears he held back and she hugged him even tighter. After a while, her father released them and Tamara, eyes wet, fled to her room. Sleep didn't come for a long, long time. When she finally drifted off, dreams haunted her.

❋ ❋ ❋

The day passed in a hell of half-aware arrangements, acceptance of condolences, and notification of her mother's death. Tamara never did have a clear memory of it. She certainly didn't get a chance to talk to Alarin or anyone else for the week until her mother's funeral.

The funeral itself passed quickly. Tamara was still in a mostly numb state. She greeted Merran in the same dull fog that had surrounded her for the entire week. He paid his respects at the funeral, then had to leave to attend a meeting.

"Is she all right?" Merran asked Greg as he stood in the doorway looking back over to where Tamara moved mechanically, her shields shuttered tight. "She won't let me in at all."

"She won't let anyone in," Greg replied soberly. "She cried the night her mother died, but she's been dragging herself through the rest of the week completely walled off from all of us."

Merran rubbed his forehead wearily. "I'm sure either Alarin or I could get through if we had some time alone with her. She's just overwhelmed and I'm sure running on pure adrenaline. See if Alarin will do it, will you? If he doesn't get the idea himself, that is. I have a meeting with the Council this afternoon, or I would, but I can't exactly postpone that."

Greg nodded. "Good luck."

"Thanks. I'm going to need it to convince the Council … again … not to recall us all." Merran sighed. "Let me know how it goes with Tamara, and tell her I'll call her later." He walked out the door.

Tamara was barely holding herself together by a thread, completely unaware of Greg, Merran, or Alarin's worry. She searched for a time to get away from the suffocating, overwhelming emotions of her relatives, and the blatantly anti-Azellian comments and conversations floating around. She finally found it about two hours later, escaping into the backyard to walk.

The silence of the trees wrapped her in a fragile, soft bubble of peace. She could still hear the party behind her, drunken people mixing with sorrow to create a mental dissonance that threatened her sanity. She took a deep breath and sat on the bench under one large oak.

With a sinking feeling of dread, she sensed the approach of someone and pulled her shields up around herself hastily.

"How are you holding up?" Justern asked, coming around the backside of the oak, obviously doing something similar—escaping into the garden to walk.

"I've been better." Tamara relaxed and rubbed her cheek with her fingers. She moved over on the bench as she looked up at him. "How do Azellians deal with the level of sheer noise humans put off?"

"Painfully. Unless we stay shielded all the time, which we usually do." Justern extended his long legs out in front of him, linking his fingers behind his head.

"I don't know how much of the funk I've been in this past week is mine and how much is everyone else's."

"Probably a combination. My philosophy is not to worry about it and focus on the birds and the trees. They're less of a pain in the ass than most people." He looked over at her, those eyes that were so similar to hers appearing uncomfortably intense. "Speaking of people, you do realize that Mer and Alari are working themselves into a frenzy worrying about you. Merran hides it better, but both he and Alari follow you around like baby *kiyyar*."

Tamara blinked at him as the image of a maternal duck being followed by a line of ducklings came to mind with the unfamiliar word. "Worrying about me?"

Justern gave her a smile that didn't match the expression in his eyes. "I'd have thought the question would be Merran *and* Alarin?"

She could feel a blush crawl up her cheeks. "I … uh … it's complicated."

"Complicated is fun. Come on, I need the distraction. And so do you. Do you really want to go back in there and face all the people whining and crying in their soup? I'm ready for a good story." Despite the harsh words, the emotion behind his offer was supportive and caring and uncomplicated. He knew what it was like, this pain of losing a parent. He also knew something none of her other friends did: it was survivable. Lowering his arms, he linked his fingers over his stomach, slouched on the bench, and watched her expectantly.

"I—I don't know what to do."

"Good place to be," he replied lightly. "It's one of the most creative places."

"Creative?" Tamara frowned at him.

"When you know what your future is, and it's all laid out in nice fixed rows, is there any creativity there?"

"Well, no …"

He spread his hands, then linked them again. "Good place to be," he repeated. "Most of the time." A shadow flittered across his face, and she knew he was thinking about the uncertainty of his own situation. "Anyway. Do about what?"

"Them. The guys … what did you call them, *kiyyar*?"

Justern studied her for a moment. "Are you having sex with either of them? Or both?"

Tamara choked. "Seriously?"

He grinned at her."What? It's a legitimate question."

"It's also a highly personal question, thank you very much."

Justern squinted at her. "Well, you have every right not to answer it. Of course, the answer's in your aura. Let's see. That aura is streaked with both brown and green, so I'd say it's both."

Tamara shook her head. "That's definitely not fair." She cocked her head at him. "How did you know I Awakened?"

"Besides the fact you have an aura when you didn't before? Mel told me." Justern shifted. "So what's the problem? From what Mel says, they've each got their talents."

The conversation had edged into the surreal, but it helped distract her from the misery she'd been steeped in for the past week, so she let it continue. "You mean you don't know personally? From what Mel said, Azellians experiment with both before settling into their preferences."

"I'm quite a bit younger than they are. By the time I Awakened, they were both pretty firmly interested in women and nothing else. Or so I thought." Justern continued to watch her with an intensity that was both unnerving and flattering at the same time. She felt as though he were dissecting her, although there was no judgment to the scrutiny, just his full attention. "Your turn."

Feeling defensive, Tamara frowned at him. "I'm not sleeping with both of them. Only Merran."

Justern gave her a long look. "That's not what your aura says."

"It's complicated. I haven't ever really slept with Alarin, he just, uh, sort of links with us when Merran and I ..." she trailed off, blushing.

Justern was silent, studying her. "And this bothers you?" he said finally.

Tamara sniffed. "Why wouldn't it? It's … not … normal."

Justern shrugged. "Why would you want to be normal? It might not be common, but I've had a few multiple links during sex myself. It's fun."

Somehow that didn't surprise her. "Fun?"

"It's not like you're married to Merran, is it?"

"No, but we're in a relationship. That should mean some exclusivity."

"Why?"

She blinked at him. "Well, because. I mean, we're in a *relationship*. It just goes with the package."

Justern shifted on the bench to face her, resting his arm across the back, his hand just out of touching distance. "You just Awakened. Why would you tie yourself to someone just because you slept with him? Merran's not thinking about it in those terms. Alari probably isn't either."

A weird feeling spread through her, a series of emotions she didn't know how to categorize. Her head spun. Maybe Merran truly didn't care if she slept with Alarin or not. She swallowed. "But Merran said … Merran said that he has no interest in sleeping with anyone else. Just me."

"Yeah, Mer's always been a one-girl-at-a-time type of guy. Pretty straightlaced in his preferences too." He shook his head. "Misses out on quite a bit, believe me."

She took a deep breath and let it out slowly. Something about Justern's attitude was making her calmer with the idea, although she had no idea why. He was certainly implying things she had never ever imagined. "So you're saying I should sleep with Alarin?"

"Why not?"

"He … he has a fiancée. Isn't that an exclusive relationship for Azellians?"

Justern snorted. "Maybe in her world, but Alari's got no interest in marrying Ida. He's just waiting for a reason to dump her. You might be it." He poked her shoulder with a finger. "Besides, it might get him out of your head if you sleep with him. Saying no is a great way to start an obsession. Especially if he's riding sex with you already. Bringing the physical into the psi is really … intense. Bringing the psi into the physical will help reduce some of that intensity. It's also a great distractor from …" he waved his hand back toward the house, "… that crap."

Tamara glanced in the direction of the house. Her Aunt Stacie stepped out onto the patio, looking for someone, putting a hand up to her eyes and peering at the yard.

Tamara returned her attention back to Justern, who seemed willing to discuss his fellow Azellians quite bluntly. Mellis would probably have been open to the discussion too, but somehow it was easier talking to someone who had never slept with either of them. Mellis's history with both young men made it odd to talk to her about them. *Not that Mel hasn't made the offer to listen several times over the past week. I just haven't taken her up on it.* "So … what's Alarin like? A one-girl-at-a-time type of guy, too? Straight-laced?"

Justern stretched and shifted so he rested his elbows on his knees. "Let's just say of all the people I know, Merran and Alari would be the last two I'd have expected to find themselves sharing a woman. Although Alarin did it once before, that was during Awakening and doesn't count." He glanced over a shoulder at the door to the house. "Relative alert. I think someone's looking for you." He shifted his weight, getting ready to get to his feet and bolt, considering the hostility he'd been facing as an Azellian in a house full of grieving humans.

"Wait a minute," Tamara protested, grabbing Justern's shoulder before he could get up. "He's done it before? With who?"

"Why Mel, Greg, and our friend Charina, of course."

"He told me it was only Mel."

Justern pulled away and got to his feet. He grinned down at her. "He's not about to shock your human sensibilities when he wants to get you into bed. Ask him again once you've slept with him." He studied her for a moment. "Although if either of them hurts you, I'll kick their asses." With that startling statement, he turned on his heel and made his way away from her, slipping out of sight with a startling suddenness, almost as if he just … disappeared.

"We've been looking all over for you, sweetheart," her Aunt Stacie said breathlessly, pulling her attention away from where Justern had gone. "Why are you sitting out here all alone? It's dinnertime. Come on up to the house. Your dad was wondering where you were."

Tamara took a breath and let it out slowly. "I wasn't …" She halted, not really wanting to explain that Justern had been out here with her. Her aunt wasn't as rabid in her dislike of Azellians as her grandmother, but watching them all dance around Merran—not only an Azellian, but the infamous Azellian ambassador no less—had been both amusing and pathetic. "I was just taking a breath of air, Aunt Stacie. I'm coming." She turned and followed her aunt back to the house, feeling better and lighter and much less stressed.

✳ ✳ ✳

It was a relief to go back to classes the next day. She missed her mother terribly, but it helped to have schoolwork to distract her from both her mother's death and the weird relationship she found herself in.

"So what's going on?" Mellis asked late one afternoon, almost two weeks after her mother's funeral as they sat in her room studying together. Tamara pushed the tablet away from her and leaned back against the wall, bringing her knees up to her chest and linking her arms around her legs. She rested her chin on her knees.

"With what?"

"You and Alari."

"Me and ... what do you mean?"

"I mean you walk around for four weeks with a turquoise aura and now you won't talk to Alari? He's been a basketcase these past two weeks, you know. I know your mom just died, and you've had a lot to deal with, but is that any reason to ignore your friends?"

Tamara stared at Mellis. "A basketcase?"

"He's been holed up in his room for two weeks, hardly coming out to attend a class. I haven't seen him like this since ... well I've never seen him like this. What happened between you two?"

Tamara swallowed. She'd seen Alarin only a couple of times these past two weeks, but she'd thought it was because she'd been avoiding him, not because he was hiding out. "Nothing really."

"Oh please. I can see your aura, Tamara. You have brown and green in it. The brown is Merran, of course, but the green has got to be Alari. You don't know any other Azellians."

"I'm telling the truth, Mel. Really, I am. Nothing happened. Not really, just a kiss. Once. And some linking when Merran and I ... sleep together."

Mellis's expression cleared and she pulled her legs into a typical crossed-legged position that all the Azellians did effortlessly. "Ah. You're linking with Alari during sex with Merran. Well, that would explain a lot."

"What do you mean?"

Mellis smiled at her and tossed her bangs out of her eyes. "Alari's pretty careful about not pressuring someone into something they aren't willing to do. He probably knows you're having trouble with it and is keeping his distance until you approach him. You are freaking out about it, aren't you?"

"Well, yes," Tamara admitted. "I mean, it's just so … weird."

Mellis laughed. "It's not that weird, especially right after Awakening, or among those who like to throw extra thrills into their sex lives."

"That's what Justy said. But I was told it's not common."

"Well, it's not usually typical to do it when the parties involved are in a relationship, but even then it's not unheard of. There have been people at home who shared a spouse before."

"Shared—shared a spouse?"

"Yeah. Two women married to one man, two men to one woman, that sort of thing. It's not all that strange, Tamara. Even on Earth, from what I've heard in my Earth history classes. Although it's more commonly multiple women and one man on Earth, it's not unheard of."

Tamara waved a hand. "Maybe, but it's not mainstream, at least not in this part of the world. On Azelle … does it ever work out?"

"Well, it can get weird, especially if one or the other thinks they're not getting enough attention, but it works as much as anything does." Mellis leaned forward, resting her elbows on her knees. "You thinking about turning the psi sex physical with Alari?"

Tamara shrugged. "I don't know. He—he'd like me to. And he's sharing it anyway. I care about Alarin. Quite a bit. More than I'm comfortable admitting. And Merran says he doesn't care."

"He probably doesn't. You've seen how often he's anywhere you can reach him, even by phone?"

"Yeah, rarely."

"He's been like that since I've known him. A rolling stone that gathers no sand or whatever the saying is."

Tamara giggled, feeling the laugh bubble up inside of her. "I think the saying is a rolling stone gathers no moss."

Mellis grinned. "Whatever. Merran's not real big on staying put. Alari, however, well, he's the dependable type. Once he gives you his loyalty and love, he's in for the long haul."

"Sexy and dependable? Wow, that's a combo."

"He's a great lover, too." Mellis shifted her weight a little. "He and Merran are about equal in that regard, but Alari's more … intense. Lets you in further, which increases the excitement factor. He'll let you see and share how hot and bothered he's getting. Merran's too controlled for that."

Tamara bit her lip. She hadn't noticed that Merran didn't share his arousal with her, but then she had nothing to compare to. "Can I, uh, ask you a question?"

"Sure, go ahead."

"Your Awakening. What was it like? If that's not too rude."

Mellis smiled. "It's personal but not rude. I was about thirteen in human years, I think. Thirteen or fourteen … I'm not sure on the exact conversion. It was summer and my friend Charina— she's Merran's niece—and I were hanging out at the beach with Merran. We'd been swimming in the oasis all morning and had come up onto the shore to rest before going to lunch. Merran had already Awakened and was messing around with someone. I don't remember who now, but it was some girl he'd met and was seducing for some reason or another. These two guys came up to us— Greg and Alarin actually—and started talking to us. One thing led to another, and the next thing I knew, I was kissing the sexy redhead," she grinned at Tamara, "and we were helping each other Awaken. Greg and Chari got sucked in too, and it sort of turned into a little more than we were intending, but it was a hell of a lot of fun."

No wonder Merran and Alarin don't think sharing me is all that odd! Tamara took a deep breath and let it out slowly. "Alarin left out a lot when he told me about his Awakening."

"Yes, he probably knew it would weird you out." Mellis shifted her weight again. "He's pretty powerful too, so it was quite a ride. I got to channel quite a bit of energy. He didn't have nearly as much to do for me."

"I always thought Awakenings were one on one."

"It is one on one. Alari and I were channeling each other and though they might have been set off by our Awakening, making it happen simultaneously, so were Greg and Chari. After we were all Awake, though … well, that was a different story." She grinned. "By the *aarya*, was it fun, although not typical. It's probably only because Greg liked men, and Chari and I aren't picky about our partners, that it went where it went. Alari sort of got dragged along for the ride. He's actually pretty conservative when it comes to sex."

Tamara swallowed, not sure she really wanted to know any more. "Oh. That's good. Because I'm probably completely tied in knots compared to what you guys are used to."

Mellis laughed. "Don't worry. For him to be this careful, Alari's very, very interested. I'd say you don't have anything to worry about."

"What about his girlfriend? On Azelle?"

Mellis shrugged. "Ask him. He'll tell you. If there's anything Alari is, it's straightforward when you ask a question. He doesn't push things on you, but if you ask, he'll answer. Are you going to talk to him?"

Tamara nodded. "Yes. Yes, I will."

"I'm certainly glad to hear that. I'd like to have him come out of his room soon." Mellis reached for her tablet again. "So, have you figured out what the professor is asking for?"

Tamara snorted and reached out for her tablet, too. "God no. That would mean she made sense. She can't possibly make sense, can she?"

Mellis laughed and they moved onto other subjects.

Although she'd made the decision to talk to Alarin, she didn't get the opportunity to talk to him right away. The only class she'd had with him was chemistry, and he'd dropped out of her class in the beginning of the semester and gone on to a more advanced level class. She would have joined the Azellians for dinner at the cafeteria in the hopes of running into him, or gone to his room Friday night, but her father called and asked her to come home for Friday dinner. Since he had to manage the relatives by himself—her Aunt Stacie was still helpfully present, trying to "take care" of her younger brother, Peter, and her nieces, and her grandmother had flatly refused to leave—Tamara agreed to come home for dinner and spend the night.

After a stressful, somewhat unpleasant dinner filled with anti-Azellian slurs and negative grumblings, she escaped to her room, wondering why she'd ever agreed to spend the night. She closed her eyes, then opened them, resting her hands on her stomach. Having made the decision to talk to Alarin, she found herself wanting to do it immediately. Had Mellis been telling the truth? Was he still interested, even after two weeks of her hiding from him? She was certainly attracted to and cared about Alarin, especially since her conversation with Mellis a couple of days ago. Lying on her twin bed, she stared up at the ceiling. Was there any reason she couldn't talk to him tonight? Turning over to reach for her phone, she pulled up Alarin's number and put her finger over the call button. *Except this isn't really phone call material,* she told herself. Removing her finger, she tapped the button to turn off the screen and then put her phone back on the table beside her.

But why can't I call him and have him come over? Picking up the phone again, she swiped the screen and positioned her finger over the call button. *Except how will he get into the house?* Asking him to come upstairs to talk to her was not going to fly real well with her family—especially with her hostile grandmother and nosy aunt downstairs. She tapped the button to turn off the screen once more and put her phone back on the table beside her.

Frustrated, she lay back on her bed, pressing her forearm into her eyes. She felt like she was in high school again—agonizing over whether to call some boy or not. Wasn't she an adult? Flipping over on the bed, she reached for the phone for the third time. Just as she swiped the screen, a soft knock on her door and familiar presence at her shields made her leap up out of bed.

"What are you doing here?" she asked Alarin, pulling him into her room, closing the door behind him and locking it.

"You worried about someone breaking in or something?" he asked, his expression neutral, but his green eyes bright with amusement. It had been a while since she'd seen him and he looked really good. His hair was a bit longer, somewhat shaggy and in need of a cut. His face was rough with stubble, as if he hadn't shaved in a day or two. It sent a thrill through her stomach. She'd forgotten just how attractive he was. She had a sudden flash of kissing him, of his body pressed against hers. "Or just afraid for my life?"

"With my relatives? Afraid for your life. I don't trust them to not come barging in here. You haven't answered my question. What are you doing here?"

He leaned against the door, looking oddly tense and relaxed at the same time. "I've been hanging out with Justy the past couple of days."

"Justy?" Although she'd spent quite a bit of time with her brother these past two weeks, he hadn't mentioned a thing about Alarin visiting. As a matter of fact, since their conversation in the garden on the afternoon of her mother's funeral, the subject of Merran and Alarin had been scrupulously avoided. "Oh, that's probably a good idea. Help him feel better ..." She shook her head and went to perch on the edge of the bed. "I was just going to call you."

"Were you? About what?" Alarin moved to sit on the edge of the desk, his long legs crossed at the ankles.

She licked her lips. "We need to ... talk."

He didn't say anything, but just looked at her expectantly.

"I sort of left things hanging about ... everything. Did you—did you talk to Merran?"

"Briefly. He mentioned that you two had talked but not what you'd said."

Tamara took a deep breath and let it out slowly. "I ... don't know how to handle this thing. Between us. All three of us."

"One step at a time is usually a good place to start."

She rubbed her cheek, feeling the blush crawl up it. "What if the next step is different than anything I've ever done or dreamed about doing?"

He went very still. "What does that mean?"

"I don't—I don't know what I want."

"Is that true?" Alarin studied her, his green eyes uncomfortably intense.

"Well, no. I do know what I want. I ... just don't want it to all come crashing down. I care about Merran. I wouldn't want to hurt him. But I ... care about you too." *There. It's been said and can't be unsaid*, she thought to herself.

He shifted against the desk but didn't move otherwise. She couldn't read his reaction. "What did you and Merran talk about?"

"About how he can't be there for me all the time, that you could offer me things he can't." She stared down at her hands.

He cleared his throat. "And what would that be?"

"Attention, caring, support." She'd missed him these past two weeks she realized. Almost more than she'd missed Merran. When had he moved into her affections so deeply? "I don't know how this is going to work. But I'd like to try."

He shifted again. "What—" He had to stop and try again. Closing his eyes, he took a deep breath, then opened them, the expression in them quite intense. Her heart leaped into her throat and settled there, pounding hard. She felt dizzy. "What ... what does that mean to you?"

She swallowed and quite deliberately thinned her shields, letting him read the turmoil and desire behind her words. He shuddered as she reached out and brushed her mind over the light that played around the edges of his physical body. "I don't know," she whispered. "I only know I don't want this to end. I want to see where it goes."

He closed his eyes and a shiver traveled through his body. His hands pressed into the top of the desk. She could feel the arousal running through him and it made her breath catch. *Well, apparently Mel's right. Alarin does share more than Merran does. I've never seen Merran like this,* she thought. His whole body was quivering with the force of his arousal. He took a breath and let it out slowly. "I told you to come back to me when things calmed down and I'd gladly join you in that bed, or in any other you might choose," he said, his hand shaking as he lifted it to brush his hair off his forehead. He was shielded, but emotion leaked around the edges of it, and she'd learned this past month that shields couldn't block her empathy anyway. "I'm still willing. Is that what you want?"

She stared down at the bedspread. "Yes," she whispered, not daring to look at him.

Her chin came up, although he hadn't moved from his position on the desk. "You're not being very convincing, Tamara."

Moving her head and breaking the telekinetic hold effortlessly, Tamara licked her lips that had suddenly become dry. Giving in to an impulse she'd had when he walked into her room, she got off the bed and moved over to stand in front of him. He watched her intently, shifting his legs so she could step between them. She walked forward, cupping his face in her hands and tilted her head slightly to kiss him. His stubble was prickly, but his mouth tasted fresh and clean and she made a sound as she pressed against him and deepened the kiss. He raised his hands up and twined them in her hair, standing up so he could pull her closer into his body. Alarin kissed her back with a passion she had never felt from Merran. His shields abruptly relaxed as his mind wound around hers in a sensual dance and his hands slid under her shirt, his warm fingers spanning her waist.

By the time she came up for air, she was dizzy and could hardly remember what she had to say. "Wait, what about—I thought you had a girlfriend? On Azelle?" She could feel his heart racing as he held her tightly against him. He smelled good too. She recognized the special "guest" soap that her mother had always bought to put in the guest room and bathroom that Justern currently occupied. A flash of sorrow shot through her.

Alarin paused, his hands stilling against her side as he shifted his grip against her body. "My ... what? Oh, you mean Ida? It's over. It's been over since I came to Earth. She knows it." He lowered his forehead to hers and she could feel the tremble in his arms as he held her tightly.

She shifted, feeling his bodily sensations against her. "I'm ... not ending it with Merran."

"I don't expect you to." Alarin lowered his head to kiss her, sliding his mouth and lips down her neck. She shuddered. "But I'd like to point out that I have considerably more free time than he does." His warm mouth closed over the skin of her collarbone and she shivered, sensations skittering over her entire body.

"Uh, shouldn't we warn Merran?"

Alarin stopped, lifting his head to look at her. A grin tugged at the edge of his lips. "I suppose that would be a nice thing to do. Much more mature than his little interruption a couple of weeks ago."

She sniffed. "I refuse to be the manner in which you two beat up on each other. Besides, isn't he in the middle of an interview? You tell me. Do you think his riding with us will enhance the interview?" When she'd decided to talk to Alarin, she'd checked Merran's schedule with Janille. He definitely had an interview tonight.

Alarin laughed, the laugh spilling through his entire body. "Nice euphemism. It would certainly be amusing, if not enhancing of the Azellian reputation. The reporter might enjoy it if she's female." He moved against her, his hands beginning to wander again, caressing a warm path up the sensitive skin of her back.

Tamara shook her head, trying to ignore the sensations flittering through her body. "No, I don't want to share either of you with anyone else."

Alarin moved her toward the bed, using his body to gently nudge her backwards. She let him, taking a few steps back. "So you're saying we have to be exclusive and you don't?"

"Yes." She didn't quite know how he'd take it, but she laid out the way she wanted it anyway.

"What did Merran say to that caveat?" Alarin didn't seem particularly upset; he was much more interested in removing her shirt than worried about the answer.

She let him pull it over her head. "That he has more than enough with a job and me. As you pointed out, you have more time than he does."

The bed bumped the back of her knees. He frowned at her bra. "What in the name of the *aarya* is this thing? And how do you get it off?" He slid his hands over the silky fabric covering her breasts.

435

Merran apparently has had considerably more experience with human women, Tamara thought, carefully behind shields, *because my bra certainly never stumped him. He's actually quite good at getting it off, even without being able to see the clasp.* "It's a bra," she said, stifling a giggle at his expression. It felt good to relax enough to laugh. She hadn't laughed much these past couple of weeks. "Azellian women don't wear them?"

"No."

She turned around. "The hook's in the back."

"Ah." After a few moments, he managed to figure out the clasp, his hands sliding up to slip the straps off her shoulders.

She held her arms to her chest, keeping the bra in place as she turned around. "Well?"

"Well what?" He didn't look like he had a brain left to process words, much less be able to answer questions, but he managed to focus. "Ah, exclusivity? You realize it's not fair taking it this far and asking me about anything right now. If you asked me for the Raderth family mantle at this moment, I'd probably happily give it to you." He took a deep breath and let it out slowly, but he didn't move back, his hands coming up to caress her upper arms. "We have something I want to explore. I'd like to see where it goes. And if it takes sharing you with Merran, I can accept that. This is complicated enough as it is. I don't think adding anyone else to the mix would be a very good idea."

A wave of capitulation washed over Tamara as she let her bra fall to the bed. She moved so she sat on the bed against the wall. "Except that he's in the middle of an interview, remember? We can't interrupt him yet." Why she was having so much fun teasing Alarin, she wasn't sure, except that her experience with Merran these past several months had given her quite a bit more confidence.

Alarin growled, the sound sending a shiver up her spine. "Fine, but he's not going to get much warning once that interview's over." Moving stiffly, he crouched and picked up her shirt. "Put that back on, or interview or no interview, I'm going to finish what we started." Climbing on the bed beside her, he leaned against the wall, resting his head against it and closing his eyes.

Tamara slipped on the shirt. "What does it look like anyway?" she asked after a few moments. "I'm always in the middle, so I would never know."

"There's actually not all that much to see if you can't sense the psi part of it. If he weren't having to juggle the political situation of our talents, Justern's trial and Healers, we'd be finishing this right now. He could hide his distraction from a human. Until he was to stand up at least."

"Do you actually … orgasm?" She could feel her face get hot.

He cracked open an eye and looked at her. "You try ignoring me having sex with you and see how far you get. It's not easy, especially when the two of you are stimulating every erotic center I have."

"Okay, got it." She shook her head. "Let's change the subject."

He grinned, opening his other eye and suddenly looking more relaxed. "What do you want to talk about?"

"I don't know. Nothing to excite the situation even more right now. What about your family? What are they like? Are they as nuts as mine?"

"Probably more. Are you willing to link with me? I can show you some memories."

She smiled at him and nodded. "Okay, let's try."

She slipped into his mind, rather surprised at how easy it was becoming. Her training with Greg was paying off. He let her read a few memories, calling them to mind and laying them out in front of her. They stayed away from touching anything too deep, although it was tempting. She lay down on the bed, her mind's eye far away on Azelle, stretching her legs across Alarin's lap. He rested his hands on her thighs, a light touch that enhanced the contact.

A knock on her door interrupted them, making her abruptly focus on the now rather than the vistas of Azelle in Alarin's head. "Who is it?"

"It's Aunt Stacie. We noticed you weren't downstairs. You came up right after dinner. Are you all right, honey?" The door-knob rattled.

Tamara exchanged a glance with Alarin. "I'm fine, Aunt Stacie. I just got really tired and came up here to sleep." She put as much sleepy distortion into her voice as she could.

"Are you sure, honey? Did you want to come down and have a snack? Spend some time with us before bed?" Tamara turned to the clock and frowned. Had so much time gone by already?

"I don't feel up to coming downstairs right now. I think I'm going to go to bed." She spoke to Alarin mentally as she got up. *I'm going to have to let her in, or she's going to think I'm lying. Could you get in the closet? I promise to make it quick.*

Alarin's grin was mischievous. He leaned forward and kissed her hard, his hands and tongue driving her almost instantly wild, besides startling her out of her wits. He broke off the kiss and slid off the bed just as she was ready to tell Aunt Stacie to go to hell. *Merran's done with his interview.*

How he knew that, she refused to ask. She got off the bed, pulled back the sheets, and as Alarin disappeared into the closet, Tamara unlocked the door. She tried to look sleepy but probably only succeeded in looking startled. Her portly aunt stood there with concern written all over her face. "I'm okay, Aunt Stacie. Really, I am. I haven't been getting much sleep lately."

"You need to eat something, honey. Come downstairs with me," her aunt pressed on.

Alarin continued his mischief. Still wrapped up in his mind, she could not escape his mental caresses. Her attempt to raise a shield between them failed miserably. "No, thank you, Aunt Stacie. I think sleep's more important."

"Nothing's more important than food at times like these, dear." Tamara couldn't stop the sarcastic little thought that bubbled up in response to her aunt's statement. She could hear a muffled noise from the closet as Alarin picked up her thought and hastily covered a laugh. "What was that?" Her aunt looked around the room.

Tamara wished now that she had never opened the door. "Nothing, Aunt Stacie." She yawned and rubbed her eyes. "Please, Aunt Stacie, I really need some time alone. I've had a long day, and I just need to take it easy."

Her aunt peered at her. "I don't know—"

Tamara felt the mental nudge that Alarin gave her aunt. It was not particularly polite or gentle. "Aunt Stacie, I'll be fine. Just tell everyone I've gone to bed. All right?"

Helpless against Alarin's will, Aunt Stacie backed out of the room. "All right, if you're sure."

"I'm sure. Thank you for thinking of me, and good night." Tamara closed the door and locked it again. Alarin opened the closet door and stepped out. "Useful talent, that," she whispered, so her aunt who still hovered uncertainly outside the door didn't hear her.

He smiled. "Well, I didn't think she was going to take no for an answer and there was no way I was going to let her get between us." He walked over to her. "Merran's done with his interview, and I have no intention of letting you change your mind." He bent over to kiss her, sliding his hands up under her shirt and stripping it over her head. Dropping the shirt to the ground, he pulled away briefly and looked down at her. She shivered at the look in his eyes. His eyes were very, very green, the heat in them enough to set her on fire. His hands trembled slighty as he lifted long fingers to cup her breast, massaging it lightly, tracing the edge of it.

"By the *aarya's* eyes, I've wanted you for a long time," he murmured, lowering his head to kiss her breast, his breath hot on her skin. Tamara's breath caught as he focused on one breast, then the other. She moaned slightly, arching back. Alarin lifted his head after a few moments.

"Like that?" he asked, a smile playing at the edge of his lips.

Instead of answering, she pulled him to his feet and kissed him passionately. He made a grunting sound that caused her whole body to contract. Alarin walked her back toward the bed, his hands pulling her against him. She could feel him pressed against her as he twirled the two of them around, pulling her the last few inches down to her bed. As she opened her shields and let Alarin slide into the depths of her mind, she could feel the arousal spilling through him—powerful, intense, and exciting. As they linked, she could feel Merran slide in to link with them also. For an insane moment, it felt as though Alarin had four sets of hands and two mouths, caressing her sensitized skin beyond anything she'd ever experienced before. She groaned and shuddered.

That sensation was a bit more than she was ready for, so she let herself get distracted by the sight of Alarin pulling back to tug off his t-shirt, unbuttoning his jeans and shimmying out of them. As he kicked off his jeans and climbed back on the bed, she couldn't help but notice he was built longer but thinner than Merran—she had to hastily hide that thought behind shields, hoping desperately neither one of them had picked it up. She'd been sharing her orgasms with Alarin for the past month, so it should have felt the same to have switched which man was in her physical bed and which was sharing the psi sex, but as Alarin slid down beside her, his body and mind quivering with nearly overwhelming excitement and desire, it didn't. It felt different—wilder and less controlled. Alarin was so incredibly responsive, reacting strongly to everything she did, encouraging her to do more. She slipped her hand down his bare chest, and lower, tracing her hand over him, indulging herself in a way she never would have with Merran. He groaned and stopped her, his hand on her wrist.

"You have to stop that," he murmured, sounding breathless. "I won't last if you do that and there's no way this is ending that soon."

"Do you have to go back to your room tonight?" she asked, rubbing against him, trying to entice him closer.

"No, I'm supposed to be spending the night with Justy."

"Then who says it has to be only once?"

He made that sound low in his throat again, a shiver taking his whole body. Tamara gave in to her own desires and rolled them over. Pushing him onto his back, she straddled him and took the choice out of his hands. He gasped, his eyelids fluttering closed as she slid over him and moved against his body, setting the rhythm. His mind curled around hers and touched her mentally in such a way that she was sent into immediate, intense orgasm, taking Tamara totally by surprise. Alarin's hands gripped her hips as he shuddered. The release when it came wrenched through his entire body, sharing her explosive climax and spilling it back into Merran.

She collapsed onto the bed beside him, pleasantly exhausted, her body vibrating with the aftermath. Alarin traced circles on her stomach, making her skin twitch as she lay on the bed propped up beside him. She closed her eyes. "Do you … uh … do you think Merran was able to get away from what he was doing? I hope he really was all right with this."

Alarin ran his fingertips lightly over her skin, the expression on his face taking her breath away. A mixture of desire and tenderness, it was erotic and stimulating and overwhelming all at once. She had to remind herself to breathe. "He was. Just ask him."

Dizzy, ready to be distracted from the intensity in Alarin's eyes, Tamara reached inward and brushed Merran's mind. He welcomed her and let her see that he had been in his office, so the side effects could be well concealed. After giving her a mental hug, he pulled shields up and returned to the project he'd been working on. "How can he do that?" she asked, confused by the ease with which he went back to work and the fact that he really didn't seem to care that she and Alarin had just made love.

"Merran can snap to focus within minutes if he needs to. He never completely gives up control. You need to be able to splinter your awareness in order to even start to do what he does. It's not easy, and is usually something only people in very sensitive jobs do. Healers, politicians, people like that. I can't do it. But considering if I could do it I wouldn't be able to share with you like this, I'm not sure I'd want to." All thoughts of Merran scattered as Alarin leaned over to kiss her again, his mind sliding through hers in a very sensual way, using mind, hands, and body to erase anything resembling thought from her mind.

Sleep came quickly, more quickly than she expected, as they snuggled together with their legs entwined. Tamara relaxed completely for the first time since her mother died.

Morning and awareness came too quickly—as did an instant complication in Tamara's plans. It was far later than she'd meant to sleep for one thing, which made getting Alarin out of the house rather problematic. She could hear people moving around downstairs. She jumped up, scrambling over a startled Alarin. "Shit!"

Alarin rubbed his eyes. "Do you always wake up that way?" He yawned.

"It's later than I wanted to wake up." Tamara grabbed a clean pair of underwear and a new set of clothes. "I still have to get you out of here, and there's a house full of nosy relatives downstairs."

Alarin sat up, the sheet falling off his body. As unselfconscious as Merran, he got out of bed. If she hadn't been so worried about getting him safely out of her room, she would have found his half-erect state enticing. As it was, he ignored it, and so did she. "Not a problem."

"Like how? I'm supposed to explain that I had you in my room for an undefined period of time, doing exactly what? They'll accurately suspect we were doing what we were doing."

Alarin grinned and came over to her. He kissed her lingeringly. "I don't think they'll ever know the full story. Besides, does it really matter?"

"Well, I think it would be considered a little rude that you spent the night with me in my dad's house." Tamara said crossly, although she did respond amorously to his kiss.

Alarin's shields hung loose, revealing a singular lack of concern as he reached for his clothes. "We'll get me out of here, Tamara dear."

They had made it most of the way down the hall when Justern came out of the room where he'd been almost completely exiled since the funeral.

He grinned at Tamara. "I see. Sneaking Alarin out, eh?"

Tamara glared at him. "Yes, and you're not helping any."

"There were some very interesting vibes floating around last night," Justern ignored her glare. "I was quite … entertained."

"Don't tell me you eavesdropped!" Tamara whirled on him. "That's disgusting!"

Justern put his hands up. "Hey, calm down, Tamara. I didn't eavesdrop, as tempting as it was."

Alarin raised an eyebrow but said nothing. Something about the quality of his silence made Tamara suddenly wonder if Justern was telling the truth. She decided she didn't want to know. Giving Justern one final glare, she motioned Alarin down the hall behind her.

They managed this time to make it as far as her father's office. Peter Carrington pulled the door open and saw his daughter standing there. Tamara flushed, certain the whole thing was over and she would not be allowed to have anything to do with Azellians ever again. "You're awake. And Alarin? It's a bit early to be visiting, isn't it?" She opened her mouth to speak.

"I asked him to stay last night," Justern interrupted, coming up behind them. "I'm sorry I didn't tell you first. We talked until late, then he fell asleep in my room. I didn't want to raise questions, so when we met up with Tamara in the hall, I had her lead him downstairs. Given the quality of sentiment around here, I suspected being with a known Azellian would be tantamount to an admission of guilt."

Tamara snapped her mouth shut and stared at Justern. He nudged her mentally. *Pay attention, you goose. I just saved your ass. Don't screw it up.*

Alarin, when Tamara touched his mind, was highly amused. Her father, it seemed, was satisfied with the explanation, or at least willing not to pressure anyone any further.

"I'm sorry you've had to deal with this, Justern." Peter ran his hand through his hair.

"Don't apologize," Justern replied quickly. "I certainly am very grateful for your hospitality and the work you're doing on my behalf. I can understand where the hostility comes from. I don't need anyone else suffering for my stupidities, however."

"This will be over soon," Peter told him. "And hopefully you'll at least be able to go home, no matter how this turns out."

Justern took a deep breath, and Tamara could read that he had gone further than he'd meant to when he originally stepped in to rescue them. "I hope you're right. There isn't much time before the court date. Let's hope I don't get a jail sentence."

That Justern was under a tremendous amount of pressure—even more than she was—crossed Tamara's mind. She extended a quick, grateful mental hug that was echoed by Alarin. Justern gave them a distracted response.

Peter shook his head. "Although we hope the court realizes your innocence, we're working toward getting you sent home if you're not cleared."

Justern closed his eyes. "You'll excuse me if I don't have faith in a system that is forced to take a person's believability as the only proof of wrongdoing."

"*Alawahea*, Justern." Alarin said in Azellian. "*Alawahea quo pi kitar me klet. Aarya di providar.*"

Justern's grey eyes were remote, his mind closed off behind tight shields. "So they say," he replied in the same language. "Maybe it would be easier if we were on Azelle. I'm not sure the *aarya* watch over Earth." He bowed to Peter, Tamara, and Alarin and switched to English. "If you'll excuse me, I don't think I'm fit company this morning. Thank you for stopping by, Alarin."

Tamara could sense Alarin's concern and sudden guilt as they watched Justern walk upstairs.

Peter frowned. "I think he's under more stress than he's admitting."

"I know I'd be a mess if I were in his position. Maybe we'd better have Greg check in on him," Tamara suggested.

"Might be a good idea. I think he's feeling isolated here, too." Alarin glanced at Peter. "Is there any way we could have him spend some time at the embassy?"

"He's not allowed to leave Earth until after his trial. The embassy is not officially considered Earth, so he has to stay here. My family is leaving this afternoon. Please tell your friends you are all welcome here at any time," Peter told Alarin. "I really was mortified by my family's behavior at the funeral and over these past two weeks."

Alarin smiled. "Azellians are no better toward humans, believe me. It is a common trait to be afraid of the unknown and hostile to newcomers." He bowed to Peter and Tamara. "I must get back to my room. I'll be back later. I think Justern will need company over the next few days." With Tamara, he bestowed a gentle mental caress that left her tingling.

The next few weeks were hectic, with little time for any kind of tender moments. As the trial drew closer, Merran got busier and the Azellians closed ranks around Justern. For the first time since she'd met them, she felt like an outsider.

The day of the trial arrived for a nervous Justern who reacted by becoming sullen and quiet, with his shields high and tight around him. It was also his first trip into the media spotlight since he'd been released from the hospital. Hidden in the Carrington house, he had been able to avoid the media hubbub that encircled Greg.

Court was scheduled to start early, so they got to the courthouse ahead of time and found a news crew already outside the courtroom. Justern's navy suit, dark hair, and downcast eyes marked him as the one on trial in the group of Azellians who surrounded him. They all followed Peter down the corridors, and Tamara trailed along behind.

Joely stood at the entrance with her lawyer. When she saw Justern, she went pale and grabbed on to what must have been her father's arm. He glared at Justern, the hostility pouring off him. Alarin lifted his hand and touched Justern's arm. Tamara could hear his mental voice in her head saying something to Justern on his private level.

The courthouse itself was an incongruously beautiful building, with soaring architecture and light pouring in through all the windows. The view from the window of the whole Front Range was breathtaking, the early morning sun playing sharp shadows over the folds of the hills. Tamara tore her gaze away as Peter pulled open the doors and peered inside. "Justern," he said in a low voice when he returned to the young man who was as pale as Tamara had ever seen any Azellian, "the judge is listening to another case right now. We have a bit of a wait, so take a seat and don't let her bother you. They're going to try to intimidate you before you even walk in. They want to put you on the defensive so you act guilty."

Tamara went over to the water cooler that stood in the corner and got Justern a cup of water. When she handed it to him, he gave her a weak smile and took the plastic cup, his hands shaking so much he almost spilled the water on himself. "I've never been on trial before," he said, in a hoarse whisper to Tamara. "The *aarya* help me."

"Do you want Greg to help?"

Justern closed his eyes. "Maybe he'd better."

Tamara motioned to the Healer, who dodged a reporter and came over. He ran his hands over Justern's aura lightly, surreptitiously, as Alarin and Mellis blocked the reporter's view. Tamara's attention wandered over to Joely. One of the other reporters cornered Joely's father. Joely herself stood against the wall, doing a fair imitation of a borderline hysterical girl. It was nearly perfect—until Tamara realized Joely really was scared. Her fear, however, was not so much of Justern, but of Alarin.

Alarin, she's scared of you, Tamara told him mentally. *Do you think you could coerce her into telling the truth in the courtroom?*

I'm certainly going to try. Alarin's mind tone was grim. *Although I'm rather limited because Merran's going to be here and he's under strict orders to keep the rest of our abilities under wraps. I also won't be able to get near enough to be sure that what I'm doing will work.*

Justern looked up at them. *I do appreciate your effort, Alari, but remember that I'm not worth jeopardizing human and Azellian relations.* Bitterness threaded through that statement, although he did try to minimize it. Tamara's heart ached for him, wishing she could help.

The sound of footsteps in the corridor made them all look up. The reporters pulled away from Joely's angry-looking father to encircle the new arrivals. Merran approached, his authority held like a mantle around him, with three Azellian assistants surrounding him. Dressed as an Azellian in an ornate robe that hung to the floor, Merran looked far more alien than Tamara had ever seen him, his brown eyes remote and cold, the short dark hair spiky and partially hidden under an elaborate hood. His aura glowed a brilliant hazel, still showing tinges of blue and green, the legacy of Tamara and Alarin's evenings together over these past couple of weeks. It was so bright that Tamara had a hard time looking at him. If he'd planned on an entrance, he certainly was making one. Every human in the hallway stared at him, drawn by a magnetism they could hardly resist. They might not be able to see his aura, but they were reacting to it nevertheless.

The reporters flocked around Merran, shooting questions at him as quickly as they could, seemingly unfazed by his … majesty. There really was no other word for it, Tamara thought to herself. He was majestic and playing up the entrance he'd made. He juggled questions easily, making it look simple, as if he hadn't rehearsed for every question they shot at him. Tamara did not hear most of the questions, except for one that resounded distinctly down the hall.

"What does the government of Azelle think of all of this?" the reporter eagerly held a microphone in front of Merran.

Merran inclined his head. "The Azellian Council is quite satisfied that Justern Memaxthal is innocent, as decided by our methods. We are confident this case will be judged fairly."

"What happens if he is found guilty?" another reported asked. "What will the government of Azelle do then?"

Merran turned cold brown eyes on the reporter, who actually turned pale as sweat beaded at the edges of her hair. "We are confident that this case will be judged fairly."

"How did the Azellian Council make a decision on this case without a trial?" Another bold reporter asked. "Without talking to the victim?"

That got an active glare out of Merran. "Alleged victim. There has been no proof of any wrongdoing at this time. As for our methods, our Healers have ways of determining the truth. The Healers are satisfied that Justern Memaxthal is completely innocent."

That got murmurs flying between the reporters. "How? Can Healers read minds?" One reporter demanded, asking the burning question they'd all been batting about for a month, ever since Justern's arrest and Greg's revelation of possessing Healing abilities.

Peter stuck his head in the courtroom again and came back out. "They're ready for us."

Justern took a deep breath and got to his feet. He followed Peter into the courtroom, sitting beside him at the long table positioned at front left of the judge's bench. Tamara, Mellis, Alarin, and Greg followed, sitting on the rows of benches just behind the table. Justern looked so young, lost, and lonely sitting up front that Tamara reached out mentally and brushed his shields. Justern turned back and gave her a small smile that faded immediately, not relaxing his shields one bit.

The jury trooped in, then Merran entered, his arrival quieter than the event it had been in the hallway. His aura was noticeably damped down as he sat behind Tamara. Sitting next to Alarin and in front of Merran, Tamara could feel the currents between the three of them clearly. She reached out and extended a tendril to both Alarin and Merran. Merran's thoughts flashed through her and into Alarin, far more worried than he'd let on to the reporters, thousands of possibilities flying through his mind along with the steps he must do to combat each. Alarin's emotions flowed the other way, through Tamara and to Merran, dominated by a strong thread of anger that someone dared to hurt one of his friends, a fierce loyalty and determination to do what he could to right what could become a terrible wrong. Her own concern for Justern spilled out, meshed with Merran and Alarin's emotions. Linked to these two men, on whom she'd come to depend so much these past few months, she stood with the rest of the court as the judge entered.

Dressed in black, seated high above the rest of the court, it was apparent that the judge was a hard man, cold and closed off to any psi abilities. Tamara's heart sank. The members of the jury were the ones to impress, but this judge would not be sympathetic to anyone, she was sure.

As the accused, Justern would be called to the stand later—after Joely's side presented their case. Joely must have recovered from her fear, because the moment she took the stand as the very first witness, she gave a flawless performance. The story she spun, complete with terrified looks at Justern and safely controlled crocodile tears, was convincing. Not too badly overacted, but just enough. Even the Azellians in the room would have had a hard time telling exactly what in the testimony was lie and what was truth. Too far away to do as he wished and force her to tell the unvarnished truth—and unsure he could have done it anyway, given how convinced she was that Justern had done her some terrible wrong for which he should pay—Alarin's simmering anger spread through Tamara and Merran.

Peter did some good, dragging up incidents of trying to get Justern alone, of her own propensity for dating lots of men. He slimed her as best he could, but the damage had been done. She even produced witnesses who told of the volatility of their relationship. The witnesses established a picture of a person Tamara did not know, cruel and careless, who might very well have beat up and raped his girlfriend, nailing his coffin shut. Peter objected that these witnesses hadn't been offered to him beforehand to investigate or depose, but the judge allowed the witnesses anyway. Peter managed to discredit them somewhat, but the very fact that she'd produced witnesses with firsthand knowledge of Justern and Joely's apparent interactions was damning, and he knew it. Justern's behavior toward her in public could have been seen as an abusive boyfriend rather than an immature young man who did not want a young woman's attentions.

By the time Justern took the stand and told his side of the story clearly and concisely, admitting that he tried to drive her away and had drunk too much that night, which gave her the opportunity to take advantage of him, no one was listening anymore. The judge called a recess in the middle of his testimony, breaking the rhythm of questioning. Tamara seethed in her chair at the ten-minute recess; Merran and Alarin were as irritated as she. Peter went over to Justern and spoke to him in a low voice. He returned to his seat when the judge returned.

"Your Honor, ladies and gentlemen of the jury," Peter said after the prosecutor got done ripping Justern apart on the stand, leaving him shaking and horrified. Tamara could feel the pain and sinking despair lacing through him. "We have heard both sides of this story now. It is apparent that there is no real evidence that a crime was committed except for the words of that young lady. There was no hospital visit after what should have been a traumatic event, even though she claims to have been slammed around by the defendant. I would like to offer a solution. You all know that Healers have abilities beyond what we as Earth humans can claim. One of these abilities is to read memories. With the court's permission, and because we have a Healer in court today, I would like to have both of these young people's memories read and the truth of this alleged event brought out in this court."

Joely went white. Tamara could feel her panic and she glared at the girl. Joely bent over and whispered to her lawyer, almost frantic. He listened and then got to his feet. "Your honor, ladies and gentlemen of the jury, I agree that should Healers have this amazing ability, it would be wondrous indeed for the justice system. I would point out, however, that the so-called Healer in court today is a very good friend of the accused and we would have no way of knowing whether or not he is indeed reading memories or just making up things as he goes along."

"Call the Healer up on the stand," the judge said to Peter. "The defendant is excused."

Tamara hardly dared breathe as Justern stepped around the stand and came to the table again.

Greg stood up, looking normal and very human in his grey suit as he walked to the front of the room. His sandy blond hair gleamed from the lights above his head as he stood in front of the courtroom, waves of serenity pouring off him.

"Please state your name and address for the court. Please be sure to speak slowly and clearly," the judge instructed him.

"Gregerin Tenricth." He spelled his name for the court reporter, then gave his address on campus.

"Gregerin, are you a Healer?" Peter asked.

"I am."

"As a Healer, what do your abilities include?"

"I can manipulate cells and molecules to help encourage physical Healing. I am trained to limited contact mentally to help Heal mental illness and to read memories to help in the treating of psychological disorders." It actually was not training that allowed him to read memories but was close enough to the truth that it could get by.

"What are your limitations?"

"I must be in physical contact with the patient to have a reading." Greg lied easily, his lie only obvious to the other Azellians in the room. There was a collective noise from the reporters and other humans in the room. "I cannot Heal anyone who does not work with me."

"Would you be able to read the memories of these two young people to discover the truth of what took place?" Peter motioned to Joely and Justern.

"Yes, I can." Greg's reply created stirs among the audience in the courtroom.

"Thank you, I have no further questions."

The prosecuting attorney stood up. "Healer. Is that your title?"

"Yes, it is."

"Healer, are Azellians capable of lying?"

"Healers are oath-bound, strictly ruled by an ethical code."

"I didn't ask if Healers had ethics. I asked if Azellians are capable of lying. Please answer the question, Healer."

Greg was caught. Without revealing more than the Council had authorized, he couldn't say more than, "Yes, they can."

"I see. Now, Healer, how long have you known the accused, Justern—excuse me if I struggle a bit with the last name—Mem—Memathal?" He looked down at his notes.

"I have known Justern Memaxthal for ten human years."

"Ten years. That's a long time. How would you consider your relationship?"

"I don't understand." Greg looked at the attorney steadily. He knew exactly what the man was driving at, but he was going to make him work for it. Tamara's stomach leaped.

"You came to Earth with Justern. Do you spend spare time with him? Did you spend time with him at home on Azelle?"

"Objection," Peter interjected, knowing it was fruitless. "Relevance."

"I'm simply trying to establish the relationship of this Healer to the accused, Your Honor."

"I know what you're trying to do, Mr. Dettner. I'll allow it." The judge leaned back in his chair. Tamara wanted to scream. Why was this continuing? They all knew where the questioning was going, and it might as well be thrown out right now. Since it was obvious that Greg shared a long-term relationship with Justern, it wasn't going to work. So why draw it out?

"What is your relationship to Justin Memthal?" the lawyer pressed, losing Justern's name completely.

"I would consider Justern Memaxthal a friend." It was hard to unnerve Greg, but he was becoming a bit rattled. Merran sent him a steadying tendril and he calmed.

"Under what circumstances would you lie, Healer?"

Greg saw the trap in the attorney's mind. "I don't."

"You've never lied?" The lawyer raised his eyebrow. "You've never given anyone false hope, misled them, made them think they were not as sick as they really were to spare their feelings?"

"I told you, Healers are governed by a code of ethics. One of those ethics is to present the whole picture to the patient, not a partial or blurred picture. We do not abuse our powers." Greg avoided that little trap neatly, and the direct question of whether he had ever lied. He had an agenda and spoke more for the reporters than for the prosecuting attorney. Tamara could read his intentions clearly. It was hopeless, however, for Justern. If the judge wasn't going to allow it, and she was sure that would be his position, why the hell was he allowing the questioning to continue? Tamara looked over at him and saw that he wasn't even paying attention. She hung on to her temper, mainly because she could feel that Alarin was very close to losing it himself. Alarin's anger appeared as a white rage in both their minds and took both her and Merran to keep him under control.

"I'm not talking about as a Healer now, Mr. Tenrick. As a man whose friend has been accused of a terrible crime, wouldn't you be tempted to shade the truth?"

"No," Greg said firmly. "If my friend had actually committed a crime like this, I would be the first one of the group to make sure he got his punishment." He was certainly convincing and Tamara applauded him to herself. Greg was a wonderful Healer, and the one thing that Healers were good at was appearing to be honest—although he had lied like a pro when he had to. Tamara clenched her hands together, praying that the judge and jury had bought the whole performance, despite the judge's lack of attention to the details.

"Are you sure? No leaning on the truth to try to get your friend off? Not even tempted?"

"No. Not even for a friend."

"Not even if it were on the orders of someone else? An ambassador, or the Council that rules your planet, perhaps?"

Peter stood up. "Your Honor, he has already answered the question."

The judge waved a hand. "Enough, Mr. Dettner. He has answered the question."

"No further questions, Your Honor."

"Your Honor, may we have the court's permission to get to the bottom of this by having the Healer read the memories of the accused?" Peter asked.

The other attorney's protest was immediate. "Your Honor, I would like to point out that no matter the personal integrity of this particular Healer, everyone has different perspectives of a traumatic memory. How can we decide what is truth and what is not based on two people's memories of the same traumatic event?"

"You have made your point, Mr. Dettner. As fascinating as this Healer's abilities may be, it is not this court's duty to test the limits of that ability. In this case, the Healer is too personally involved to offer an objective opinion. I will not allow it. You may step down, Healer."

Greg gave the judge a slight bow and stepped down.

"I think we have listened to enough. Please be prepared to offer your closing arguments after a ten-minute recess." He smacked the podium.

Tamara was shaking when Greg returned to the seats. "Oh God, if he'd let you read her memories. Did you feel her terror when Dad suggested it?"

Justern joined them, still pale and shaken. "You did really well, Greg. Thank you."

Greg smiled at Justern. "I know you're innocent, Justy, but if you weren't, I still wouldn't lie for you."

"I wouldn't want you to." Justern shook his head. "That would be against everything Healers have ever stood for. Not that the humans understand any of that. I do wish humans would allow a scan that would reveal her for what she is, though."

Tamara snorted, darting a hostile glance at the other side of the room where Joely and her group stood. "Someone like that will go through life doing whatever she pleases and getting away with it because she's got people all figured out and she knows exactly how to manipulate them and the system."

Merran nodded to Greg. "You did wonderfully within the limits that were imposed upon you."

Greg inclined his head. "I've gotten really good at it during the past few weeks. No matter what happens here today, we've made some important points that will get back to where they need to go." He glanced at the reporters who took out their handheld computers and typed away. Greg then turned to Justern. "Are you all right?"

Tamara, too overwhelmed by everything else that was happening, suddenly realized Justern was not looking very good at all. She came around the benches and slipped an arm around his waist, offering physical as well as mental comfort in that touch.

Only Azellian control allowed him to prevent the desire to cry. Tamara could feel him fighting the tears, although nothing showed on the surface. "I hardly recognized myself by the time they were done with me." His voice shook a little, the only visible show of his emotions. He coughed. "I'd hate myself too, if I were the person they painted me to be." He coughed again and Tamara could feel his nausea rising, a result of the huge bursts of adrenaline that had poured through him. She coughed in sympathy and tightened her arm around his waist. "She was so convincing, I almost question myself and what really happened. I know I didn't do what she claims, but based on her description of all that took place it makes you wonder, how could I not have done it? Could she really have made it all up? How could she hate me that much? I'm Azellian and I couldn't even tell where the lie ended and truth began in her words. She twisted it all so completely, how will anyone believe me?" His arm tightened on Tamara, flexing his muscles under her touch. "What if they find me guilty?" he whispered the words.

Greg ran a hand over him lightly, and Tamara could feel the Healer's soothing warmth pour through him, easing back the reactionary nausea and reinforcing his control. "*Alawahea*, Justern. We know you haven't done anything wrong, and so does the Council. That girl hates herself and life so much that she has to spread her hatred to everyone else rather than take responsibility for her own mistakes. We Healers have seen it many times in people. She is trying to destroy your life because then it validates the destruction she has created in her own."

Justern smiled at him weakly. "Knowing why she's dragging me through this doesn't help all that much. I just wish she'd leave me alone."

"Hang in there, Justy," Tamara said softly. "No matter what she says, we know you better than that." The judge's assistant returned.

Justern disengaged, giving them all a mental hug, then hastened back as the judge returned.

Closing arguments were addressed to the jury, Mr. Dettner's full of lots of emotional appeal. Peter's argument was masterful, well thought out—and a failure. The jury deliberated, then returned an hour later with a guilty verdict.

Justern sat in his seat stunned. Although he had known there was a good probability for this outcome, given the fact the media had doused everyone in fears of Azellians and that Joely's performance had been masterful, it still came as a complete shock. He looked over at Joely who hugged her father, her attorney, and every other nearby person as tears streamed down her face. In between hugs, she cast hostile, fearful glances over at Tamara and the Azellians.

"Mr. Memaxthal, you have been convicted by a jury of your peers," the judge said, getting his name right, at least. Tamara put her hands over her mouth, feeling sick and dizzy. "However, we are aware that during your previous incarceration, you were drugged heavily enough to nearly kill you. This court is willing to accept your word that you will remain in custody until you are sentenced one week from today and forego the dangerous alternative of drugging you senseless to ensure that you remain in custody. I understand the Azellian Ambassador is present today. Ambassador?"

Merran got to his feet and bowed. "Your Honor?"

"Does the embassy support the court's decisions?"

"It does, Your Honor," Merran said flatly, without any hint of emotion.

"Then will you aid us in ensuring that this young man will remain in custody until sentencing?" the judge asked.

Stuck where he did not want to be and knowing that the alternative of keeping Justern drugged was not acceptable, Merran inclined his head. "By my word as an ambassador, we will, Your Honor."

"So do you offer your word that you will remain in custody until sentencing, Mr. Memaxthal?" the judge returned his attention to Justern.

"I will remain in custody," Justern said in an almost inaudible voice. His head hung low as the bailiff approached and led him away.

Merran leaned over to the others seated beside him. "My job continues," he said. "Peter and I have to get him sent home... or it's going to kill him."

The reporters mobbed them at the door of the courthouse. This case had become much higher profile than it should have been. As Merran fielded question after question, taking their attention away from Greg, Tamara looked over to where Joely held on to her father, staying within the shelter of his arms as they hurried out of the courthouse. She longed to race after them to tell Joely exactly what she thought of the young woman's accusations. Peter ushered Mellis, Tamara, Greg, and Alarin into his car. Shocked silence reigned as they drove to Tamara's father's house, still reeling from the verdict.

"Dad, you can get him sent home, can't you?" Tamara asked later as the group of them sat in her father's house. "He doesn't need to stay here and be in jail for something he didn't do. It will ruin his life!"

"It depends on the judge. He may be willing to accept that Justern really was convicted incorrectly and let him have his life, or he might want to be firm, to make an example of him. I suspect that the Council will have something to say about this. Unless they leave Justern to hang out to dry, which I believe is highly unlikely, I am hopeful that we can get him sent back to Azelle. I started laying the groundwork for that weeks ago, and Merran is doing his part as well. Human law is fairly clear in rape cases, but date rape is something else entirely. Ultimately, it will be up to the judge, but we will continue to do what we can to influence the decision to send him home." Peter rested his head in his hands. Suddenly, he lifted his head and looked steadily at Alarin. "And you, young Raderth. I know what the Raderth talent is, and I suspect you have it in spades. Forcing her to admit that she lied in court won't do any good, unless we can get evidence to substantiate that position. To say nothing about revealing to the world more than what I understand the Council has okayed."

Alarin's smile was almost predatory. Tamara shivered, having far more access to his thoughts than she wanted right at that moment. "I will not force her to do anything."

"Be sure you don't. Leave her alone," Peter said sharply, "or we'll be fighting charges against you next. Stay away from her, all of you. That's an order. Merran is trying his damndest to make sure you aren't all sent home. If any of you have anything to do with her you are going to endanger his efforts. She's spoiled and dangerous and we're lucky Justern is the only one who has been affected by this."

Tamara expelled an explosive sigh. She knew her father was right, but she had to admit the thought of using her abilities to harass Joely into a confession was a temptation. It would not be difficult, not at all. A thousand revenge thoughts raced through her mind and she swallowed them all with tremendous effort that left her shaking.

❋ ❋ ❋

Exactly one week later they were all in court again, sitting in front of the judge. Justern was wearing the hidious orange suit and humiliating chains. He barely looked up, sunk in an apparent deep depression.

"There is considerable political pressure to have you deported and sent home immediately. While I am constrained to some extent by the politics inherent in this situation, I do not feel that you will be appropriately chastised for the harm you have done to this young lady, whom you used so cruelly. I have no knowledge of the type of punishment you will receive on Azelle, nor is that within this court's purview. I am, however, allowed by law to assess damages. I hereby fine you the sum of a half million dollars, or the equivalent in Azellian money, to be paid to the young lady who brought these charges against you. Maybe you will learn in the future to restrain yourself. You are hereby remanded to the custody of the ambassador, who will make sure you are sent back to Azelle on the next shuttle. He will also ensure that the fine is paid."

Justern didn't seem to have heard, but Tamara's stomach dropped as she thought of the judge's decision. *As a student, there is no way he has that kind of money! As an Azellian, where money is not the focus of life the way it is here, there is no way he'd ever get that kind of money, either!* Tamara was horrified.

"Dad!" Tamara protested as the judge banged his gavel and dismissed them. "How can they? There weren't any damages requested! She didn't miss classtime. She didn't even go to the hospital!"

Peter shook his head, his obvious anger written across his features. "He can't, honey. We're going to have to appeal this," he turned and spoke to Merran as the ambassador came forward and Justern was taken away to get dressed into his street clothes.

Merran sighed and rubbed his temples. "I know. There's no way Justern can make that kind of money on Azelle, and he's innocent to boot. I don't think the courts can force a foreign power to collect a fine, though. The judge knows it, which is why he instructed that I will guarantee it. However, if the Council tells me to ignore the fine, which I believe will be their position, there isn't much Earth can do but try to pressure us to pay up. We're not done with the political process on this, not even close."

Peter nodded. "Or the court process. I've already readied an appeal."

When Justern came out again, Tamara's heart went out to him. Physically, he was there as he walked toward them, but it was obvious he was not there emotionally.

Merran moved closer to Justern. "I'll take Justy back to the embassy with me."

"We'll fight this, Justern," Peter said to the young man.

Justern lifted his head and looked at Peter. "*Alawahea*," he whispered. "The *aarya* tell me that this will never be over until I die."

Something in the way he said it and the faraway look in his blue-grey eyes scared Tamara. *Merran, watch him. All night. Maybe we should have Greg spend the night with him too. He's making me nervous. Do you think he's suicidal?*

I'll watch him, Merran said grimly. *Greg, Alarin, Mel. You too, Tamara. You're all welcome to join us. We're going to have to watch him for a few days until he goes home.*

They arranged shifts for the following three days. Merran managed to whisk Justern to his apartment rather than the embassy, so he could stay there until the next shuttle arrived three days later. Tamara sat over Justern for the early morning shift on the third day, watching him as he lay sprawled on Merran's bed.

"How long have you been there?" Justern asked as the sun spilled into the room and across his face. He lifted his head and sounded semi-normal for the first time in three days. "Where am I?"

"Merran's bedroom."

He looked around. "Nice. Well, at least he doesn't have to come up with half a million dollars to pay to that lying bitchface."

Anger. Much better than the semi-comatose depression of the past three days, Tamara thought.

"Dad's fighting it. And Merran's going to see if the Azellian Council will help. Not that human authorities can do much when you return to Azelle except ask the Council very nicely for you to pay up."

Justern snorted, turning over on his side. "I may be High Council on both sides of my parentage, but I'm also the boy responsible for the death of his mother and disowned by his father."

Tamara shifted on her chair. "You've said that before. What do you mean by that? You're responsible for her death? I thought you were only ten! How could you possibly have caused her death?"

Justern was silent. He was quiet for so long that Tamara wondered if he would answer her. "There ... was a place at the Uzor oasis that I was not supposed to go. None of us non-psi children were. It was dangerous."

"But you went anyway."

Justern shrugged. "I went anyway. It was the only place I knew where I could be alone and get away from my parents' fighting. It was either that or the High Desert, and even I wasn't that stupid. Only acolytes or those trying to die go into the High Desert. Mother came to look for me. While she searched for me, she slid on some rocks, hit her head, and died immediately. I found her and tried to get her back to Uzorantxl, but I was too small and too weak to manage ... and I had no psi." There was a wealth of guilt and self-castigation in his confession.

Tamara shook her head. "You were just a child! It was an accident, Justy. It wasn't your fault."

"Well, my father certainly blamed me ... and so did the Council. The rest of Azelle wasn't far behind." He shook his head. "In light of all that I've just told you, I don't think the Council will jeopardize Azellian-human relations over me."

"They were ready to recall the students and their ambassador over you. They are really not happy with you being convicted when the psi evidence is so clear. It's taken a lot of effort on Merran's part to keep the Council from retaliating on your behalf."

"But we have no way to prove it to the satisfaction of the humans. I honestly don't think much of the human court system, Tamara." Justern sat up. He brushed his hand across his eyes.

Tamara looked at him sympathetically. "I know, Justy. I'm sorry. I wish …" She trailed off.

He closed his eyes. "So do I, believe me." Taking a deep breath in through his nose and releasing it out his mouth, he swung his legs over the edge of the bed. Tamara hastily averted her eyes, but she stood up and followed him to the bathroom. "Are you going to watch me?" he asked, standing at the toilet. He flashed her a faint grin. "Not that I mind, but besides our consanguinity, I think you already have enough with Merran and Alarin in your bed."

"Uh, we're supposed to keep an eye on you at all times." Tamara blushed. "I'll turn my back."

Justern shrugged. "I'm not going to kill myself, if that's what you're afraid of," he said as the tinkle of water made Tamara wish desperately she hadn't been the one to be present when he woke up. The toilet flushed and the sound of running water splashing into the sink allowed her to relax slightly. "It was tempting for a while, but my soul isn't quite ready to quit this life for the next turn of the wheel."

Tamara turned around. "It was a concern. You haven't been exactly yourself."

Justern smiled at her in the mirror above the sink. "I'm better now. Unless I'm mistaken, I'm going home today, right?"

Tamara nodded. "The shuttle arrives at five tonight. What are you going to do when you get back to Azelle?"

"Well, I'll be able to piece together some of my life again. Finally. At least I hope I can. I haven't had much luck at avoiding attention on either planet," Justern said, returning to the bedroom again. "The only thing I'm going to miss about Earth is you."

Tamara followed him, and when he stopped, she gave in to her desire to hug him tightly. His arms wrapped around her, and she could feel the slight tremor that went through him. "I've been glad to know my brother too. I'll come to Azelle, I promise. It might take a fight, but I am going to get there. This isn't the last time we will see each other. You will write or call too, won't you?"

Justern grinned and ruffled her hair. "You betcha. I have no intention of losing my sister now that I've found her. Now, if you want, you can have Greg come in and certify me healthy, but can I take a shower without an audience?"

Tamara laughed. "I'll call Greg in. I have no intention of watching you take a shower. Thanks anyway. As you said, to say nothing about our blood tie, I've got more than enough to deal with already with Alarin and Merran." She moved toward the door.

"Tamara," Justern said as she rested her hand on the door.

"Hmm?" Tamara turned toward him.

"Thank you. You know my mother's fairytales about her daughter and my sister? The real thing's even better," he said softly.

Tamara smiled, tears welling up in her eyes. "I'll get Greg."

It had not gotten any easier to say goodbye eight hours later when the shuttle stood in the spaceport yard. It took a mighty effort for

Tamara to hold back her tears as Justern boarded the shuttle. Mellis, not having anything to keep her on Earth, had decided to go back too, making Tamara feel a little better to know Justern would not be alone back on Azelle.

"His cousin, our friend Charina, is still there too. Justy will be fine," Alarin said from behind her.

"One day that will be you getting on that shuttle," Tamara told him, her throat thick. "It's going to come sooner than I'll ever be ready to have you go. What will I do when you leave?"

"Incentive to follow," Alarin grinned at her, pulling her close to him and kissing her lightly. "I'm still here next semester and through next year too, thanks to Merran."

"Thanks to me, what?" Merran came up to them. He dropped a kiss on Tamara's lips and stood on her other side.

"Thanks to you, Greg and I get to suffer on Earth for another year. Do you think next semester will be anything like this one?" Alarin asked as they watched the shuttle start to taxi toward the runway.

"The *aarya* damn it, I hope not. I don't think I could survive another year like these past three months."

"And Greg? What happens with Greg?" Tamara asked as the noise of the shuttle disappeared into the distance. "He's a celebrity. Why did he decide to stay?"

Merran shrugged. "I suspect our Healer has a large dose of the prima donna in him."

"I do not!" Greg protested, sauntering forward in an exaggerated way, his hands waving dramatically in the air. "I am a diva!"

"You don't sing," Tamara said, laughing. "You can't be a diva."

Greg grinned at her and resumed walking normally. "Well then, maybe Merran's right. Maybe I'm just a camera hog."

"I'm just glad you guys are still around." Tamara opened her mind to include all of them. "Here's to hoping things actually calm down and settle into a routine. Let's get a drink that doesn't affect us."

"The *aarya* grant," the three men chorused, and they walked arm in arm to the same bar where Tamara had spent her first evening with the Azellians. No longer the same person as she had been then, Tamara leaned back and stretched, a smile spreading across her face. Life might have dealt them all blows this year, but maybe there was something to this *Alawahea*. She tipped her chair back and ordered a drink.

✻ ✻ ✻

Across town, in the tall highrise that housed the Earth Liaison Office, Ellen Pearson signed out of her email and leaned back in her chair with a sigh. A light knock on the door made her look up.

"Come in," she called.

Her assistant, Lori, pushed open the door. "Did you hear about the verdict?"

"Yes. Kendra at the courts just sent me an email."

"Guilty. Do you really think he was?"

Ellen shrugged. "I really doubt that the ambassador of Azelle would have sent anyone with any violent tendencies to Earth. And I know Jed Smythe. His daughters are rather ... notorious for what they will do to get attention. I suspect the boy got caught in a mess he probably should have avoided." She let out her breath slowly. "At least we were able to get him sent home, despite Jed's efforts. He doesn't like Azellians at all, and his daughters know it. I'm sure that's part of why this young man got caught up in this drama."

"Yes, but they have fined him severely."

Ellen laughed. "Good luck getting the Azellian Council to collect that fine. Between Ambassador Corina, the news media, and myself, I'm virtually certain that the president will hear about this."

"You think we can get an official pardon for him?"

Ellen shrugged. "If Ambassador Corina doesn't require it before they allow that Healer to work on any of our sick people, he isn't the political star that we all know and love. I'm certain they'll ask ... and they'll probably get one. Did you see what the Healer managed to do? They can Heal virtually anything."

Lori nodded. "That Healer's going to be the focus of so many demands ... I'll be surprised if he sticks around. Do you think they'll send more Healers to Earth?"

"We'll definitely be asking for more when we ask for the next set of exchange students for next semester."

"So we're doing it again?"

Ellen sat up. "Yes, and I have full support from those above. If it weren't for the Healers, I might have had a harder time with it, but as it is, fantastic mental abilities or not, we want those Healers."

"And it's amazing how flexible the powers that be are when it comes to something we want." Lori headed for the door. "Ellen, do you think all Azellians share those abilities? Or do you think it's limited to Healers, like they're saying?"

Ellen frowned. "I don't know, Lori. I don't know." Her assistant accepted that answer and stepped out of the office, closing the door behind her. After she'd left, Ellen stared out the east-facing window in the direction of the airport. She imagined she could see the shuttle launch straight up into the sky, bearing the disturbing presence of the young man who got caught in the coils of political maneuvering. *But any of us who have ever worked closely with Merran Corina know that it's highly unlikely their Healers are the only ones with these talents. Although I'm certain the man will never admit to it. That is, until he can't avoid it anymore.* She smiled and closed down her computer for the night. There was plenty of time to worry about the following semester and the next batch of thorny political questions ... tomorrow.

STAY TUNED FOR
BOOK TWO ...

DON'T MISS OUT on the next chapter in Tamara, Merran, and Alarin's lives in the second book of The Azellian Affairs in early 2016.

In Gratitude

AS WITH ANY artistic endeavor, this was a long time in the making and involved large numbers of people to whom I am extremely grateful. Jill and Sue, without your early enthusiasm for the World Girls, I don't know if I would have embarked on this journey so many years back. All my friends and relatives, who never doubted I could do it and who have been patiently waiting a very long time for it to happen, thank you for your faith. It might have been a really long time in coming, but it's finally here! Donna, my incredible heart-centered editor, you have been an inspiration and the main reason I've gotten to where I find myself today. Without your skills and support, this would still be a raw attempt to convey a story. Chuck, wonderful friend and videographer: thank you for your supportive enthusiasm and belief in this story, as well as your invaluable help with the visual and audio aspects of story production. Thank you, Meghann, Lisa, Diana, Alissa, Danielle, the loving sisters of my meditation groups, for your support as I step into an entirely new world of who I am. Your love and willingness to share your own joys and fears have made my shifts so much more powerful for the sharing. Meghann, the Mistress of Marketing, for your contributions and guidance in the mysterious world of marketing and social media: I would never have dared to embark on this journey without your encouragement and support. I love you! Rikka, Zach, and Nikole, the Adventures In Oneness team, thank you for your guidance and loving presence as I follow my heart and discover magic and miracles beyond anything I could have imagined. Josh, Theta Healer extraordinaire, thank you for helping me break through the fears and limitations that occasionally sweep the rug out from under me. Without your abilities to help me discover where I'm getting in my own way, I would have found this journey so much more difficult. My group of fellow entrepreneurs at 3 to 5 Club, thank you for providing an awesome community as I stretch my wings and soar. And last, but not at all least, my wonderful husband, Troy. You helped me realize this story had something to say and encouraged me to say it.

This story would not exist without all of you and I am forever thankful for every one of you! Life really is all about love, and I'm surrounded by some of the most amazing people in the world.

About the Author

SARA L. DAIGLE has been creating stories since she first forayed into the world of writing at the age of eight. As an avid reader growing up in a small town without much access to a library, and before the birth of the Internet, Sara devoured her mother's extensive stack of science fiction and romance novels to keep her literary thirst quenched. Soon afterwards, she began writing her own stories and entertaining her friends by composing plays for them to act out.

A passionate interest in astronomy, anthropology, and linguistics, coupled with this early background in science fiction and romance, led Sara to merge the two fields and create a series of interlinked stories built around a fictional planet's culture and its interaction with ours.

Sara currently lives in Denver, Colorado, with her husband and three very loving but energetic dogs.

Let's Stay Connected

TO STAY CONNECTED, please be sure to find me online by visiting my website at www.SaraLDaigle.com. You can also contact me at Sara@SaraLDaigle.com. I would love to hear from you!

And one last favor ...

If you have enjoyed *Alawahea*, please leave a review on Amazon, Barnes & Noble and Goodreads.

Thank you!

About the Press

Merry Dissonance Press is a book producer/indie publisher of works of transformation, inspiration, exploration, and illumination. MDP takes a holistic approach to bringing books into the world that make a little noise and create dissonance within the whole in order that ALL can be resolved to produce beautiful harmonies.

Merry Dissonance Press works with its authors every step of the way to craft the finest books and help promote them. Dedicated to publishing award-winning books, we strive to support talented writers and assist them to discover, claim, and refine their own distinct voice. **Merry Dissonance Press** is the place where collaboration and facilitation of our shared human experiences join together to make a difference in our world.

For more information, visit http://merrydissonancepress. com/.

Merry
Dissonance
Press